PRAISE FOR JOHN MATTHEWS

"Matthews maintains the suspense... an engrossing odyssey into the seamy side of a world that is so near, yet sometimes seems so far. Compulsive reading."
  The Times on *Past Imperfect*

"With *Past Imperfect*, Matthews shows that he is already a novelist of real accomplishment."
  Barry Forshaw on *Past Imperfect*

"'One of the most compelling novels I've read... an ambitious and big novel which will keep you enthralled to its last page."
  Cork Examiner on *Past Imperfect*

"Matthews certainly knows how to keep the reader hungry for the next revelation."
  Kirkus Reviews on *Ascension Day*

"Ascension Day is like a narcotic, paced with danger, and totally addictive. Impossible to put down. This is what thrillers are meant to be."
  Jon Jordan from *Crime Spree* magazine on *Ascension Day*

"Goes to the wire... a gripping thriller."
  The Scotsman on *Ascension Day*

ALSO BY JOHN MATTHEWS

JOHN MATTHEWS

LETTERS FROM A MURDERER

EXHIBIT A
An Angry Robot imprint
and a member of Osprey Group

Lace Market House,
54-56 High Pavement,
Nottingham
NG1 1HW
UK

Exhibit A/Osprey Publishing,
PO Box 3985
New York,
NY 10185-3985
USA

www.exhibitabooks.com
A is for Argenti!

An Exhibit A paperback original 2013

Cover photograph: Steve Meyer-Rassow; design by Argh! Oxford
Set in Meridien and Franklin Gothic by EpubServices

Distributed in the United States by Random House, Inc., New York

ISBN: 978 1 90922 337 0
Ebook ISBN: 978 1 90922 338 7

Printed in the United States of America

9 8 7 6 5 4 3 2 1

*To a stylish, bygone era, of which my mother was part;
and to all those among my family and friends
who remember my mother and that era with fondness.*

FOREWORD

With a series of murders of prostitutes in London's East End in the late 1880's, the reputation of the killer later to become known as "Jack the Ripper" was secured in the annals of criminal history as the most notorious serial killer of all time.

Murders undisputedly attributed to the Ripper, subsequently termed the "canonical five" – Mary Ann Nichols, Annie Chapman, Elizabeth Stride, Catherine Eddowes and Mary Jane Kelly – all took place between August and November 1888 in London's Whitechapel. However, there were eleven "Whitechapel murders" in total between April 1888 and February 1891, and investigators both then and since have been sharply divided on which of those – Emma Smith, Martha Tabram, Rose Mylett, Frances Coles and Alice McKenzie – should have been included as "Ripper" victims.

The last murders possibly attributed to the Ripper were in fact not in London at all, but in New York, with one similar murder also in New Orleans. Intriguingly, these all took place after the murders in London had ceased and have drawn increasing attention from investigators re-examining the mystery of "Jack the Ripper".

1

New York. November, 1891.

The first place Camille looked as she walked in the room was towards the bar manager, Delaney.

One look from Delaney and she immediately knew the lie of things. If he glanced worryingly to one side then back again, it meant that either local ward detectives, Pinkerton agents or the hotel owners were present; eyes cast down meant there were already too many girls working the bar; eyes up and even if you found a client all the bedrooms were busy. It was only if he simply smiled that you were welcome to stay.

Delaney smiled tightly and had already turned to serve someone as Camille nodded back in recognition. The bar was heaving, noisy – the strains of a piano in the far corner barely audible above the cacophony: porters, bricklayers, peddlers, stevedores and sailors from the nearby dock steamships. Camille recognized at least six working girls she knew; but perhaps Delaney thought the heavy Saturday night crowd warranted it. More flouncing skirts and petticoats, the longer the men stayed, the more drinks they ordered.

But as Camille saw one of the girls go upstairs with a client and Delaney raised his eyes and shrugged, she wasn't sure whether it was worth the wait. She scanned for any likely customers who might buy her a drink to bide the time – but nobody caught her eye or smiled back. Ah, ten years ago I'd have made your heads turn, she thought. More and more she was finding her trade on the street these days, where the darkness and shadows hid her age.

The warmth and ambience of the room felt welcoming though after the cold outside, and she lingered in its embrace a moment before snapping herself out of it. She couldn't risk another night without a customer – especially not a Saturday night. Already her two little ones had had nothing but flour porridge for three days.

She'd work the streets nearby for a while, then if she was still empty-handed she'd return; the men might be drunker then, less fussy.

She was only ten yards out the door when she heard his voice.

"Hello… were you looking for someone?"

Camille turned: she hadn't seen or heard him follow her out; and looking at him now – medium height, brown hair, trim beard and moustache, as unassuming as he was non-descript – she hadn't noticed him in the bar either. He'd simply merged with the crowd. But he looked respectable enough, not too dirty or rough-looking. He'd do.

"I might be at that, kind sir. And were you looking for a lady tonight?"

"Yes… yes I was."

His eyes shifted down for a second, as if ashamed of admitting it. She liked that. "Did you want to go back inside? We might have to wait ten minutes for a room."

"No… no. It's okay. It's a bit too noisy in there for my taste."

Maybe so, she thought; but more likely he was embarrassed being seen going to the rooms with a girl.

She followed his gaze past her shoulder to the alley behind.

"Okay. One dollar." She smiled, and waited for the money to be in her hand before adding, "No biting. And rip my dress and it'll cost double."

She led the way midway down the alley, leant back against the wall and lifted her dress up. She looked sharply to one side; sudden commotion as three men burst from the bar talking loudly.

Her customer leant in closer to cover her modesty. He didn't look their way, but seemed to be aware of their every movement in his peripheral vision – his body rigid, tense. For a moment she feared he'd been unnerved and would ask for his money back. But as finally their voices drifted away, he relaxed again. The only sounds on the night air were the clip-clop of hooves of passing cabs on Catherine Street and the funnel hoot from a steamer in the nearby docks.

"Come on, then," she said, and hiked her dress and petticoats up higher to her waist. She wore no underwear, so simply waited for the usual fumbling for him to get inside her.

Except this felt somehow different; deeper, higher than she'd ever known before, taking her breath away, and a sharp stinging and strange wetness on the outside too.

As she gasped, he looked deep into her eyes. "Don't move," he said. "You'll just make it worse."

And as she felt the shudder of him ejaculating and realized it was a blade inside her, starting to shake and scythe deep in her gut, her gargling scream barely reached her throat before the hand at her neck gripped tight, choking it off.

When the pathologist, Jacob Bryce, got to the third stab wound, he knew that it was no ordinary back alley robbery, which constituted most of the murders in the city's notorious Fourth Ward.

Most of the blood, concentrated around the woman's chest and stomach, had coagulated into a thick skin, indicating that death had taken place several hours beforehand. Bryce had to use alcohol to clean and loosen the blood in order to view those first puncture wounds.

It was the practice at Bellevue hospital that whenever a body was brought in for autopsy, one of the crime scene detectives should also be present to pass on key information when queried. Bryce looked towards the attending detective, whose name he couldn't recall and who still looked somewhat in shock.

"What time did you discover the body?"

"Uh, we got there, myself and a colleague from Mulberry Street, at just before midnight."

"And the first people to discover the body – when might that have been?"

The detective briefly consulted his notes. "Another girl from the Riverway Hotel first noticed her in a side alley forty minutes before we arrived."

"Much activity in the area that time of night?"

"Yes. Quite busy still."

Bryce nodded thoughtfully. Add on at most half an hour for her body to first be discovered, then the two hours since midnight taken up with initial forensics at the crime scene and transporting the body in an ambulance wagon to Bellevue.

The deep gash to the side of the woman's neck, severing the carotid artery, wouldn't on its own have been unusual for a street robbery; it was the fact that it was combined with so many stab wounds – Bryce had counted eight so far. Blood flow from the neck wound was less, indicating that the stomach wounds had come first.

By the time Bryce had located the fourteenth stab wound, he realized he was in unchartered waters; it was like nothing he'd seen before. The smell of body waste mixed with carbolic and alcohol was heavy in the air. The young detective was now even more wide-eyed and looked slightly nauseous, one hand going to his mouth.

Bryce noticed a small "X" marked on the woman's left shoulder. He'd get a photo taken of it later. A keen follower of Virchow's principal, Bryce had a neat line of glass jars prepared and labelled, ready – once they'd been initially examined and weighed – to take each of the body's internal organs. But he soon discovered that two of those jars would go unfilled. He looked towards the detective.

"Were any body parts removed from the scene? Perhaps bagged and taken elsewhere for examination… or inadvertently left at the crime scene?"

The detective looked flustered, had to think for a second. "No. None that I know of."

"The scene was searched thoroughly – nothing left there?"

"Yes… yes. I'm sure it was."

Bryce wondered whether the scavenging rats and dogs of the area might have run off with or consumed the woman's liver and kidney. Half an hour? Unlikely in such a short period, but regardless the killer had first removed those organs. Yes, like nothing he'd seen before, although he had *heard* of something similar.

Bryce looked at the clock on the wall. Five hours before Inspector McCluskey was in his office for him to pass on the information.

St James Club. London.
"Come now. This Darwin fellow was clearly deranged." Viscount Linhurst swirled his brandy balloon. "Evolved from monkeys? We're clearly the far higher species."

With a captive audience of two of London's leading surgeons – Sir Thomas Colby and Andrew Maitland – he thought it an apt time to air such views.

"You'd never guess it from any of my household staff," Maitland commented.

A light guffaw from Linhurst, but Colby remained serious. "I don't know. I see the similarities daily in autopsies. Every single organ in the same place – liver, stomach, spleen – and every bone and joint the same too, right down to the little finger." Colby held up a pinkie. "I wouldn't discount it so hastily if I were you."

"I'm not convinced." Linhurst tapped his forehead. "It's all here, you see. And Darwin hasn't adequately explained how a monkey could possibly–" Linhurst broke off as a club usher approached.

"I apologise for the intrusion, gentleman, but there's an urgent call for Sir Thomas."

Colby unfolded the note held out on a silver tray. "Sorry. Excuse me a moment."

He followed the usher towards the vestibule call booth, and at the other end Police Commissioner Grayling wasted little time with preamble.

"There's been another one." Silence; and Grayling wasn't sure if it was purely shock or Colby hadn't immediately made the link. He added, "Similar to the other eight."

"Where? Whitechapel again?"

"No. You'd hardly credit it when I tell you. It's across the sea. New York."

But Colby wasn't that surprised. With the last murder more than a year ago now, the supposition was either that the Ripper was imprisoned, dead, or had moved on.

"Who is handling the investigation there?"

"McCluskey." Octave lower, derisory. "But, no matter – you'll need to go over as soon as possible."

"I see. I hazard he didn't request my involvement."

"No. *I* did. Your contribution is invaluable to match the crimes. There's also the possibility that it's a copycat murder. As you're well aware, there has been far more in the press about this than we'd have liked. But if a link is proven, we still have by far the heavier case burden. Eight murders that remain unsolved."

Colby didn't need reminding. Three years that had consumed his life like never before. The number of murders attributed to the Ripper ranged from five to as many as eleven, but eight was the number Colby had personally cited as having links. No past investigation had attracted such strong public furore, and a Fleet Street eager for fresh readers hadn't helped.

"There was also a mark left on this one," Grayling said. "A small 'X' on her left shoulder."

"Oh?"

"It might be significant, it might not. Or indeed mean that this is a different man entirely; not the Ripper at all. We won't know until we get the full details."

"Yes, I see." Colby sighed. "One problem, though. I have an important speech at the Royal College of Surgeons in two weeks' time that I must be here for. I won't be able to go until after that."

"I'm not sure matters will hold that long – aside from the politics. McCluskey would no doubt start bleating about our incompetence again. Can't you delay it – speak there later?"

"No, it's an annual event. But that's not the only problem." The rest of Colby's hectic social calendar flooded in: his son's upcoming investiture at Sandhurst, a dinner-dance invitation from Lord and Lady Northbrook that he'd face untold woe from his wife for missing. "I fear I'm not going to be able to go over."

"I'm sorry to hear that. I suppose I'll just have to tell McCluskey the bad news – or probably *good* from his point of view. He'll be relieved no doubt that we aren't interfering, as well as now have first-hand proof of that incomp-"

"I have a suggestion," Colby cut in. The thought had struck as Grayling started riding him. "One of my best students went over to New York four months ago. An aunt who he was close to – she raised him after his mother died – was very ill. He could stand in for me."

"But would he be competent enough?"

"Very much so. My main protégé, you could say. Of all my students, he was the only one to identify crucial links in the Ripper case without my constant prompting. Uncanny – almost as if he knew the man personally."

"I see."

Colby could sense some residual doubt. The one blot on his protégé's copybook, Colby liked to think of as reflecting more on his personal life than his competence – so hardly worth mentioning.

"And of course I could give him added consultation by telegram and letter from London."

"Yes, I... I suppose it could work," Grayling said at length. "But if he's picked up on any of the scuttlebutt in London, tell him not to use our pet-term, Inspector McClumsy – get us off on the wrong foot. And what's his name, by the way?"

Colby swallowed back a chuckle. "Jameson. Finley Jameson."

New York, November, 1891.
"Mr Jameson... Mr Jameson!"

The voice had a slight echo, as if it was at the end of a tunnel, and it took Finley Jameson a moment to focus on the wizened Chinaman hovering over him and realize where he was. The smell of opium smoke and incense was heavy, and Jameson wasn't sure if the mist was just in the air or behind his eyes.

"Mr Jameson... Lawrence is here. Says he has an urgent message for you. Shall I show him in?"

That snapped Jameson to. His assistant, Lawrence. Jameson sat up, rubbing his head. Years back in his university days he'd had a shock of wavy, wild blond hair, but now cropped short it looked much darker.

"No, no. Tell him to wait. I'll be out in a few minutes." He didn't want Lawrence to see him like this. He wouldn't understand.

"Do you want me to get Sulee to bring you some tea? Help you waken?"

"Yes... thank you. An excellent suggestion."

Sulee, more distant through the mist, gave a small bow as she went to make him tea. Her lithe beauty was apparent despite the plain high-collar shirt and loose trousers of any laundry worker.

He recalled Ling offering for a dollar that Sulee give him a scented oil massage while he smoked; for another dollar she'd apply the oil with her naked body and then lick it off inch by inch, "Like a cat."

Jameson thought he'd politely declined, "Perhaps next time" – but when later he seemed to remember Sulee's oiled body writhing against him, he wasn't so sure. Then halfway through her eyes became vertical ovals and her skin transformed to that of a tiger's, complete with stripes – unless it was the candlelight throwing shadows through a nearby palm – so perhaps it had been a dream after all.

That was the main thing to attract Jameson to these dens, that wonderful merging of dreams and reality. But was *death* always what triggered his visits? Certainly, the first time he'd visited one had been not long after his mother's death, and it couldn't be sheer coincidence that his visits since had often been following his and Colby's most traumatic autopsies. Now too, this visit to Ling's had come straight after his aunt's death, and often his past visits to dens had taken place when other problems had arisen in his life.

Personal demons he was escaping or merely a harmless distraction? After a moment, he shrugged the thought away. As often, he found himself more at ease studying the intricacies of the lives of others rather than his own.

He smiled as Sulee handed him a jasmine tea.

2

New York. January, 1892.

I thought a short note was in order, since I heard you were in New York. And no less than Colby's star pupil. It will seem as if the spirit of Thomas Colby himself is here, continuing the game we started in London. Send him my regards, will you.

They appear not to have identified the previous marks, so I've put this one where it can't be missed. Has Colby sent you over especially because of me? If so, I'm flattered. You know, I used to watch you all with Colby, playing out the final moments of those poor girls.

Ah, now you are wondering which one I was amongst those looking at you: butcher, baker, candlestick-maker? So many people milling past day and night. And New York is the same. Such a press of humanity flooding in from every corner of the globe. At times invigorating, but at others like bedlam. Bedlam? Now there's a word to conjure with. How is your assistant, Lawrence, by the way?

Though you probably couldn't have chosen a better time to be in New York. All these fast-rising new monoliths and now the first electric lighting bringing its streets to life. Wrap yourself in the warmth and bonhomie of its bars, theatres and music halls and you could almost be in London.

19

*Almost, my friend. I'm sorry to hear about your aunt
dying. As you'll no doubt soon discover, it's hard being
separated from friends and family. Strange fate that the
closest bond we might have in this new city is with each
other.*

Detective Joseph Argenti sipped a thick black coffee as he
read the letter, then looked across the table at New York
Mayor George Watkins.

Ruddy and bold would best describe Watkins,
he considered: Ruddy complexion, bold handlebar
moustache, and while not that tall at five feet seven
inches he appeared almost as broad. In contrast, Argenti
was thinner, wirier, taller, sallower, and his moustache
and beard were cropped tight.

They were seated by the front window at the Vendome
tea room. Outside on 41st Street passed an incessant hoof-
clatter and rattle of hansom cabs, dray horse drawn coal or
brewery carts and the occasional horse drawn tram.

"When would Jameson have first read this letter?"

"Just this morning. It was sent directly to *The Times*.
Our man obviously wants to keep the challenge public
– as with many of the past letters sent first to the press.
He doesn't want to run the risk of Jameson keeping the
letter private."

"How might our man have known that Jameson's aunt
died? Was there anything in the newspapers about it?"

"I don't think so. We're checking now. But there'll
have probably been an obituary notice. He could have
made the link."

"Also, does Jameson have an assistant called Lawrence?
And what's the significance with Bedlam, if any?"

"Yes, he does. But we don't know yet of any significance.
As I say, it's too early. The letter arrived just this morning."

Argenti nodded thoughtfully. "And Jameson will be at this meeting now with McCluskey?"

"Apparently so." Watkins checked his pocket watch. "Anyway, we'd better get a move on. I'll fill in the details on the way."

They took seats at the back of the music hall on 23rd Street. On its raised stage Inspector McCluskey and Finley Jameson fielded questions from the press and leading City Hall representatives and clergy. A hotchpotch of "concerned citizens" filled the rest of the room, from the Salvation Army to the local Grolier club.

A *New York Post* reporter near the front was on his third question about possible suspects, and McCluskey was starting to get flustered.

"As I said, our initial information regarding the suspect known as Frenchy One appears to have been incorrect. He couldn't have been in the bar that night because his steamer had set sail two nights before."

"And the other suspect – Frenchy Two?"

"We haven't been able to locate him as yet. So we can't confirm anything one way or the other."

A *New York Times* reporter lifted his pen. "And do you have any other suspects from other nations? Perhaps Italian, Russian or Dutchy One and Two? Or, seeing as we're in New York – Irish or American One and Two?"

A ripple of laughter ran through the room. McCluskey held a hand up to quell it. "Let me make this clear. There was only one man seen leaving the bar around the same time as Camille Green, and two other girls we spoke to thought he was a man with a strong French accent they'd met a few weeks before. We're now trying to ascertain just who that might have been."

Watkins leant close to Argenti. "You're looking at a dead man."

"Why? Is he ill?"

"I meant career-wise. He made no friends spouting about British police incompetence – who we're now reliant upon for case history – then compounds that by making our own force look like the biggest incompetents on earth with all this wild-goose Frenchy nonsense. That's why I showed you that letter this morning – to get you involved."

"You want me to assist McCluskey with the investigation?"

"No. I want you to *take over* the investigation from him. In fact, I was speaking with Commissioner Latham about the matter just the other day."

Argenti fell silent. He should have known there was more to it. Private meeting with Watkins at the Vendome, then the fact that Watkins was sitting at the back with him rather than at McCluskey's right arm.

Watkins grimaced. "Look. Let's be clear about this. McCluskey's days are numbered. Not just because of the fiasco he's making of this investigation, but the corruption storm sweeping his department. As you know, Michael Tierney rakes off from the docks, gin houses, bordellos and half the construction projects in this city, has half of City Hall and the police in his pocket, possibly including McCluskey. Whereas you stood apart from that corruption, stood against it." Watkins looked towards McCluskey. "And trust me – that's been noted."

Argenti nodded, pensive. "Did you hear the street rumour that Tierney's put a price on my head for daring to go against him?"

"Yes, I did. All the more proof of how you stood your ground." Watkins studied him soberly. He knew that Argenti had a wife and three children. "I know it wouldn't have been an easy decision for you to make."

Cigar and pipe smoke was heavy in the air, swirls of it illuminated as it drifted past the hall's gas lighting.

On stage, Finley Jameson was elaborating on his earlier autopsy comments. "To clarify, strangulation didn't cause death, merely rendered the victim unconscious. Evisceration of the lower abdomen and stomach and subsequent loss of blood was the likely cause of death."

"And this appeared similar to past Ripper attacks in London?"

"Yes. Almost identical to the mode of injuries in at least four of the past cases."

"Is there a significance to the mark he said he left on Camille Green's body?"

"It appears to be an 'X' on her left shoulder. But it could be anything. A crude form of signature mark, or perhaps even the Roman numeral ten."

"Were any of the other bodies marked?"

"No, they weren't – not as far as was seen. They're checking again now in London."

A moment's silence as notes were made, then a *Herald* reporter raised his hand.

"And that girl cut in two by a tram last week. Could she have been another victim, the murderer simply placing her there to disguise his handiwork?"

"No, not possible. I saw her not long after the Coroner, and blood lividity in the autopsy proved that she was alive when struck by the tram."

Watkins turned to Argenti. "What's your impression of Jameson? Someone you could work with well?"

Argenti contemplated Jameson: early thirties, neatly trimmed beard and moustache, and no particularly striking features, except his eyes which appeared almost light grey and were constantly darting, alert, taking everything in. And an easy smile, which was endearing.

Curious though, that only hours after such a personal letter had been aired publicly, Jameson was handling himself so competently, seemed untroubled. Clearly either a sharp mind, able to calmly separate his emotions; or strangely detached from those emotions – which would be more worrying.

"As well as any, I daresay." Non-committal; he saw little point in being blunt and voicing the obvious that he and Jameson were poles apart in culture and manner. But as Watkins looked at him intently, he sensed it wasn't just a casual query.

"Because it looks like you'll get the chance sooner than I thought. Fresh lead's just come in, a friend of Camille Green's. I'd like you and Jameson to go and see her, question her."

"Through McCluskey's department?"

"No. This has come directly through a contact I have at Pinkertons. He's been trailing some of the working girls from the same bar for a while now."

"Won't that be seen as stepping on McCluskey's toes?"

"Leave McCluskey to me and Commissioner Latham." Watkins looked wistfully back towards the stage. "Like I say, in a month's time he won't have a leg left to stand on – let alone any toes."

3

On the way to see Camille Green's friend, Finley Jameson's hansom cab stopped at the junction with Fifth Avenue to let a horse drawn tram pass. He turned to Argenti.

"Lawrence has come to know his way round the city quite well. We should be there soon."

Argenti had seen Lawrence only briefly as they'd got in the cab – fleeting impression of gaunt, dark eyes beneath the shadow of his derby hat – then again now as Jameson gave fresh instructions through the roof hatch.

As Jameson shut the hatch, Argenti raised the subject of Lawrence's mention in the letter. "Any idea how the writer might have known that?"

"Ah, the infamous letter." Jameson waved one hand theatrically. "No idea immediately. But public records being what they are... and of course my name and photograph have been in the papers a few times since I joined this investigation. No doubt all will become clear in time."

"If you don't mind me saying, I thought you handled the meeting well. Especially considering that only this morning you'd viewed such a personal letter."

"I don't mind you saying that at all. But I didn't actually read the letter until after the meeting. Lawrence sorts my mail and morning newspapers and made me aware of the letter, but advised it might upset me before the

25

meeting – for which in any case I was busy preparing notes. I decided to read it later."

Argenti nodded, looking over for a moment at some flower sellers on the corner of Washington Square. That partly explained Jameson's earlier reaction.

Argenti prided himself on being a sharp, stylish dresser, but Jameson's light-grey herringbone was a cut above his own black suit, looked like it cost a month of his own salary. Jameson's burgundy derby had a soft sheen to it, as if it was made of velvet, and the head of the ebony cane in his grip looked like solid silver, fashioned in an Anubis head. No doubt it could be a formidable weapon against footpads.

They had to wait at the next junction for two horse drawn buggies and a handcart laden with fruit and vegetables to pass. Further down the street could be seen other traders in Gansevoort Market packing up for the day.

"Regarding the X-mark on Camille Green's body, is a Roman numeral your favoured supposition?"

"No, that suggestion came more from London. I'm more sceptical, or at least I remain open about it. Though we'll soon know. They're now looking for a IX or VIII on the past two victims."

"And his comment about Bedlam? Did that have any significance?"

"Ah, yes. Bedlam." Jameson sighed. "London's notorious lunatic asylum. He appears to have got that right too. It's where I first found Lawrence."

"I'm sorry."

"Don't be. He's far from mad – just that his mind works in a different way to yours and mine." With the roof hatch closed and the clatter from the road, they couldn't be heard from the driver's position behind them. "Many a case, he has many more facts memorized than me and is also my main sounding board. I don't know what I'd do without him."

They rode in silence for a moment down Wooster Street. One of the new electric trams passed them heading the other way, crammed with passengers. They were still a novelty in the city, though word was that one day they'd take over from horse drawn trams. Personally, Argenti couldn't see it.

Jameson took a fresh breath. "And you? From your name, I'm guessing your family originally came from Italy. How long have they been here?"

"Almost thirty-five years now. My family came here when I was just seven."

As they turned into Broadway, the first gas lamps were being lit. At this time of year wood and coal smoke mellowed the smell of horse manure on the night air. Four tons of it deposited daily on New York streets. On the main thoroughfares it was shovelled into roadside troughs for people to use for their gardens, but in the summer it turned to dry dust which, along with that produced by ash barrels on the sidewalks, would carry on a strong wind and sting eyes.

"The city probably holds few surprises for you then," Jameson commented.

"Probably not." Argenti smiled tightly.

In areas like the Fourth Ward, though, with sanitation poor or non-existent, human faeces and urine became the stronger smell. Turning off from Chatham Street, Jameson involuntarily cupped a hand over his mouth, biting back a retch.

"Looks like we're there."

The symmetry of buildings had deteriorated street by street, and now it was simply chaos, four- and five-storey tenements juxtaposed against one- and two-storey dwellings with tumbledown board shacks wedged in between, foetid piles of rubbish piled against their sides, often waist-high. The last of the city's gas lamps were over a mile behind them, and the only light was from occasional coal braziers on street corners. The shadows were heavier, more foreboding.

By the nearest brazier two women were begging, one with an infant wrapped in a shawl, and halfway down the alley a drunk was prone on the ground; or perhaps he was already settling down for the night.

Argenti felt a twinge of apprehension as he looked towards the warren of alleys. Not because of the neighbourhood. He'd spent the last decade hunting down rakes, thieves and murderers in such streets – knew that the sudden rustling in the shadows behind you could as easily be a thief with a knife as rats and dogs sifting through the garbage – but because he suddenly realized that he'd only conducted interviews in the company of department colleagues. Not only did he hardly know Jameson, he had little idea what a "criminal analyst" actually did. It was uncharted waters.

Argenti tapped his pencil on his notepad. "How do you wish to proceed?"

"Simply ask your questions, as normal. Consider me just as an observer. If I have anything to ask, it won't be until the end of the interview."

Michael Tierney's web of vice and extortion touched almost every corner of the city and so required a virtual army to keep it in operation, collecting dues from dockworkers, shopkeepers, clubs, bars and gambling halls, and prostitutes like Ellie Cullen.

The Fourth Ward was at the lower end of Tierney's empire, so was entrusted to a young foot soldier called

Jed McCabe. Not the brightest, but he was fast gaining a reputation for being fiery and unpredictable, which was perhaps just what was needed to keep the chancers and lowlifes of the Fourth Ward in line.

He'd already received two payments light and had one not show that day, so his patience was worn when he got to Ellie Cullen. He looked at her sourly after counting.

"What game d'yer think yer playing? There's only half here."

"I'm sorry. We had a bad month… what with Camille dying." She saw he looked vague, and added, "You know – that Ripper killing. It's been in the papers an' all. Yer must have read 'bout it."

"Of course I have." He wasn't about to admit to any of these girls that he couldn't read, though he'd heard talk about it. "But whatya got here? Five girls, six? The rest o' yer shoulda worked harder to make up."

"That's the thing, yer see. One of the other girls, Anna, was very close to Camille. She was so grieved by what happened, we couldna get her out the house for two weeks."

To one side was a baby in a cot and in the corner a girl no more than five stared at McCabe with haunted eyes. Through the door to the kitchen, an inch ajar, two more kids peered out, and how many more beyond? Even if true, it sounded to McCabe like a line being spun – one that wouldn't go down well when passed on to Tierney – and as the baby started crying his nerves finally snapped.

He grabbed Ellie by the blouse, pulling a billy club out of his belt. "Doesn't Michael do right by you girls? Smooth the way f'yer to work his bars and clubs? How would it be if yer didn't even get entry to those bars? How would you even eat?"

"I know. Michael's been good t'us. We'll make it up to him next month."

"And St Patrick's. Pouring his money in f'the community so y'all got a place to pray. And y'know what God does to those who don't thank him for his mercies, don't yer?" But as he raised the billy club higher, saw her shrink back in fear, he suddenly realized how pretty she was. Probably the prettiest here, the highest earner. If she was marked, income might drop for yet another month. But still he felt the need to do something, give *some* message, and as the baby started wailing louder, he swung out with the Billy Club at it.

Ellie gasped, pushed against him, but McCabe was too strong. He threw her back, and as she fell to the floor he moved in and started kicking her in the ribs and kidneys, where it wouldn't show. He paused suddenly; voices approached. Through the window he could see two men in suits heading down the alley towards the house.

He waved the billy club at her. "Next time yer better not be light. Otherwise y'know what'll happen."

She leapt towards the cot the second McCabe was out the door, saw the pillow imprint of the billy club an inch to the side of her baby son Sean's head. She picked him up and hugged him tight as she started crying.

When the knock came at the door, Ellie sent one of the kids to answer it and meanwhile spent a moment in the kitchen composing herself.

True to his word, Jameson remained silent in the background while Argenti conducted the interview, first of all ascertaining the movement of the other girls in the house that night and who might have been last to see Camille.

"I think Jessie. She was at the Dungarvan with Camille jus' an hour before."

"Jessie didn't go to the Riverway hotel as well?"

"No. She picked up a client at th' Dungarvan, so Camille went on alone."

"And you? When was the last time you saw Camille?"

"About eight o'clock. I was workin' uptown in the Tenderloin with two o' the other girls, yer see. And Anna was here takin' care of the kids." Ellie went on to explain the structure of their little commune, how they'd take turns caring for the children while the others worked. She nodded towards the girl in the corner. "We're still takin' care of Camille's two little ones – couldn't jus' leave 'em to the streets."

"I see."

"And times when they wen' short on food, I'd get some extra butcher's bones and boil up some broth for 'em – but never tell Camille. She was too proud." Ellie looked down. "It was tough for Camille these past few years. As she got older, customers were gettin' harder t'find."

Argenti was reminded that it wasn't far different to the support amongst families in Hell's Kitchen. "That's very commendable of you – helping out like that."

"It was the leas' I could do."

At intervals Jameson dabbed a handkerchief at his nose, as if the stench of sewerage was still assaulting his sinuses. But there was an overlying aroma of lavender in the room; at least the girls here were making an effort.

Argenti glanced at his notepad. "And did Camille mention any clients that concerned her in the weeks before her murder? Perhaps had been violent to her?"

"No... none I can think of."

"Or any strange or odd in their manner?"

"No. Can't say she did." A dry smile creased her face after a moment. "Mind you, lot o' our clients are odd or strange. Goes wit' the job, yer could say. That might not a got a mention."

Still silence from Jameson, and it was starting to unnerve Ellie. Her livelihood largely dependant on assessing men quickly, she couldn't work out his purpose here. One hand fidgeting on a silver-topped cane, his pale grey eyes seemed to bore right through her – but then occasionally he'd smile and his countenance would soften. It was like two completely different people – not entirely comfortable with each other.

And while she found herself warming more to Argenti and knew that unlike Jed McCabe these two presented no danger to her, she was reminded of the many times she'd had to slip silver dollars to the police to keep working some clubs. They were almost as bad.

"And tell me," Ellie asked Argenti. "Are the reports of what that man did t' Camille true? How he tore her apart?"

But this was more Jameson's territory. Argenti looked towards him, and Jameson finally spoke.

"Yes. Unfortunately they are. Some embellishment, but what you've read in the papers is for the most part accurate."

"I don't read, mister. Now with Camille gone, only Anna does – and not that well, either."

Jameson was incredulous. "*What*? Only one of you in a house of five that can read, and even then not competently?"

Ellie smiled slyly, shaking her head. "What world d'yer live in? You obviously don't know much."

It was as if a switch had suddenly been thrown in Jameson. His face flushed. "A far better world than this, I can tell you. You girls off all hours with your faces painted – while these poor little wretches are left to their own devices. No doubt another generation coming up that won't be able to read!"

But Ellie gave as good back, wagging a finger at him as she admonished that Camille had actually been very well read and used to tutor the children when she could. "Came from a good family upstate. Well-educated... used t' recite from Emily Dickinson an' Shakespeare, I'll have yer know. And which you'd a known yourself if you'd *read* those same highfalutin' papers."

Jameson found himself smiling halfway through. He liked her spirit, and he was struck with actually how beautiful she was, an almost pre-Raphaelite quality to her wild red hair which flowed in ringlets over her shoulders.

"Which Shakespeare plays were her favourites?" he asked, and Ellie was off balance for a second.

"Uh... Twelfth Night. And Romeo and Juliet, I think."

"Not Merchant of Venice?"

"No, don't think so. Why?"

"No reason."

Ellie became pensive, the first shadow of concern crossing her face. "Are any of us here in danger from the same man?"

"No. That's highly unlikely." But then Jameson reminded himself that in fact two of the Ripper's past victims were known to each other, and went quiet.

He stayed silent in the background again as Argenti finished with a few perfunctory questions about the other girls in the house and their movements if they should want to speak to any of them later.

But then halfway up the alley from the house, Jameson suddenly turned. "Oh... I appear to have forgotten my cane."

He headed back while Argenti waited, and as Ellie let him back in and he picked up his cane: "Look, I'm sorry for my severe tone with you earlier. It was ungracious of me. Take this."

Ellie cocked an eyebrow. *Ungracious?* When had anyone used such a word with her? She looked at the two silver dollars held out. She doubted he'd accidentally forgotten his cane, it had looked knitted to his hand. For whatever reason, he'd wanted an excuse to come back, perhaps didn't want to show his generosity in front of his colleague. But still a hint of suspicion stayed her hand inches from taking the coins. "Do you wan' something in return fo' this?" She slowly smiled, as if in fact she quite liked the prospect.

"What? Like a receipt?"

Ellie's laughter could still be heard as Finley Jameson walked from the house, and only then did he allow a dry smile to crease his deadpan expression.

4

Lunch at Delmonico's was a grand affair. The first New York restaurant to have its menu in French, diners were treated to such unpronounceable delicacies as *Tournedos de Boeuf Languipierre* and *Aiguilletas de Sole Dieppoise*. Liveried footmen in front watched the hansom cabs of diners while they ate, so Lawrence had joined Finley Jameson and Argenti for lunch.

Jameson looked at Argenti expectantly as he took the first two spoons of his *Lobster Bisque*. "What do you think?"

"Yes. Very good... very good."

"Thought you might like it. In my opinion, the best Lobster Bisque outside of Brittany."

Jameson had been halfway through explaining about criminal analysts* when their entrees arrived. Jameson had chosen oysters. He slid down the third before continuing. "Or 'criminyst' as Colby terms himself and others of the same trade. Because indeed it could be argued that it all started with Colby."

"And before that he was a surgeon and pathologist?"

"Still is. He's still one of London's leading surgeons called upon for autopsies. And of course I suppose it's

---

* *What became termed a "criminal profiler" in later years.*

a natural extension of that. Having examined a wound, what sort of man might have done that? Was he tall, short, left-handed or right-handed? Heavy or light blow – strong or weak? Or was it perhaps a woman? Or, in the case of particularly violent murders, as we have now with the Ripper – what sort of mind might have produced that? Was the attack frenzied, or steady and methodical? A demented mind or a calm and calculating one?"

"And what sort of mind did Colby decide we were looking at with the Ripper?"

"Oh, very much a calm and calculating one. As cold and iced as these oysters." Jameson slid down another one, grimacing. "And just as slippery."

They ate for a moment without saying anything, then Argenti asked, "And was this the first letter directed at you from him?"

"Yes. Colby was the subject of three letters previously when he became involved, and there were five other general letters sent to the press before that." Considered in that light, Jameson supposed he should have felt flattered rather than disquieted, the bloodiest and most intense criminal investigation in British history, and he now was at its forefront rather than simply in Colby's shadow. Jameson slid down the last oyster, dabbed his mouth with his napkin. "Though two of those were thought to be hoaxes – not attributed to the Ripper."

Lawrence looked across, spoke for the first time, "Three if you also include the early 'Jack' letter. Opinion is divided on whether that letter was from the Ripper or not."

"Yes. Ironic that the letter to have given him his nickname, signed 'Jack', might not have in fact been from him." Jameson nodded in acknowledgment. "And if I ever omit any information or get my facts jumbled –

you can always rely on Lawrence to furnish the correct information. A veritable memory man."

From Jameson's tone, he was clearly praising rather than admonishing. Argenti nodded and smiled too at Lawrence.

"Indeed," Jameson added, "you could ask Lawrence directly anything concerning the Ripper. Particularly the more obscure points which might have escaped my attention."

"Certainly. I'll keep that in mind."

The question hung in the air, but Jameson asked Lawrence's permission before explaining when he'd first met Lawrence, while visiting another patient at Bedlam, he'd been mumbling something in the background. "As I got closer, I recognized it as the Pi multiple square root... possibly the eleventh or twelfth multiple." Jameson gestured. "I couldn't be sure because I'd never got beyond the eighth myself. I asked if he could tell me the fourteenth and nineteenth multiples. He recited them instantly, without fault.

"Successive British Monarchs over hundreds of years, the composer and date of major symphonies, the names of horses and jockeys in numerous derbies – a dazzling flood of data I tested him on that no normal mind could sustain. I then realized he was far from mad, he had what was known as 'Itard's syndrome'*, yet with a particularly strong eidetic memory. His family thought he was possessed, had him exorcised three times before finally

---

* In later years this became known as "Savant Autism", or more specifically "Asperger's Syndrome". But at this stage, in the late Victorian era, the only studies of the syndrome done were by Jean Marc Gaspard Itard, a French physician.

having him committed. I realized that with the right care and medication, he could live an almost normal life." Jameson sighed. "But still it took another two months to get Lawrence out of that Godforsaken place, get him signed to my care. I promised that I'd never let him go back there."

With the look that went between the two men at that moment, Argenti realized that they weren't just master and assistant, they were close friends.

"Lawrence's input on the Ripper case and others has been invaluable."

Lawrence smiled graciously as he turned to Argenti. "As flattered as I am that Finley praises me so – in recounting in that manner he omits his own *invaluable* contribution."

"What Lawrence is trying to say is that he just provides facts. It's up to me to interpret those and come up with some answers." Jameson looked up as the waiter approached with their main courses. "So thus far on the Ripper case, while he's played his part admirably, I'm failing miserably at mine."

Argenti smiled at the self-deprecation, even though it was probably by now well practiced. Yet other traits of Jameson's were at odds: his complete lack of social awareness with Ellie Cullen's illiteracy. His ability to talk so casually about these girls being butchered over this sumptuous banquet, straight after leaving a district where people ate rats to avoid starvation. Perhaps that was an element of British class he hadn't yet grasped.

"It's good that you're still able to be so objective." Though Argenti was equally thinking, so *cold*, detached.

"Yes, I suppose so." Jameson looked at Argenti steadily; then after a second a dry smile rose. "Though I daresay someone has to in order to try and save these poor wretches."

Argenti nodded, but inside his thoughts were in turmoil. Jameson had obviously picked up on the edge in his voice, but then his inbred arrogance had quickly taken over. And if a key part of their investigation was going to be interviewing girls in areas like the Fourth Ward, they'd make little headway if Jameson was going to be such a social oaf. He should tell Mayor Watkins as soon as possible. He didn't think he was going to be able to work with Jameson. They were simply too different, poles apart.

Though despite his conflicting thoughts, and feeling uneasy in such an establishment, as his own plate was put before him he couldn't help admiring it. Never before had he seen food so artistically arranged.

"Anyway, enough about us and the Ripper," Jameson said, cutting into his *Tournedos Rossini*. "Tell us more about yourself, Detective Argenti."

As they exited the restaurant, the clatter of cutlery and general murmur of conversation was replaced by the heavier clatter of iron wheels and horse hooves on cobbles.

Jameson took a measured breath of the outside air. "Let's go for a walk. Lawrence, you stay here with the hansom."

Jameson set off at a brisk pace down William Street. Argenti fell in step alongside.

"Where are we going?"

"Indulge me a little." Jameson had first noticed the man as they came out of the warren of alleys from seeing Ellie Cullen. A non-descript man in a brown suit and matching derby, he'd have blended in and become lost in most streets. Perhaps it was the fact that he'd been trying to act nonchalant, combined with the fact that there were less people in middle-class garb in the Fourth Ward, which had led to Jameson noticing him. Then in his peripheral vision he'd spied the same man across the road as they'd come out of Delmonico's. "Don't look behind you. But I believe we're being watched."

Argenti halted an involuntary look back halfway, and fixed on a passing hansom. "Are you sure?"

"We'll soon know."

Jameson kept his eyes resolutely ahead as they maintained a steady pace, made sure not to glance back and give the game away. Only as they took the next turn at Exchange Place was he able to surreptitiously catch a glimpse of the same man, about eighty yards behind, trying to look casual amongst a dozen or so people on the same stretch of sidewalk – but definitely following them.

Jameson felt his chest tighten. *Ah, now you are wondering which one I was amongst those looking at you: butcher, baker, candlestick-maker?* Jameson wondered whether the Ripper's boast of playing cat and mouse with them would now lead to his downfall. "He still appears to be with us."

"Who do you think it is?"

"You know the mention in that letter of him watching me and Colby…" Jameson said no more. He saw the realization hit Argenti. "As I said – *don't* look back! We're just out for a casual stroll. If he thinks anything is untoward, he'll be off. We'll lose him."

"Okay. I understand." But Argenti's mouth felt suddenly dry.

"Follow my lead at the next turn. Do exactly as I do."

"Yes… okay." For the moment any thoughts of conflict with Jameson had to be set aside; suddenly the investigation had come to them, was upon them. Unless it was one of Jameson's wild imaginings.

Hanover Street was busier, and as they took the next turn into Beaver Street, Jameson couldn't tell this time without glancing back whether the man was still following through the people milling behind.

Jameson's eyes darted at shop fronts in the street, and forty yards down fixed on one which fitted the bill, a patisserie with its entrance deeply recessed between two bow windows.

"Here. This one! Tuck deep in out of sight."

Argenti mirrored Jameson's actions, pressing back tight against the doorway. The two of them, breath held, waited expectantly.

The man in the brown suit paused for a second as he turned the corner, perplexed. Then he continued at a steadier, more cautious pace, eyes scanning for anything he might have overlooked in the street ahead; the two men shielded perhaps by a group of three talking further down.

The man noticed another turning thirty yards past the group. He put on a spurt, and had hardly got into stride before his eyes shifted to the side and rested on them.

A frozen moment as the recognition sparked, then Jameson and Argenti bolted from the doorway towards him.

He lost a couple of yards turning to run away. He headed the other way down Hanover Street, and they were only seven yards behind as they hit the junction with Pearl Street. He decided to cross it, hopefully lose them weaving through the passing hansoms.

Argenti noticed that the man was quite portly, but he was running like a man possessed, determined to keep the distance between them. And, as if fearing he might escape from their grasp, Jameson put on an extra burst too, ran a couple of paces ahead of Argenti.

They bobbed and weaved frantically through the traffic, a couple of horses pulling a butcher's cart rearing up in front of the man at one point, startled. The man picked up stride again down Pearl Street and turned into Hanover Square – but as he reached Water Street, the traffic was even heavier.

He darted through a gap between a bicycle and a hansom – then saw the approaching electric tram. He paused for thought only a second, then raced for it, making it past the tram by barely a foot, the driver sounding his bell in warning.

Jameson knew it was impossible to follow, and had to wait in frustration as it passed, peering through its windows and the gaps between passengers to try and pick up the man's progress the other side.

Jameson was so engrossed, he didn't see the tram approaching the opposite direction, only heard its bell along with a startled shout.

"Finley!"

Argenti's full weight hit his shoulder in that instant, bundling him through the split-second gap between the passing tram and the one approaching. The driver braked and it rumbled ominously past with a screech of metal behind them as they hit the ground, breathless.

Jameson glared at it, brushing himself off. "Infernal things. You can't hear them approaching. Thank you. I owe you my–" Then he was quickly reorientating, focusing again on the man running the far side. "Come on!"

The man looked back anxiously at them. He'd gained five yards due to the tram, but now lost a fraction waiting for a horse drawn coal truck to pass before running on. He went off at a tangent, darting into a service alley – but Argenti could see that he was beginning to tire. He looked increasingly over his shoulder as he noticed Jameson gaining on him, Argenti just behind.

The rapid patter of their footsteps echoed in the narrow alley, a butcher in bloodied apron breaking off from tipping offal into a garbage can to look at them.

Halfway along the alley, Jameson by then only four yards behind the man, became suddenly tired of the chase; or perhaps only then did he feel he was close enough to try the trick.

He swung his cane and hurled it, spinning from the momentum, towards the man's legs. One part struck his right calf while the other caught in front of his left foot, tripping him into a stumble.

As the man sprawled to the ground, Jameson was on him quickly. He picked up his cane, raising it threateningly above the man's head.

"Okay. The game's up. Why were you watching us?"

The man, gasping for breath, stared blankly at them.

"You pushed your luck just a little too far with that last letter – boasting how you were observing us."

The man's brow knitted. "What... *what* are you talking about?" He went to reach inside his suit jacket, but Jameson gripped his wrist.

"Don't even consider it. Allow me."

As Jameson pulled out only a wallet, Argenti saw his expression fall. Clearly he'd been expecting something else, a long knife, perhaps.

"I... I'm with Pinkertons," the man spluttered. "I was told to keep an eye on anyone visiting the other girls at Camille Green's house. Follow their movements."

Argenti tied the threads together. As Jameson checked the man's Pinkerton's identity card in his wallet, Argenti showed his own Detective's badge.

"Didn't Mayor Watkins inform you that myself and Mr Jameson would be visiting the girls at the house?"

"No. No, he didn't."

So much for liaison between departments, Argenti thought.

5

Flaming torches cast long shadows as the men entered the dilapidated warehouse and took their seats.

Wedged between Battery Park and the East River Docks, it was one of many earmarked for redevelopment now that the immigration terminal had moved from Castle Garden to Ellis Island, for which one of Michael Tierney's construction companies had the main contract.

For now, though, it served as the ideal venue for Tierney's other interests: cock, dog and bare-knuckle fighting. His favoured breed was a Canario crossed with a Pit Bull or Bull Mastiff, which he had personally bred and trained for fights. His favoured bare-knuckle fighter, Tom Brogan, also happened to be his main enforcer and head of his street gang army.

Brogan had a fearsome reputation, now almost folklore, though nobody seemed sure which had come first; unbeaten bare-knuckle fighter or Tierney's right-hand man? All anyone knew was that Brogan used to be a fireman and his favourite method of dispatching victims was with a fire-axe, an account that Tierney made sure to share with anyone tempted to cross him.

Tierney gloated as Brogan ambled into the chalked square which served as a ring, muscles flexing, glistening in the torchlight glow. Cheers rose from around the ring, and Brogan held a fist up in acknowledgment.

Bench seating was arranged in four tiers on two sides. On one side sat Tierney's entourage along with a few city officials he wanted to keep sweet, and on the other was a mixed crowd and the opponent's supporters – an enthusiastic cheer arising to compensate for their lesser numbers as he entered the ring.

Fools and their money, Tierney thought, as he watched his bookie taking the bets. To one side of Tierney was his pet canary in a cage; on the other side sat Inspector McCluskey, perhaps a measure of their respective positions within New York's power structure that McCluskey had come to see Tierney rather than the reverse. Although McCluskey waited until the fight was well under way in its second round before broaching the "urgent matter" he wished to discuss.

"If Argenti makes good progress with this case, he'll gain more prominence, start rising up the ranks."

"And why's this particular case so important?"

McCluskey gave Tierney a potted history of the Ripper case. "Shaping up to become the most notorious case in criminal history. And now it appears he might have struck in New York."

"My, my. Violent murder coming to New York. Who would have ever thought?"

McCluskey arched an eyebrow. Now wasn't the time for flippancy. "Argenti's got no less than George Watkins behind him. And if he makes a challenge for my position, we've *both* got problems. You've already had your own little run-in with Argenti, I understand."

"Yes, I have at that." That gave Tierney more pause for thought. He looked levelly at McCluskey before bringing his attention back to the boxing.

Brogan's opponent, a bull-necked stevedore in his mid-twenties, looked every bit as burly and strong as Brogan – but despite the seven-year age gap, Brogan looked wirier, quicker, and was a country mile ahead in technique. Tierney had instructed him to take the fight its course, give the crowd value for money, and so it was a measured, mechanical demolition, a dozen body and facial blows each round, enough to draw a torrent of blood without knocking his opponent out. In return, Brogan had taken only a couple of glancing head blows.

"Go on, Tommy. Show him what you're made of!" Tierney shouted as Brogan landed a heavier flurry of punches. Then, when the bell sounded, more calmly to McCluskey, "So what exactly d'you think I should do about Argenti? Make good on that price I put on his head? Maybe get Tom to chop him into pieces and feed him to the pigs on my farm?"

"I was actually thinking of something a bit more imaginative and subtle."

"Oh, imaginative I can do – but nobody's ever accused me of being subtle." Tierney smiled dryly. "I'll give it some thought."

They sat in silence through the next couple of rounds. But then as Brogan went in for the kill and the clamour from the crowd rose, Tierney's canary started chirping stronger. There was a canary tattoo also on Tierney's neck, distorted by raised veins as he shouted his support. When he first arrived in America, he'd originally been a Pittsburgh miner. A canary had saved his and seven other miners' lives from a gas explosion. Ever since, he'd carried a canary with him as a good-luck charm.

Brogan knew he'd knocked his opponent unconscious the moment the blow landed – but he didn't want it to end there. So he came in close with a couple of uppercut stomach blows to keep him on his feet, another to the kidneys as he grappled him, and then a final crunching jaw haymaker which sent two teeth flying on a gout of blood. He hit the ground like a felled tree as the crowd rose to their feet, the roar deafening.

"Puts on a good show, eh?" Tierney said to McCluskey. "I can't see him being beaten easily."

"Yes. Quite formidable." McCluskey wasn't sure Tierney had fully grasped the seriousness of the situation. He'd brought the clipping with him, so he might as well show it. "And if you needed any reminder of just how cosy Argenti is getting with Mayor Watkins."

Tierney looked at the newspaper article McCluskey handed him, headlined: "FRESH INITIATIVE IN THE RIPPER CASE". Beneath it three men stared sternly at the camera.

"Who's the man on the left?"

"Finley Jameson. A man sent to advise from the Ripper case in London."

"Okay." Tierney sighed. "I'll put Tom straight on it, tell him to start numbering our Mr Argenti's days."

In the row behind them sat Jed McCabe, along with a number of other street collectors. He hadn't paid much attention to Tierney's conversation with McCluskey – until the news clipping was folded out. Although he didn't want to say anything in front of McCluskey. He waited for the two men to part before approaching Tierney outside of the warehouse.

"Sorry t'rouble yer, Mr Tierney. But I couldn't help noticin' that news story yer were lookin' at."

"What about it?" he said impatiently.

"I… I saw two o' those men. They were visitin' one o' the girls on my fourth ward round."

"I see. And who might that have been?"

"Her name's Ellie. Ellie Cullen."

••••

Ellie looked worriedly at the clock on the far wall.

Where on earth was Anna? She knew Ellie had an important date in the Tenderloin and she'd promised to take care of little Sean. Now Anna was almost two hours over the time she said she'd be back.

The clock was one of the few luxuries they had in the house. Vital, given how much of their daily activity revolved around *time*; time they should be out working, time to feed and take care of the children, shop, launder. There never seemed enough hours in the day and that schedule wound ever tighter as night-time approached, their most intense working period. One person late, not being back when they should, and the clockwork harmony of their little commune fell apart.

Ellie looked out the window along the alleyway. Mist seemed to be settling heavier now that night had drawn in. When she'd first arrived with her family from Cork twelve years ago, she hardly recalled nights like this. But with more wood and coal fires burning in the city, they were becoming more frequent. And as she watched the mist swirls appear denser by the brazier burning at the end of the alley, giving the light an almost spectral hue, another thought suddenly froze her heart.

God, *no*. "The sort of night the Ripper might favour," the toff had commented. "He can hide more effectively, get lost in the mist and shadows." The toff and the detective had said it was unlikely the Ripper would seek out another of them, but what if they'd been wrong?

It had taken nearly two weeks to get Anna out the house again after Camille's murder. And then not just because of having to pay Tierney's dues, but the fact that they'd run out of food in the house, surviving on just scraps. With the children always getting fed first, at one point she'd eaten nothing for two days.

Yet despite that necessity, now she started to feel guilty urging Anna back out on the streets. She'd been one of the most vocal in assuring Anna that everything would be okay.

Ellie looked back at the clock, then out along the alley again. Still no sign. She could feel the chill of the night air seeping through the windowpanes. She started to fear the worst.

Straight after leaving police headquarters that evening, Argenti joined Jameson at his regular club, The Lotos, for brandy and a cigar. Jameson had received a telegram from Colby in London, and he'd also been making his own notes. He touched on why he'd picked up on the Pinkerton's man earlier.

"He was essentially nondescript, blended in. How many men of average height with brown hair, trim moustaches and derbies are there in any major city?"

Argenti nodded. "You think the Ripper is such a man?"

"Very much so. It has always been Colby's contention – and I agree unreservedly with him – that this is why the Ripper has gone undetected for so long. He simply merges into any street scene. Disappears." Jameson drew on his cigar, blew out a slow smoke plume. "Don't forget, here we have a man who managed to kill four of his victims no more than twenty yards from a milling mass of people. Whitechapel streets teeming with hawkers, peddlers, tramps and other prostitutes at all hours of the day and night – yet he slipped away undetected. And now we have much the same here at the Riverway hotel, a fresh victim killed within yards of a busy hotel bar with people constantly in and out."

Argenti took the first slug of his brandy, felt its warmth trickle down. "What is this, by the way?"

"Thirty year-old Napoleon. Only the best for the Lotos. Why?"

"It's good. Very good indeed." He smiled in appreciation. A world apart from the grappa he was used to. His eyes drifted for a moment to the bookshelf to one side.

"Ah, yes. Mark Twain. He's one of the founding members of the Lotos, and it remains his favourite club." Jameson sipped at his own brandy. "Unfortunately the club wasn't inaugurated until three years after Dickens' last visit to New York. Although there was a dinner in his honour at Delmonico's."

Argenti nodded. Apart from the fine cuisine and liquor in Jameson's company, he was learning a few things about his own city he didn't know. "And as with Camille Green, I understand the other girls weren't sexually assaulted either?"

"No. None were. Somewhat contradictory, picking up a prostitute, but then doing nothing with her." Jameson shrugged. "But time might be a factor here too. Would there be sufficient time for him to sexually molest *and* kill them with so many people close by – at least without increasing the risk of detection."

"So you're saying that time constraint was the reason there was no sexual contact with the girls?"

"No. I'm not saying that at all. I'm saying that was *one* factor." Jameson leant forward, then he paused, considering whether to elaborate. After all, this next theory was far from widely held. "Colby thinks that our man might be a virgin; the stabbing in itself some form of sexual release. But by no means everyone agrees with that theory."

"I see." Argenti recalled one of his early cases. A boy of eighteen had been arrested for killing an aged prostitute. In the interview the boy's story had been that they'd both been drinking heavily and he'd felt disgusted with himself for sleeping with such an elderly woman. His sexual performance had also been lacklustre due to the drink, and as she poked fun at his lack of potency, he picked up one of her high-heeled shoes and struck out repeatedly, killing her.

Argenti initially had sympathy for the boy, could imagine how that unfortunate action had been brought about by a combination of drink, self-disgust and the woman's taunting. But then the pathology report had uncovered that the woman had also been sexually assaulted an hour or so after death. And it transpired that the boy had gone back to the same bar to continue drinking, then had returned to have intercourse with the dead body again later. For Argenti, it was his first major loss of innocence with cases; now, little surprised him.

"It's certainly a theory I wouldn't discount out of hand," Argenti said.

Jameson looked thoughtfully at his brandy balloon as he swirled it. "There's one other factor with the timing. He appears to be a man perfectly in tune with his surroundings. Almost as if there's a metronome in his head timing his own movements and those of everyone around him. And if everything's not absolutely perfect, he'll walk away. Won't do anything." Jameson took a slug of brandy, grimacing. "For every girl he's killed, there are another one or two out there whose lives he's spared. Only they don't know it."

6

If the ticket collector had continued straight on, he might not have chosen that particular girl.

But halfway down the corridor something made the collector halt, an oddity on a past ticket perhaps, or not enough time before the next station to do an entire carriage, and he'd rather not cut off halfway. He turned back again.

The man coming down the corridor the other way slid into the girl's compartment a moment later. Only seventeen, she gave him a pretty smile, but nevertheless reserved. Perhaps her mother had told her not to be too friendly with strangers.

He nodded, smiled tightly back, and opened out his newspaper, The *New York Times*. After a moment he noticed her gaze drift away, looking out at the woodland and farm fields of New Jersey rolling by the train window.

"A fine day," he said.

"Yes. Yes, it is."

"Uncommonly good for the time of year, you could say."

"Yes… I suppose you could."

He could tell that she felt hesitant talking to him, and as she turned to look through the train window again, his eyes were drawn to her legs; a hint of dark stocking beneath her petticoat, which had a red lace trim. And as his gaze rose slowly up and he saw the same matching red in her lipstick, it became a crimson flow spreading out.

He knew then what was going to happen, knew that as he asked his next question she'd call out and scream, and so he covered the distance quickly between them.

She was quick though too, leapt back with a gasp, back pressed against the train door as he clamped one hand hard over her mouth.

He looked searchingly into her eyes. "You're not a virgin, are you?"

Wide-eyed, terrified, she just stared back.

"Tell the truth. I'll know if you're lying."

Barely able to speak with the hand clamped over her mouth, she mumbled and shook her head.

"Such a shame not to be a virgin any more," he said. "And at such a young age."

Her eyes darted frantically and he could see that she wanted to say something. He lifted his hand barely an inch from her mouth, ready to clamp back tight if she tried to call out. He leant closer to hear.

"It… if it's money you want," she spluttered.

One hand fumbled in her jacket and she held out her pocketbook.

He glared at it disdainfully. "No. No, that's not what I want." He knocked it from her grip and it fell to the floor. The crimson seemed to spread down her neck, touch the collar of her dress.

He felt insulted that she thought he might be a common thief, and looked hard into her eyes again to try and get the mood back, that first moment when they feared he might enter them. He shifted his grip to her throat to strangle off any sound she might make, and made as if to fumble at his trousers to complete the impression.

He saw the change in her eyes then – a blend of fear and fervour that he found no other moment brought – and disguised by his fumbling the knife was already in his grip from inside his coat. He thrust swiftly and deeply, and along with her short gasp saw yet another subtle change in her eyes, a far deeper surprise, yet somehow abandoned, as if nothing else mattered in the world in that instant. He could see why the French called it *"Le Petit Mort"*.

He felt the first tingle of his own orgasm rising – but then it was suddenly cut short. He felt her falling back away from him, and he had to frantically grip at the train door frame to stop himself falling out with her. The train door swung and flapped wildly on the wind as billowing steam and the train's piston-wheel rumbling assaulted his senses.

He saw her body strike the side embankment awkwardly and roll down. He stared at it for a second as he leant out and swung the door shut again. Would the wound and her falling have been enough to kill her? If it wasn't, she'd be able to identify him.

He felt his heart beating hard and fast. Had anyone seen the girl fall? He waited apprehensively for the emergency cord to be pulled, the train start grinding to a halt – but nothing came.

He looked down. Three visible blood spots, her pocketbook still on the floor. Another potential problem. He wiped away the blood spots with a handkerchief and picked it up, but bided his time until the train was a couple of miles down the line passing some woodland with thick undergrowth at the side. He opened the window and threw his hankie and the pocketbook out.

Still his heart pounded hard, anxious that any passing passengers might see him and later be able to identify him. He went along the corridor, careful to keep looking out towards the passing landscape, away from two passengers in the end compartment. He slipped into the toilet at the end of the carriage and stayed there until the train reached the next station at Maplewood.

He cast an anxious eye over the Maplewood platform before getting out, in case there was some police presence. *Nothing.* Only three other people departing and another two getting on. He went past the hansom cabs waiting outside the station, decided to walk the half-mile to the town centre. The fewer people who remembered him in the area, the better.

Argenti and Jameson convened a small conference at Police HQ on Mulberry Street. The room also doubled as a presentation room for visiting pathologists and criminologists and could hold thirty. Today, there were only eleven people present: six reporters and a handful of other city and police officials, including George Watkins. Inspector McCluskey was notable by his absence.

They made quick work of it and only fielded a few questions. The girl on the train was apparently visiting her aunt in New Jersey. She was young and wasn't a prostitute. Her pocketbook was taken and there was only one visible knife wound, indicating a robbery. It looked like she either jumped or was pushed from the train. Conclusion – it wasn't the handiwork of the Ripper.

Argenti held up a hand as the questions started to become repetitive. "I think that covers it for today, gentlemen. I suggest any further questions be saved until after our official report, which will be issued tomorrow."

Afterwards, Argenti and Jameson retired to a café round the corner, where Lawrence also joined them.

"So, we've covered the official version," Jameson said. "Let's see what we might have overlooked. This aunt she was apparently visiting in Bernardsville. How far away is that?

Argenti shrugged. "Forty or fifty miles."

"Forty-four to be precise," Lawrence interjected.

"And New Jersey is mainly a rural, farming district?" Jameson looked at both of them, but it was Lawrence who answered first.

"Sixty-one percent natural green space and woodland, four percent urban or industrial, the remainder farms. Mostly pasture for cattle and sheep grazing, some dairy farming."

Jameson smiled tightly at Argenti, as if excusing the excess information. "You can see now why Lawrence finds his way around the city so admirably. Within only days he had every Manhattan street and its grid system memorised." He took a fresh breath. "Okay. So with her pocketbook gone, it looks unlikely to be the Ripper – he's never robbed before. But let's look at other possibilities. What if in their struggle it fell? It could then have been picked up by anyone passing."

"A possibility, I suppose," Argenti agreed.

"And what if immediately she was knifed, she decided to jump from the train to safety."

Argenti was doubtful. "That's quite a fast moving train."

Jameson looked at Lawrence. "Any idea what speed the train to New Jersey would have been travelling?"

"It's a second generation Baldwin... so probably forty to forty-five miles an hour."

Jameson whistled softly. "Yes, that's quite a speed to make the decision to jump – at least without the certain knowledge that you'd incur serious injury. But if the alternative was facing death?"

Argenti appeared to sway, but then another thought anchored him. "But she wasn't a prostitute. And as you said, all the Ripper's previous victims have been prostitutes."

"Unless we include what might have been his first victim, Sarah Kelly. Sarah's husband, James, was a strong Ripper suspect at one point. But how might the Ripper have known whether this girl was a prostitute or not? You see, I examined her along with the Coroner, and I noticed that she was wearing lipstick and quite heavy rouge. A bit garish and forward for a seventeen year old, wouldn't you say? Especially just to see her aunt. And what time was she supposed to be seeing her aunt?"

Argenti checked his notes. "Uuuh… four o'clock."

Jameson looked up as their waitress in a formal black and white maid's uniform approached carrying a tray with their coffees. She poured from a silver jug, but left them to help themselves to cream and sugar. Jameson was lost in thought for a moment.

"And yet the time of her death was not long after eleven, so she'd have been scheduled to arrive in her aunt's town of Bernardsville certainly before midday. That leaves four hours spare. Was she seeing a beau perhaps? Or a more illicit meeting with a man, married or otherwise, that she might have made herself up for? And, appearing like that, heavily rouged – she could easily have been mistaken by the Ripper for a prostitute, or at the very least a woman of questionable virtue. We can't be sure whether that's the line he draws with victims, it could be simply that prostitutes are the most visible representation of that."

"Yes, good point." Argenti stirred a cube of sugar into his black coffee. "But that raises another aspect. You mentioned before about the potential victims the Ripper might have spared. But how many murder victims might there be not attributed to him, simply because he got disturbed halfway through stabbing or changed his mode of attack?"

"Indeed. There have been a number of other cases loosely attributed to the Ripper." Jameson took his first sip of coffee. "But the truth of the matter is we might never know."

Sir Thomas Colby spent four long hours late into the night after his day's surgery at Westminster Hospital looking methodically through the organ specimens for Alice McKenzie and Mary Jane Kelly. Every organ was in labelled glass jars suspended in formaldehyde.

He could find nothing resembling a IX or VIII mark on the organs of either of them, nor any alphabet letters; only a short vertical straight line cut on the pancreas of Alice McKenzie, but it could as easily have been where a stab had passed through. Still, he made a note of it, then passed everything over to his assistant, Christopher Atkinson, to continue the search.

"How far back should I look?" Atkinson enquired.

"Three more victims back, to Annie Chapman, then call it a day. Let me know if you find any other similar marks; which, as I say, could merely be as a result of one of the many stab wounds."

"And if we still find nothing?"

"Then we're left with only a few options. Either it's a complete ruse or the marks were left elsewhere. If it's on the victim's skin, then it will be lost to decomposition by now, unless it can be seen on forensic photographs taken at time of death. And if it's on their bones, it will mean getting an exhumation order." Colby grimaced. "But let's see how we go before drawing any conclusions."

It was tedious, painstaking work. Atkinson examined each organ through a magnifying loop, then if necessary a microscope.

He found one more simple vertical incision on Elizabeth Stride's kidney, then an hour later what looked like a "U" with a strange inner branch on Catherine Eddowes's heart. But in amongst the veins of the heart it had been difficult to discern; and while again it could have been the result of the numerous stabs wounds, the "U" formation struck Atkinson as too neatly formed. Perhaps the "U" had been the intended letter and the branch off had been merely from a random knife cut.

He worked for a further two hours without finding anything else before finally putting down his magnifying loop and turning off the lab's gas lights.

7

I see the newspapers are full of conjecture: was it the Ripper or not? Only one knife wound, plus appears to have been robbed. Also a nice young girl simply visiting her aunt, not a lady of the night.

And you think now that I might cast some extra light on the matter, clear up the mystery? Perhaps say something that only the murderer might know. But then that would be partly doing your job for you, wouldn't it? What would be the fun in that? Ending the mystery before it's run its course.

That mystery, that puzzle, is now part of what bonds us, an almost invisible energy running between us. Can you feel it? Perhaps not as intensely as I, not yet. But as you know life takes us on some strange paths and that could soon change.

Did you know that you missed one of the girls I killed in London? Ah, now I have you wondering which one. You and Colby diving again for long hours into the old case files. And have you and Colby discovered the other letters yet and made the link?

Perhaps Lawrence will work it out before you, or this new detective Argenti. Thing is, you never did tell the truth about why you ended up meeting Lawrence, did you? Or about yourself, for that matter. The other thing which appears to bond the two of us, we both have our secrets.

In the week after the *New York Times* received the letter, Joseph Argenti only saw Jameson once – a chance meeting at the newly built Madison Square Gardens where Argenti had taken his eldest daughter, Oriana, to see a piano recital.

Jameson gave profuse apologies. He had a speech on pathology to give at the Bellevue, and he'd been bogged down preparing notes. But it struck Argenti that Jameson had been stung by the letter's contents, seemed harried beyond purely a work burden.

Argenti had spent much of the day going through the files on the two recent cases and comparing notes on the past Ripper murders in London, and ended up bringing the files home with him. Could Jameson possibly be right? The delineation simply how garish they appeared rather than them being prostitutes. There was enough public furore as it was – but if the public realized their own womenfolk might not be safe, that all it might take was a touch too much rouge?

Argenti looked up as piano strains reached him from the next room. My goodness, that last girl had been only a few years older than his own Oriana.

He heard his wife Sophia cross the hallway and the piano become louder as she said to Oriana, "Can you help Pascal and Marco get ready soon. Supper is in half an hour."

"Yes. Okay." Then, as a jauntier style of music drifted through the open door, Oriana called out, "Papa! What do you think of this?"

He put the file in his lap to one side and dutifully got up. Crossing the hallway his youngest, Pascal, only four, sped past him and ran up the stairs, calling out.

"Marco... Marco! Momma says if you haven't finished your homework soon, you're in trouble!"

Argenti smiled to himself. Often too hectic to work at home – the house filled with music, voices calling out, laughter – but he wouldn't have it any other way.

The house where he'd been raised on Mott Street had often been filled with excitable voices and laughter, with his three brothers and two sisters, his parents and a grandmother crammed into just three small rooms. But there'd been other sounds too, his father's groans at night as his back-breaking foundry work became too much for his age; his mother's tears when he'd died and also when she lost his youngest brother, only three, to tuberculosis; their breath-held fear as they hid in cupboards or under the kitchen table some days when the rent collector called. Long days without food that Argenti vowed would never happen when he had a family. It had been the death of his sister, Marella, that had finally crushed his mother.

Their house on Charlton Street was a world apart from that. Once Oriana had been old enough to take care of Pascal and Marco, Sophia had taken a job in a grocers and provisions store a block away, and his own wages had risen with promotions; the piano they'd bought for Oriana three years ago as if confirmation of their more respectable status.

Oriana beamed as he walked into the music room. "What do you think?"

"Uuh. I don't know. What is it?"

"It's Sousa's 'The Thunderer' – but in a new style my music teacher says is becoming popular."

As Argenti listened beyond the uneven syncopated rhythm, he recognized the popular march. Uncomfortably, it reminded Argenti of the music in dance halls in the Tenderloin. Ellie Cullen and Camille Green dancing to it as the Ripper picked out his mark. Or, years back, Marella. He forced a smile.

"Very lively indeed. But I don't think it's the sort of music that will help you become a concert pianist. Can't imagine it being played at Madison Square."

"No, I suppose not."

Oriana continued playing the same tune for a moment after he left the room, but as he put the Ripper files back on his lap and resumed reading, he heard her start playing Moonlight Sonata again.

When Jameson had bumped into Argenti at Madison Square Gardens, he'd in fact only just started preparing his speech for the Bellevue. Soon after seeing the letter in the *New York Times*, he'd disappeared to Ling's for two days.

It had all started when his new maid brought him tea.

Jameson was very much a creature of habit. In London he'd had a wonderfully reliable Scottish housekeeper in her late fifties, Megan, but she felt she was too old to make the trip to America and be parted from her remaining family in England.

He'd wanted to replicate Megan as closely as possible and so asked the Manhattan agency if they had any Scottish housekeepers of mature age. The closest they had was a half-Scottish, half-Mohawk woman in her mid-thirties. "But she's been in service for ten years now and we have very good reports on her," the agency said.

Jameson took Alice on and found her diligent enough, if at times over-attentive and fussy for his liking; or perhaps it was the fact that nobody would ever adequately fill Megan's shoes.

Then that morning Alice had put his tea on the table before him. But as he came to spread out some of the papers he was working on, he moved his cup and saucer and placed it on the edge of the fireside hearth.

A moment later he watched Alice come up and move it in a few inches. He looked at her curiously.

"Why did you do that?"

"I... I was concerned it might tip and spill. It was very close to the edge."

He took this as an affront to his unassailable grasp of mathematics and Newton's Principles. "No, it wasn't. It was perfectly balanced!"

"But... but you might have tipped it yourself as you reached for it."

Jameson's face flushed. "And now you're compounding your error by suggesting I might be uncoordinated or clumsy. Insufferable woman!"

She bit at her bottom lip, close to tears.

Lawrence, sipping at his own tea, looked up, concerned by the exchange.

"And this isn't the first time you've done this, is it?" Jameson chided. "Why, just days ago you moved some papers of mine. It took me hours to find them!"

"I'm sorry."

"When I put something somewhere, it means I've done it for a reason. A perfectly good reason!"

"I understand..."

"It means I *don't* want it moved!" he snapped.

"I'm sorry if I've displeased you, sir," she murmured. Then, unable to hold back the tears any more, she fled from the room.

Lawrence's concerned gaze stayed with her a moment before he looked back at Jameson. "That was uncalled for, Finley. You were being totally irrational."

Jameson waved a hand dismissively. "Hah! That's all I need. Being told I'm irrational by a madman."

Lawrence got to his feet, glaring. "When you're like this, it's *you* that's insufferable, Finley – not anyone else."

Jameson realized that he'd stepped too far. "I'm sorry, Lawrence, I..."

He reached a hand out, his expression softening. But it was too late. Lawrence was already halfway out the room.

It was then that he'd decided to go to Ling's, sensing he wasn't going to be good company to anyone for a while; too many demons haunting him.

But at one point in his opium-hazed two days at Ling's, he found himself staring into a mirror as Sulee massaged him, wondering about his own possible madness.

Colby had encouraged them to retrace every moment of the Ripper's actions; the position he'd been in when he'd stabbed the girls, the position of each girl and where and how he'd approached them, his likely escape routes; going line by line over his letters to the newspapers, trying to discern what type of mind might have written them.

Finley had decided to take it a stage further. Rather than just applying textbook analysis to what the cramped letters or exaggerated loops might mean, he'd tried to actually copy the writing, hoping to get closer to the man. What sort of man might write in such a manner, with such a flow to the hand? And when he'd commenced the same with the last letter to the *New York Times*, he suddenly paused halfway, how mad was that? Copying the writing of a letter to yourself.

Maybe Lawrence was right. It was he himself who was irrational and mad rather than Lawrence. Pushing himself so close to the Ripper's mind that he'd stepped over the edge. There was a book recently, *The Strange Case of Dr Jekyll and Mr Hyde*, and at times Jameson feared the same was happening with himself. He was splitting into two entirely different personalities.

"Do you want me to be naked now?" Sulee asked, and this time he had no resistance. Or perhaps he thought it might help clear the cobwebs from his mind.

"Yes, I would. That would be nice."

Though as he felt her oiled body sliding against him, he wasn't sure if it was better than his earlier dream about her or not.

"A fine man he was too. Real gent. So I got carried away a bit wit' time. I'm sorry."

Ellie nodded as Anna explained why she'd been late. She'd been relieved to see Anna at first, but her annoyance at the pall of concern that had settled on her as the minutes of waiting had become hours quickly resurfaced.

"You shoulda sent a message. Got Kenny over with one at least." Kenny was a thirteen year-old street kid who ran messages between the Bowery clubs they worked. "We were worried."

"Kenny wasn't on his usual corner when I firs' looked out for him. And by the time he was back, I was ten minutes from finishin' up." Anna became thoughtful. "Besides, I've been late before and yer haven't worried so."

"I know. But it's different now since–" Ellie stopped herself short. Almost two weeks to get Anna back out of the house, one of her first night's truly relaxing again in a man's company, and here she was bringing back the spectre of the Ripper.

Ellie forced a smile, waved one hand discardingly. "Make no mind o' me. Jus' one of my mother hen moments – worrying fer nothing."

While Jameson was out, Lawrence consoled Alice in the kitchen. She'd wiped back her tears sufficiently to start washing up, but he could see she was still upset.

"I'm sorry about Mr Jameson. He has these... these turns at times which make him very difficult to be around."

"Why do you make excuses for him? I've seen the way he speaks to you, and often that leaves much to be desired too."

"You have a point, I suppose." He'd never really judged it from the viewpoint of others, and of course there was only so far he could go towards explaining why he felt bound to be more forgiving of Jameson. "But I daresay I balance that against his general good nature. His heart's in the right place."

Alice looked over as she finished stacking another dish on the drainer. "Then he should try and be more consistent."

Consistent? He himself was far from consistent, and the conversation was quickly getting into areas he'd hoped to avoid. He grimaced. "His work isn't easy at times."

"Maybe not. But that's still no excuse for him being so rude."

Lawrence couldn't help smiling, seeing her take her residual anger out on the pan she was scouring. "And of course this hasn't been an easy year for him with his aunt dying."

He saw her soften, her movements suddenly less aggressive. "Yes. You told me before they were very close."

"Very much so."

Alice continued scouring, thoughtful; then her expression brightened after a moment. "Still. She left him this lovely house." She cast her eyes around. "Didn't she have any children of her own to leave it to?"

"Her husband died four years ago and their only son, Giles, was killed in the second Afghan war. Finley lived with them since the age of nine, so became almost a replacement son. They looked upon him as their own."

She paused for a moment in her pan scouring.

"Yes, easy to see I suppose how he'd have been so grieved by his aunt's passing, what with her being like a mother to him."

"My advice, for what it's worth, when he's in one of these moods, simply keep clear of him. That's what I always do. A few hours later he's right as rain again."

"Sounds like good advice." Her washing up picked up rhythm again. Then, as if an afterthought, "But what happened to Mr Jameson's mother and father, for his uncle and aunt to take him in like that?"

"That's a long story," Lawrence said. And one, he reflected, probably more at the root of Jameson's darker moments than his aunt's death. "Best left for another night when we're both not so tired."

"I understand." From the shadow she saw cross Lawrence's face as he left the kitchen, she could tell it was a story she'd probably never get told.

8

As Ellie Cullen saw Jed McCabe heading down the alley towards her, she picked up her baby son, Sean, and went into the kitchen, passing him to the oldest girl there, nine year-old Sarah.

"If McCabe comes in the kitchen, head out th' back way with Sean. Keep 'im safe, and don' return till McCabe's gone."

Sarah nodded numbly and Ellie went back in the front room. She told the other four children there to go into the kitchen too, just in case, and looked again through the window. What the hell did he want this time? More threats, another beating? But he seemed to be held up talking with some tramp on the ground.

The tramp, a cripple with just stumps for legs, tugged at McCabe's trouser legs as he begged him for money. "Whatever y'can spare, kind sir."

McCabe held out a nickel so the tramp could see its glint, then spun it in the air. The tramp's eyes followed it hopefully, reaching out, but it was a yard distant, and as it hit the ground spun and rolled further away.

"If yer can reach it befo' me, it's yours." McCabe's smile widened. A trick he'd played a few times before, he knew that only those on makeshift trolleys could move with any speed.

The tramp grunted and lunged for it nevertheless. McCabe was ahead of him, though one thing he hadn't foreseen this time, another tramp close by who looked crippled but had his legs folded double underneath a blanket. He leapt for the coin from the other side, and McCabe had to stretch to make sure he got to it first.

McCabe pressed his boot against the man's hand inches from the coin. "Did I offer th' challenge t'you? No, I fokin didn't. Now, out my way."

He put his boot against the man's chest and pushed hard, and as the man tumbled back gave him another kick in the side for luck. He picked up his nickel and strode on to Ellie Cullen's.

Watching McCabe's display with the tramps, Ellie was already fearing the worst. So when he didn't even mention the money or start threatening, she was off balance for a moment.

"What? The two dapper gents 'ere?"

"That's right. They came jus' a minute after I left last time. What were they here fer?"

She was guarded again, feared that if she gave the wrong answer the billy club would be quickly out. Perhaps McCabe knew that one of them was a policeman. "Nothin' to do wit' Michael's business, cross m'heart. We'd never rat on 'im." And as McCabe's eyes stayed on her, clearly losing his patience: "It... it was t' do wit' Camille – yer know, followin' up on those Ripper murders I was tellin' ya 'bout."

McCabe slowly nodded. Her account tied in with what Tierney had told him.

"Did they say they'd come back t' talk to yer again or any o' the other girls here?"

Ellie pondered for a second. "They only said they *might*. They asked a few questions 'bout which girls mighta seen

Camille that night and when they'd be here t' talk to. But no firm promises o' anythin'."

"If they *do* come back, Michael would like t'know. It'd be worth somethin' to him."

"Oh, right."

As McCabe saw her eyes brighten, he didn't like the idea of it at all, but it was what Tierney had told him to offer. "We could overlook the last payment bein' light, and let yer off the next one entirely. Plus a few silver dollars and a drink o' two for yerself at any o' Mike's places for yer trouble."

"And that's all I have t' do? Let yer know they're here if they should come back?"

"Yeah, that's all. While they're still here, min' you."

Ellie was used to anything to do with money in her life having more attached to it than that. Then the catch hit her: *still here.* "But how would I even let yer know? Las' time they were here jus' half an hour."

McCabe looked towards the kitchen and a face peering through the crack in the door, whisper of voices beyond. "Yer got lots of kids here. Send one o' them t'get me. I'm never more 'an four blocks away at any time. An' lunch time I'm always at Fennelly's. Also, try an' keep 'em here as long as yer can. Give us time t'get here."

As Jed McCabe left the house, he paid little attention to the other tramps and drunks in the alley, including one wrapped in a grimy black blanket halfway up, slouched against a wall as he sipped at a bottle of liquor.

Lawrence waited for McCabe to be out of sight, then slipped the bottle of cold tea back in his pocket and headed away in the other direction.

The idea had come to Jameson from seeing the Pinkertons man. Having someone watching Ellie Cullen's was a good idea, but a man in a smart suit stood out too much in the Fourth Ward, particularly the grubby warren of alleys leading to her house.

Lawrence looked gaunt, sallow and wide-eyed at the best of times. Some coal dust smeared on his face and old, soiled garb, and he blended right in. Nobody would give him a second look.

"And you're sure it was the same man we saw coming out of Ellie Cullen's just before we visited last time?"

"Yes, of course," Lawrence said tiredly, as if the suggestion that his recall wasn't anything less than perfect was ridiculous. "I also saw him at a house further along the alley two days back. Came out counting some money. And the same as I followed him to another house just round the corner."

Jameson nodded, pensive. "Obviously a rent-man, or perhaps a more ominous form of money collector."

But Jameson had to wait a few days before Ellie was next there, if they kept to the house rota she'd imparted of when the other girls took care of the children. Also, he had something else he wanted to discuss with her.

Ellie's greeting was one of faint surprise as she opened her door. She looked at him and then past his shoulder.

"What? All alone t'day. No friend wit' yer?"

"No, I... I came alone. It was more a private matter I wished to discuss."

"Decided yer forgot somethin' more than yer cane, have yer?"

Her sly smile, one hand on her hip, unsettled him. She really was a pretty girl, a flower in this compost heap of a hovel. He cleared his throat.

"Uuuh, no. It was more to do with what you mentioned last time about... about your reading."

"My *reading*?" Still that hand challengingly on her hip as her brow knitted. Then she suddenly remembered about getting the message to McCabe. "Oh, one minute... gotta send one o' the boys to the groggery."

She went in the kitchen and shut the door behind her. She went over to Pete, only ten years old and probably the fastest runner. She leant in close as she whispered to him to find McCabe. "Either makin' calls in the streets aroun' or at Fennelly's. Tell 'im the toff is here. Right now! An' fast about it!"

As Pete ran out past Jameson, Ellie asked through the half-open kitchen door whether he would like some tea.

"No, no. It's okay, thank you." He wasn't sure if it was because he didn't want to put her to the trouble or reluctance to have any food or beverage in such a place.

"I'm makin' for myself, so it's no trouble."

Leaving her to take tea on her own though might look rude, unsociable. The two of them sharing tea might also help smooth the way for what he'd come to discuss. He smiled tightly. "Yes, very well then. Thank you. I will."

The tea seemed to be taking ages, and he found himself unconsciously tapping one finger on the rough table he was sat at. Outside, the cries of a rag-and-bone man as his cart rattled by. A baby crying and the murmur of other children's voices came from the kitchen. Finally, the clinking of her stirring the teapot just before she brought it through. He stopped his finger-tapping and smiled at her as she put the teapot and two cups down between them.

"This reading problem you mentioned," he commented as she poured their teas. "I think I might be able to help with it."

"In what way? Oh... milk."

He waited patiently again as she went back in the kitchen and returned a moment later with a milk jug.

"Thank you." He nodded as she poured. "Thing is, I appreciate how difficult it is for you – all these children and nobody here who can read properly." He took his first sip of tea. "Now I've got some time spare, and so has my assistant Lawrence. We're both extremely well versed in English grammar and literature. And once you were tutored properly, you could pass it on to the children... pick up from where Camille left off with them."

Ellie was incredulous. "What? You'd tutor me yerself. Take out yer own time t'do it?"

"I... I realize it's somewhat unconventional. But I haven't been in New York long enough to know of any reliable tutors, and–"

"No, no. It's not that. It's jus' that..." She stopped herself then. How to explain to this toff that no man had ever offered her any help outside of a quick grope or sweaty hour on a lumpy bed. One regular who'd taken a shine to her once had offered marriage, but then she later discovered he was a bigamist with a wife already in Boston. And with that reminder her suspicion came to the fore again. "An' what would yer want in return fo' all this tutoring?"

"Why, nothing." He smiled softly. "Not even a receipt."

She returned the smile hesitantly. This toff was a strange one, without question, hardly saying anything on that first visit as he stared at her with hawkish eyes, but she was beginning to warm to his style.

He took another sip of tea. "We can start any time you like. Have the first lesson today, if you want?"

Today? It suddenly reminded her that Pete might return with McCabe at any moment. Give us time t'get here, she thought. She hadn't thought much about what Tierney wanted with this toff and the detective – but it certainly wasn't for a tea dance. The only man to trouble to try and help her, and she'd betrayed him for a handful of silver.

"Oh, no. Not today. In fact, jus' remembered – got someone else callin' soon. You can't stay." She stood up to usher him out.

"Someone calling?" Jameson was reminded of the other subject he wanted to raise. "Is it perhaps that man who was here last time just before we visited?"

"No, no. Not at all." But she fired another anxious glance through the window.

"You seemed troubled then too. Is he bothering you, pressing you for money perhaps?"

Ellie looked at Jameson keenly. Could he possibly know already about McCabe and the link to Tierney?

"What, Bobby? My cousin?" She laughed disarmingly. "Whenever he's 'n trouble, he comes roun' fo' an extra penny, but rarely gets it." She looked again through the window. "Look, yer gotta go!"

Jameson stood up. "But if he's just a relative, why so bothered?"

She realized she wasn't covering well. She pondered for a second, made as if the connection had only just dawned on her.

"What this, now? This isn't Bobby callin', silly – it's a customer. And if he sees yer here, he'll think I'm already busy wit' one."

Jameson was sure she was lying. She wouldn't entertain clients in a hovel like this with all these kids around. For whatever reason, she was eager for him to leave.

She reached for the front door and opened it.

Jameson touched his derby rim as he went out. "Don't forget – those lessons. We can start as soon as you like."

"Yes… I appreciate. An' I'd love to. Jus' not today, tha's all."

She fired one last anxious glance each way – still no McCabe, thank the Lord – and shut the door.

Pete had run faster before, but never so haphazardly, darting from street to street like a jack-rabbit. Within no time his breath was ragged.

He found McCabe in the end at Fennelly's, his regular lunchtime watering hole. He was sat at the bar supping a stout next to Martin, who handled the neighbouring collection area for Tierney.

McCabe wiped the froth from his mouth, peering sharply at the boy as he gave him the message.

"Are yer sure she didna say the toff *and* th' detective were there?"

Pete pondered for a moment. He'd have remembered if she mentioned a detective. "No. Jus' the toff."

McCabe turned to Martin. "Mike seemed keen t' know, either way. So if yer can run and tell 'im the toff's there right now, I'll head back there with the boy."

"Okay, gotya."

McCabe burst through the saloon door with Pete headed in one direction just ahead of Martin running through the other.

If McCabe had got there a moment earlier, he'd have run right into Jameson. As he approached the alley leading to Ellie Cullen's, he caught a glimpse of Jameson's distinctive burgundy derby hat fifty yards past the alley heading away from him.

McCabe eased to a walk following in the same direction, shuffling into the road at one point for a better angle past the melee of people and handcarts in between to make sure it was Jameson. Ten yards further along Jameson turned into another street.

McCabe kept following. Tierney would be disappointed that Jameson had already left Ellie Cullen's; if he could point them to where Jameson had gone, it would make it less of a wild goose chase.

But as he turned into the next street, there was no sign of Jameson. His eyes frantically darted and scanned. There were less people on this street, and the smart suit, derby and cane would have been easy to pick out. A couple of hansoms were rolling away eighty yards down the road past the normal collection of open trucks and handcarts. Could one of them be the toff's?

He walked twenty yards deeper into the street, eyes scouring for any hidden recesses, turn-offs or alleys. Nothing.

He turned and headed back to Ellie Cullen's, one hand going to his billy club. Obviously he hadn't made the arrangement between them clear enough.

The second McCabe was through Ellie Cullen's door he had one hand at her throat, the billy club raised in the other.

"One fokin' thing I ask of yer, and you can't even do that right. I tol' you t' keep him here."

"I tried," she pleaded; barely a gasp with the pressure at her throat. "But he said he couldna stay long."

"Not near hard 'nough. Mike's men'll turn up, and I got nothin' to show 'em. I'm gonna look a fool." He raised the billy club higher.

"I tried, I promise." She tried to shrink back from the anticipated blow, but the grip at her throat was too tight. Her eyes shifted desperately to the table. "Made 'im tea an' everything – see. But he said he'd jus' called by fo' a minute. Had t' leave."

He glanced at the table then back at her. He brought the club down hard on her shoulder, then another sharp blow to her thigh. She groaned with the pain.

"Next time he calls, yer make sure t' keep "im here longer." He raised the billy club high again. "Otherwise next time it's yer pretty face or yer bairn's skull."

Wide-eyed, she nodded as McCabe stared the message home. But as he gave one last blow to the soft flesh at the side of her stomach, winding her, the door burst open behind them and Jameson was there.

"Unhand the girl! This instant!" Jameson brandished the Anubis end of his cane threateningly.

Jameson had noticed McCabe following fifty yards behind him, so as soon as he'd turned the corner he'd ducked into the first open door, his back tight against a wall as McCabe passed only feet away at one point.

McCabe turned with a sly leer. "My, my. The magpie returns fo' the jewel." He raised his club again so that their positions almost mirrored each other.

"And away with you, if you know what's good for you!" Jameson shook the cane.

McCabe looked him up and down disdainfully, his leer now almost incredulous. "You're out o' yer depth here, dandy boy. The turf for miles aroun' belongs to Mike Tierney, and this little patch jus' happens to be mine. So I make the rules here o' who comes and goes, and how much they pay fo' the privilege."

"I won't warn you again," Jameson said.

McCabe looked to one side, as if sharing his disbelief with someone unseen. Then he moved like lightning, lunging and swinging his club straight at Jameson's head. Jameson parried with his cane and the blow slid off and brushed his shoulder. He struck back quickly, catching McCabe squarely on the shoulder; but the Anubis ears were sharp, pierced McCabe's jacket and drew a speck of blood.

McCabe quickly shook off the surprise – the toff had landed a lucky blow, that's all – and swung back again. A full parry with the cane this time, the blow didn't even connect. But no return blow came, and McCabe raised his club to strike again.

Jameson appeared to step back then lunge with the cane, and at first McCabe thought, What's the point in that, prodding with his cane? Then he felt a sudden numbness spread through his arm.

As McCabe's arm had lifted with the club, Jameson had pulled out the head of his cane. A swordstick. Not a full sword, but half-length, a slim razor-sharp sixteen-inch blade which he plunged into McCabe's shoulder. McCabe looked in shock at the blood welling there.

"Yer stabbed me. You fokin' stabbed me."

"How observant of you." Jameson smiled dryly. He pulled the blade out, poised *en guard* to lunge again. "Now, as I said: be off with you! And if I see you here again, I'll cut out your liver and throw it to the dogs in the alley."

McCabe's arm started to tremble, and the billy club dropped to the floor. He shuffled cautiously around Jameson and picked up his club with his left hand. Then, as he was by the front door and felt braver out of the blade's reach:

"Yer not heard the last o' this, mister. An' you'll be a dog's dinner all right once Michael hears 'bout this."

Jameson made as if to thrust again with the blade, and McCabe swiftly opened the door and ran out.

The pride of Michael Tierney's empire was a brewery he'd taken over four years back on Pearl Street, McLoughlin's. Serving fine ales and stouts to bars throughout New York, Tierney's plan was to spread that network to Boston and beyond. Word had it that it wasn't a friendly takeover, Tierney squeezing out the past owners with increased book debt and "security" fees.

In the brewery yard were standard carts with dray horses, but he also had three for express deliveries with sprightlier colts for runs to Brooklyn and New Jersey.

Tierney thought it likely that in continuing their investigation, Jameson and Argenti would visit Ellie Cullen's again; and when he got news they had, Brogan with his fire axe would load into one of the "express" carts with a few other men armed with billy clubs, shotguns and pistols.

They'd cosh the two men as they came out of Ellie Cullen's so that to any onlookers it might look like a robbery. Their original target was Argenti, but they realized it would be too risky to leave a witness like Jameson alive. So they'd load both onto the cart and take them somewhere remote where Brogan could hack them into three sections – head, torso and legs – at leisure.

Then most likely a burial at sea. Tierney had an undertaker friend who also had a range of lead-lined coffins specifically for sea burials. Slipped some extra money, he'd put another body or body part in the same coffin before sealing it.

McCluskey had asked for "subtle", but this was as subtle as it got with Tierney; the only deference being that an attack with coshes on the two men would be far easier staged, and go practically unnoticed, in the back alleys of the Fourth Ward than on Fifth Avenue or Wooster Street. Thus the eagerness to know when the two men were at Ellie Cullen's.

As Martin ran into the yard at McLoughlin's, Tierney was in his office with his bookkeeper going over that month's figures. He looked up as Tom Brogan opened his office door.

Ellie was close to tears with thanks, but equally eager that Jameson get away.

"Tierney's men could b' here at any moment."

"It's not safe for you to stay here either." Jameson looked anxiously through the window. No sign of anyone approaching yet. He suggested that Ellie head out the back way, take the kids to Battery Park for a while. "I know there are a lot of you, but the older children can help with the younger ones. And don't come back here until you're sure one of the other girls will be here."

"And you?"

"I'll hail a hansom and head off the way I came in. Stop off at Mulberry Street on the way and get a policeman at your door meanwhile."

9

Mike Tierney's favourite tipple was one of his own brewery's black stouts with a dark rum chaser. He was midway through his first of the day when Brogan led Martin through and he heard about the toff being at Ellie Cullen's.

Alone? The information threw him for a moment. Either the toff was very brave or very foolish. Obviously Argenti hadn't warned him of the dangers of venturing into the Fourth Ward alone.

But he reminded himself that Argenti was his main target, and if he sent Brogan with a team now that might forewarn them of what he had in mind.

"My interest is in the detective. The toff's just a side dish." He got up and patted Martin's shoulder. "So we won't be payin' the man a visit, not today."

Jed McCabe hustled quickly away from Ellie Cullen's heading towards McLoughlin's brewery. Hopefully Brogan and his men would come speeding round the corner in a brewery cart at any second, and he could point them in the direction of the toff before he got away from Ellie's.

Then he thought about what had just transpired, the lesson in swordsmanship the toff had given him. If Tierney found out, it would reflect badly on him, would seriously dent his street authority. He'd need a cover story.

He glanced at his shoulder, the blood still streaming from it. With his left hand, he took out his billy club and rubbed it in the blood, then slipped it back into his trouser belt.

So when Martin on his own ran towards him and told him that Brogan and his men wouldn't be coming, he was relieved; although he feigned disappointment.

"Tha's a shame. Didn't like the look o' that toff. It'd been good to see 'im get his ass kicked."

"Oh, and Mike said fo' yer not to do anythin' with him either," Martin said.

"Course not. I know well enough that th' toff an' the detective's Mike's business. Mine's jus' with the girl."

As they turned the corner towards Fennelly's, Martin asked, "What happened to yer shoulder?"

McCabe looked at it as if he'd only just noticed it. "Oh, that? Ran into a coupla o' the Shirt Tail gang on the way back." He held up his bloodied billy club. "They won't be doin' that again in a hurry."

10

When Argenti put his gun on the high shelf in the bedroom cupboard after hanging up his jacket after work, he couldn't help noticing the look his wife Sophia gave him. He removed only his derby hat and jacket; as usual he would stay semi-formal and keep on his waistcoat and tie for dinner.

The NYPD didn't supply guns to its men. It was therefore up to each officer to buy his own. As a result, on scant pay, only a third of the NYPD carried guns. Argenti didn't usually keep a gun at home, but with the increased activity with Tierney he'd decided to break that rule. The normal arrangement in his section was to share the use of three guns, with the key to the gun drawer held by that day's duty officer.

Sophia didn't say anything immediately; she waited until they were sat at the table after dinner and the children had gone to bed before she softly enquired, "Is something wrong at work, Joseph? Something troubling you?"

"No, not at all." He pulled a tight smile. "Everything's fine."

"No street problems or riots expected?"

As with himself, the Draft Riots had defined a part of Sophia's childhood. Hundreds had been killed or injured, and smaller pitched street battles were still periodic events. Argenti blew out a soft plume of smoke from the cheroot cigar he'd lit after dinner.

"Well if there are, nobody has troubled to tell me about them."

He could see the concern still etched on Sophia's face. She was still in her early forties a very beautiful woman, just the first touch of grey in her dark hair; to Argenti, every bit as beautiful and serene as the first day he'd met her. But occasionally worry lines in her face would show her age more: as now, as she tried to come to terms with why he'd brought a gun home, when for the children's sake they'd agreed he wouldn't. He realised he'd been too flippant.

"Just some increased troubles between a few street gangs. We've been told to be more cautious going into some areas." He didn't want to go as far as telling her about the price on his head from Tierney, worry her unnecessarily.

"And that's all?"

He looked across at her more directly. She knew him so well, could no doubt tell that something deeper was troubling him. He hadn't planned to say anything, in part because he hadn't got his own thoughts clear on the matter, but now with the question laid bare between them he told her the bones of the Ripper case and his concerns about Jameson.

Sophia was silent for a moment. "And is it just differences between you that you see as the main obstacle to you working together?"

"No, not just that. It's his attitude with some of the people we'll be dealing with as well. If his own world is so removed from theirs, how effective can he be in interviewing them? And something else too..." Though now he was getting to the nub of what he hadn't quite pinned down himself. It hadn't simply been Jameson's abrasiveness with Ellie Cullen the other day, the thought that his social oafishness might hamper the investigation; or Jameson coolly sliding down oysters straight afterwards. It was the sudden change in moods that he found unsettling. The fact that he was unsure what Jameson might do next. "We simply have different working styles, which I fear will clash."

"But this case might help your advancement?"

"Yes, very much so, *if* handled correctly."

Sophia fell silent again, glancing at the oil lamp between them as if for inspiration.

"Then don't you think it might be worth giving the case some time? Those differences might later not appear such an obstacle, or you'd reach some sort of working compromise."

"Yes. That's a possibility, I suppose." He blew out another cigar plume. She knew him so well. Sophia had deftly drawn out what was already half on his mind. Was that why he'd balked at saying anything to Watson or Latham straightaway – the feather in his cap of such a high profile case outweighing his own personal disquiet? In the end he knew Sophia's advice was right, give it time.

The previous night he'd brought the Ripper files home with him, but for the next few nights he delved into them with more gusto. Cut off from his family – Oriana's piano playing, Marco and Pascal playing board games or doing their homework, Sophia gently humming in the kitchen – as alone in his study he delved deeper into the mystery and the various hypotheses of the British Police, Colby and the newspapers: a butcher or surgeon, a visiting merchant seaman, a local, a master of disguises or showman, possibly a Jew or a Mason, lowly, high-class. In short, they didn't have a clue.

Argenti found himself wavering between the varying theories; and now there were possibly two more murders in New York to work into the equation. What common element might bond all of those?

The thought dwelled on his mind with no answer, until the next night when Sophia asked him to check the date for Oriana's next conservatory music lesson. He leafed through his diary. He knew he'd written it down.

"Appears to be the third of next month."

"Are you sure?"

"Yes, I..." And as he flicked forward a month and back again, the thought suddenly hit him. The way that notation of day and month differed between the USA and Britain. "I just checked."

He looked towards the wall clock. Would it be too late to disturb Jameson?

Finley Jameson's house at 1334 Greenwich Avenue was an impressive Georgian brownstone left to him by his aunt. In their last couple of meetings, Argenti had learnt more about Jameson's background. After the Crimea, his uncle had commanded an engineering regiment in India, part of the network of British army engineers who built the railroad there.

On return to Britain he'd joined London and North Western Railways and subsequently became a founding director of the New York Central Railroad, moving with Jameson's aunt to New York just two years after Finley left medical college. His aunt and uncle had only one son of their own. He'd followed his father into the military and been killed in the Second Afghan War.

The centrepiece of 1334 Greenwich Avenue was an impressive drawing room with gallery library above. Jameson admitted that when he'd first arrived at his aunt's house he'd had trouble getting to grips with the high street numbering in America. "Along with, yes, you're right – the difference in the day and month order." His voice raised to reach Argenti in the gallery library above. "Fifth or sixth in the shipping registers there, I think you'll find."

"Sixth," Lawrence said, surer of his ground. He was alongside Jameson in the drawing room below as between them they searched through the earlier shipping registers. "Three along from *Great Expectations*, the last in the Dickens row."

Among the Dickens, Twain and Thackeray volumes, Argenti couldn't help noticing some darker books too: Edgar Allen Poe and Marquis de Sade; *The Necromancer*; *Pseudomonarchia Daemonum*; Goethe's *Faust*; *Melmoth the Wanderer*; Thomas de Quincey's *Murder considered as a one of the Fine Arts*. He took out the fifth and sixth shipping registers, just to be certain, and walked back down the stairs to the drawing room.

As he started looking though the sixth volume, Lawrence prompted, "Looking at the sequence in these earlier volumes, I think you'll find it just after halfway through – the *Frisian*, 4,782 tons. Built 1878 at Harland and Wolff shipyards."

Argenti tapped his finger on a page after a moment. "Got it here. And you were right about the transfer date to Blue Crest Lines being in April too. All I could presume for my theory to hold was the transfer being made some time in 1889."

Lawrence looked at him blankly. The suggestion that he might have got the date wrong simply didn't compute.

Jameson nodded. "So your theory is that when Blue Crest replied about the dates queried of when the *Frisian* was in London – the Americanization of the dates caused confusion?"

"Yes. In London there was the theory that the Ripper might be working on a cattle steamer, because the murders all took place at a weekend and usually these steamers arrived for the weekend and set sail again on the Monday." Argenti leafed through one of the files. "They managed to tie in a ship sailing from Rotterdam for three of the dates, the *Frisian* – but they needed to link at least two more dates for the premise to hold. But remember, they didn't consider this possibility until a year later, and in March 1889 the *Frisian* had transferred from De Voort Lines to American-owned Blue Crest. So the query on those last two dates would have come through to Blue Crest's offices in New York."

Argenti passed Jameson the telegram answer that had come from Blue Crest's offices. It read simply: DATES FOR LONDON: 4/10/1889 & 10/5/1889. He then handed Jameson the initial request: GIVE DATES FOR FRISIAN DOCKING LONDON CLOSEST TO 2ND WK IN APRIL AND 1ST WEEK IN OCTOBER 1889?

Argenti leant over, pointing. "Now in London they no doubt read those dates as 4th October, a full week adrift, and 10th May, more than three weeks adrift. So, no date match. Whereas the Blue Crest clerk in New York who sent the answer probably meant April 10th and October 5th – a match for both."

Jameson nodded slowly, a wry smile rising. "I can see now why Watkins was keen to have you replace McCluskey. He looked up as Alice approached with a large silver tray with their tea and coffee, along with two bottles.

Argenti was the only one having coffee. As Alice poured, Jameson asked Argenti, "Would you join me in a brandy with your coffee? Or would you like whisky?"

"A brandy would be fine, thank you."

Argenti noticed that Lawrence didn't have any spirits and wasn't offered any; nor had he shared any of their bottle of wine at Delmonico's. Perhaps alcohol conflicted in some way with his medication.

Jameson swirled his glass thoughtfully for a second. "Did you know that this initial theory with the cattle steamers came from no less than Prince Albert, Queen Victoria's husband?"

"I... I saw a note about that in one of the files." Argenti shrugged. "I wasn't sure whether it was a real claim or not."

"Oh, it was a real claim, make no mistake, along with the accusation that went with it, that Prince Albert only came up with the theory to divert suspicion from his own family." Jameson sighed. "Started off purely as an ugly street rumour, but eventually the press got hold of it and started speculating the same, that Queen Victoria's grandson, the Duke of Clarence, was somehow implicated."

"Yes. I saw something to that effect too."

"Along with the Queen's surgeon, the Masons, half the Jews of Whitechapel and Uncle Tom Cobley and all."

Argenti smiled, said nothing. Jameson looked back at the telegrams.

"Marvellous invention, but the extortionate cost leads people to be brief. And brevity, as we now see, can lead to errors." Jameson took a fresh breath. "Fine. We tie in those two cattle-steamer dates – which at least gives us a firm link to the original canonical five murders. But where does that leave us on this attack here at the Riverway Hotel? I understand that the *Frisian* was shipwrecked off the English coast almost a year ago now."

"Broke up on the Lizard in February, 1891," Lawrence interjected. "Salvaged and scrapped four months later."

Argenti leant forward. "That's the thing. Blue Crest have another two cattle steamers – the *Delphinius* and the *Union Pride* – both of which do regular runs to New York."

"I see." Jameson was pensive as he tied the threads together. He took another slug of his brandy, closing his eyes for a second as he savoured it. "So what's left to determine now is if one of those boats was in New York the weekend Camille Green was murdered, and if it was, when it will be back here."

11

When they called at the Blue Crest Lines offices the next day, a clerk confirmed as he studied the telegram that the dates written in that manner, 4/10 and 10/5, would have in fact referred to April 10 and October 5.

"And out of these two vessels of yours," Argenti enquired, "the *Delphinius* and the *Union Pride* – which one might have been in New York harbour the weekend of 14th November of last year."

The clerk, a dapper young man in his early thirties with a cheroot moustache, took a moment to check a register at a side desk. Jameson stood just behind Argenti, and Lawrence waited in the hansom outside. The clerk looked up after a second.

"Looks like the *Delphinius* was here that weekend. Arrived on Friday, the twenty-first, sailed back once laden again on first tide Monday the twenty-fourth."

Argenti and Jameson exchanged a look.

"And pray tell us," Jameson enquired, "when the *Delphinius* might be back in New York?"

The clerk didn't need to consult the register this time. "It's mid-voyage right now, due to dock in six days."

Argenti asked, "Also, would you happen to have a crew list for the *Delphinius*?"

"For the past voyages, yes. But not for the current one. There are often a number of last minute crew changes –

so we won't get that list from the Captain until after the ship's docked."

"Well, if you have that list for the November 21 passage to help assist us. Also for those past two dates on the telegram when the Frisian was docked in London."

The clerk checked his pocket watch. "If you return before our offices close today, I will ensure the lists are ready."

Argenti knew that either they'd make ink-press copies or someone would have to painstakingly write or type each name.

"Thank you. You've been most helpful." Then to Jameson as they were heading out and getting in the hansom, "Six days? Do you think that's going to be enough time to get that final list from London?"

"It's going to be a close call," Jameson admitted. They'd had two of the past crew lists from the *Frisian* matching past London murder dates on file, but were missing the third which they'd requested by telegram earlier that day.

Lawrence flicked his whip and the hansom set off into the traffic along Fifth Avenue.

When that final list arrived from London, sent by courier on a Blue Ribbon contender liner to hopefully catch up with the lumbering *Delphinius* in passage, they had another problem – the *Delphinius* had made good passage due to fair weather and had arrived four hours earlier than scheduled.

They'd planned to get to the boat as it docked and was starting to unload, all of its crew still present and correct, but by the time they got there it was partly unloaded and some of the crew already ashore, including the Captain.

"Though after a shot o' rum and hot tea at the nearest bar," the burly First Mate, Nick Squires, commented, "he'll no doubt be back. Make sure this rabble don't break half the Jerseys' legs unloading."

Longhorns, grain and cotton one way, Jerseys for milk, canned goods and general provisions the other, Squires had confirmed as the main cargo. Though Argenti couldn't help noticing that a few of the Jersey Bulls also had long horns, the waxed handlebar moustaches of many of the burly men handling the steers mirroring them.

The first deck had already been cleared of cattle and the remaining crew were part way through clearing the deck below. Two large sections in the upper deck had been pulled back to create an access well to that lower cattle deck, but it was a far more delicate operation craning them out. The hoist with straps had to be lowered practically out of sight of the dockside crane operator. The crew below would then strap in a fresh cow and on the top deck a fellow crewman would whistle and signal to the crane operator that it was secure to lift.

Argenti and Jameson were alongside Squires on the Bridge deck, looking down into the well as the men loaded the cattle.

"Do you have a list of the crew for this current voyage we could view?" Argenti enquired.

"No, sorry. Only Captain Burrows has that, keeps it private in his desk. It'd be more than my life's worth to– No, no! Keep that lot more on the left!" he shouted to the crew below. Then calmly again as he looked back at Argenti. "Sorry. You'll have to wait till he gets back."

They'd been so engrossed in their conversation with Squires, they'd hardly noticed the crew member in a plaid-shirt below looking at them worriedly as they arrived; in particular as Argenti had shown his NYPD badge.

"I thought at first you mighta been calling about that river pirate incident we had last year," Squires said. "Two o' my men were seriously injured in that."

"Sorry. Different department," Argenti said.

Jameson raised a brow. "River pirates?"

"Yeah. Bastards operate right outta there." Squires pointed to the ramshackle tenements a block from the dockside. "Sneak out at night in rowing boats and use kids no more than eight to get through any open portholes. Smaller, see."

Argenti nodded. He went on to explain to Jameson how they'd then let in older gang members to rob the crew. "Or often murder them if they get in the way."

Squires had meanwhile been filling a clay pipe. He lit it and took the first few puffs. "That's right. Damn fortunate that amongst the crew we had left on that night, one of them had a rifle. Saw 'em off."

But Jameson had been distracted halfway through. As the man below had looked a second time with consternation towards them, Jameson had noticed him from the corner of his eye; and as the man did the same again now, Jameson met his gaze directly. Alarm rising in the man's eyes, Jameson knew instantly something was wrong.

"Hey, you!" he shouted.

The man bolted for it, weaving through the steers towards the aft deck.

Jameson ran down the two flights of steps towards the lower cattle deck, Argenti catching on a second later and following.

"Stop, I said!" Jameson shouted as he hit the cattle deck. The man was close to its end and the door there leading to the aft section and lower decks.

Most of the cattle were still in their wooden pens, eight or ten to each, but there were still six loose Jerseys from the last pen emptied and they were getting more agitated with the men running and the shouting.

Perhaps if Jameson had asked Squires, he'd have advised against the action, but the desperation of the moment seemed to call for it. If the man got through the end door, he'd disappear into the warrens of the boat or dive through a porthole and escape. Jameson took out his pistol and fired just above the man's head.

"*Stop!*"

The man kept running, swung the door open and ran through it. The shot echoed heavily in the iron hull, the agitation amongst the cattle mounting quickly to panic, one group burst out of their pen, and the growing thunder of hooves spread that panic like a tidal wave through the rest. Another pen burst, then two more, and within no time the deck was a mass of stampeding cattle.

Crew members jumped for safety to the sides as more pens were broken through. Argenti tucked in quickly behind one of the last intact pens, looking desperately ahead for any signs of Jameson. Dust from straw and dried cow dung kicked up from the stampede hung in the air, and it was difficult to see clearly ahead.

"Finley!" he called out.

No answer.

"*Finley!*"

But as still no answer came, he feared Jameson had been trampled in the stampede. Looking at the madness of the rush of cattle through the dust ahead, it was hard to imagine how anyone could have survived it.

Three piers and two hundred yards away, but a million miles in ambience, was Tom Dexter's river showboat.

An old-style Mississippi steamboat, it plied a passage between New York and Charleston, spending five days in each before setting sail again. It had shows with dancing girls, magicians and comedians on the main foredeck and gambling aft deck, with supreme-class cabins above and first-class below.

Gambling was only meant to take place once the boat was in passage, but as with Dexter's other two clubs in downtown Manhattan, he paid city officials and policemen to turn a blind eye. It also wasn't necessary to be a travelling passenger to partake of the shows or the gaming, and *Dexter's Showboat* would attract numerous visitors when docked in New York or Charleston.

Not least because of the number of pretty girls on board. Show girls and working girls, the line between them thin, worked the affluent crowd, getting them to part with as much money on champagne, gambling and illicit sex as they could. A number of cabins were always vacant, rotating every hour or two with visiting clientele.

The man on the upper promenade deck appeared to gaze absently over the East River. He in fact had half an eye on the drunken man behind him slumped over a lifeboat trunk, a quarter bottle of champagne still in his grip. Was the man gone enough yet, would he notice him approach? As finally he watched the man's eyes drift shut, he moved in and slipped the key from his jacket pocket. It was a passenger key, which explained the man's drunken state. If he was heading to a cabin for a quick sojourn with a girl, he'd have made sure to be in better shape.

He slipped back into the shadows and then joined the activity in the showroom, watching a magician on stage as he put his female assistant in a trunk and started to run long swords through it to gasps from the audience. He observed a few girls at the back of the room watching the show like him, but none of them seemed to have noticed him.

Then one girl in particular caught his eye, rich red lips and rouge to match a red and black bolero top. But it wasn't just that splash of red that stood out from the sepia of the smoke-misted room in that moment, but the fact that she looked a lost soul. Not far different from how he'd felt a moment ago, he thought, their fates intertwined.

As she left the room and took the stairs to the upper promenade deck, he followed.

"What's your name?"

"Lucy," the girl said, easing a smile after a second, her initial reserve gone.

She'd been leaning against the rail looking out over the river as he came up on the promenade deck. He stood by the rail just a yard to her side, admiring the same view. There was nobody else on deck.

"I'm sorry if I'm being presumptuous, but you seemed a bit of a lost soul in there."

"I've seen that trick before," she said.

He nodded, silence between them for a moment.

"Is that because you're here often to see these shows?"

"Could be," she said, smiling slyly.

A coy one, he thought. For whatever reason, she didn't want to admit she was here regularly. Maybe she wasn't right. He'd need to test more. He took the cabin key along with five silver dollars from his pocket and held them out.

"Is this a trick you've seen before?"

She arched an eyebrow, her face not giving much away – and then her gaze suddenly shifted past his shoulder. Two men had come out onto the deck twenty yards along.

He slipped the key and the money back into his pocket.

She picked up on his anxiety, the way he turned stiffly away from the two men so that he couldn't be seen.

"Why, are you ashamed to be seen with me," she teased. "And we've only just met."

"Not, it's not that, I…"

"One of Manhattan's gentry? Afraid to be seen where you shouldn't be?"

"Something like that." He felt himself tremble. Perhaps he should just leave. Suddenly it didn't feel right.

She appraised him more steadily, then her expression eased again, possibly because the two men along from them headed back inside or because she'd made her own decision in that moment. She leant close to him, touched one hand against the pocket where he'd put the key and the money.

"Even if it is a trick I've seen before, that doesn't mean it's one I'm tired of."

When they got to the cabin and she started to take off her bolero top, he halted her.

"No. Please leave it on."

He asked her to take off her remaining clothes and as she lay on the bed he admired the contrast between her bolero top and the darkness of her pubic hair: black, red, black, red. It had a certain symmetry to it.

A look in her eyes in that moment made him pause for thought again whether this one was right: the girl *and* the moment. Maybe he should just let her go. After all, he'd probably never get the symmetry perfect.

Darkness. As Jameson focused on the faint light coming through a porthole at the end of a passage ahead, he wasn't sure how long his blackout had lasted. How much time he'd lost.

Just after being barged against the hull by a couple of the stampeding Jerseys and banging his head on an iron rivet, he'd managed to squeeze through the door at the end. Breathless, he took stock. A few bruised ribs, one of them felt as if it might be broken. The last thing he recalled before the darkness dragged him under was the deafening clatter of the stampeding cattle on the other side of the door and feeling nauseous.

He focused on the porthole light. Which way had the man gone? If he'd been unconscious for a while, the man might be long gone by now. He edged along the corridor cautiously, looking into doors each side as he went – two empty cabins, a scullery, a store cupboard with shovels and brooms. He opened the door at the end, an open aft deck, two capstans with heavy ropes trailing down to the dockside. A sailor in blue dungarees by the back rail glanced at him disinterestedly, flicked his cigarette butt into the water below. Not the man who'd run.

Jameson looked over the side. No sign of anyone swimming or scampering away across the dockside. Jameson took the stairs down to the lower deck.

Darkness again. It took a moment for Jameson's eyes to adjust to the scant light. He ventured along cautiously. Smaller compartments here, stacked with flour bags, calico, engineering parts, sacks of wool, railway sleepers.

Jameson realized that he'd dropped his cane in the stampede. He felt naked without it.

A sudden rustling sound ahead. He tensed, edging forward more cautiously. As he came to the next compartment and his eyes adjusted to the dim light, he saw two rats nibbling away at some grain where a sack had split open.

He eased his breath, but short-lived, more rustling behind him. He half-turned, catching only the shadow of the shovel swinging towards him. It glanced off his shoulder – but he was already off balance, tumbling forward onto the grain sacks.

The rats scurried off. He saw the shovel swing at him clearer this time, though the man behind was still in shadow.

Jameson rolled quickly aside, grabbed a handful of grain as he went and threw it in the man's face.

The shovel hit the sacks, throwing more grain dust into the air. The man coughed as he swayed a fraction, rubbing his eyes with his left hand.

Jameson seized the opportunity – sprang up and rugby-tackled the man hard while he was still off balance. The man went sprawling, hitting the compartment side partition. The shovel clattered from his grasp.

The man dived for the shovel again, and Jameson aimed to kick it away. In the confusion of shadows the man came in between and Jameson's boot struck him squarely on the jaw.

"You've got some explaining to do," Jameson said as the man slumped back against the grain sacks.

But the man was unconscious.

12

When the crewman came to, Captain Jim Burrows was back from his dockside tipple. Having ascertained the man's name, Bill Doyle, the first thing Argenti and Jameson did was check it against the crew lists they had for the three past key dates the *Frisian* was docked in London. He wasn't on any of them. The only list with his name was when the *Delphinius* had been docked in New York the weekend of Camille Green's murder.

Argenti and Jameson interviewed him in Captain Burrows' cabin with Burrows present to observe.

"So, why did you run from us?" Jameson asked.

Doyle was silent, and remained so until Argenti said they were investigating a series of murders of prostitutes and he was on board when the *Delphinius* was docked in New York last November. "And a woman named Camille Green was murdered only a few streets away from here."

As it dawned on Doyle they might want him for something far more serious – he'd seen Camille Green's murder linked to past Ripper killings in the newspapers – he opened up. He'd been in a bad fight at their last docking in Liverpool. "Th' man was left in a fearful way."

"What, you think you killed him?" Argenti pressed.

"I dunno... I dunno." Doyle cradled his head, rubbing it. "There was a lot o' blood, tha's all I know. I got out o' there quick when the rozzers came. When I saw yer here, I feared the worst. If he wasna already dead, that he'd died while we were in passage."

Jameson had retrieved his cane from the cattle deck on his way back. He tapped two fingers against its top. "Is there anyone else who can vouch for this account?"

"Tom Chilton, he was there too at the time o' the fight… saw most of it."

"Chilton's already onshore," Burrows interjected, "along with half the rest of the crew."

It was left that First Mate Squires would keep Doyle under guard in a locked cabin until Argenti could get two policemen to escort Doyle to nearby Tombs jail; to be held there until they got the necessary corroboration both from Chilton and the Liverpool police.

Squires escorted Doyle out and they turned their attention to the other names on the crew list. One in particular had leapt out at Argenti and Jameson as being present at all but one of the key *Frisian* docking dates in London, plus also the November New York docking for the *Delphinius*: JF Taylor. They scanned quickly down the current crew list Burrows handed them. It was there, two-thirds down. Argenti stabbed at the name, eyes brightening.

"This crew member here, JF Taylor – may we speak to him?"

"By all means, *when* he's back on board. Jack Taylor's a linesman and pilotman, was first ashore once he'd seen us safely docked – three hours ago now. Came by O'Grady's to join me and my navigator Ben not long before I left there." Burrows puffed at his pipe. "Suppose there's a chance he's still there – but he said he was heading off to lodgings."

"Do you know which lodging house he might have gone to?" Jameson enquired.

"No, sorry. I don't." Burrows sank into thought for a moment, puffing again at the ornate clay pipe partly nesting in his grey beard. "The only thing he mentioned was that it was just round the corner on Cherry Street."

Argenti's eyes narrowed. "Beginning or end of Cherry Street?"

"Beginning, I suppose – otherwise he wouldn't have said 'just round'. One of the bar girls at O'Grady's seemed to take a shine to him – she told him about it." Burrows smiled, a faint twinkle in his eyes. "Between you and me, I think it was more the promise of what she had waiting for him there that enticed him."

Jameson saw Argenti's face pale. "What's wrong?"

"I'm not sure our friend, Jack Taylor, has been 'enticed' to a proper boarding house." Argenti looked keenly at them. "Come on. We might not have much time."

To identify Taylor, Captain Burrows accompanied Argenti and Jameson as Lawrence raced them in the hansom from the dockside to O'Grady's. Argenti explained that running a "crimp house" was another popular activity of the same dockside gangs who operated as river pirates.

"They put up a sign in the window as if they have rooms – but it's not a real lodging house. Visiting sailors don't know any different, they take a room… and while asleep later, usually heavily drugged from a "bedtime" drink, one of the same kids they use to slip through portholes will sneak in through a false back panel and rob him – or worse." The normal complement of staff to run a crimp house was a barman and a prostitute. "Usually the same girl that has enticed the sailor there from a nearby bar."

"Or *worse*?" Jameson quizzed.

"To prevent him later telling on them and their operation, they'll often kill him. Dump his body in the sewers." Argenti sighed heavily. "And of recent they lack the patience to even wait for him to go to bed. They'll knock him out with that first drink at the bar, rob and kill him right there."

Jameson was horrified. "Do you catch many of them?"

"Very few. We send men in, and they disappear into the sewers – not far behind the body they've just dumped."

As they got to O'Grady's, a group of men and a bar girl were outside, bantering and laughing about something. Burrows cast a cursory glance their way – Jack Taylor wasn't amongst them – then led Argenti and Jameson into the bar.

A crowd of thirty or so, most didn't pay them any attention, the general hubbub staying at the same level, only a group close by the door fell quiet, looked their way with curiosity. Burrows looked past them, picked out his navigator Ben and another seaman at the table where he'd left them. He went over.

"Jack not with you any more?"

"No. Left about ten minutes back." Ben took a swig of his ale, smiled. "With that bright-eyed girl giving him the come-on."

"Okay. Thanks." Burrows turned away and they headed out, Ben pulling a face as to what the panic was about.

Argenti commented that it was only half a block. "We'll go on foot."

Jameson instructed Lawrence to stay with the hansom, and they sprinted off.

Argenti knew of only one proper boarding house in the early part of Cherry Street. They checked there first, no Jack Taylor. Next they headed to the five houses that Argenti knew had been used before as crimp houses; dark, no sign of life at the first two. They found Jack Taylor at the third house.

Behind a rough wooden bar stood a man in a dark-blue apron to complete the image of a barman, and at Taylor's side was a sharp-eyed brunette, heavily rouged. Taylor smiled uncertainly as he spotted Burrows, raising his glass.

"Hey, Captain – whatya doing here?"

Argenti saw that Taylor's glass was already two-thirds empty. He strode over and knocked it from Taylor's hand before it reached his lips.

"What did you put in his drink?"

The barman and the girl exchanged glances; this wasn't how it was meant to go.

"Don't know whatya talkin' about," the barman said.

They heard the sound of someone scurrying from a room at the back, probably the kid they'd hired to sneak in Taylor's room or help dump his body in the sewers.

The barman lurched towards a door to his side as if that suddenly looked a good option for him too, but Jameson was alerted to it, drew his cane blade to block his way. He put the blade inches from the barman's throat.

"As my colleague just asked, what did you put in his drink?"

The barman's eyes shifted anxiously. "Nothin... *nothi'*."

But to put the lie to that Taylor at that moment started swaying, holding one hand out as he tried to balance. His muscle control rapidly going, his legs started trembling and then finally buckled. He clutched desperately at the makeshift bar as he slid to the ground.

"Opium or chloral hydrate?" Argenti barked.

The barman didn't answer. Jameson pressed the blade against his neck.

"Chlora... chloral hydrate," the barman muttered.

"By the heavens," Jameson exclaimed. "In large doses, that's more of a poison. How much?"

The barman fell silent again. Jameson pressed the blade point harder against his neck, drawing blood.

The barman held a forefinger and thumb an inch apart. Jameson knew that if that's what he was admitting to, it was probably twice as much.

"He could be dead within minutes." Jameson looked at Burrows. "Would you be so kind, Captain Burrows, to tell Lawrence that I urgently need my medical bag from the hansom?"

"Yes... of course." Burrows stepped lively, ran out.

Taylor started to convulse, a white froth trickling out one corner of his mouth. Argenti drew his gun to guard the barman and girl while Jameson tended to him.

Jameson sat Taylor up and wrapped his arms around him, pulling hard at his stomach to make him retch. Nothing. He tried again; only a heavier trickle of white froth.

Argenti caught Jameson's eye in that moment. Was he thinking the same thing? If this was the monster who'd savagely murdered eight women or more, would it really matter if he died here now in this grubby room?

But what would then be missed was due process, the weeks of police interviews, the evidence trail to seal beyond doubt that it was the Ripper, then the final trial and press reports to sate the public. Argenti knew that Jameson would do his best to save Taylor's life.

It was Lawrence who burst back in the door a moment later. "I thought I might be able to assist more competently. Captain Burrows is with the hansom."

"Yes, you might," Jameson said, and a symbiotic cooperation took over, each of them knowing what the other's role should be. Lawrence drew a vial of adrenaline into a syringe while Jameson raised a vein and then injected.

Jameson fed a tube down Taylor's throat while Lawrence attached a bottle of saline water to its end. And as the last of the bottle emptied, Jameson tried the abdominal pulls again.

The barman and the girl watched the activity anxiously too; after all, the difference between prison and the gallows was being played out right before them.

Jameson pulled hard again four times at ten-second intervals. Still nothing, only the same steady white froth trickle. Taylor was shuddering violently now, his eyes rolling upward to show only the whites. Jameson feared the worst.

"I think we've lost him," he said, breathless from exertion. "One last try!"

He clasped afresh at Taylor's stomach and pulled once, twice, and on the third Taylor gave an almighty retch, covering himself in vomit, some of it splashing onto Lawrence and Jameson.

"Okay, hold him," Jameson said. They switched position and Jameson pulled the tube out of Taylor's throat as Lawrence pumped back twice more at Taylor's stomach.

Another, lesser surge of vomit and Jameson wiped Taylor's face clean with a cloth and shone a candle from the bar into his eyes. The pupils had half-rolled back into position, but there was still no life in them. Jameson slapped Taylor's face a couple of times and shook him. A cough and a small retch from Taylor, and his pupils finally settled back and slowly focused.

He blinked and peered at Jameson. "Who are you?"

"Why, Jack Taylor, I'm the man who just saved your life." He smiled tightly and gestured towards Argenti. "And my friend here has a few questions for you."

13

Jameson autopsied the girl at 7.22 am. Lawrence assisted and made notes while Argenti observed from the side of the room.

Lucy Bonina's body wasn't discovered until after 5 am. It took almost an hour to raise Argenti and he spent half an hour at the crime scene with five other policemen before Jameson, having got Argenti's message, arrived with Lawrence. It had been a long night for both of them. Argenti had found two policemen patrolling at the corner of Madison Street and together they'd escorted Jack Taylor to Mulberry Street. He was still slightly groggy from the chloral hydrate, so it was decided that he'd have a medical examination and spend the night in the Tombs, to be questioned at first light.

Jameson had meanwhile asked Lawrence to run him to the Lotos, said he wanted to grab a nightcap and that Lawrence should head home and not wait for him; he'd get a street cab when he was finished. But as soon as Lawrence was out of sight, he'd headed to Ling's where Sulee had gently massaged his aching ribs with scented oil.

He'd lost himself in the opium haze at one point, wasn't sure if it was just Sulee's oiled body against him or a score of maidens, bodies intertwined like a mass of writhing serpents. And then suddenly it was blood rather than oil lubricating that slithering mass of bodies. He shook the image away.

Jameson refocused his eyes on Lucy Bonina's cadaver. He was still tired, hadn't shaken off the last of the night's opium haze. He squinted, tried to concentrate.

"Tongs. Scalpel... retractor."

Lawrence passed each across as they were requested. Jameson leant in closer.

"Six puncture wounds to the stomach and two to the spleen." He asked for another retractor and a probe, and peered at an angle. "And three more visible on the liver. The intestines, which have for the most part been removed and laid across the subject's left breastbone, show signs of five further punctures prior to evisceration."

When Jameson had cut through the girl's bolero top, he'd had trouble telling where the red cloth started and the mass of coagulated blood finished. The wound area was so large that he'd only needed to cut a few more inches into the chest cavity to gain full internal access, and his first main observation was that the heart and kidneys had been removed.

Although Argenti had been present at several autopsies before, none had affected him like this one, possibly because it brought home the savagery of the attack. On the scores of photographs of other Ripper victims he'd leafed through, it was still possible to regard them remotely.

Or because the girl was young and had been very beautiful. He'd talked to a bar manager and one of the other girls to find out about her: Lucia Bonina, only 23, an Italian immigrant, she'd used the name "Lucy Bonnie" as a stage name. Neither the bar manager nor the girls would admit to Lucy being a working girl, "She was just one of our showgirl dancers." Perhaps so as not to reflect badly on the *Showboat*'s activities, perhaps to protect Lucy's modesty in death.

But he couldn't help picturing Marella or his wife Sophia when he'd first met her, and at one point had to look away. As Jameson started slicing out the girl's remaining organs to weigh and examine them, Argenti excused himself to have a coffee in the Bellevue canteen. "I'll return shortly."

He closed his eyes as he brought the steaming coffee to his lips. *Dio la aiuta… Dio lo aiuta.*

The autopsy was vital before they questioned Jack Taylor, in particular the time of death. If Lucy died after he appeared at O'Grady's, Taylor couldn't possibly have killed her.

Argenti left it as long as he could before returning, but still had to wait through almost another hour of Jameson removing the girl's organs, examining them and putting them in jars. Jameson dabbed some sweat from his brow with one sleeve, looked over.

"From blood lividity and level of digestion of a meal we understand the subject ate around seven or eight in the evening, we have time of death; at least within a three hour span, sometime between 9 pm and midnight last night."

Lawrence made a note and Argenti nodded. That meant Jack Taylor had almost two hours to murder Lucy Bonina before arriving at O'Grady's, only five hundred yards from Tom Dexter's Showboat.

"What's your full name?"
"Jack Frederick Taylor."
"Your age and date of birth?"
"Thirty-nine. Born 19th May, 1853."
"And where were you born?"

"Saratov, Russia. My family moved to London when I was thirteen."

"And is Jack Taylor your original name?"

Argenti conducted the interview while Ted Barton, one of his most trusted colleagues, made notes. Finley Jameson observed from the side of the room. Taylor paused briefly, this question was obviously linked to the last.

"No. No, it's not. My original name was Jalek Telyanin. It was changed when my family came to England."

Argenti nodded. Jameson had confirmed that the same happened as in the USA, names were anglicised, often at point of entry by immigration officials who found the original name unpronounceable.

"Are you married or single?"

"Single. I was married when I was young for a while." He gave a bittersweet smile. "But that's been over near on ten years now."

"And in which area of London do you now live?"

"In Stepney, East London."

Argenti looked at Jameson, who commented. "For the purpose of the record, Stepney is about two miles from the Whitechapel area."

Taylor looked from one to the other, his brow knitting; he hadn't yet made any connection. All he'd been told so far was that he was being held over the alleged serious assault of two girls in New York, one when the *Delphinius* was docked in New York last November, the other just last night.

Jack Taylor had lank, dark-brown hair and eyes only a shade lighter. Nose slightly crooked, possibly broken at some time, but otherwise no distinguishing features. About five-foot-nine, average height and build; as Jameson had said, a man that could merge into a crowd and disappear. Argenti noted that Taylor would often look to one side before answering, getting clear recall, or working out the best deception?

"And how long have you been living in Stepney?"

Taylor thought for a second. "Uh, five or six years now."

A more meaningful look from Argenti to Jameson. That answered the one *Frisian* voyage where Taylor was missing from the crew list, listed as "onshore". He lived only two miles from the murdered girl.

Taylor was vague about his movements for when the *Delphinius* was docked in November, "That was three trips back. Been a fair few places in between." But he was more certain about where he'd been the previous night before arriving at O'Grady's. "I went to see a girl called Julie at a club in the Bowery, the Peacock."

"Do you know her surname?"

"No, I don't. I... I saw her last time we were docked in New York, but in the end she wasn't there last night." Taylor shrugged, a win-some, lose-some gesture. "So I ended up staying with a couple of the other girls there."

"Do you know their names?"

"No, sorry... didn't catch 'em." Taylor smiled meekly, and as he saw the doubt settling on Argenti's face. "But I was there for sure. Why else would I dress up in my finest? I'm sure the girls will remember me."

Argenti contemplated Taylor's dark grey hacking jacket, now looking the worst for wear after last night. Why else, he thought, except if you wanted to look like gentry to get on board Tom Dexter's Showboat.

Argenti looked at his watch. He'd started the interview after lunch, having used the morning for a search of Taylor's cabin on the *Delphinius* and confirm some details by telegram to London. Two letters found in Taylor's cabin and some crew book notes they'd passed to a handwriting expert to compare with the letters to the newspapers.

Five hours before the Peacock Club opened. Tomorrow morning before the handwriting report. Little more to be done till then. Argenti addressed Barton as if suddenly Jack Taylor no longer existed.

"First interview suspended at 3.28 pm. Suspect to be held in the Tombs for later questioning."

Argenti ignored the plea in Taylor's eyes as he got up, and shut the interview room door halfway through him calling out what this was all about.

"I've done *nothing...*"

After the second interview the next day, Mayor George Watkins wasted no time in calling a press meeting at Mulberry Street. Having put his weight behind his golden boy, Detective Joseph Argenti, he was keen to declare victory.

It had been an eventful twenty-four hours. Argenti and Barton had taken a fresh police photograph of Taylor along with his identity book photograph to show the girls at the Peacock Club. None of the girls they spoke to recalled Taylor from the night before. Most damning, a girl they showed the same photos to at Tom Dexter's Showboat thought she might have seen him.

Jameson had accompanied a police officer and they'd taken more items from Taylor's cabin: items of clothing, another letter and two ink sketches Jameson thought might be significant. At the second interview, Jameson seemed particularly interested in Taylor's ink sketching abilities and had asked Taylor to imitate a handwriting sample. Soon afterwards, Watkins had called his meeting.

A small gathering of press reporters, city and police officials, Watkins nonetheless knew that within twenty-four hours the headlines would be spread across the City, then worldwide. The significance of the meeting wasn't lost on those present. Watkins and Commissioner Latham sat one side of the conference table with Argenti and Jameson the other. McCluskey was in the front row amongst other police and City Hall officials, the press directly behind.

The room was quiet as Argenti made his official statement, a gentle hubbub only rising as a Sergeant went round and handed out press statements. A *Herald* reporter was first to raise his arm.

"So you have a positive identification of the suspect, Jack Taylor, at the Showboat on the night in question?"

"No, not exactly," Argenti corrected. "The girl in question said she couldn't be *absolutely* sure."

"But nobody to support his alibi that he was at the Peacock Club at the time?"

"That's correct."

A *Times* reporter looked up from the press release. "Though you have a date and place match for all the previous attacks, including Camille Green's attack at the Riverway?"

"All except one. But while the suspect was onshore at the time of Catherine Eddowes's murder, we discovered that he lived only two miles away."

That led to a few questions about Taylor's nationality, age and background, then attention turned to his handwriting and the letters.

"What exactly does 'Proximal Scribe Dexterity' mean?" the *Herald* man asked, reading directly from the Press release. Jameson answered.

"It means that while we didn't find a direct match to the letters to the newspapers in his handwriting, we believe he has that ability."

"What led you to that deduction?"

"Some letters and sketches in his possession, plus we also conducted a test."

The handwriting report had concluded that while Taylor's natural style was clearly different, some loops and letters had similarities. But Jameson had become intrigued by Taylor's ink-pen sketches of fellow crew members, a skill which Taylor boasted had helped supplement his income between voyages selling sketches by London's Green Park. Jameson had complimented him on the skill, said that it must take a steady hand. He then passed across a letter and asked if Taylor could copy it as closely as possible.

Jameson hadn't wanted to use one of the Ripper's letters to the newspapers; at that stage they hadn't revealed what the questioning was about and didn't want to forewarn him. He'd asked Taylor to copy the first few lines of one of Lord Byron's love-letters to Lady Caroline Lamb. Taylor's copy was uncannily accurate.

"I understand you also found some bloodstains."

"Yes, we did," Jameson said. "We found some old bloodstains on one of Taylor's shirts, not entirely washed out."

A *New York Post* man asked, "What excuse did Taylor give for those?"

Argenti answered. "He said that he got caught by one of the steer's horns a few trips back."

A light guffaw ran through the room, some smiles and head-shaking.

"When do you expect to lay charges, or have you already done so?"

Argenti paused for a second, and Watkins cut in. "Very shortly. We await some information from London to decide the total number of charges, and then those will be made. We firmly believe we have our man."

The *NY Times* reporter picked up on Argenti's hesitation. "Is that a view you share, Detective Argenti? Do you believe you've finally apprehended Jack the Ripper?"

It wasn't awaiting the final details from London that had given Argenti pause for thought, but Taylor's reaction when they'd revealed the purpose of their questioning and the Ripper connection; total shock, disbelief. Could Taylor be that good an actor? But the weight of facts against Taylor was heavy, and the bandwagon Watkins had started rolling heavier still. Argenti was loath to stand in its way.

"Yes, I believe we have."

McCluskey slapped the *New York Times* down on the gaming table at Tierney's side. The headline read: "RIPPER ARRESTED IN NEW YORK". Underneath was the quote from Argenti, "I'm confident we have our man," along with a photograph of Argenti, Jameson and Mayor Watkins at the Mulberry Street conference table.

Tierney looked aside briefly from his poker hand, gave the article only a cursory glance. Wildcard poker was his favourite backroom game with his men at his club on Lafayette Street. He left standard poker, faro and "21"* to the peasants on the front salon tables. Tierney didn't like his private card games disturbed, but McCluskey had told him it was urgent.

"So whatya expect me to do about it?"

"I warned that if you didn't take the wind out of his sails this would happen." McCluskey was red-faced, flustered. "Argenti's promotion is almost certain now.

---

* *Victorian term for "blackjack".*

And like I said, once he starts challenging my position, I might not be able to give you the level of protection you now enjoy."

"Yeah, and you also said 'subtle'." Tierney smiled dryly. A muscle tick teased the canary tattoo on his neck. "Now if yer wanted me to send one of my lads to slice his guts out at the Mulberry Street front desk, I coulda done that day one."

"I know." McCluskey sighed, rubbed his forehead. "But maybe we haven't got the luxury of time to be as subtle as I first thought."

"Maybe not. But if you wan' me to move sharpish, I'm gonna need to know a bit more."

McCluskey gave him the background with Taylor and his failed alibi of being at the Peacock Club.

"So if this guy's alibi looked good, that'd do the trick?" Tierney confirmed, putting two cards face down and taking fresh ones from the dealer.

"Yes. That is, if the Peacock is one of the clubs on your rounds."

Tierney smiled slyly. "*All* th' clubs are on my rounds. But you're in luck. I happen to know the local Madame, Vera Maynard, who runs the place along with a fleet o' girls 'tween the Peacock and a few other clubs. I'll have a word with her." Tierney looked back at his cards. "Now if you don't mind me gettin' on with my game."

"Yes. Yes, of course." With a perfunctory nod, McCluskey left.

An hour later Tierney sent one of his runners to tell Vera Maynard to expect him at the Peacock that evening, so when in top hat and tails he walked in with Brogan and two other henchman, she had on her best dress and smile to greet him.

"Michael, long time since we've seen you. What brings you these parts?"

She had a waitress fetch him the best malt whisky, and left the whole bottle by the glass on the table. Vera nodded understandingly as Tierney explained the situation and passed across *The Times*. A large woman by any measure, Vera Maynard covered it well with exotic, flowing smock-style dresses. Her auburn hair tied in a bun, ornate earrings and sometimes a tiara, she was always immaculately turned out as an example to her girls.

"So a little story from me or one of my girls wouldn't go amiss?"

"That's right. A little story." Tierney smiled and took a swig of his whisky.

Vera looked back at the news article. Tierney usually only went out of his way for his own, whereas it looked like this Jack Taylor was just a merchant seaman.

"This guy Taylor important to you, is he?"

"No. More t'do with sticking the knife in Detective Argenti. A little score I have with him, plus the hoi-polloi at Mulberry Street don't want him to rise up the ranks any higher than need be."

Vera nodded knowingly. She glanced at the photograph with the article. "I thought for a moment it might have been payback for the wrangle that sidekick toff of Argenti's had with one of your men last week."

Tierney's eyes narrowed. "*What* wrangle?"

Vera realized that Tierney hadn't heard about it, and she didn't want to be the one to break the news. She shook her head hastily. "It's nothing."

"Oh, but it *isn't*, Vera. It obviously isn't."

"Just scuttlebutt, loose talk." She shrugged. "I'm sure it doesn't mean anything."

"I think I should be the judge o' that." He noticed Vera's earrings were large gold hoops with small clusters of diamonds dangling from them. He reached across and touched one. "My, these earrings. You could almost swing a trapeze artist from 'em. But very pretty mind you." He tugged at it, glaring at her. "Now tell me what it is you've heard."

Wincing with pain as her earlobe was dragged down, Vera passed on the story from her girls about Jameson seeing McCabe off with his swordstick. "Stabbed him bad in his shoulder, and apparently McCabe went running off with his tail between his legs."

"And jus' which girls might that be?"

Vera fell silent, and Tierney tugged harder.

Vera let out a sharp gasp with the pain, but met Tierney's gaze steadily. "You can pull my ear off if you like, Michael, but still get nothing from me. They're my girls, and it's my job to protect them."

Tierney held her gaze challengingly, a smile slowly rising. He eased the pressure. "I understand, and I admire you fo' that loyalty. One thing we have in common. I feel the same 'bout my men – except when they try an' dupe me."

He gave one last tug at her earring in warning before letting go, his expression dropping. It hardly mattered the last in the chain on that scuttlebutt, he reminded himself, it had obviously started with the girls at Ellie Cullen's and spread like wildfire from there. His authority was being challenged, people starting to laugh up their sleeves at him. There was only one way to stem that tide. He'd have to teach the toff and the girl a sharp lesson, but first he'd take care of McCabe.

14

London. March, 1892.

Commissioner Grayling dabbed his mouth with a napkin as he looked across the restaurant table at Sir Thomas Colby.

"So. Do you think they've got the right man in New York? Do you think this chap Taylor might be the Ripper?"

"Some things fit well. Others I'm not completely convinced about – could be purely circumstantial."

Colby observed Grayling sink into thought again. There must have been a good reason for Grayling to invite him to the Café Royal to discuss the matter; only the second luncheon meeting they'd ever had. Perhaps after four years of tracking the Ripper, Grayling was keen to close the matter.

Grayling took a fresh breath. "I suppose when we hear about this last possible alibi for the Tabram murder, we'll have a clearer idea. Sergeant Hoskins of the Southend Police has promised to get back to me tomorrow about it."

"Yes. I daresay." When presented with the various docking times for the *Frisian*, Taylor had claimed that the weekend of Martha Tabram's murder he'd gone to stay with an old friend, Albert Mattey, in Southend. "Debates about Tabram not being one of the Canonical Five aside."

Colby smiled tightly as the waiter cleared away their hors d'oeuvres. As he took a sip of his wine, Grayling commented.

"It's a Bordeaux seventy-five. I thought you might appreciate it."

"Yes, indeed. A very fine year." One of his favourites, as was the restaurant, with its Baroque décor and gold-brocaded columns, one of the few places in London to feature French haute cuisine, and reputedly boasting the best wine cellar worldwide.

"At least one good thing if it does prove to be the Ripper," Grayling said with a resigned sigh. "It takes all the pressure off us over all that letter and symbol nonsense."

"Yes, I suppose it does."

After Atkinson's findings, Colby had consulted an expert in letters and symbols: two marks could have been Hebrew letters, or simply a chance cut for one and the other a crudely cut "U".

Given past problems with semitic links, Grayling was eager to avoid the Hebrew letter suggestion and had pressed whether indeed all the marks could be random. Colby had agreed that they could.

"Then that's the option we shall go with. Our remit was purely to find specific Roman numerals, no point in going on an unnecessary diversion."

An hour later, Colby had sent a telegram to New York:

ROMAN NUMERALS IX OR VIII NOT FOUND ANYWHERE ON PREVIOUS VICTIMS. NO MARKINGS FOUND ANYWHERE ON INTERNAL ORGANS THAT AREN'T CONSISTENT WITH STANDARD STAB WOUNDS.

Grayling took another sip of wine. "Are you concerned that with this announcement in New York, they might steal our glory?"

"No, that's not been my concern." Though now they were probably getting more to the heart of Grayling's business, Colby thought. "More simply to make sure of our ground so that we're not forced into a hasty backtrack later."

"Yes. Good point."

Grayling looked up in appreciation as the waiter approached with their main courses, but Colby sensed some lingering doubt.

"And of course in Finley Jameson we have the factor of having our own man there," Colby commented. "He played an equal part in this, as we did in supplying both Jameson and the New York police with vital information. Without that it's doubtful they'd have had this breakthrough at all."

Grayling waggled his fork in agreement after the first mouthful. "Yes, certainly. I think we need to play up that factor as much as possible. Put the main focus on our man Jameson as being at the forefront of this breakthrough now. New York will no doubt blow their own trumpets over this, so we need to blow ours equally hard."

"Yes, I... I suppose." Colby suddenly realized that avenue had been all-but decided. Grayling had merely wanted to get his accord too, thus the luncheon.

"And I have just the Fleet Street man for that," Grayling said. "I always ensure he's first to be fed the main murder stories, so he owes me a few favours."

Colby simply nodded as he continued eating, a twinge of concern at the mention of increased press focus on Jameson. He only prayed that they didn't make the connection to the last time Jameson had appeared in the newspapers.

••••

"Follow the trail. See where it leads," Jameson commented. "Piece together minute by minute Taylor's movements that night, then see if any parts of that jigsaw puzzle don't fit – Colby's usual instruction to first year pupils. At least in that respect his advice now is predictable."

Jameson pushed a taut smile to Argenti as Lawrence canted the hansom slowly down Market Street.

"Do you think it will help?" Argenti quizzed. "As you said, it's already been established from past Ripper cases that here we have a man who can murder in only minutes and escape unseen. In this instance, Taylor had almost two hours."

"Yes. But some setting up was required this time. He needed to get a cabin key without being seen; also to meet his target out of view of others, so that they weren't seen together. Those factors converging might still have boiled it down to only a few opportune moments. And if those moments hadn't arrived, he'd have simply slipped away again and chosen another night."

Argenti nodded, surveying the heavily shadowed street and alleys running off each side. Jameson's comments made perfect sense, but it didn't make him feel any better knowing that young Lucia Bonina had lost her life purely by random chance.

Eighty yards ahead was O'Grady's, its gas lantern the only light in that half of Market Street. The only other light was from a hotel three hundred yards behind them on the corner with Madison Street. In between it was pitch black.

"So, having left the *Delphinius*, Taylor probably headed up Pike Street," Jameson pointed to his left, "because another of the crew said they saw him heading away from the docks. Then he rounded the block at Madison, and came back down here at Market Street, which would have put him closer to where the *Showboat* was docked."

"But Captain Burrows and his navigator were at O'Grady's. Wouldn't they have seen him pass?"

"In this light, doubtful. All he had to do was cross the road and he'd have been all but lost in shadow. Also, Burrows and his navigator didn't arrive at O'Grady's until forty minutes later. Taylor was linesman and pilot assist, so he was first off."

"Or to play safe he could have taken the next road along at Catherine Street and doubled back."

"Yes. That's a possibility," Jameson agreed. "*Dexter's Showboat* is moored almost equidistant between the two."

As the hansom turned out of Market Street onto the East River dockside, they could see the *Showboat* a hundred yards to their right. With gas lamps at regular intervals along its decks, it stood out as a bright and garish beacon amongst the drab hulks of neighbouring freight ships. It was due to sail to Charleston the following night, so their last opportunity to visit the boat was now.

"No doubt Taylor saw the *Showboat* as the *Delphinius* was docking," Jameson commented, looking at the nearby vessels.

"You think he planned it?"

"Certainly at the stage he decided to don smart apparel, I believe he had it in mind, yes. Captain Burrows and his navigator were still in their working clothes, you might have noticed."

Lawrence pulled the hansom alongside the *Showboat* and they went up its gangplank. Argenti nodded brief accord to their doorman, who knew him from his past two visits. They'd chosen the same time they estimated Taylor had visited to mirror the situation as closely as possible, and the show area inside was crowded and noisy.

On stage, a bare-chested man in gold harem pantaloons juggled flaming torches to gasps and applause from the audience. Argenti saw that fire suddenly reflected in Jameson, enlivened by the crowd, eyes darting around the room.

"Do you think he met her in here?" Argenti asked.

"Unlikely. He wouldn't have wanted to have been seen with her here or stay too long for people to notice him. Unless..." Jameson's gaze shifted to the far side of the room. "Look over there. Can you see the back few rows of people?"

Argenti looked. Only the first few rows were lit by the stage lights, the mid-rows indistinct, and the back was shrouded completely in darkness. "No. No, I can't."

"Darkness and light. Darkness and light. He plays with it, you see. He could have stayed there safely for a while – completely obscured except from those practically next to him. Also, a couple of the girls thought they saw Lucy go to the outside deck."

"So, there's the possibility that he also saw her go out and followed her."

"Yes. After, say, a discreet delay. Or he was already outside on deck waiting for her. Don't forget, it was on the aft portion of the promenade deck where the cabin owner, Mr Tullet, believed he'd fallen asleep or on the way lost his key. Let's go up."

Outside, the noise of the showroom and casino floor was quickly lost, just the gentle lapping sound of the East River waters against the *Showboat*'s hull. Argenti looked the deck's length. Two men and a woman were near the fore end talking, nobody else on deck. Jameson's gaze followed his for a moment before fixing on the East River waters ahead.

"Yes, perfect... absolutely perfect." The darkness of the river seemed to draw him in, and he was lost in reverie for a moment as he had a flashback to the Whitechapel alley where Annie Chapman had been murdered, Colby describing how she'd been savaged only eight feet from passers-by and nobody had seen a thing. Colby had walked into those same shadows to demonstrate, asking his students if they could see him, repeating like a mantra, "Come on, try hard to put yourself in the moment... put yourself in the moment. Only by getting inside the mind of the Ripper do we stand a chance of catching him." However hard Jameson had tried he hadn't been able to see anything of Colby in that darkness close by. But now as he drew his focus back to the river ahead it merged with the darkness when he'd blacked out on the cattle steamer and the dark haze of the opium den and Sulee writhing against him with the blood fresh from Lucy Bonina's cadaver.

"Are you okay... are you okay?"

It took him a second to return from his reverie and focus on Argenti. "Yes, yes... fine. This side of the boat is perfect, you see." He pointed. "The darkness of the river, scant light from Brooklyn beyond. The other side he might have felt too exposed to people on the dockside or approaching up the gangplank."

Jameson led the way round to the port side of the promenade deck to illustrate his point – the activity there of people up and down the gangplank was more intrusive – then they headed back down towards the showroom and casino.

"When's the final search of Taylor's cabin being done?" Jameson enquired.

"Tonight. My men are there now. We couldn't wait until the morning because the *Delphinius* sets sail at first light."

"Okay. Let's finish up here and then join them."

They spent forty minutes more on the *Showboat* checking the casino, show floor and the cabin where Lucia had been murdered, then a last moment back on the promenade deck looking out over the East River before leaving the boat.

Halfway back down the gangplank, they could see Ted Barton and two men heading their way. And as Barton caught Argenti's eye, he beamed and held something aloft. It looked like a notebook.

15

Tom Brogan wedged one oil-soaked flaming torch into an empty beer crate and held the other as he watched Jed McCabe and Martin unload the ale barrels off the cart and stack them onto a pallet at the side of the warehouse.

"Come on, putya backs into it, yer nancies," Brogan teased. "We gotta have this lot loaded ready for the barge up t'Boston by midnight."

"Yer not helpin' us load then," Martin joshed back, smiling, and McCabe gave him a sharp look. Brogan wasn't noted for his sense of humour.

Brogan looked stern for a moment, then a sly smile creased his face. "I done my bit bringin' the cart from th' yard. So now I'm jus' foreman and finger-pointer here, and dontya forget it." He waved his flaming torch. "Come on, step lively. Was'nt four silvers and all th' ale yer could drink enough fo' yers?"

"Yeah, was right 'nough," McCabe said, grunting with exertion as he helped Martin with another barrel. "Very generous o' yer."

He'd been halfway through his supper at Fennelly's when Martin came in and told him Brogan wanted help shifting some barrels. The smell of fish was heavy in the warehouse from previous consignments and the nearby fish-yards and trawlers. Brogan nodded towards his pint of ale left on a nearby pallet.

"Don' seem t' have supped much of yer ale so far."
Brogan noticed that the dark stout was only a fifth of the
way down.

"Savin' it fer when we're finished." McCabe smiled
tightly.

"Come on now, don't be shy. This is thirsty work 'ere.
An' there's mo' where that came from."

Brogan waved his torch, as if it was more a command
than polite suggestion. McCabe got the message, and after
dropping the next barrel on the pallet with a grunt, he
dutifully went over and took another heavy swill from his
pint mug. Martin's mug was already halfway down, but
nevertheless he joined him for another swig. Brogan's eyes
seemed to be fixed on them keenly, and McCabe didn't stop
until he was two-thirds down. He sighed in appreciation,
belched and wiped away his foam moustache.

Brogan smiled. "Feelin' better now, no doubt."

"Yeah, thanks," McCabe said, and got quickly back
to shifting the barrels. Half a dozen more, the cart half-
unloaded, maybe he'd take another sup.

As he was carrying the third barrel across, he started
to feel groggy. Martin facing him appeared to blur, and
only yards from the pallet his legs felt weak and started
trembling. Maybe he shouldn't have had that drink after
all, but this now was different, groggier than he'd ever
felt even after six or seven pints.

"Sorry, I..." He struggled to keep going to the pallet,
but as his legs finally buckled he dropped the barrel a
yard short.

With the extra weight, Martin dropped his end too,
looking at him with concern as he slumped to the ground.
"Are yer okay?"

"I don't know, I..." His jaw muscles felt tight too, making
it difficult to speak. Martin receded into the shadows as

Brogan came into view and looked down at him. The last thing McCabe recalled before sinking into blackness.

Searing brightness awoke him. Brogan's face was above him again, but now he'd brought the flaming torch in close. He waved it again in front of McCabe's eyes. McCabe could feel its heat against his face and neck.

"Yer wake yet?" Brogan asked.

McCabe coughed, squinting at Brogan through the light of the torch. "Uuuh, yeah... yeah." He shook his head. He still felt groggy. But when he went to sit up or move his arms, he realized he couldn't.

For a second he thought they were still numb and paralyzed, but when he looked to each side and down, he saw that he was spread-eagled on his back, his wrists and ankles tied to the edges of the pallet he was laid flat against. His shirt had been torn off, his chest left bare. Brogan ran the flaming torch close to it, grimacing.

McCabe shook his head again, as if it was all a bad dream. "Wha's this all 'bout?"

"Good question." Another voice – Mike Tierney's. He stepped into view, peered down at McCabe. "I could ask much the same about what happened 'tween you and the toff at Ellie Cullen's, couldn't I?"

McCabe, still desperately trying to clear his head, squinted at Tierney. "What she tol' yer? No doubt a pack o' lies."

"Oh, I daresay she embellished a bit, and the story mighta got a bit o' dressing too as it passed from girl to girl on the Tenderloin. But then I heard the same story from my contacts at Mulberry Street." Tierney sighed, his countenance darkening. "So tell me what happened with the toff, Jed."

McCabe's throat felt suddenly dry. He moistened his lips with his tongue.

"Jus' a bit of a tussle, tha's all."

"And what happened in this tussle?"

"He... he pulled this silly-lookin' blade from his cane – so I showed 'im what fer with my billy club."

"Gave him a good seein' to, did yer?"

"Tha's right. I did." McCabe smiled crookedly, the first hint that Tierney was starting to buy his account. "Saw 'im off no trouble."

Tierney looked away again for a moment before contemplating McCabe steadily. "Now that story might wash, yer see – except fo' one problem. When I saw a picture of the toff in the newspapers the next day, he looked fine an' dandy. Not a mark on him. Whereas you appear to still have a serious stab wound."

Tierney pressed hard against the dressing on his shoulder, and McCabe hissed in pain. "And, yer see, that appears to tie in more with the story out there. That the toff stabbed you one real good, and you ran off with yer tail between your legs."

"No, *no*. Not true. I got 'im a coupla good 'uns too." He could hear Tierney's canary chirping stronger in the background as their voices rose, but couldn't see it.

Tierney rolled on as if McCabe hadn't spoke. "Cos what happens out there with you also reflects on me. And I don't like people talking 'bout me on the street. Laughin' at me." Tierney leant in close, as if he was sharing a confidence. "And I like it even less when my own men hide the truth from me." His voice lowered to almost a whisper. "Then continue to lie t'me."

Tierney straightened up and nodded to his side.

McCabe saw another man step from the shadows and hand Brogan his fire axe. And in the corner of his vision, he could see a brazier burning by that third man.

"No, Mike... *no*. *Please*. Yer got it wrong."

Tierney arched a brow sharply. "Have I now? I don't think so." He nodded at Brogan.

"For God's sake, Mike... I'm beggin' yer." Tears stung his eyes, ran down one cheek. He tensed against the ropes, shuddering with fear.

But Tierney just stared back at him solemnly as Brogan raised his axe, and McCabe's breath fell in gasped bursts as he realized what was about to happen, his body chopped into pieces and thrown into the brazier. His stomach heaved, and some vomit ran out one corner of his mouth. He coughed and spluttered. "At... at leas' let me have a slug o' that ale to knock me out."

Tierney leant in again, softly stroking his brow. "Did yer think of softening the blow to me when you had half the town laughing up their sleeves at me? No, you didn't. Now which hand do you use t' collect my money fo' me?"

McCabe had to think for a second, thrown by the sudden change of subject. "Uh... uh, th' right hand."

Tierney stroked his brow one last time, smiling gently as he straightened up and signalled to Brogan.

Brogan brought the axe down hard on McCabe's left hand. McCabe let out a guttural cry of pain. Brogan grimaced. He'd hoped for a clean slice just below all four finger joints – but on two fingers there was still some joining sinew and skin. He swung again, severing cleanly.

McCabe started to shiver in shock, still expecting the following blows but praying he blacked out before they came. But the next thing he felt was on the same hand. The man with Brogan pressed a red-hot branding iron against his bloodied finger stumps. His own singeing flesh overlaid the smell of fish for a moment, the pain like nothing he'd known before. As the echo of his strangled scream bounced back from the warehouse walls, Tierney leant over him again, gently stroking his brow.

"Let that be a lesson to you. And thank yer lucky stars that I still see some value in you collecting fo' me."

McCabe attempted a weak smile in appreciation, but at that moment he finally, thankfully, blacked out.

"So where did you first meet Lucy the other night?" Argenti pressed. "Where the show was or on the promenade deck?"

"I told you. I didn't meet any Lucy. I was never on the *Showboat*."

"That's not what one of the other girls said. She claims she saw you there."

"Then she's mistaken or she's lying. I told you, I was at the Peacock Club."

"So why didn't any of the girls there see you? Why is it that you were only seen at the *Showboat*?"

Taylor clutched his hair in one hand. "I don't know... I don't know. I was there at the Peacock, I tell you."

Four nights in the Tombs and now the third round of questioning, Argenti knew that his best chance of breaking Taylor's account was now. Finley Jameson and Ted Barton were to his side. It had been agreed beforehand that they could fire questions at Taylor too; anything to keep him rattled, off-balance, Argenti had emphasized, "Hopefully get the contradictions to show."

"So what time did you leave your friend Albert Mattey in Southend?"

"Uuuh. Five or six o'clock. I told you before."

Argenti flicked back in the file before him. "No, you didn't. Before you said seven or eight o'clock. You've brought it forward two hours."

"I... I don't recall exactly. It was a few years ago now."

"Let's see what your friend Albert says, shall we?" Argenti turned to another page in the file. "He says it was just after lunch."

"No, no... it was later."

Jameson interjected. "Is that when you decided to bring your time forward? When you knew your friend had said it was earlier?"

"No. It was later than he said. At least four-thirty, five."

Jameson: "You see that's where the timing is critical. Because if you'd left your friend's house in Southend just after lunch or even, say, four-thirty – you'd have still had time to get back to London in time to murder Martha Tabram."

Taylor's eyes darted between them anxiously, pupils dilated, he looked worn down with fear and tiredness. He shook his head. "I told you. I don't know any Martha. I don't know any of these girls."

"Is that correct?" Argenti said, taking the notebook out of a folder and sliding it across. "Then why do you have the girls' names written down in here, including Martha?"

Argenti hoped he'd timed it right. He felt the pressure as much as Taylor. The final telegram from London about the Mattey alibi came the morning after the notebook discovery. Barton and his men had found it tucked in a sock in the bottom of Taylor's cabin trunk. He watched Taylor blink slowly as he observed the book.

"Don't know what you're talking about."

"Their names are all here." Argenti prodded the notebook with one finger. A bluff. Only four of the names were there. Martha, Catherine, Elizabeth and Mary along with the names of another six girls. But if in the heat of the moment Taylor suddenly blurted out, "There are only four there", they had him.

"I don't know what you mean." Another slow blink from Taylor. "They're just some old lady friends and acquaintances."

Jameson: "Are those all your old lady friends there, then? Or do you just write down those you choose to murder."

Taylor shook his head. "No... no."

Argenti could sense they had him reeling, unsteady. "Quite a coincidence, don't you think? Their names matching like that?"

"I... uuh... it wasn't me." Taylor looked between them desperately. "I promise on my life."

Argenti averted his gaze from the pitiful plea in Taylor's eyes; with everything now on a knife edge, he couldn't risk softening.

"So why did you keep the notebook hidden like that? What were you keen to hide?"

No answer for a second. Taylor's eyes flickered uncertainly. "There... there's personal things in there."

Jameson arched a brow. "Personal, or incriminating?"

Silence again.

Argenti: "As in a list of women you killed."

Taylor's bottom lip started trembling. He shook his head. "No... *no*. I didn't touch them. It was poems and notes to a few of the girls. That was what was personal."

Jameson reached for the notebook. "Indeed. And let us look at some of those, shall we: '*You cover your pain well, but I'm sure a part of it will always remain in your heart*'." He looked at Taylor. "Does that seem familiar? Where did you get that passage from?"

"I... I didn't get it from anywhere. I wrote it myself."

"Or this one, '*The thought of winning your hand makes me tremble, if along with it came the utmost passion of your heart.*' Whose words are those originally?"

Taylor stared at him blankly.

"Let me tell you, shall I? Give or take a few words, these are passages from Nathaniel Hawthorne's *The Scarlet Letter*. A novel about forbidden passion and sin, but particularly of women." Jameson tapped the notebook. "Sins which you decided the women here should be punished for."

Taylor closed his eyes for a moment and seemed to shrink inside himself. "No.... no! I didn't touch them. I don't even know any of them."

"You write down the names of women you don't even know? Curious."

"It... it's not the same Martha."

"A different Martha, then," Argenti said. "What's her surname?"

"Uh... Turner, I think."

"You *think*? And the others?"

"I... I don't recall now. Not all of them."

Jameson: "So you recall the one you needed to separate from Tabram, yet still starts with a T. But not the others? How convenient."

Silence. Taylor's haunted eyes shifted rapidly from one to the other.

Argenti: "So which one did you murder first? Did you write them down in the sequence you killed them?"

Taylor clutched at his hair as his head sunk down. He started slowly shaking it after a second.

"And why did you mark Camille Green's body, but not the others?"

Silence. Only that continuing slow head shake.

"Why keep up the pretence any longer," Argenti pressed. He sensed he was close to breaking him. "We *know* it was you. So what's the point in holding back from telling us the details?"

Still that slow, steady head shake. Then after a second a low guttural murmur. "No... no. *Please.* I didn't do it."

Jameson: "You know at heart you want to tell us. Revel in all the glorious detail you hinted at in those letters to myself and Colby."

Argenti and Jameson exchanged a brief look. The Ripper's vanity. He might not be able to resist the temptation to boast about the murders and how he'd been able to fool them for so long. But Taylor only looked up fleetingly, nonplussed, as if he didn't know what Jameson was talking about.

The tension in the room was stifling. Argenti knew that after playing this final ace card, they'd be left only with tossing a coin in the courtroom. He turned a few pages in the notebook to a folded newspaper clipping. He ceremoniously unfolded it and spread it out on the table.

"And then we come to this item here in your notebook. Do you recognize it, Mr Taylor?"

Taylor simply nodded.

"Answer clearly yes or no!" Argenti barked.

"Yes... yes I do."

"It's a clipping from the London *Daily Telegraph* about the murder of Elizabeth Stride, is it not?"

"Yes," Taylor muttered, barely discernible.

"Speak up!"

"Yes, it is."

"And what was it doing in your possession?"

Silence again. Argenti's icy stare made it clear it was taking all his willpower not to reach across the table and throttle the answer from Taylor.

"She... she was a friend of a girl I knew. That's why I had it."

"I've heard some stories in my time." Argenti grimaced sourly. He prodded at the notebook. "One of the girls whose name you've written down? Because you have Elizabeth's name written down, and here just a few pages on you have the news clipping about her murder."

"No. That's another Elizabeth I wrote down – not Stride."

"What's this *other* Elizabeth's surname?"

"I don't recall now, I…" Taylor broke off, startled, as the door behind Argenti burst open.

Argenti swung round, glaring at the young duty sergeant standing there. "I thought I made it clear. No disturbances – under *any* circumstances!"

"I'm sorry. I… I thought you'd want to hear this immediately," he stammered.

Argenti went out and shut the door behind him. "Okay. What is it?"

The sergeant pointed along the corridor to a rotund woman with gold hoop earrings, who smiled meekly back at them.

"Says she's a manageress at the Peacock Club and heard you were asking about Jack Taylor amongst some of her girls." The sergeant was red-faced, anxious, sensing Argenti wouldn't like the news he'd brought. "She claims that he *was* at the club the night you were asking about."

16

It was too bright here, he thought. Too bustling and noisy, three girls outside of one club, gents in top hat and tails drawing up in a hansom, two sailors calling out from across the road to the girls.

As a man in a derby passing brushed against him and looked round, he averted his gaze; too many people who might notice him. He kept walking rapidly, taking the next turn at 29th Street. It was just as busy. Forty yards along, a woman in a bright blue evening dress was hawking for the show inside. He went eight doors down to another club and opened the door.

The women outnumbered the men in the club two to one, the atmosphere warm, vibrant. In the corner a self-playing piano played *Clementine*. But looking round, there weren't enough quiet, dark corners where he could talk to a girl without being noticed; worse still, there was a bright gaslight by the stairs leading to the rooms. He'd be seen going up with anyone. As a couple of girls looked his way, he hastily closed the door again.

He walked on. Maybe he should choose another area. This was all too bright and busy for his liking, not enough shadows and darkness. He felt suddenly conspicuous on the street, as if too many people were noticing him. He started looking round for a hansom, and was just about to raise a hand to one approaching when he saw her. She was shrouded in the shadows of an alleyway to his side, and he doubted he'd have noticed her but for the bright red garter on her thigh.

She was leaning slightly forward, examining it keenly as she adjusted its position. She'd just come out the back door of a club and thought that nobody could see her in the darkness of the alleyway.

He walked towards her to get a clearer look. "Very pretty," he remarked.

She looked up, slightly startled. She hadn't heard him approach. She smiled slyly.

"The garter or my legs?"

"Both." He looked up and saw that she had a matching red silk ribbon round her neck holding a glass pendant. Inexpensive adornments, but effective, they caught the eye at a distance. "And *you*, of course."

She had a lazy, slow smile. It was difficult to tell if she'd been drinking or was just naturally slow to respond. "Thank you."

"What's your name?"

"Daisy."

"Daisy... Daisy," he repeated, thoughtful for a second. "That's a nice name."

"Thank you."

She was pretty too with light brown hair and a fleck of green in her doleful brown eyes. But he'd seen that look before, a few years ago she might have had more life and light in her eyes, as if with each dollar and man that had laid with her, some light had been washed from them. Even if he'd met her away from the Tenderloin, he'd have known from her eyes what she did for a living.

He glanced to each side. Nobody else in the alley, and the people passing hadn't paid them much attention. But he needed more time with this one, somewhere private.

"I wondered... could we go somewhere, perhaps?"

She appraised him for a moment. "We can go back in the club, if you like. They have some private sections at the back."

"No. I was thinking of somewhere different."

"Your hotel room?"

"No... no. Maybe your place or a room you know nearby."

She sank into thought. "I don't know, I..."

"*Daisy!*"

She broke off and turned towards the girl who'd called her name from the club doorway.

He turned his head away.

"You seen Bernard?"

"He's down below changing a barrel, I think."

His whole body was suddenly tense, rigid. Had she seen him? The club's back door was ten yards along, shadows heavy in the alley, little light. But he could sense her still there, as if something else was on her mind.

"You gonna be long?"

"I don't know yet. That depends."

Daisy smiled back at the girl and he felt her touch on his arm. He hoped that she hadn't discerned his anxiety. He was tensed so tight he'd started to tremble.

"You want one too?" Daisy asked.

It took him a second to realize she was offering him a cigarette, and her next action was so quick he didn't have time to stop her. She struck the match and it briefly illuminated their faces.

"No. No, thank you." The flame died as quickly, but he knew with certainty that the girl by the club door had seen him.

"Okay. See you in a while." The girl went back inside the club and shut the door.

Daisy let out soft plume of smoke. "Now, you were saying?" She reached out and touched his arm again, her face dropping after a second. "My, you're shaking like a leaf. Are you okay?"

Her eyes searched his face, and he looked quickly away, fearful of what she might see. If he could read their dark souls through their eyes, could they read his?

"Yes, uh... just a bad cold I've been trying to rid myself of these past days. I... I shouldn't have come out tonight."

"It's okay. I'll warm you up." She stroked his arm, but he pulled it brusquely away. "I'm sorry. *Sorry.*" He turned and strode resolutely away.

"I'm sorry too, mister," she called after him. "When you're rid of your cold, let me know."

But he'd already turned the corner, heading back the way he'd come along 29th Street.

Ellie found the man by the Monroe Street junction with Market Street; or, rather, he found her.

He'd stayed thirty yards shy of the corner, looking each way along the street at intervals and checking his pocket watch, as if he was waiting for someone. And as she felt his eyes slide across her for a second time, she ambled towards him.

"Were you waitin' for someone in particular?"

"I'm not sure, I..." He looked flustered for a second, looking anxiously past her shoulder.

"Or if she's not comin', would my company perhaps take the sting outa bein' let down?"

She held his gaze more directly. She knew she'd have to be forthright to put him more at ease. Too many awkward moments could pass before he got round to admitting, as much to himself, that he was in a part of town he shouldn't be. Monroe and Market were notorious pickup areas; unless he'd got lost or picked an odd area for a meeting, there were few other reasons to be here.

"Could be..."

His eyes slid over her again, weighing her up, and as they shifted anxiously past her shoulder again to some people passing the corner, she felt a chill as it suddenly struck her that there *was* another reason.

It hadn't only been Anna balking at going back out on the streets after Camille's murder. Half the girls in the house had stayed in for two or three days after, herself included. And when she had finally ventured out, she'd found herself looking over her shoulder more. Finley had said it was unlikely the Ripper would come back for another of them, but what if they came upon him by chance? Now she was only two blocks away from the Riverway Hotel.

What was it Finley had said about the Ripper? Nondescript, blended in, but looked like a city gent, sought out the darker street areas for his liaisons. An opportunist, who would keep a keen eye on nearby activity.

The chill gripped her deeper. The light was stronger on the corner, but he'd purposely kept twenty yards away where the shadows were heavier. And he did seem particularly on edge, his eyes shifting anxiously to anyone who might pass and become visible within that corner light.

She studied him more keenly – brown hair and matching brown derby. Dark grey suit, black wool coat. A study in shades of brown and grey, he could pass for a hundred city gents and you wouldn't recall him a moment later.

And as he suddenly reached inside his coat and she saw the glint of silver, the chill leapt up and gripped her throat. She gasped, took a step back.

"What is it?" he asked, alarmed.

"Uh...uh. Nothing." She saw then that it was the silver pocket watch she'd seen him looking at before. "Jus' this chill night air. Gets to me at times."

She would have cosied back into him, continued her play for him. But she was still unsettled, unsure.

And as his eyes drifted past her shoulder again, this time she followed his gaze. Surely not? Only a split-second glimpse before the figure was lost again amongst the shadows, but in that instant she'd thought she'd seen a crimson derby. Surely there couldn't be two men with those? But what on earth would Finley be doing in this neck of the woods this time of night?

Ellie hustled back to the corner for a clearer view. People passing were as quickly lost in shadow again the other side of the junction. She caught a vague shape moving away, but she could no longer tell the colour of the hat. It could as easily have been brown rather than crimson.

She had to wait for a hansom clip-clopping past – but as the view became clear again, there was nobody in sight. She eased out her breath. It probably hadn't been Jameson after all. As with her imaginings about the Ripper these past nights, she was starting to see too much among the shadows.

She turned back towards her potential customer, but he'd gone too, disappeared back into the darkness of the night.

He found her on the edge of Five Points. Everything was wrong about her, but the moment was right; whereas conversely everything had been right about the previous girl, but the moment had been wrong.

His first thought had been to get away from the Tenderloin as quickly as possible. If he attacked another girl in the same area that night, Daisy and her friend might make the connection. He walked three blocks away, then hailed a hansom cab and asked to be taken to the Bowery.

As the hansom turned into the Bowery, its horse suddenly reared up, disturbed by an elevated steam train chugging past. Its tracks raised on iron parapets above the sidewalk each side, it pumped copious billows of steam at the buildings it passed.

"Sorry about that. Infernal things," the driver said. "You'd think they'd give some thought for the horses when they invent these contraptions, wouldn't yer?"

"Yes, you would."

But looking out each side, the brightness of the street and the bustle of people wasn't much less than the Tenderloin, and then he suddenly remembered it was also where the sailor had initially claimed to have gone the night he'd killed Lucy Bonina. He asked the driver to take him on to Five Points.

"Five Points?" the driver quizzed. "I'm afraid I don't go in there."

Almost as notorious as the Fourth Ward, a warren of gangs, footpads and cutthroats, few ventured into the area this time of night unless they lived there. He nodded his understanding.

"Okay. Leave me as close as you can."

He'd walked the rest and found the girl two blocks from Five Points.

She looked lost at first, like a waif or stray, rather than looking for a man. Gaunt with dark, sunken eyes as if she hadn't eaten for days, lank black hair and a smock dress that had probably been white at one time but was now a shade between yellow and grey. Disturbingly young, she looked Italian or gypsy Irish, and so poor she'd used coal dust for eye make-up.

She smiled at him as he came close. "Yer lookin' for some time, mister?"

There wasn't even a touch of red about her, she was just a sketch in grey against the black night, and he'd almost walked on. But time was pressing; if he left it till the next night to find a girl, it might be too late.

"Do you have a place nearby we could go?"

"Yeah, I do at that." She pointed. "Jus' left off the next alley."

"Anyone else be there?"

"No. We'll be alone."

As they undressed in the drab room, he wondered why apart from one girl none of them ever realized until the last moment what was about to happen. Was it being so impromptu that kept the girls off-guard? One girl lights a match and escapes, another smiles at him at the wrong time. Fate.

He noticed rags and old clothes piled waist-high one side of the room, and torn clothes and garments were also piled on the only two chairs there.

"Oh, one thing," he said. He reached into his coat pocket and took out a small vial of red liquid. He dipped his little finger in it and touched it against her mouth. "You should have some colour on your lips."

Her lips trembled as he touched them and she smiled softly at him; as if nobody before had ever taken such care with her. He felt tears well in his eyes as he looked at her. She looked so beautiful now, the red appearing to leap out of the drab room. It was vital this time to link the two attacks, so he'd brought a vial of Lucy Bonina's blood with him to put it on her body afterwards; now this sudden impulse.

"Does it look good?" the girl asked.

"Yes, it looks perfect."

••••

There had been a moment later when he thought of stopping and letting her go. As he gripped her throat, she stared back at him with wide, pleading eyes as if to say, "Why are you doing this to me?"

She looked so young and pitiful that he thought she deserved a second chance in life. But he knew by then it was too late, she'd seen the blade in his hand and could identify him later.

He tried still to savour that first knife thrust of entering her and feeling her warm blood spill out and bathe him, but even that felt wrong this time. A faint flicker in her eyes told him she was still alive as he'd made the first few knife thrusts, and tears were streaming down his cheeks as he continued thrusting, muttering like a mantra under his breath, "I'm sorry, I didn't want to do this. I didn't want to kill you. You weren't the right one... weren't the right one..."

17

*I didn't want to kill this one. So you have her blood on
your hands as much as mine. If you hadn't gone on
that foolish excursion with the sailor, she wouldn't have
died. But I had to do it while you still had him held in
the Tombs, see. If you'd already released him, you might
have thought he'd killed another one and so would have
arrested him again. You left me with no choice.*

*You're beginning to disappoint me. I thought you were
a worthy adversary, but now I am beginning to wonder.
I killed that last girl, Lucy, only a hundred yards from
where you and Argenti were on board the Delphinius,
yet you both then went on that fool wild goose chase with
that sailor, Jack Taylor? Didn't you know from the start
it couldn't be him? Don't you know me well enough by
now? You've forced me to link the two girls' deaths now
so that there can be no further doubt.*

*I also marked that last letter on Camille Green's body
where it could be easily seen, but even that was misread
and you headed in the wrong direction. So I've left this
one now where it can't be missed. But don't forget, I'm
watching you, so I know when you put a foot wrong
probably before you do.*

*Still, I'm surprised at Colby, usually so thorough,
missing those markings and not making the link
previously. They were subtly hidden, yes, but not totally*

obscure to someone of Colby's calibre; or yours, for that matter.

Also ask Colby why the writing near Catherine Eddowes's body was removed so hastily with no mention of it since? Could he have misread that message too?

"Heavy bruising and contusion to the right side of the victim's neck and shoulder. Two lateral cuts to the left side of the neck, severing the carotid artery."

Jameson leant back and Lawrence, making notes at his side, moved in and measured the wounds.

"Five and half inches and four and a quarter inches, respectively."

"Likely cause of death, haemorrhage from afore-mentioned severance of the carotid artery."

Light was intense in the morgue examination room, four ceiling gas lamps and another suspended by a copper tube directly above the cadaver. Their soft hiss was the only noise in the lull from their voices and the clink of probes, clamps and retractors against enamel dishes.

Argenti stood at the back of the room observing, having passed on details from the crime scene at the outset. She'd been discovered by Samuel Gerson, landlord of the small ground-floor room where she'd been murdered. She was employed by him there as a rag-picker until 9 pm six nights a week, so he was at a bit of a quandary as to what she was doing there almost two hours later.

Argenti didn't share any details with Mr Gerson, but he then had the victim's name, Laura Dunne, and where she lived.

"One smaller cut to the right side of the neck, only superficial. Deeper, oblique cut running from the left-corner of the victim's mouth to her jawbone…"

"Three and a quarter inches."

"Blood apparent following the exact contour of the lips. From level of coagulation, could have preceded death. To be confirmed following further analysis."

Lawrence leant over and scraped some of the blood from Laura Dunne's top lip into a Petri dish. "I'll bottle and label this sample separately."

When earlier Argenti had seen Laura Dunne's mother, Brenda, after her initial shock and tears she'd had trouble fathoming why anyone would attack her daughter at Mr Gerson's place.

"You don' think Mr Gerson's responsible, do yer?"

"No, we don't. We believe Laura met a man outside."

"Why would she do that? She worked at Gerson's place till eleven at night. She's a good girl."

Argenti hadn't wanted to shatter Brenda Dunne's illusions about her daughter, leave the last thing in her mind after her death the fact that she'd been lying to her, and why. He'd merely asked why Laura might have been working such long hours or wanted some extra money, and Brenda Dunne went on to explain how her youngest, Daniel, had scurvy only a few months back.

"Doctor tol' us unless he got proper fresh food, he'd get it again and next time he'd be a gonna.... but we can barely afford scraps, see, so Laura she–" Brenda Dunne had paused then, the stark reality of Five Points suddenly hitting her, where girls as young as twelve sold their bodies on the street. *"You're not sayin' that?..."*

Brenda Dunne couldn't bring herself to say the words and Argenti couldn't either, so he'd just nodded and held her with a solemn stare.

She'd turned away then with a gasp, one hand at her mouth, and he'd got a past image of his own mother when she'd first learned that Marella had been working in a Tenderloin club.

"Was she hurt bad?" Brenda Dunne asked.

"Her injuries were very serious...."

"Primary cut to the abdomen runs from just below the breastbone to the right of the groin by the appendix, then runs horizontally to the left side of the navel and up to just below the left side of the ribcage."

A large, cavernous aperture, it took more time for Lawrence to measure it. "Length, eleven and a half inches. And at its lowest, abdominal point, a width of eight and three-quarter inches."

"The cut at its upper extremity divides the enciform cartilage. Everything in between has been laid open, most internal organs exposed."

"But we believe most of these came after her death."

"You believe? Are yer tryin" to tell me that she didn't suffer fore she died?"

"If it's any consolation... yes. Yes, I am."

"The intestines to the large extent have been detached from the mesentery and laid over the victim's left shoulder. Large cut to the surface of the liver on the left, another smaller cut at right angles to this."

"Three and three-quarter inches and... two and a quarter inches, respectively".

"Liver itself appears healthy. Further small cuts to the pancreas and spleen, to be examined in more detail upon later removal. Right kidney somewhat pale but intact. However, the left kidney has been fully removed. By, from appearance, someone with at least basic medical knowledge. The left renal artery has also been fully severed."

Argenti contemplated Laura Dunne's broken body, only seventeen, born in the wrong part of Five Points at the wrong time – whether it was to put food on the table to save her baby brother's life or just buy her first pair of shoes – she'd never had a chance. Rag-picking had probably paid her less than eight cents an hour, and pitifully he could see where she'd smudged ash-barrel dust around her eyes to try and look more attractive to men.

Jameson's voice snapped him out of his thoughts.

"I think we all need a break, don't you?" His look towards Argenti held a tinge of concern. "We can finish up here straight after. Right now I think some of Bellevue's best canteen mud, better known as tea and coffee, is in order."

The Bellevue was Manhattan's oldest and one of its largest hospitals. Now, approaching mid-morning, its second-floor canteen was as busy and hectic as its emergency rooms. They took a corner table away from the main bustle and clatter.

Jameson grimaced as he put down his cup after his first sip of tea. "One hell of a liberty, trying to blame her death on us. I can see it's had an impact on you."

"Yes, certainly the accusation doesn't help, on top of all else." Argenti sighed. "But I think it was more the autopsy straight after seeing Laura Dunne's mother, how she reacted to knowing that her daughter was..." Argenti's voice trailed off as he realized he was getting too close to home, too close to his mother and Marella.

Jameson shook his head. "Typical mental misfit. Unable to take responsibility for his own actions, has to blame it on others."

Their table was solid marble and the floor made of large flagstones so that both could be easily washed down. Not far different from the morgue they'd just come from.

"What are your thoughts about the letter?" Argenti asked Jameson.

"The letter he left on the steps of Tammany Hall this morning or the letter marked on Laura Dunne's left kidney that accompanied it?"

"Both."

Jameson dipped a biscuit in his tea, applied thought. "Certainly he's becoming bolder, leaving the package there right under Mayor Watkins's nose – but possibly he wanted to ensure it was seen immediately. Didn't want to lose any time."

"You said you believe it's a Hebrew letter or symbol?"

"Yes, but I can't be sure until we've consulted someone more knowledgeable in the language, and also uncovered whether, as he claims, there have been past similar marks left on victims."

"But I thought the mark left on Camille Green's shoulder was a simple 'X'?"

"Possibly not," Lawrence cut in. "Its appearance is similar to '*Alef*' in Hebrew – equivalent to our letter 'A'. The mark running diagonally down from the right isn't a completely straight line – it has a slight curve to it."

Jameson nodded. "And if indeed there are similar marks on previous victims, why were these missed in London? Or, as he suggests, if they *were* seen – the more thorny issue of why that wasn't made public?"

Argenti's brow knitted. "But why would they do that? Did they wish to hold back something private so at to confirm with certainty it *was* the Ripper?"

"Unfortunately, some of it became public before they had that opportunity." Jameson exchanged a brief look with Lawrence. "You might recall from the files the mention of a bloodied leather apron left at the scene of Annie Chapman's murder. The favoured protective garment of many butchers and upholsterers – but particularly of the many newly arrived Jewish immigrants from Russia and Poland to the area."

Argenti nodded. "Yes. I remember some notes about that."

"As a result, there was already a degree of agitation in the area aimed at these immigrants. So when near the scene of Catherine Eddowes's murder an inscription was found which could have related to Jews, but with an odd spelling – J-U-W-E-S – it was hastily removed by the police before the press got there."

Lawrence elaborated. "The exact wording was 'The Juwes are the men who will not be blamed for nothing'."

After another sip of tea, Jameson continued. "Now with that spelling, a few possibilities arose. Either it was written by an illiterate and did indeed relate to Jews, or it was a reference to Jubelo and therefore had a Masonic link."

Lawrence said, "Jubelo is the second in the chain of Masonic blood oaths, Jubela, Jubelo, Jubelum. It describes what should happen to those who betray the oath. Their left breast to be torn open, vital organs removed and thrown over their left shoulder."

"Similar indeed to the almost ritualistic killing of many a Ripper victim," Jameson picked up again. "However, that hypothesis then led to an even more worrying conspiracy involving the Royal Family, masons and the hierarchy at Scotland Yard. Either way, whether it was to avoid anti-semitic street riots or protect the reputation of the Royal Family, there was sufficient reason to have that wall writing removed." Jameson shrugged. "Apart from which it appeared unlikely it was from the Ripper himself. If he was Jewish or indulging in some form of Masonic ritual, it would be a strange way to refer to himself in the third person or point the finger at his purpose."

Argenti tied the threads together. "So you're saying that announcing a Hebrew letter has been marked on the victims might give rise to the same problem of anti-semitic street protests?"

"*Both* problems in fact. Hebrew also features in many Masonic rituals, particularly initiation. It could reflect on that thorny issue too." Jameson sighed. "We'll know more when we've heard back from London. And if indeed they *did* find anything on past victims, just why it was covered up."

After dinner, Jameson announced that he was going for a walk.

"Do you want company, or is there anywhere I can run you in the hansom?" Lawrence enquired.

"No, it's okay. Just a few things I need to work out on my own. I won't be long."

But only two blocks from the house, he hailed a hansom and headed to Ling's. The day's autopsy still weighed heavy on him, the images too fresh, too *real*; as if in reconstructing the murder, he imagined himself actually there at the time. His own hand becoming that of the Ripper's knife hand. He needed to clear his thoughts.

Ling stayed by the front desk dealing with another client as Sulee led him through. In the far corner of the room were two other men, but they paid him little attention. Jameson sat on an Ottoman sofa as Sulee prepared a pipe and lit an oil lamp. Kneeling, Sulee held the end of the long pipe over the lamp, and Jameson started sucking up the first vapours. At this point he'd usually be left alone for a while until his later massage – but as Sulee got up to go, Jameson held up a hand.

"No, please. Stay with me for a while and talk."

"Okay. As long as it doesn't involve any deep philosophy, I won't charge extra." Sulee sat at his side, and Jameson saw from her return smile that she was joking. "What do you wish to talk about?"

Said like that, Jameson suddenly wasn't sure what he wanted to discuss, if anything. He sighed. "Perhaps my recent problems and frustrations, perhaps something deeper – such as why I come here in the first place."

"Ah, but if I got you to face that, you might stop coming here. Not good for business."

Jameson nodded. Sulee's smile was enigmatic this time, as if she was only half joking.

"There are some things I can't talk to Lawrence about, you see. They would burden him too much. It's not just my coming here that I can't tell him about."

"And do you wish now to talk about those other things?"

"Yes, I believe I do." Jameson took another heavy draw, felt the opium's warmth suffuse him. "It's to do with my mother. How in fact I came to meet Lawrence in the first place. But I can't talk to him about it, you see, because it would just remind him of a past he's still battling to forget."

"And are you battling to forget too?"

"Yes, I... I suppose I am."

"And so you come here?"

Jameson sank deeper into contemplation as he sucked on the pipe. It was a moment before he answered.

"That isn't the only memory that haunts me, what happened with my mother. It's also my work, dealing so much with the dead, trying to solve the mysteries of why they died. Often pieces of those puzzles and their haunted faces are still raging through my mind late into the night." Jameson sighed and took another puff. "Without the oblivion offered here, I wouldn't be able to sleep."

Sulee was thoughtful. "And do you take anything else to help you sleep?"

"Yes, I... I do. For the past almost four years now I've been taking laudanum."

Sulee nodded. She noticed Jameson's eyes becoming glassy, start to flicker.

"Whenever you want to be alone, just tell me. I'll leave."

"No, no... stay a little longer. I was about to tell you what happened with my mother." Jameson's gaze drifted to one side, as if he was having trouble getting clear what he wanted to say.

"Yes, that's right. You were."

But halfway through the next sentence, she watched Jameson drift off completely, glazed eyes fixed on some distant plateau. She waited a moment more until there was just the gentle fall of Jameson's breathing, then got up and left the room.

18

The pressure of the investigation intensified with the collapse of the case against Jack Taylor, with a reporter pressing Mayor Watkins whether he'd be seeking a review of Argenti's role heading the investigation. Watkins had been quick to defend, pointing out that under his predecessor there had been three past suspects for the Camille Green murder, each far more tenuous than Taylor.

But Jameson had sensed something else weighing Argenti down. Perhaps the sheer brutality of Laura Dunne's murder, her young age or dire poverty; she hadn't been wearing shoes and her mother had told Argenti she didn't in fact own a pair. Or the fact that after thirty long years in the city, Argenti had seen it all – the endemic corruption, the cruel gulf between rich and poor – so there was no reaction left but tired scepticism. The city had finally worn him down.

Whereas to himself it was all fresh and exciting, a vibrant new city, and so he could observe that social injustice at arm's length. Like the wealthy benefactors who gave a few silver dollars each month to the workhouse poor, but didn't think about it beyond that. Didn't relate that to the reality of the fetid beggars and street urchins they brushed aside daily with their ivory canes.

Now, visiting Ellie again, Jameson liked to think that his efforts were more than that. He smiled as Ellie

Cullen finished her tea. After their first few lessons and now twenty minutes of her battling through word pronunciations in passages of *Little Dorrit*, he'd decided upon something different for this one.

"We're goin' out today, yer say?" Ellie asked.

"That's right. We'll do the rest as a practical lesson on the streets of New York. We'll go in my hansom."

"Okay. Won' be a jiffy. I'll jus' check with Anna if she'll be okay wit' little Sean for a while, then fix me hair up."

As they went out the alley, Jameson noticed the two policeman on their regular beat between the Riverway Hotel and Ellie's approaching forty yards away. He touched his hat at them and one of them nodded in acknowledgment. Jameson's head turned sharply, sensing someone looking at him from behind – but as he scanned the alley there was only a beggar sat against a wall.

"Yer okay?" Ellie enquired.

"Yes, I'm fine. Fine. Let's go." He had something important to give Ellie, but it would wait until their return.

Lawrence headed the hansom uptown, along Canal Street and then onto Lafayatte Street. Halfway up, Jameson picked his first test.

"What's the name on that shopfront? The green sign on the right?"

"Mart-in-sons."

"Yes. Martinson's. Very good." He'd decided that names rather than words familiar in her daily vocabulary might be a stronger test of her phonetic ability. "And the sign on the left – gold on a brown background?"

"Bee-u-man's."

"No. That one's Beauman's, pronounced Boman. The eau gives an 'o' sound. But that's a more difficult one, derives from the French. We'll come back to those later."

They turned into Broadway and a hundred yards along Jameson pointed to another sign. "And that one?"

"Brown's thee-atree."

"Think in terms of what you know that building to be and how it would be pronounced."

"Oh, right. Theeater." Ellie smiled gently, then twenty yards along pointed to another sign. "Look! I see that one's been spelt right. Theater!"

Jameson smiled in return. Incorrigible. He'd noticed that while a number of theatres had kept the old English spelling, others had adopted the more phonetic spelling.

"Fair point. Let's leave the occasional 're' pronunciation along with the 'eau's' until later, shall we?"

"Soun's like a good idea. You're th' teacher."

She had a twinkle in her eye as she said it, and Jameson couldn't help finding her teasing side endearing. They rode in silence for a moment, Ellie appearing lost in thought before she turned to him again.

"By th' way. Was it you that I saw by Monroe Street the other night?"

"Don't believe so." Jameson's brow knitted. "What makes you ask that?"

"Oh, jus' that I saw a man with a crimson derby across the way there. Thought it might have been you."

"No, I'm afraid not." He smiled primly. "Obviously I'm not the only one in the city with outrageous hat sense."

Jameson resumed his test after the next junction, picking out a dozen more random signs as they travelled uptown; and while Ellie got most pronunciations right, they were still a struggle for her. Though when they got to the corner of 59th and Lexington, she pronounced Bloomingdale's without any hesitation.

"That's very, very good!" Jameson exclaimed. "You're getting the hang of it now."

"Tha's cause I know that shop t' be Bloomin'dales, silly." She smiled, but from the pause she wasn't sure if he'd taken it as an affront. "Well, yer did say to think 'bout what we knew words and places t' be."

His smile slowly rose, and they both burst into laughter at the same time. Lawrence frowned at what all the commotion was about, and Jameson felt Ellie lean against him as they laughed, suddenly aware of her body heat and perfume.

The silence following felt awkward, so Jameson quickly resumed his pronunciation tests on shop signs they passed. As they headed back down Broadway, Ellie pointed to the opera house.

"A... a man I knew once, he said he wen' to th' opera regular. Says they sing in nothin' but Italian there."

"Yes, most of the time. But not exclusively. If it's light opera such as Gilbert and Sullivan, it will be done in English."

"My, my. Italian. An' here's me still strugglin' with English."

Jameson smiled tightly, his gaze lingering on the Grand Metropolitan for a moment before shifting for the next shopfront test.

They stopped off at Gansevoort Market and he brought her a fresh pineapple and a bunch of bananas to take home as treats for the children. Then they sat on the steps of Burnham's clam cannery overlooking the market while they ate ham and smoked beef jerky rolls from the covered market behind.

Most of the traders in the open cobbled area sold their produce from the back of their carts with the horses still hitched. Jameson got Ellie to read some of the names on carts and stalls, but at one point with the surrounding bustle his thoughts drifted, again struck with the sensation that someone was observing them. *Don't forget, I'm watching you.* He scanned the square.

Watching? Ellie had indeed been right in her observation, it had been him the other night. But he thought it might be awkward admitting he'd been watching her.

He'd been close to the area and called by Ellie's place impromptu to rearrange the time of their next reading session. But as he'd approached, she was going out. By her bright finery, it looked like she was starting work. She hadn't seen him. He decided to follow.

And, sure enough, two streets from the Riverway Hotel, she'd soon struck up a conversation with a man who'd been standing close by. He'd questioned in that moment why he'd followed her. Curiosity, or because he feared she was still in danger? That this man now might be the Ripper. What did he feel as he'd observed them? Discomfort, fear for her safety, jealousy? He focused more keenly on the man in the dull light, as he had many times following the Ripper's path in Whitechapel, visualizing the man leaning closer, the blade in his hand. But the scene in his mind suddenly transformed to himself with Ellie, his own hand on the blade as he thrust, and he knew that he shouldn't have followed her, knew that–

Lawrence's voice snapped him out of it. "We should head away soon. It will probably be there by now."

"Yes. Yes, of course." Their main reason for taking this diversion, to be able to pick up the telegram reply from London en route.

Lawrence and Ellie stood at the back of Great Eastern's main reception hall at the corner of Broadway and Liberty Street as he read the five-line telegram.

Jameson was unusually quiet as they returned in the hansom to Ellie's, still preoccupied with the telegram's portent. He should share its contents with Argenti as quickly as possible. Only Ellie's parting kiss on his cheek in thanks for the day broke him from his thoughts. He almost forgot what he'd planned to give her.

"Oh, before you go." The policemen weren't by her door, but Jameson looked round in case they were approaching, again that sensation of someone peeking from a doorway at them. Nobody there. Nevertheless, he shielded with his body from any possible onlookers as he handed Ellie the small pearl-handled revolver. "I've noticed that the police patrol isn't here all the time, so you should keep this with you for protection. Keep it safe on you or in a drawer."

Ellie fingered the revolver nervously for a second before tucking it into her handbag. "Anyone would think you cared 'bout me."

"Yes, they might," he said, riding the tease with a soft smile.

Martin pulled sharply back into the doorway sixty yards along from Ellie Cullen's, his pulse racing. Had the toff seen him?

The last thing he wanted to do was get into a scrape with the toff and end up with a hand chopped off with an axe. But with the mood Tierney was in, getting seen by the toff and then lying about it might lead to the same result.

He'd swapped two blocks of his collection area with McCabe because Tierney didn't want McCabe going anywhere near the toff. Likewise, Tierney had told him not to go near the toff either, "Jus' keep a sharp eye out for him when yer by her place, tha's all. An' let me know the second he shows there."

Martin gave a final look to make sure the coast was clear, then sprinted off in the direction of McLoughlin's brewery.

Joseph Argenti had been home only half an hour when Jameson called at his door. Sophia hadn't returned yet from the store where she worked and so Oriana went to answer it. As he heard Jameson's voice, he came out of his study.

"Come in, Finley. Come in." Argenti beckoned him in; then to Oriana as she shut the door behind Jameson. "And Oriana, would you be so kind to arrange some tea for my guest?"

Jameson smiled in appreciation. "Sorry to trouble you at home. I was hoping to catch you while you were still at Mulberry Street, but then I got held up at the hospital." Argenti led the way back into his study, and as they took their seats Jameson passed the telegram across. "The reason for the urgency."

"I see." Argenti unfolded it and started reading:

YOUR PROMPT WAS OPPORTUNE. WE HAVE NOW DISCOVERED SOME OTHER LETTERS. TOO SENSITIVE AND TOO MUCH DETAIL TO DISCUSS BY TELEGRAM. MY INTENTION TO TRAVEL TO NEW YORK. WILL ARRIVE APRIL 24TH ON THE BRITANNIC AND PLAN TO STAY ONE WEEK. CAN YOU ARRNAGE FOR A HEBREW WRITING EXPERT FOR MY ARRIVAL?
YOURS, THOMAS COLBY

Argenti looked up. "The twenty-fourth. That's Tuesday week?"

"Yes. I would have caught you earlier, but I had to wait on Laura Dunne's tests." He looked up as Oriana approached with their tea on a tray and set them down on the table between them. "Thank you."

"My pleasure." Oriana smiled and curtsied as she left the room.

"Charming girl. Is she your eldest?"

"Yes. My two younger ones are both boys."

Argenti brought his attention back to the telegram. "It appears there *have* been some other letters marked on victims. Although he says 'now', as if it's a recent discovery."

"Unless of course he's being diplomatic. Doesn't want to give away that some markings were discovered earlier." Jameson sipped at his tea, grimaced.

"Seems like you could be right about the letters marked on Laura Dunne and Camille Green being Hebrew."

"It was actually Lawrence who noticed that. Latin for my Hippocratic oath was quite sufficient, thank you. Though we'll obviously know more when we've consulted an expert in Hebrew." Jameson became contemplative. He reminded himself how Argenti had been affected by the two autopsies; but had was little way of softening the information. "We found something strange too from testing the blood on Laura Dunne's lips; it isn't her own."

"Whose do you think it is? *His*?"

"Unlikely that he'd take the risk. We can't fully tell blood types yet – all we can run is a test for agglutination* to prevent mortality during blood transfusion. If blood from a donor and recipient agglutinates clumps together,

---

* *Though distinctive blood types were not identified by Carl Landsteiner until 1901, agglutination tests were run from 1880 in several hospitals prior to blood transfusions.*

then it's not suitable. The blood from Laura Dunne's lips did agglutinate with her other blood samples, meaning it's not hers. We ran the same test with Camille Green's, and it did the same. However, with Lucia Bonina's blood it didn't." Jameson sighed. "So it appears it's either from Lucia Bonina, or someone else."

Argenti simply stared at him, blinking slowly, as if he was having trouble assimilating the information. As it finally dawned on him, his eyes closed for a second. "I suppose that's the link between the two murders he referred to in his last letter?"

"It would appear so. But that also means there's no doubt a mark too somewhere on Lucy Bonina's body, only we haven't so far managed to find it."

When Martin caught up with Mike Tierney, he was in the middle of his regular inspection round at the brewery. The heat from the copper boilers was intense, the smell of fermenting hops and malt heavy in the air.

Martin had to raise his voice to be heard above the noise of the boilers and the mash tun. Tierney pulled his attention from inspecting the temperature gauge on one of the copper boilers as Martin finished.

"Looked like they'd been off somewhere, yer say?"

"Tha's right. All dressed up fine she was."

"But no Detective Argenti with 'em?"

"No." Martin shrugged. "Leas', couldn'a see 'im."

Tierney was thoughtful as he continued along, Martin half a pace behind. From what he'd seen in the press, Argenti and the toff were meant to be working on this "Ripper" case together. So what was the toff doing seeing Ellie Cullen on his own?

As he approached the first in a row of four large fermentation vats, the worker at its side dipped in a long-handled copper ladle and held it towards Tierney. Tierney inhaled from the dark liquid in the ladle bowl.

"We got the yeast level right at last," Tierney commented. "Jus' a touch more malt though, I think."

The worker nodded and they moved on. Tierney turned again to Martin. "So, the coppers guarding Ellie's door. Who'd they put on the beat?"

"Bill Payne and Josh Rawlings, by th' looks of it."

Tierney nodded. He had Rawlings in his pocket, but Payne was another matter. He'd have to give that more thought. "And the timin' of their watch between there and the Riverway?"

"Looks like they spend twenty minutes in fron' of each, and the walk tween's maybe twelve, fourteen minutes."

Tierney arched an eyebrow. "An' are yer sure you're telling me everything now, and the toff didn't see yer?"

"No, tha's everythin'. An' he didna see me, I swear."

Tierney savoured the fear in Martin's face for a second, then put a comforting hand on his shoulder.

"No worries. Yer did well." As they continued walking along, Tierney slipped his arm fully over Martin's shoulder, as if they were old friends. He nodded towards the fermenting vats. "Yer know there's an old story goes round that one of the night-workers once fell in a vat. Whether jus' from the fumes or having a tipple mo' than he should, nobody ever knows. Looked like a pickled walnut when they foun' his body in the morning. Not a pretty sight." He smiled tightly as he patted Martin's back in parting. "Jus' shows you – yer can't be too careful, eh?"

19

Jameson's maid, Alice, didn't register the sounds at first; they took a moment to drift from the edge of her sleeping subconscious and wake her.

Her eyes blinked slowly in the dark, trying to place where the voices were coming from, little more than muted mumbling, as if they didn't want to be heard, it sounded as if they were coming from the kitchen.

Her first thought was that someone had broken in. She sat up sharper in bed, holding her breath so that she could hear them clearer. Certainly she'd never known Master Jameson to venture into the kitchen; and Lawrence would usually only come in if she was already there to talk to. But it was still too subdued to make out clearly.

She got up, opened her door and edged her way to the top of the stairs. From there, she could just make out a thin slat of light spilling into the hallway below. They'd left the kitchen door a few inches ajar. She started making her way slowly down, careful not to make any noise on the staircase.

Two voices, she could make out as she neared the bottom of the stairs. And as she moved across the hall closer to the door, the person doing most of the talking certainly sounded like Master Jameson. But what on earth were they doing in the kitchen at this hour? It must be close to three in the morning.

The sight that met her eyes as she peered through the gap in the door took her breath away. Jameson was holding up what looked like a human heart, his hands thick with gore, sleeves rolled up and blood running halfway down his forearm as he admired it. His voice drifted out.

"Very difficult to see markings clearly on here, especially close to either of the ventricles."

"So, along with the kidney and stomach, a lesser choice."

She saw Lawrence come briefly into view, his hands also thick with blood as he picked up another organ from a dish on the kitchen table.

"Yes. Appears that the liver or spleen are always going to be prime choices – at least from the point of view of clarity and ease of identification."

There were three dishes in front of them, she could now see. Each contained two or three organs and were thick with blood. Spots and trails of blood could be seen on the table where they'd lifted out organs to inspect them.

She must have unconsciously held her breath because it came out with a sudden gasp as the full horror hit her.

Jameson and Lawrence looked sharply her way. Lawrence started towards her, reaching one bloodied hand out.

She ran, and was halfway back up the stairs as Lawrence swung the kitchen door open. He looked out after her.

"Alice..."

She was too gripped with fear to even look back in acknowledgment. Breathless, she slammed the bedroom door shut behind her.

The smell of wood and coal smoke on the air was heavier at night. Not just from more fires burning then, but because with the cooler night air it would settle lower.

Argenti liked the smell, and blew his own contribution of cigar smoke towards it as he sat on the veranda. Their house was raised five steps from the street and at the back was a small veranda leading from the dining room. Argenti liked to sit there after dinner as the days got warmer.

He looked out over the neighbouring yard fences towards the only gas lamp in view in their street. Mist and smoke seemed to be settling around it, and as Argenti looked up he wondered if there were fewer stars visible now than when he was a child, the city's smoke becoming heavier as it filled with more people.

"Are you okay?"

Argenti looked round as Sophia approached. Dinner had finished almost two hours ago and the children were in bed.

"Yes, fine. Busy day, that's all. Just relaxing a while."

Sophia nodded as she took a seat beside him. She gave him an understanding smile.

"Just that you seemed troubled. Oriana said you had a visitor earlier, so I wondered if it might have been to do with that."

"It was only Jameson. More on this Ripper case."

"Oh, I see."

Argenti sensed she was expecting more. She knew only the bones of the Ripper case and that if successful it would mean a promotion for him, but he hadn't gone into detail beyond that.

"The murder details are upsetting, yes, but I'm used to that." He shrugged. "It's the fact that some of the girls are so young, the youngest only seventeen, only a few years older than Oriana. And one of them was from an Italian family."

Sophia looked at him, pensive. "I can see how that might have raised your concerns, Joseph. But this is a good neighbourhood, it's why we moved here."

"I know. I know." He looked straight ahead, blew out another cigar plume.

"And while it's upsetting what happened to those girls, they *were* putting themselves at risk out on the streets like that. Oriana's a good girl."

Argenti looked at her sharply. "*Good girl*? But what defines that? That last girl, Laura Dunne, was only seventeen and was out trying to scrape together money to save her young brother's life. Is that not good?"

"Oh, my." Sophia put her hand to her mouth as the reality hit her.

He could hardly blame her for the misconception. In all the newspaper articles he'd read, the victims were portrayed simply as soulless, misguided wretches, women who'd fallen from grace, almost as if to say, "If you turn to a life of prostitution, this is what might happen to you."

"Sometimes, Sophia, that dividing line between what's good and bad is thinner than we'd like to think, and for some of these women there's..." He stopped himself then – too close to home – realized that if he got too close to the real reason, he'd have to explain about Marella; about how the city's police corruption had played its part, and so the reason now he was driven against it, saw it as a way of making amends. It would have been so easy to just accept money on the side to turn a blind eye like half the rest of the department, come home one day and tell Sophia she didn't have to work so many hours in the shop. But that would have felt like giving in, admitting defeat, joining those he saw as responsible for Marella's death. He could explain none of that, so in the end he simply said, "But yes, you're right. I'm worrying for nothing."

••••

Of all the seedy bars and low dives close to the East River docks, Dirk's Tavern had the reputation of being the lowest.

A regular gathering place for whores, sailors, thieves, fences and assorted gang members and drunkards, brawls were a frequent occurrence, and Dirk Sullivan boasted one of the longest behind-bar billy clubs in the area. He also had a musket there, reputedly lifted by his father from a soldier's dead body during the Draft Riots, but so far he'd only had to loosen some ceiling plaster above the heads of brawlers. He hadn't yet killed anyone with it.

But even Dirk Sullivan had his standards, and Sewer Charlie was decidedly below them. The last few times Charlie had peeked his head in the doorway, Dirk had sent him packing sharpish. It was only because this time he was with a couple of city gents that Dirk abided his presence.

As Argenti and Jameson had walked into the bar with Charlie, a few drinkers had left soon after. Possibly they'd recognized Argenti and knew he was a detective, but it might well have been Charlie's smell. Spending most of his days and nights between the sewers and Sweeney's Shambles, Charlie reeked of them.

The smell of raw sewerage was heavy in his black wool coat and on his black matted hair and beard; the only relief to the black was a tinge of grey in his hair and a few rotting brown teeth.

"Ah, tha's good. Tha's good," Charlie said with an appreciative sigh as he put his ale tankard back down on the table after the first few heavy slugs.

"And where did you first see him?" Argenti asked.

"Like I said, down in the sewers. Has his own place down there, jus' as I do."

"How much time does he spend down there?"

"Maybe same as me." Charlie shrugged. "Maybe more... maybe less." Charlie went on to explain that he also had a room he'd go to in Sweeney's Shambles when the tide was too high or it became too damp. "Don't know if he does the same. Only seen 'im once in the Shambles before."

"And what does he look like?"

Charlie's eyes shifted, as if he was trying to get a mental picture. "Brown hair... not that tall. Dresses smart when he goes out, but wit' a black police cape over – says he bought it in London while there. Keeps his beard neat trimmed." Charlie shook his head. "Doubt you'd notice 'im that much in a crowd."

Argenti glanced at Jameson before bringing his attention back to the notes he'd made earlier. Some elements struck a chord, but if this was just a local tramp trying to get a few free drinks from spinning a wild story, this supposed "Ripper" would no doubt evaporate as soon as they asked to be pointed in his direction.

Ted Barton had rushed into his office with excitement after luncheon with the news that a local tramp, Sewer Charlie, said he knew who the Ripper was. "Claims he's someone like himself who hides down in the sewers, and has openly boasted about killing these girls and how we'll never find him."

The information had come through a local stevedore who gave Barton tips on stolen goods in the dock area, and in turn a note was passed back through Barton's informant for the tramp to meet them at Dirk's Tavern.

"So why New York after London?" Argenti enquired. "And why in particular the East dockside sewers?"

Charlie leaned across the table, as if he was imparting a vital secret. "He used to be a merchant seaman, yer see. An' while on a trip here, he heard 'bout how the river pirates operate – plunderin' ships, then disappearing back down the sewers where they couldna be found." Charlie tapped a finger against his wizened forehead. "An' that tickled somethin' in his mind, see, 'bout how he used to operate in London."

Jameson asked, "And just how might that have been?"

"I see from your accent, yer might be familiar with that neck o' the woods yerself." Charlie took another slug of beer as he appraised Jameson. "That's how he did it, yer see. Through the sewers."

"What? He got to the girls through the sewers?"

Charlie smiled slyly. "Oh, gettin' to them was no trouble – he said he followed and picked 'em normal like. An' killin' them only took minutes. It was the gettin' away that was the problem. Covered in all that blood as he was."

"I see."

Charlie watched the dawning realization on Jameson's face. "Didn' it ever occur to any o' yer how he got away so quick from all those killin's without being seen with all that blood on 'im?"

"Yes, you have a point." The main theory had always been that the intense darkness and poor visibility, especially on fog-bound nights, had provided the main cover. Also the many butchers and slaughterhouses of the area, which meant that someone walking round with a bloodied apron wasn't that unusual a sight.

"He'd just slip down the nearest manhole, see. Escape through th' sewers which by then he knew so well." Charlie took a slug of ale, belched. "An' now he knows the East dockside sewers equally well."

"But what if the nearest manhole cover was some distance away?" Argenti asked. The theory had merit, except for the Lucy Bonina murder where the killer had to leave the busy and brightly lit *Showboat*.

"That's where he'd use the cape, see. Either to cover th' blood already on his clothes, or he'd put the cape on before killin', then put it in his bag after."

Argenti nodded. If this was an invented story, then certainly Sewer Charlie had gone to a lot of trouble just for some free ale.

"And you say that he told you all this over a drink one night. Opened up on how he did everything?"

"Tha's right. Shared a bottle o' rum with him one night and he tol' me the whole nine yards. Confession's good fo' the soul, as they say. An' ninety-proof rum's better than communion wine fo' that." Charlie knocked back the last of his drink. "On the subject of which."

"Yes, of course." Argenti eyed the empty tankard slapped back on the table. "But first we need to know where we can find this man; question him immediately."

This was the juncture where Argenti expected Charlie's account to lose steam. He'd say something about the man apparently boarding another merchant ship, "Probably halfway to Australia by now," and they'd just be left with another mythical Ripper suspect to add to the files. But instead Charlie said, "Tha's easy. He's no doubt where I saw him in the sewers last night and has been fo' the past two months now."

With the light suddenly ignited in Argenti's eyes, Charlie held up a calming hand.

"But I'll have t' guide yer there – otherwise you'll have a hellish time findin' yer way through the passages down there. That is, if you don't mind me bein' yer guide?"

"No, of course not."

Argenti signalled to Dirk for more drinks.

Commissioner Grayling nodded to the waiter for the bill.

"I think this little chat before you catch your train for Southampton has been helpful, don't you?"

Colby smiled tightly. Grayling had invited him to cream tea at The Ritz to ensure they had all their ducks in a row regarding what should be said in New York.

"I suppose *one* benefit of not revealing exactly what the letters are; it precludes any copycat murders, and also allows us to be sure which ones are Ripper victims."

"Yes. And not mentioning the Hebrew link – *if* that's what it turns out to be – also lets us off the hook with further public agitation. Hopefully satisfies *both* aims."

The waiter brought the bill on a silver tea tray and Grayling paid. Grayling lapsed into thought for a second after the waiter left.

"How many past Whitechapel victims have we now found marks on?"

"Three."

"And in New York, you say they found a letter marked on the first victim and now this latest one. But what about the second victim, Lucy something?"

"Jameson inspected again all of Lucy Bonina's vital organs held in store at Bellevue Hospital, *nothing*. It's been left that I'll conduct a more in-depth examination along with Jameson when I arrive in New York."

"And if you *still* find nothing?"

"Well, I daresay then we'll have our first real acid test of how to differentiate Ripper victims from non-Ripper victims."

They'd arranged to meet Sewer Charlie by the entrance to the alleyway which ran alongside Sweeney's Shambles. Once they entered the alleyway, news of their presence would spread like a bushfire through the thieves, gang members and river pirates of the Shambles.

The most run-down, decrepit tenement block in a city now synonymous with them, the only inhabitants of the Shambles were those who had no place else to go. With sanitation non-existent, hundreds of bedpans and trashcans full of excrement were emptied daily into open sewer holes – their manhole covers long gone – at ground level in the Shambles.

It was this connection with the sewers and proximity to the dockside that had made it particularly popular with river pirates and thieves. If the police ventured in after them, they simply disappeared into the labyrinth of sewers beneath. It was also why Charlie kept a small room there for when the tide became too high for him to stay in the sewers. Charlie pointed as they entered the alley.

"My room's near the back, jus' past halfway."

Argenti nodded, following just behind Charlie. He looked round briefly at his men, some of them giving their guns a last check. He'd emptied his department's gun drawer plus called on more to make sure all his men were armed. Ted Barton and four others: Brendan Mann, John Whelan, Tom Donnelly and Jeremiah Lynch. Entering Sweeney's Shambles unarmed was a sure death sentence. Jameson was last in the line as they went along the heavily shadowed alleyway. Mid-afternoon, but with five-storeys encroaching so closely each side, the light was dim.

Charlie nodded towards the kerosene lanterns they were carrying.

"Like I said, don't light em till I tell yer. Jus' gives more warnin' of our approach."

Sudden scurrying behind dusty, brown-stained windows as they passed; regardless, it appeared that some had already been alerted in the tenement block.

"This one." Charlie indicated to the side. "This one's the best door."

Argenti nodded and followed Charlie through the door. A dark hallway, it took Argenti a moment to adjust to the scant light and see that it was empty.

Charlie led them along, and fifteen yards ahead they hit a T with another corridor. Charlie turned left. Argenti followed, and the movement from behind caught them by surprise.

Argenti moved out the way, but John Whelan behind him only managed to half stoop – the wildly swinging club striking him high on the back, winding him.

Ted Barton, next in line, raised his gun to the man. "Swing again, and I'll drop yer."

Early twenties, with a sidekick also armed with a billy club. As they saw how many were in Argenti's team, their bravery rapidly waned. But Argenti noticed the first man looking past his shoulder.

Argenti wheeled round, and barely discernible in the shadows ten yards away was a boy no more than eighteen with a gun pointed at them.

Argenti raised his own gun. The boy looked uncertain, his arm starting to waver. Dressed the same as the others – loose shirt and derby – they looked like members of the local Shirt Tails gang.

Argenti said, "If you wish to see another day, I suggest you get away while you can."

A frozen, tense moment between them before the boy lowered his gun, turned and scampered away. The other two, suddenly realizing Argenti's team hadn't come for them, followed.

"Sorry 'bout that," Charlie said, as if he was partly responsible. He gave a toothless grin. "Neighbours aren't what they used t' be."

Charlie's room was four doors along the corridor, and totally bare save for a single chair, small kerosene heater and a few dingy blankets on the floor. In one wall was a ragged hole three foot high, pitch darkness beyond. Charlie pointed.

"We go through there. An' you'll need yer lanterns now."

They lit the lanterns, but still a few of Argenti's team looked at the dark hole with apprehension. Charlie led the way and Argenti followed.

Beyond was a small coal storeroom with an open manhole at its centre. Charlie led the way down through the hole and Argenti and the rest followed, Jameson the last in line.

Iron rivets embedded in stone formed steps. The stench of faeces and urine from Sweeney's Shambles had been strong, but as they descended to its source it was excruciating and had an ammonia back-bite. Brendan Mann, just ahead of Jameson, swallowed back the bile he felt rising.

The walls were tight each side for the first fifteen feet of their descent, then the passage widened out and they could hear the trickling of water below.

As Argenti stepped down following Charlie, he could see that they were on a small ledge running one side of a four foot wide sewer trench. Charlie looked back to check the last man was down, then nodded ahead.

"Follow me."

Thirty feet ahead was the dark wall of another sewer tunnel running crossways. As they approached the end, Charlie directed them.

"We turn right here."

Argenti had hardly stepped into the fresh tunnel behind Charlie when a bullet zinged off the wall close by, the gunshot booming loudly in the tunnel. Argenti pinned himself tight against the sewer wall. It was pitch black ahead, he couldn't see who was firing. As another shot zinged off the wall, Argenti and Ted Barton, the only two to have so far made the fresh turn, also ducked back for cover. Charlie quickly followed, breathless. He peered into the darkness of the fresh tunnel after a second.

"Give 'em a minute to get clear. They think we followed 'em down here and we're after 'em."

They waited expectantly. Argenti began to wonder if this might be the ruse. Charlie would say that they weren't going to be able to get to the Ripper because of all the gangs down in the sewers. But sure enough after a moment they heard the scurrying of footsteps receding. After a moment, Charlie peered out again.

"Seems like th' coast is clear now." He beckoned and they edged out cautiously.

Argenti noticed that every sixty yards or so a fresh shaft led up; presumably to other manhole covers. Ahead, the narrow ledge suddenly tapered off.

"We're gonna have to wade the rest," Charlie said. "Don't worry. It's shallow."

Argenti followed Charlie into the freezing water. It came to just above his knees. Barton and John Whelan were suddenly startled by some movement in the water at their side. They shone their lanterns closer. Two shiny brown rats, the largest almost a foot long. The rats swam past and then scurried up onto the nearby ledge.

The seven of them in line with their lanterns cast heavy, ominous shadows on the sewer walls. After a moment, Charlie became alerted to it.

"When we get closer, yer might have to kill a few o' those lanterns. Don't wanna warn him that a crowd's approaching, possibly frighten him off. He's used to only me payin' him a visit."

As they got to within twenty yards of the next sewer junction, this one running off diagonally, Charlie held a hand towards them.

"Jus' hold back there a moment. I gotta check somethin'." He waded to within two yards of the junction and appeared to be listening out for something.

Deathly silence, just the trickle and dripping of water. After a moment, Jameson hissed from behind.

"What on earth are you listening out for?"

Charlie held a finger to his lips. "I need t' listen out fo' which direction he might be."

Argenti's brow knitted. He thought Charlie had said this man had stayed pretty much in the same place the past couple of months? But whatever it was Charlie was listening out for, he appeared to finally hear it. His expression lifted, and he looked keenly back at them.

Although to Argenti it didn't sound like somebody moving about, it sounded like the rush of water; unless it was somebody wading heavily through the water.

The realization hit Argenti almost at the same time as he saw the wall of water surging towards them, its frothing top edge the first thing visible in the lantern light.

Charlie turned sharply from them, his eyes suddenly fixed on the vertical shaft ladder five yards ahead as he dashed for it. He'd obviously done this many times before, escaping advancing tide surges, and timed it perfectly. But Argenti and his team were caught in no-man's land, too far to get to the ladder ahead and too far from the one behind.

The natural instinct though was to head away from the advancing water – so that was the direction they frantically turned and started running. Argenti got a last glimpse of Charlie disappearing up the ladder, the oncoming surge of water just swilling Charlie's ankles as he leered back at them.

"Come on... we can make it!" Argenti urged his men on. But the knee-deep water hampered their progress. Panicked shouts and exclamations from a couple of them, any words and breath gone from the others with the shock. Jameson was closest to the nearest ladder eighteen yards away, but the rest of them were straggled at intervals behind.

Argenti felt the wall of water hit his back after only a few strides, throwing him forward. He thought he saw Jameson get a hand on the ladder as he was washed along, but he couldn't be sure as he felt himself dragged under, the foetid water filling his nose and mouth. He coughed and spluttered, fought to surface. But his kerosene lamp had been extinguished, and he could no longer tell in the pitch black surging water which was up, down or sideways.

He caught a faint glimmer of light and pushed towards it. He surfaced with a gasp, focused. Jameson was eight yards away, clinging to the ladder. He seemed to be the only one with a lantern still burning. Was that another set of legs going up the ladder just above Jameson? Argenti couldn't be sure. He couldn't see the others. As Jameson spotted him, Jameson called out.

"Here! Swim over, Joseph... grab my hand!"

"I... I'll try."

But for each two yards he made, the surging water seemed to pull him back almost as far. As he got to within three yards, Jameson stretched out his arm as far as he could. Although Argenti noticed Jameson take a step higher up the ladder, and he realized with panic what was happening. The water had risen so high there was only a foot gap between its surface and the sewer roof. Jameson shouted again.

"Almost there, Joseph! One more hard push – then reach for my hand!"

Just a bit further. Argenti's chest and arms ached as he thrashed at the water. He gasped like a landed fish in the last remaining air gap as he made one final desperate bid to grasp Jameson's hand.

But at just a foot away, the water swilled fully over his head, and the blurred image of Jameson and his lantern started to drift away again.

At the point he realized he was no longer going to make it, that lantern light was just a faint dot. And as it faded completely, Argenti wasn't sure if it was the blackness of the sewer waters or his lost consciousness giving him welcome release.

20

As soon as Thomas Colby got out on the promenade deck, he lit a cigar and looked out over the dark, brooding Atlantic.

Dinner on board the *SS Britannic* was a formal affair, and he and his wife, Emilia, had been dressed in their finest for the occasion. Colby felt privileged that they were sat at the Captain's table, but towards the end of the third course an iron foundry proprietor started to bore him with a potted history of Bessemer furnaces, so he'd decided to have his after-dinner cigar early and grab some fresh air.

He'd brought Emilia along on the trip to enjoy some shopping and socialising while he was busy in morgues and hospital labs, but when earlier she'd started rambling on about the new Canadian furs in New York stores, he'd cut her short.

He exhaled cigar smoke on the salt air. With the turn the investigation had taken, he realized his impatience with small talk and niceties unrelated to his work was more acute than usual. Drawing a veil over the Hebrew nature of the body marks had been Grayling's idea, and so he felt uncomfortable continuing the subterfuge of why they hadn't picked up on that earlier; besides, it reflected badly on his professional acumen.

Though later when the ship docked and Jameson was there with Lawrence to greet them, Jameson too indulged in small talk. How was their voyage, was it Emilia's first visit to New York and what did she have planned? Jameson nodded back towards the dockside.

"I believe these great ocean liners will be the making of New York. You can walk to the heart of Manhattan from them, whereas the closest the big liners can get to London these days is Tilbury or Southampton."

"Yes, good point," Colby agreed. For once Colby welcomed some diversionary talk, because it tiptoed round the thornier issues at hand. Though when they did finally turn to the investigation and he enquired, "I understand you're making some strong progress with this fellow Argenti," Jameson's face clouded.

"I'm afraid there's been some bad news."

Joseph Argenti had hovered close to death for much of the past twenty-four hours, and if his fever didn't break soon Jameson feared the worst.

The pull of the current had increased and forty seconds later there'd been another air gap before Argenti, along with Jeremiah Lynch, had finally been sluiced out into the East River dockside. They were quickly spotted by nearby stevedores and fished out. A sailor watching the commotion assisted in reviving them.

After dropping Emilia off at their hotel, the Brunswick, Jameson brought Colby up to date on their way to Bellevue hospital.

A nurse cooling Argenti's body with a damp towel gave a courteous smile and stepped back from attending to him as they approached.

"How long has he been unconscious now?" Colby enquired.

"All but the first eight hours. As the lung infection took hold, his fever steadily rose and finally he slipped under.

If it wasn't for the water's high salt content I fear we'd have lost him already."

"How are you treating the infection?"

"Tartar emetic and paregoric." Jameson gestured towards the nurse. "And regular cooling for the fever, which has ranged between 103 and 105 degrees."

Colby nodded, thoughtful. "I think you're right. Tonight will be the most critical point. Does his family know? Are any of them here?"

"His wife. She's returned home for a couple of hours to see to her children. I said I'd wait here until she returns." Jameson checked his pocket watch. "Probably still forty minutes or so. She said she'll stay with him overnight along with the duty nurse."

It was arranged that Lawrence would take Colby back to the Brunswick and they'd reconvene at the Bellevue again in the morning.

"Not the best circumstances under which to be doing Lucy Bonina's second autopsy," Colby remarked. "But time is pressing and I only have a week here."

"I understand."

Jameson was left alone with Argenti and the duty nurse. When she went to change her water and towels ten minutes later, Jameson reached across and gently stroked Argenti's brow. He could feel his fever burning against his palm.

"Fight against it, Joseph. Your wife and children are saying their prayers for you, and miss you dearly. As do I, my friend."

"He lost two o' his men, but he's survived it – still in th' hospital. An' the toff got clean away."

Tierney was in the brewery yard inspecting a new horse as Tom Brogan brought him the news. The horse brayed and pulled back as he checked its teeth and molars. He had to hold it steady with the reins.

"An' what's the outlook from th' hospital?"

"Word goin' round Mulberry Street is not too good." Brogan waggled one hand.

Tierney brought his attention back to the horse, an eleven- or twelve year-old Clydesdale mare, so a good ten years more service before it was ready for the knacker's yard.

"When are yer set to meet with Sewer Charlie again – give 'im his last bit o' payment?"

"He's done as tol' and laid low for a coupla days. He'll send a kid from th' Shambles to let us know where he is. Prob'ly some time later today."

Tierney nodded thoughtfully as he checked the horse's flanks and fetlocks for injuries. Tierney figured that since the main bond with Argenti and Jameson was the Ripper investigation, they'd vigorously pursue any fresh leads on that front. The rest had been worked out through his contacts at Sweeney's Shambles and Sewer Charlie's knowledge of the East River tides. A group of policemen lured down into the sewers and drowned in pursuit of the Ripper? No possible connection to himself.

"With the way things have turned out, we're obviously gonna have to rethink." He took a fresh breath as he stepped back and gave the horse one last appraisal. "Also, slight change o' plan fo' when yer see Sewer Charlie."

21

Jameson came to see Argenti at first light and stayed with him for an hour to allow Sophia to have some breakfast in the canteen. His fever had reduced to 102 degrees, but he was still unconscious.

"I'll be in the east wing basement of the hospital for a while," he informed Sophia when she returned. He left to meet Colby for Lucy Bonina's autopsy.

Argenti came to forty minutes later, and after Sophia's tears of thankfulness and him orientating himself to where he was and what had happened, one of his first questions was how many of his men had survived.

"I... I don't know, Joseph. You need to rest more."

He gripped her hand. "How many did I lose, Sophia?"

"Uh... two I think."

"Do you know *who*?"

"No, no I don't. Finley is in the basement of the hospital now with another man who arrived from London last night. Perhaps he'll be able to tell you when he returns."

"Yes, of course. I'm sorry." He released his grip, could sense that his sharp tone was starting to worry her. But at least he had part of the picture, Jameson had been one of the survivors, and if Colby had already arrived that meant he'd lost two days. "Perhaps some more water?"

He'd already drunk a glass after coming round. Sophia reached to the side table and poured another glass. He tried to clear his mind more and focus as he sipped. Jameson was probably conducting the Lucy Bonina autopsy with Colby, which meant he'd have to wait another hour or two to get the details of what had happened to the others. And Jameson would probably be keen on keeping him in the hospital a while longer for rest and observation.

The duty nurse tended to him for a while, taking his temperature and applying the cooling cloth again, then minutes later a doctor came to see him and took his blood pressure and listened to various positions on his chest with a stethoscope.

The doctor made some brief notes. "You're in Doctor Jameson's charge, so no doubt he'll want to make his own observations."

As the doctor left, Joseph asked Sophia how the children were. Oriana had taken care of Marco and Pascal overnight, and she commented that Finley had seen to him for a while earlier that morning while she had breakfast in the canteen.

"When he returns, I'll go home and see them. They've been worried about you too, Joseph... praying along with me."

Seeing the tears well in her eyes in that moment, he felt a stab of guilt at what he was about to do. He held her hand in comfort. The mention of the canteen had sparked the thought, but he waited until the nurse went out again for another towel change before he asked whether it was far. "Just that I'd love a cup of coffee, if it isn't too much trouble."

"Yes, yes, of course."

Sophia went one floor down and along the corridor to the canteen to get the coffee, and was no longer than eight minutes before she returned. When she walked back into the room, it was empty.

••••

"What do you feel might have precluded the Hebrew markings being picked up earlier in London?"

Colby looked up from examining Lucy Bonina's spleen on a Petri dish. Her cadaver was laid on one morgue table and her internal organs arranged in a row of Petri dishes on the adjoining table. The gas lights suspended from poles above each table were on, lending their faces a ghostly pallor as they leant in close.

Colby wore pince-nez glasses with a special magnifying loop attached to its right lens. He took a fresh breath.

"Two reasons, I suppose. First of all we were originally looking for either Roman numerals or letters from the English alphabet. Nothing uniform fitted in with that, could have just been random cut and stab marks. Secondly, I left much of the re-examination to my assistant, Atkinson." He smiled tightly. "You know what it's like with assistants. Often they simply follow instructions to the letter."

"So, to recap, two Hebrew letter markings we've so far found in New York, and now three in London?"

"Yes."

"And is that the reason for your trip now, to keep the matter as secret as possible given the implications?"

Colby moved on to the dish with Lucy Bonina's right kidney, started examining through his magnifying loop. "I leave such things as 'implications' to the likes of Commissioner Grayling." He looked up after a second, sighed. "No marks there either. You have to admit, though, keeping the matter under wraps also has distinct forensic and procedural advantages."

"Why's that?"

"The issue of possible copycat murders. If we let the cat out the bag regarding Hebrew letters marked on the bodies we risk other murderers copying that. We wouldn't know where we were. At least by keeping it under wraps we'll know which ones are Ripper victims and which are not."

Jameson nodded his accord after a second. Some discussion had obviously taken place on the matter in London.

"Any particular pattern you've noticed about these New York murders?" Colby enquired. "Either consistent or unusual?"

Jameson could sense that Colby was keen to change the subject. "Their ages are very different. One approaching forty, one in their early twenties, the other only in her teens."

"And what does that tell you?"

"It tells me that age is of no consequence regarding his victims. They're just random selections." As Colby looked at him, Jameson recalled the opportunism stressed in past lectures. "That random nature is often driven by opportunism."

"Exactly. Given the number of prostitutes on the streets, if he had a particular type of victim in mind – whether in her twenties, thirties or forties, or a certain hair colour – he had plenty of time to choose them. So another factor had to be the key. Namely, whether they were in the right shadow and obscured at the right time for him to kill them and escape undetected." Colby placed the kidney back on its dish. "All clear on that one too."

"There's one other possible factor," Jameson commented, suddenly struck with the thought. "The colour red featured on two of the victims, Camille Green's dress was red and cream and Lucy Bonina was wearing a bright red bolero top. I recall that also being a feature with a number of the London victims."

"I see." Colby mulled it over. Jameson could see that he'd caught him off balance, and it was strangely gratifying to reverse for a moment their mentor-pupil roles. "Well, I suppose red is a popular colour for ladies of the night. But you said on just *two* of the victims?"

"Yes. But with the third girl, Laura Dunne, while she was dressed quite plainly and drably, he painted some blood – probably from the victim we have here, Lucy Bonina – on her lips."

"Oh my." Colby adjusted his pince-nez, appeared to look at the cadaver before him in a different light for a second. "Yes, possibly a telling factor."

Jameson could tell that Colby was still off balance, and used the opportunity to return to their prior subject.

"In regard to keeping the letters marked on the victims under wraps, is that now the recommended official line from London?"

"Yes, it is." Colby started examining Lucy Bonina's heart. "Or at least the Hebrew nature of the letters. The suggestion is that we announce that marks have been found on *some* victims – even if we go on to find them on *all* the bodies – but not the exact nature of those markings."

"And if we find Hebrew letters on the others and it appears to form a message?"

Colby looked up from studying the heart. He fixed keenly on Jameson above the rim of his pince-nez glasses.

"Then if and when we do find such a message, at least we'll know how many more victims we're facing. Unless he can be stopped in the meantime."

When Argenti got to his office at Mulberry Street, John Whelan informed him that they'd lost Ted Barton and Tom Donnelly in the sewer tidal flood. "And Jeremiah Lynch is still in hospital."

Whelan was hesitant as he spoke, not just due to the tragic nature of the news imparted, but Argenti's appearance.

Argenti had grabbed the closest-fitting clothes he could from a wardrobe in the next ward, but only the trousers were a good fit; the shirt was too tight and a brown wool coat at least a size too big. His hair was unkempt and his eyes red-rimmed and bleary. Perhaps it was the shock too of seeing him so soon, one minute they heard he was at death's door in the hospital, the next he was there in front of them.

"Good to see you, Inspector," Brendan Mann offered.

"You too." Argenti went over to the gun drawer. He took out a Smith and Wesson .44 and a Remington .38. "See what you can raid from Hadley's department. And if he can spare two good armed men too, it will help."

"Are we going back into the Shambles?" Whelan asked, his hesitance now tinged with incredulity.

"Yes, we are." Argenti checked the Smith and Wesson and loaded it. "Unfinished business, you might say."

"Are you sure you're well enough for this?"

"I might not be." Argenti smiled tightly. "But I've just lost two good men and have no intention of letting that ride." He looked up as voices trailed down the corridor.

Brendan Mann walked in brandishing two guns with Jake Hadley alongside.

"Pistols are no problem," Hadley said. "But I've only got one man I can spare right now – unless you can wait till mid-afternoon."

Argenti had lost track of time in the hospital. He glanced at the wall clock. "No time to waste, I fear. We might already be too late. Sewer Charlie might have gone to ground straightaway."

Hadley nodded. "Okay. I'll send my man to–"

Another voice crashed in from behind him. "What's the meaning of this?" Inspector McCluskey, drawn from his office by the activity, stepped into view.

"A return party for the Shambles, before we're too late."

McCluskey, red-faced, surveyed the men priming their guns and getting ready. "I can see that. But firstly I doubt you're well enough, and secondly I have to question the wisdom of such a reprise action especially after you've just lost two men."

"Your concern is noted, sir." Argenti slipped the gun into his coat pocket.

McCluskey felt the sting of those words, the open reminder that Watkins and Latham had passed the Ripper investigation from himself to Argenti. He was powerless to stop Argenti. All he could do was delay.

"Look, I can see you're set on it, but you're still a man short. No point in increasing the risk more than need be. One of my men, Bill Griffin, is just finishing up something for me. Wait eight or ten minutes, and he can be your extra man."

Argenti's instinct was not to waste more time. But he could tell that John Whelan was already concerned about his condition, and endangering his men just for the sake of ten minutes would look unreasonable. "Yes, okay. Thank you."

McCluskey went back to his office and quickly briefed Bill Griffin, instructing him to look busy with some filing for ten minutes before joining Argenti's team. "If you see them getting close to Sewer Charlie or any of Tierney's men at the Shambles, try and delay or create a diversion." To Griffin's raised eyebrow, he added, "Use your imagination!"

McCluskey scrawled a quick note on a piece of paper and rushed out, huddling his collar against a light rain.

He was out of breath by the time he found the boy he was looking for a block away on Bayard Street, Frankie, one of three young teen message runners he used regularly. He handed Frankie a silver dollar with the message.

"Take this hotfoot to Mike at the brewery. The usual, he'll give you another dollar when you give him the message. If I hear later you were longer than four minutes, I'll take the extra dollar back off you."

A block a minute, Frankie made it with twenty seconds to spare, and was only half as out of breath as McCluskey had been minutes back from walking just one block.

Tierney handed the boy the dollar. The advantage of using boys like Frankie: they couldn't read, so couldn't pick up on anything sensitive or incriminating. He unfolded the note:

If you haven't already gone to see Charlie, make it quick! Argenti is on his way to the Shambles with a fresh team of men right now.

Tierney looked out the window. Brogan was still in the yard, tying down a tarpaulin over a barrel stack in the rain. Tierney's face was a mask of fury as he ran out, taking the stairs two at a time. They'd received a note from a river-pirate kid Charlie had sent an hour back, a crude map of Sweeney's Shambles, with an "X" marked on a room in its north-east flank, and underneath:

I'll be here till midnight.

They'd planned to be discreet and go at dusk, when dockside activity was less, but now they'd have to change their plans. He hailed Brogan as he burst into the yard.

"Looks like Argenti's made it out the hospital, and we could be facin' a problem sooner than we thought."

He handed Brogan the note; no other explanation was necessary. Within a minute, Brogan had a cart loaded with three armed men racing towards Sweeney's Shambles. They parked north of the Shambles on Madison Street and ran down.

"Ah. I think I might have finally found something," Colby announced.

He'd finished examining all of Lucia Bonina's organs before turning his attention to the torso. He peered at a section of her pelvic bone.

"Can you swab a bit more, please?"

Jameson leant across and cleaned the area with more alcohol. With Lawrence busy cleaning the iodine and bicarbonate mix off the organs already examined, Jameson had assumed the role of Colby's assistant.

Colby pointed. "See. There! As the pelvic bone curves towards the back, a small mark."

Jameson leant closer and picked up a loop. "Looks like the letter 'U', but with an inner branch on its left-hand side. The same letter found on Catherine Eddowes's body, if I recall."

"Yes. In her case marked on her heart." Colby straightened up, gave a gratified breath. "At least it provides some explanation of why all the organs have been removed. Without doing so, this area would have been impossible to access."

Jameson was contemplative. "And here we were all this time thinking it might be some form of ritualistic killing."

"Ah, now you're starting to subscribe to the newspaper theories." Colby grimaced. "I'm not sure we ever did really believe that. Our first thoughts – well, mine at least – were pure savagery, whether to overtly shock or satisfy some strange blood lust was never clear. And of course the removal of some organs which he later sent to us. Ritual elements were always a secondary consideration."

Jameson nodded. "Yet we have him engaging in the same drastic removal of internal organs even when he's left marks on organs which are quite easily reached."

"Yes, you have a point." Colby appeared momentarily put off his stride by the observation, or perhaps it was also the distraction of a nurse entering the door at the far end of the morgue. "Possibly in his frenzy he killed each one in the same manner, then decided afterwards where exactly to leave the mark. Perhaps also guided by the time he felt he had in each case. And of course the prior removal of the organs and intestines would have allowed him that choice."

The nurse was mumbling something to Lawrence who was closest to the door. Jameson was keen to keep hypothesising with Colby, but he could see the nurse looking his way and pointing. Lawrence looked his way too, his countenance suddenly grave.

"What is it?" Jameson called towards them.

"There's good news in that Detective Argenti has awoken," Lawrence said. "But unfortunately, he appears to have disappeared from his hospital bed."

22

Argenti had decided that the first place to check was Charlie's previous room, so they approached the same way as before, from the south side of Paradise Alley. A biting wind from the dockside drove the rain at an angle and at least the damp, foetid alleyway gave some shelter from that. They went in the same doorway as last time, a third of the way along.

There was no armed gang waiting in the shadows of the corridor this time, and they made their way swiftly along. Argenti was first in the door of Charlie's old room, gun pointing, John Whelan and the other three close behind.

The room was empty. The blankets and small kerosene lamp there before were gone too.

"I've got an idea which other room he might be using," Bill Griffin offered. On the way, he'd thought of a possible diversion. "This way."

He led them back the way they'd come, then left into another corridor. The light grew dimmer as they got deeper into the warrens of the Shambles.

"Okay. Put the lamps on," Argenti directed. Whelan and Mann had brought kerosene lamps in case they had to go down into the sewers. The glow of the lamps radiated no more than six yards to the front and the back of them.

Bill Griffin figured that Charlie would keep clear of anywhere near his old room, so he should be safe picking rooms on the south side. He chose a door at random three along.

"This one." He held one finger to his lips as he gently turned the handle. Locked. He stepped back to barge it open – but at that instant a grimy, dark-haired man opened the door. The man was covered in ash and coal dust, and beyond him they could see two other men sorting through ash barrels.

"We're looking for Charlie," Griffin announced sharply. "Where is he?"

"Charlie... don't know no Charlie." He had a thick Italian accent and his eyes shifted between Griffin and the men behind, perplexed.

Argenti and Brendan Mann exchanged glances.

"Come on, don't play games," Griffin pressed. "He's used this room before, I know."

The man started to look unsure. He looked round at the others. "You know a Charlie?"

Head shakes and shrugs, and Griffin knew he'd milked the diversion as much as he could. Argenti was getting impatient.

"They don't know anything, let's–"

A door five along from them suddenly opened, a ragged thirteen year old peering out. Seeing the group of policemen, he started running.

"Hey, *you*!" Argenti shouted. The boy paid no heed, kept running. But his friend behind had only started his run as Argenti raised his gun. He stopped after a second, tentatively raised his hands; perhaps didn't want to chance the odds on Argenti not firing.

Argenti moved closer, speaking reassuringly. "I haven't come for you or your friend. Not interested in what you might be doing. We're looking for a man called Sewer Charlie. You know where he is, there's a silver dollar in it for you."

The boy looked at Argenti and his men, weighing up. Then his eyes fixed on the coin Argenti took out, glinting in the light from their lamps.

"Two, and it's a deal."

Approaching from the north, Brogan and his men took one of the first doors down on the east flank of the Shambles.

Brogan edged cagily along the corridors. First sign of Argenti's men and they would get away. They'd just have to then hope that any police team wouldn't find Charlie, or if they did he'd be wise enough not to say anything.

Brogan studied the crudely drawn map, there were two doors that it could be. He knocked on the first. No answer.

He tried the second door, and after a moment came a hoarse voice: "Is that Mike's man?"

"Yeah. It's Tommy."

Charlie opened the door, brow raised faintly at the entourage. "How many bags o'silver yer carryin'?"

"Jus' the one." Brogan fired a quick glance back down the corridor before shutting the door behind the last man. "We get more passage than mos' in the Shambles. But still yer can't be too careful. 'Specially when yer carryin' money."

"I moved to a differen' room, so if the coppers come lookin', they won't find me. An' I won't be stayin' here long – so no worries." Charlie grinned a toothless grin.

Brogan noticed his men looked uneasy; the concern that Argenti's men might be close behind or the stench coming off of Charlie.

"Oh, Mike doesn' a worry. He leaves all those t' me." Brogan took the drawstring purse out of his pocket. "Thirty pieces, as agreed."

Charlie opened it and took a few coins out, as if to ensure they were real. Never before had he seen so much money.

He was so engrossed, he didn't notice Brogan take his gun out until it was too late. The shot hit him squarely in the chest, throwing him back.

Brogan leant over to take back the purse, slipping back in a few coins that had spilt out. But Charlie's grip was tight, his eyes flickering in defiance, as if letting go of it was the last thing he'd do.

Brogan obliged that wish. He fired a second shot at point-blank range into Charlie's right eye socket.

Brogan took back the purse and was already halfway out the door as two of his men lifted Charlie's body and dropped it through the hole at the back of the room into the sewers.

There were two other possible rooms which Charlie might have chosen on the corridor. Argenti and his men were halfway through checking the first when they heard the shots from the far end of the building.

Argenti looked sharply that way, they appeared to have come from the other possible location, but the boy suddenly looked hesitant.

"You don't have to lead us all the way there," Argenti said. "Just take us to the end of the corridor with the room, and point."

The boy nodded after a second, and they sprinted off – through a dog-leg, another long corridor, then a right turn. With the sound of the shots and then their running, some doors opened as they passed, but most closed as quickly again; just a regular day at the Shambles, the lesson long learned. Don't get involved.

A final left turn and the boy pointed along another shadowy corridor. "Seventh door up on th' right."

Whelan stepped up front to shine his lamp that direction and Argenti flipped the second dollar coin to the boy. The boy touched a finger to his imaginary cap and ran back the way they'd come.

Argenti was out of breath from the run and could feel the strain already in his legs, his weariness from his illness and hospital stay beginning to tell. He lagged a couple of paces behind Whelan and Mann as they raced to the door. It was a foot ajar. They burst in, gun barrels pointed as they frantically scanned the room. It was empty, a few splatters of blood on its rough stone floor, a short smeared trail and then more blood spots leading to a hole at the back of the room.

Argenti concentrated on the sounds of the building around, picked up rapid, scuffling footsteps after a second.

"Come on! They're not that far ahead!"

He led the way, but with his increasingly weak legs Whelan and Mann took the lead again as they took the next right into another corridor in pursuit of those frantic footsteps.

Their shadows danced crazily along the walls in the light of their lamps. Everything beyond their glow was lost, they were guided purely by sound, confused at one point as a man halfway along opened his door and looked out at the commotion. The man's image swayed and blurred in Argenti's vision as he ran past. His legs were aching and he started to feel dizzy, getting his balance back by bracing a hand briefly against one wall.

And then as they turned into the next corridor there was a clear view again, only a fleeting view, but as the last two men running from them opened the door to the street at its end, their silhouette was clear.

"Hey, *you*!" Whelan shouted. "Police! *Stop*!"

The door was already half closing behind them as Whelan squeezed off his shot – some wood splitting near its top hinge. Argenti doubted he'd have done better. The shaking in his legs had now spread up to his arms.

A long alleyway as they burst out of the same door. Sixty yard stretch one way; the men would have still been visible if they'd gone that way. They chose the shorter twenty-yard length in the opposite direction.

But the problem was those running steps ahead of them could no longer be picked out, they were lost among the clatter and bustle of people on Madison Street.

As Whelan and Mann ran out on to the street, Argenti and the others close behind, it was impossible to home in on anything suspect, four or five carts heading in each direction, half a dozen hansom cabs, a horse drawn tram and a coal truck blocking part of their vision east – the men they were pursuing could be anywhere.

Argenti sighed. "Thanks, men. We did our best."

Though it was clear that they saw that as a poor consolation, and they were mostly silent as they ambled back to their wagon parked on the south side of the Shambles.

Argenti was glad of the slower pace after their madcap run, but his legs seemed to be aching now worse than ever and he still felt light-headed and dizzy. He'd broken into a hot sweat too, the rain against his face feeling icy in contrast.

As they approached their wagon, there was a commotion by the dockside with a huddled group of people looking into the water.

Brendan Mann ran ahead to see what they were looking at, a stark and horrific sight in the grey water, Sewer Charlie's body with two gunshot wounds floated not far from where Argenti had been washed up just two days ago.

"Oh, jeez. Come look!"

Mann beckoned the rest of them over, but Argenti never made it. His legs finally buckled halfway across and he collapsed in a heap on the rain-washed dockside.

23

Between autopsies and tending to Argenti, Jameson had spent more time than he'd have liked to in Bellevue Hospital the past few weeks. A proud edifice eight storeys high, it was the first hospital nationwide to have a maternity wing, ambulance service or include a sanitary code.

In Jameson's opinion it matched the very best of London hospitals such as St Thomas's or Guy's; normally he'd have felt at home there, but it was its psychiatric wing that unsettled him. Argenti's ward windows overlooked the gardens with the pavilion for the insane constructed twelve years ago, and now with the warmer weather some of its inmates ambled there with their carers.

The flat, placid faces of those termed "mongoloids", who he knew shouldn't be there any more than Lawrence shouldn't have been at Bedlam. And as the disturbed screeches and repetitive chanting of the more serious cases drifted up towards him, he got a brief image of his mother with her hands over her ears rocking gently back and forth, and had to look away.

"Something troubling you?"

Argenti's voice from behind broke him from his contemplation. "No, everything's fine – just admiring the gardens. Temperature down and your last blood test was good. You appear now also to be in far better form."

He glanced back at the window. "The noise through the window doesn't disturb you?"

"No. I hardly noticed it."

"Good. That's good." Jameson recognized that this anxiety was his personally and covered quickly. "Just that you need as much rest as possible."

"As you've kept reminding me."

Jameson smiled tautly. Argenti probably had a stomachful of him playing mother hen over his illness the past two days, admonishing him for leaving his hospital bed while still ill and putting himself at such risk, as well as the additional worry and grief caused his wife and family.

Jameson didn't want to strain their relationship any more than need be, so changed the subject. He'd told Argenti on his last visit about them finding a letter marked on Lucia Bonina's pelvic bone, and now fleshed out the details.

"Colby telegrammed London requesting exhumation of three previous victims there to take place upon his return. Did you have any luck in finding an expert in Hebrew?"

"I've spoken to one possible candidate – head of a Jewish seminary in the city, Sabato Morais. So as soon as I get out of this infernal place, I can arrange a meeting. When will that be, by the way?"

"All things being equal, tomorrow morning. A couple more tests, ensure your temperature's remaining stable, and I can sign you out." Despite his efforts, they'd returned full circle to Argenti's "under sufferance" hospital stay. Jameson shifted topic yet again. "Oh, and Colby is keen for us all to have a night out together before he leaves New York, so I suggested the opera. *La Traviata* is playing at the Grand Metropolitan. He'll be with his wife Emilia, and I'm sure your Sophia would love it."

"Yes. And you? Who would you take?"

"Oh, I'll think of someone." He already had, but now wouldn't be the time to say. "And you'd probably enjoy it too – it being in your native Italian."

"I'm sure I would."

Jameson could tell from Argenti's tone that he was as keen on opera as he was on hospitals.

Argenti arranged a meeting with Sabato Morais for the afternoon before they were due to go to the opera. A chief rabbi visiting a police station was seen as inappropriate as them visiting a synagogue or religious seminary, so Jameson suggested the neutral ground of the Lotos Club and sent a note to Mulberry Street offering to pick up Argenti and they'd go together. "Something I wish to discuss on the way," it had said.

As Lawrence cantered the hansom along the Bowery and into Fourth Avenue, Argenti enquired, "Something delicate regarding the investigation that you didn't want discussed in front of Colby, perhaps?"

"No. It's nothing to do with the investigation. Though I suppose 'delicate' could be a way of describing it." Jameson took a fresh breath. "The woman that I'm planning to take to the opera tonight... it's Ellie Cullen, Camille Green's friend whom we questioned in the Fourth Ward."

"Oh, I see."

"I thought I should tell you beforehand, because I wouldn't want you to act surprised when I appeared with her and possibly embarrass her. Especially with Colby and his wife there too."

"Well, yes, it does come as a surprise and a bit..." Argenti was about to say "odd", but perhaps that was too strong a term, and much about Jameson's erratic behaviour had struck him as odd from day one. He put it down simply to the class divide between them. "...unconventional, to say the least. How did this come about?"

Jameson explained how he'd taken pity on Ellie when he'd heard she wasn't able to read, "Especially when I learned that in Camille they'd lost their main tutor teaching the other children there, including her own. That next generation growing up without the skill that I admonished her over." He grimaced awkwardly. "So I've taken it upon myself to give her some private lessons, and in the process we've become good friends."

Argenti noticed Jameson's hand working the top of his cane as he spoke – rotating back and forth, gripping, rotating again; this was obviously a topic that had troubled him deeply. "And was one of your concerns that some people might think this 'friendship' had crossed procedural lines?"

"Yes, that had occurred to me. But certainly not enough to prevent me helping her." Jameson shrugged. "Besides, we avoid all matters pertaining to the investigation – stick strictly to spelling, *Sense and Sensibility* and *Little Dorrit*."

"Safe enough ground, it seems." Argenti smiled tightly. It added some extra light to why Jameson had the run-in with McCabe while visiting Ellie Cullen that day; his previous account had been that he'd gone there purely because Lawrence had seen someone suspicious call by her door.

A sudden clanging of bells and rumbling of trucks from behind disturbed them. Lawrence pulled into the side as a fire-truck rattled past followed closely by four others. All were drawn by three sprightly fillies for speed rather than the slower dray mares of coal and milk-churn trucks. Crammed with men, ladders and buckets that looked as if they might fall off at any second, the noise was deafening.

As the last fire truck passed, Lawrence set off again. Fourth Avenue merged into Park Avenue, the shops and residences finer and more salubrious the further they travelled away from the Bowery. They rode in silence for a moment before Jameson spoke again.

"For a girl like Ellie Cullen, this will be a special night for her – one that she usually wouldn't get to enjoy. So I didn't want it marred by her possibly feeling awkward or embarrassed."

"Don't worry. Your secret's safe with me."

"And you understand why I'm doing this, don't you?" From the look in Jameson's eyes, Argenti could tell that Jameson saw his approval as vitally important.

"Yes, indeed I do. Very noble of you." Though was he starting to question Jameson's altruism. After all, Ellie Cullen was a very pretty girl.

Jameson looked ahead, suddenly distracted. "What on *earth* is he doing? Why doesn't he pull forward?"

A bakery van pulled by two drays had stopped and was blocking them from pulling into the Lotos Club. Argenti leant out and noticed that in turn it was held up by a hansom cab stopped while a stocky grey-haired man in top hat and tails fumbled with the change in his hand, unsure which coins to give the driver. As the bakery truck moved, Jameson saw the man too.

"Ah, Colby appears to be here already. Last time you two met, you were still unconscious. I'll introduce you."

Sabato Morais was approaching seventy, and while the years had weathered and lined his face and grown his bushy white beard almost a foot long, his eyes remained sharp and, unlike Colby, he read without the aid of glasses.

As head of the Jewish Theological Seminary in New York, Morais was not only an expert in Hebrew but a leading figure in the city's Jewish community. Jameson had arranged a private function room at the Lotos and the four of them grouped around the baroque dining table at its centre. Jameson summoned a Lotos waiter to bring Morais his requested lemon tea while they awaited his deliberation.

Morais looked up briefly from the piece of paper on which they'd written the sequence of letters.

ה נ _ _ ה ש _ א ש מ _ _ _ ?

"You've put down the letters here as they would appear in Hebrew – running from right to left?"

Argenti nodded. "Yes. The first letter in the sequence is on the far right."

"If you wish to make notes as I go?" Morais waited for Argenti to poise a pen over his notepad. "The first letter is *'Hei'*, equivalent to the English letter *'H'*, then *'Beth'*, equivalent to *'B'*; then after the two spaces *'Hei'* again." Morais paused and looked up. "I presume the spaces are for where you mentioned you don't yet have letters?"

"Yes, that's correct," Argenti said.

"But you expect them to arise and be in these spaces here?"

Argenti shrugged, and Colby interjected, "Well, of that we can't be totally certain yet. It's only a supposition at this stage."

Jameson: "Presuming also that the letters are being provided to us in the correct sequence."

Morais looked from one to the other. "It's difficult enough to make anything of this as it is – without it being a random jumble of letters. Is it this person's intention to give you a puzzle, not make it easy for you?"

Colby smiled dryly. "You could say that. Let us go with the assumption that the letters are in order to begin with. If we get stuck, then we can start looking at the alternatives. If we knew all the English letter equivalents, it would be a start."

Morais nodded and took a fresh breath. "Then we have '*Shin*' – '*S*' in the English alphabet; then after the following space, '*Alef*', an '*A*'..."

Morais's lemon tea arrived and he thanked the waiter and broke off to sip at it before continuing methodically through the sequence. Argenti wrote them down, as did Colby, while Jameson at his side seemed preoccupied with his own thoughts, glancing only briefly at Argenti's notes. Morais looked up again as he finished.

"As you mentioned, the dashes at the end indicate further spaces to be filled – but what does the question mark signify?"

"Simply that we're not sure how many more letters there are to come," Jameson said. "It could be two, three, four or more. Or indeed none at all."

Colby scrutinized the line of letters through his pince-nez glasses, let out a tired sigh. "Nothing which appears to make any sense in English. Anything that strikes you in Hebrew, Rabbi Morais?"

Morais studied them again. "It would depend where the divide came between letters and words. For instance, *Hei* and *Beth* together as a separate word would translate to *hen* in English. And later on, *Alef* and *Shin* together translates to *fire*. But add on other letters in each case and the meaning is changed." He shrugged. "Either nonsense or another word entirely."

Colby exchanged looks with Jameson and Argenti. They'd known at the outset they were chancing their luck. They'd just have to wait and see what the three exhumations in London yielded.

"You've been most helpful," Jameson said. "May we prevail on your good nature again, Rabbi Morais, to help with further Hebrew letters we may find?"

"Why, certainly." Morais finished his lemon tea, then reached for the leather folder to his side. "Oh, and there is one thing I've brought with me which might help you with that." He opened it and handed across a single sheet of paper. "The Hebrew alphabet."

24

Inaugurated in 1883, in just nine years The Grand Metropolitan had managed to carve out a reputation to match the world's best opera houses such as Milan's La Scala, London's Royal Opera House or Venice's La Fenice.

La Traviata was among its most popular operas and its auditorium that night started filling rapidly. With leading soprano Adelina Patti in the role of Violetta, it was anticipated that not a single seat would be empty.

Jameson was first to arrive with Ellie Cullen, as if taking the role of host to greet Joseph and Sophia Argenti and the Colby's when they arrived. Jameson had ordered a bottle of champagne to mark the occasion, and as he took his first sips and surveyed the grand reception hall he remarked to Colby that there were a few notables present.

"I see." But as Colby looked around, it was clear that he didn't recognise anyone in particular.

Jameson indicated with his champagne glass. "James Pierpoint Morgan and his wife over there. The railroad financier."

"Marvellous, I'm sure."

It was clear that anyone less than Joseph Koch or Louis Pasteur would fail to impress Colby. Among the notables was also a young oil engineer from Oklahoma, Nathan Galen, but it was the woman with him that caught Jameson's eye. Colby had turned in response to something from Emilia, so Jameson made the comment to Ellie.

"What a remarkable looking woman, if I may say." He smiled graciously. "Present company accepted, of course."

Early twenties, in an elegant opal blue ball gown to match her eyes, her auburn hair was piled high into a tiara, giving her neck a swan-like grace. Ellie knew the girl, but paused for a moment before saying anything.

"That's Olandra. One of Rosie Miller's girls."

"Oh, I see." Jameson nodded, took another sip of champagne.

It was evident that Jameson wasn't au fait with such matters, so Ellie went on to explain that Rosie Miller furnished a number of high-class escorts to out-of-town businessmen for functions like this.

"We call them 'fallen debutantes'. Girls that might have made it on the debutante circuit if they came from the right families – but don't. So they end up workin' for their money. Every now an' then one of them will get lucky and be taken on as a bride." Ellie smiled tautly. "If their background doesn't come out, that is."

Background doesn't come out? It reminded Jameson of the tightrope he himself was walking with bringing Ellie here tonight. He checked his pocket watch; seven more minutes until curtain call.

Argenti, with Sophia a few yards away, smiled tightly his way; as if to say, noticing his consternation, that he would have no worries from Argenti's quarter. But Jameson was more concerned about Colby; that with his intuitive nose for character traits, he'd pick up that something wasn't quite right about Ellie Cullen.

Jameson found himself tensing as Colby turned from Emilia and approached.

"I think it went well this afternoon, don't you? It was useful that extra hour we put in deliberating after seeing Rabbi Morais."

"Yes, I believe it was." Jameson relaxed again. He should have realized that everything with Colby was one-track. Matters not pertaining to his work held scant interest for him. "If nothing else to share our thoughts with Detective Argenti. Often a fault with us criminysts, I find, we spend so much time consumed with fine details – some of it seemingly inconsequential – that we neglect to pass that on fully to investigators."

"Yes. Certainly it helped fill in background details from London of which he might have previously been unaware."

Jameson smiled his accord. Earlier, they'd got a map from the Lotos library to guide Colby through the geography of the murders. Five Points was just over a mile away from the East River docks and Colby commented that, as in London, they'd all taken place within a close radius. And the victims had all been of a similar class, apart from Lucia Bonina, whom, while her background was no different to the others, had been working on a more elegant showboat.

Jameson had pointed out that Camille Green had also been from a decent family in upstate New York. "Indeed, was reasonably well-read."

"Yes, but I understand that as the years advanced she had fallen from grace."

"Not dissimilar to Catherine Eddowes's background, in fact."

"Yes."

Jameson had noticed that Argenti appeared uncomfortable as they'd indulged in their seemingly offhand discourse about the class of the victims. Jameson wondered whether that was because Argenti was originally from such a background, or because as Jameson was now consorting with Ellie Cullen, he saw the comments as somewhat hypocritical.

Colby revisited the topic. "I wondered. We've always assumed that the varying ages and social backgrounds of the women was driven by a combination of suitable locations and time constraints, in short, places where he could murder swiftly without being seen." Colby took a breath. "But what if this link with the colour red you brought up earlier was also a factor? That would certainly be more limiting, forcing him to be less selective regarding age and class."

"And the significance to him?"

"I don't know. Possibly something or someone from the past he associates with the colour red." Colby shrugged. "Or it could simply be something that stands out for him on a drab and foggy night. As butterflies attract mates with bright colours, these women inadvertently attract a killer."

The term "drab" struck a chord with Jameson. "Perhaps also why he indulges in such gore with them. We've always assumed that it was base brutality and bloodlust, but what if he's simply spreading that colour red? Brightening up their drab and wasteful lives as he sees them?"

Colby arched an eyebrow sharply. "What? Some sort of social redeemer, rather than simply a brutal avenger punishing them for their sins?"

"Why not? As we both know of old, murderers rarely see themselves as bad or evil, or even misguided. There's always some explanation, some rationale in their minds, however warped and..." Jameson's voice trailed off, suddenly gripped with panic. He loved these deeper deliberations with Colby, but he'd got so engrossed he hadn't noticed that Emilia Colby, seeing Ellie alone, had drifted her way and struck up conversation.

"Yes, you could have hit on something," Colby commented.

But Jameson had already half-switched off. As he overheard Emilia comment something about Ellie's accent, he held a hand up to Colby. "Sorry. Excuse me. Something I neglected to mention to Ellie."

He went across, cut in. "Promises to be a splendid night. Some wondrous stories circulate about the lead soprano, Adelina Patti. Apparently she demands to be paid five thousand dollars in gold coins for each performance."

"My goodness, that's a princely sum," Emilia Colby remarked. But she wasn't to be deterred. "I was just saying to Ellie that I was having trouble placing her accent."

Jameson tried to think of something inventive or another subject change, but Ellie beat him to it.

"Yes, forgive me. English is somewhat new to me. Coming from a noble Southern Irish family, we originally spoke in Gaelic – so English was a second language. And of course the American influence probably hasn't helped."

"I see." Emilia was lost in thought for a second. She gestured with a gloved hand. "Cullens? Would that be the Cullens of Waterford by any chance?"

"No. The lineage bestowing privilege comes from my mother's side – the McElroys, from Cork."

"McElroys... McElroys? I don't believe I know them."

"Literally translated, it means sons of the Kings of Ireland."

"Oh, my. Yes, you can't get more noble than that." Emilia smiled tritely. "So with Gaelic being your main language all those years, no doubt you still speak it now?"

"Yes. But, like I said, only the old version."

Jameson intervened; she was clearly getting out of her depth. "I think, ladies, we should head to our seats now, avoid the–" Thankfully the bell went for curtain rise. "Ah, there we are."

As they made their way with the crowd up the grand stairway and were out of earshot of both other couples, Jameson turned to her.

"Incorrigible. Sons of the Kings of Ireland." He smiled. "Can't take you anywhere."

"Oh, that's the thing, Finley – you probably *can*. Comes from long years of fooling clients I'm anyone from Lillie Langtry to the Queen of Sheba."

"Now *that* she probably wouldn't have believed."

Their chuckling echoed off the high-domed ceiling as they made their way up.

They took their seats in one of the twenty-four private boxes that flanked each side of the top fourth tier of seating closest to the stage, with the orchestra pit almost directly below them. Their private box had capacity for eight people, but many of the smaller boxes were occupied by only two people paying the four-ticket price for the additional intimacy and privacy.

Jameson knew that Argenti had gone mainly for Sophia's sake, but at one point he seemed to get wrapped up in the drama and music too. As the "Drinking Song" hit its rousing chorus, he noticed Argenti tapping his fingers on one thigh.

By contrast, Jameson found himself increasingly distracted. Colby's earlier comment about the colour red possibly linking the girls preyed on his mind, and he had a quick flashback to the beautiful girl in the reception hall, a bright red ruby or garnet had been the centrepiece of the tiara she was wearing. Which direction had she gone, what seat had she taken with her partner? Last thing he remembered she wasn't far behind them heading towards the upper circles and boxes.

Jameson looked frantically around, scanning the circle and the boxes opposite – but everything seemed to be swallowed up in darkness beyond the first few feet. Though as he scanned, he had the feeling he'd had before, that someone was watching him from those shadows.

But surely if they were masked in shadow, he would be too? He tried to shake the thought away, but the uncomfortable feeling of invisible eyes watching him from among the audience stayed with him. And while before the orchestra and the sailing voices had uplifted him, now they seemed to press in on him.

He felt Ellie lightly touch his hand. "Are you okay?"

"Yes, I'm fine." he said. "Very good. And you?"

"Oh, my, yes. It's a grand spectacle."

He gently squeezed her hand back, smiling. Ironic, he thought. He'd worried that the opera's theme, that of a fallen woman, might touch too much of a raw nerve in her. But in the end it had been the colour and spectacle of it all that had captured her most. Perhaps not surprising, he reflected, that after her drab surroundings of the Fourth Ward, this vibrant splash of colour and life now would enliven her, would...

Drab? His chain of thought suddenly faltered. "It could simply be something that stands out for him on a drab and foggy night," Colby had said. "But what if he's simply spreading that colour red? Brightening up their drab and wasteful lives...?"

His throat felt dry, constricted. He scanned the auditorium below and the rising tiers of seating. What was he hoping to see? A glint of red from that tiara shining out like a beacon? Amongst the darkness, progressively deepening with every yard from the stage, there were probably scores of tiaras, red dresses and rubies.

Suddenly he didn't feel well and feared another blackout was close, but he managed to hold out until the intermission – the rousing music and singing seeming to press in tighter against his temples with each passing minute – then with a gentle touch to Ellie's hand and a nod to the others, he excused himself.

"I won't be a minute."

The noise of the auditorium and the soprano's soaring voice still spun in his head as he walked along the corridor. His skin felt clammy, a cold sweat breaking out on his forehead and he wondered whether he'd caught Argenti's earlier fever.

He took one of the private cubicles in the washroom at the end and sat down. The voices continued to spin in his head, and the images were quickly there too.

Now even the laudanum to help him sleep wouldn't hold them at bay, all those murder victims he'd examined over the years; though not just their stark, frozen faces in death repose, but in their final moments – screaming, pleading, eyes flickering in their death throes. When he'd first been haunted by them, he thought it was simply a by-product of getting too close to the Ripper, "Getting into his mind", as Colby urged.

And as those images gripped him now and he felt the first misty edges of blackout swilling in, he realized that unconsciously he'd been rocking back and forth – and the image suddenly there was of his mother, rocking back and forth as she clamped her hands over her ears to shut out the hubbub and screaming of Bedlam.

She was trying to say something to him, reaching out, and he leant closer to hear.

••••

"Oh, I'm sorry. I came to see my friend."

The girl looked round at the man by the opera box door. "Nathan? Mr Galen?"

"Yes, Nathan."

"He shouldn't be long. He's just gone to the bar, I believe."

"Ah, I wondered if I might wait for him?" He smiled graciously. "Once the opera starts again, I might not get the chance, you see."

"Yes, I... I suppose. Certainly." Her initial hesitation went. A friend of Nathan Galen's, he might be upset upon his return if he learned she'd sent the man packing.

He took the seat one away from her, left a discreet distance, in observance too that it was Nathan's seat when he returned. He surveyed the private boxes opposite, saw that they were mostly shrouded in darkness except for a few people close to their edges, one or two now observing the auditorium below through their opera glasses rather than the stage. He presumed that their view in turn was similar towards the boxes his side.

He looked towards the girl, his eyes drawn to the red ruby in her tiara. He noticed too that she had a matching ruby ring on her left hand. Without doubt she was a rare beauty, probably the most beautiful of all the girls so far. How could a girl like that fall from grace? It was like a trick, a deceit – her beauty belying what she'd become. In that regard, she was worse than the others. The defilement of such beauty...

"A splendid evening," he remarked.

"Yes, it is."

He knew that he had limited time, knew that those would be her last words. He swivelled towards her swiftly, pulling the blade from his jacket in the same instant. He plunged so deeply that he feared for a moment he'd run right through her to the seat behind. His other hand clasped hard over her mouth to mask any sound, but there was little more than a muffled gasp of surprise, no scream – drowned out by the noise rising from the auditorium.

He was sure that they were shrouded in darkness, but still he was careful to keep her shielded by his body, his back to the auditorium behind, face unseen. To anyone observing, they'd think they were embracing.

He held the first thrust deep inside her until he felt himself ejaculate, then pulled out and lunged again, working the blade higher through her insides as he watched intently the flickering death throes in her eyes.

The first thing Argenti became aware of was raised voices and shouting from one of the private boxes opposite.

Nathan Galen hadn't shouted when he first saw Olandra's bloodied body, he was frozen with shock. That had come from a floor usher who'd glimpsed her body past his shoulder. The shouts of alarm became increasingly frantic, and then someone blew a policeman's whistle. Whether an off-duty policeman, one of the Metropolitan's security men or just a passing opera patron, nobody ever found out, but it sprang Argenti from his seat.

He ran round the semi-circular corridor, Colby close behind. He showed his badge as he pushed through the small group of people that had gathered around her body.

The blood patch on her blue dress spread from her breasts to her navel, the centrepiece of which was a wide open gash, a foot-long trail of glistening intestines spilling out to one side. A woman behind Argenti got her first view of the body and let out a piercing shriek.

Argenti turned sharply to the people around. "Was anyone seen leaving the box?"

Head shakes and mumbling, and Argenti was already keenly scanning past them for anyone slinking away, moving hastily or looking suspicious.

"Who was first to see her?"

Nathan Galen was still too shocked to speak, and the young usher pointed at Galen and then himself.

"He was... *we* were."

"And did you see anyone leaving or in a rush close by?"

"No, sorry," the usher answered, but Galen's gaze was distant, lost.

Argenti shook his shoulder. "*Sir*? Did you see anyone?"

All that Galen managed was a numb head-shake. Argenti turned to Colby.

"Where's Jameson?"

"I don't know. I thought he'd gone to the bar – haven't seen him."

Argenti looked back at the girl. "He's done this because we're here. One of the other girls, Lucia Bonina, was killed just a hundred yards from a boat we were searching."

Colby's brow knitted as he grappled with the implications. "You think so?"

Argenti broke him out of his contemplation. "But if we hurry, he can't be far away!" He turned to the usher. "You come with us. Show us every possible exit."

They were already at a sprint, pushing through the milling crowds, as the usher said, "The central staircase is the main way in and out – apart from fire exits on each far flank of the building."

"As soon as you see one of your colleagues or a security man, instruct them to check one fire exit and you go check the other. We'll take the main stairway."

They found a security man twenty yards along, and the usher had just finished passing on instructions, frantically pointing, as they saw Jameson heading towards them. He looked flustered and out of sorts.

"Where have you been?" Argenti asked.

"The… the washrooms. I wasn't feeling well." Jameson looked round at the frantic activity – increasingly excitable voices and shouting. "What's happened?"

"Another girl." Argenti closed his eyes solemnly for a second. Nothing more needed to be said. "But come on – he might still be close."

The usher and security man raced off towards the fire exits at each end as Argenti led the chase down the main stairway. It was busier than normal, panic spreading that it might be a fire and the alarms had failed.

If the man in a grey suit and matching derby halfway down the stairway hadn't looked back with consternation at that point, a second later an urgent voice booming from behind them, "Hey – *you*!" – they might never have picked him out.

Argenti saw the grey-suited man look frantically towards the man in top hat and tails who'd shouted behind them, then at himself and Jameson forging their way through the milling crowd his way. The man started running, barging his way haphazardly through the crowd.

Argenti put on an extra spurt, taking the marble steps two at a time. Jameson was close behind, but Colby with his extra weight and age lagged a few yards behind.

The grey-suited man was quick and sprightly, and kept his distance twelve yards ahead of Argenti. He pushed and barged his way through the crowd desperately, seemingly running for his life, and as he swung into the stairway from the second floor, he collided with a waiter walking up. The tray full of champagne flutes he was carrying went flying, smashing in a cascade down the steps. A woman further down shrieked as the man pushed her brusquely aside.

Argenti felt glass crunching under his feet as he hit the same patch, but Jameson's feet slid from him on the wet marble, and he stumbled briefly before righting himself. Argenti was breathless as he reached the last stretch of stairway, but the man was still the same distance away as he crossed the entrance vestibule towards the main doors onto Broadway. They weren't going to catch him, and once the man was out on the main street Argenti feared they'd lose him completely.

"Stop him! Stop that man!" he shouted, hoping to get one of the doormen's attention.

But by the time the nearest doorman had spotted the running figure and fully focused on what was happening, the man was already half past him and barging through the doors onto the Broadway sidewalk.

A confused mass of people were there, for a moment the man's eyes darted in each direction, wondering whether to lose himself in the crowds. He decided to cross the road and thought he'd timed it right to dart in between the traffic. He didn't notice until too late the man on a penny-farthing bike approaching on his nearside. He collided with it, sending its rider and himself sprawling in a tangle with the bike's frame.

He righted and got to his feet quickly, and had just started into his stride again as Argenti, still at full run, hit the small of his back, knocking the wind from him as they tumbled to the ground.

The driver of a fast-approaching milk wagon, startled by the two figures suddenly sprawling in front of him, pulled sharply to one side on his reins. Horse hooves thundered past, the cart's iron-rimmed wheels missing the man's head by only inches.

Argenti grabbed the man by one shoulder, turning him to face him; younger than he'd expected, no more than mid-thirties, dark sandy-hair, his startled eyes focused on Argenti, then shifted past his shoulder to Jameson and the man in top hat and tails who'd initially shouted from the stairway.

"Thank goodness, you've got him. Well done," the man in the top hat said. "The scoundrel ran off with my wallet."

One of the many pickpockets that regularly worked the city's music and opera halls, he was taken away by two policemen to be held in a cell at Jefferson Market for later arraignment.

Argenti conferred with the usher and security man. They hadn't seen anyone on the fire exits either. Colby returned to the murder scene. "Let's see what might be gleaned while it's still fresh," he said. Meanwhile Argenti and Jameson watched the remaining people exit the opera house with growing despondency.

The management called off the performance, offering return tickets for alternative nights. A few men looked their way as they left: purely curiosity or one final defiant snub? – *I killed her right under your noses and still you couldn't get me.*

Argenti sighed. "Yours and Colby's theory that he's nondescript and blends in well with a crowd – he's surely putting it to the test now. He could be *anyone.*"

Jameson joined Argenti briefly in surveying the milling mass of people, merging with yet another swarm of people on Broadway, a sea of derbies and top hats with suits in matching brown, grey or black – one man couldn't be discerned from the next.

"Yes, I see what you mean."

But Argenti couldn't help noticing that Jameson seemed somewhat numb, distant; not his normal exuberant self. They waited for the crowds to thin out, then decided to join Colby. Halfway back up the stairway, Argenti observed Jameson's right hand and cuff as he gripped the brass rail.

"You appear to have some blood on you."

Jameson looked at it, as if he'd only just then noticed it. "Ah, yes. I must have cut myself on some glass when I stumbled on the stairs."

As they rejoined Colby, he looked up from examining the girl's body. "It appears as if an internal organ might have been removed in this instance too. Probably the pancreas. I can't be sure until her autopsy is completed."

Argenti nodded, chewing at his bottom lip as he surveyed her torn body. "Does anyone know her name? Know who she is?"

Nathan Galen was still in shock and it took him a moment to focus on Argenti's question. Jameson too appeared in almost as much shock as he observed the girl and saw who it was, flashback images of her tiara with its red ruby once again assaulting him, but he was first to answer.

"Her name's Olandra," Jameson said.

25

She was a prize this one, wasn't she? I saw the way you looked at her, could see that you thought so too. But you also knew in that moment exactly what she was, as did I. I could see it in your eyes.

Oh, yes. I was standing just yards away from you all at one point. You, Argenti, and no less than the illustrious Thomas Colby all the way from London. Four long years now you and Colby have been studying me, you should know me better than your own family. Should be able to pick me out at a distance, let alone only yards away. But in your case, you never really had a family of your own, did you? And now with your aunt dead, the only family you have left is Lawrence.

If Colby has come over just on my account, I suppose I should feel flattered. But certainly not an auspicious night for you; all the top men on the case in one place, all supposedly expert in crime detection, yet none of you had the first sniff that I was there. If you can't track me down even when a girl is killed right under your noses, what chance do you have with the others? The press will have a field day.

I daresay I should thank you for picking this girl out for me. Without that look you gave her, I might never have noticed her. You all but killed her yourself with that look. But little point in torturing yourself over that. If it had not have been her, it would have been another girl. All I can advise is in future be careful what you covet and prize.

The meeting was convened at Abbey's Theatre on Broadway the afternoon after the letter arrived at *The Times*. Opera patrons and local theatre managers swelled the numbers of concerned local businessmen, Tammany Hall officials and Press reporters, and Argenti couldn't help noticing that there were more top hats and tails in the audience now that a murder had occurred uptown.

Argenti sat facing the audience behind a long table on the stage flanked by Jameson, Colby, Mayor George Watkins and Police Commissioner Bartholomew Latham.

"You had an earlier strong suspect, I understand. A certain Jack Taylor. Is he still a suspect?"

"No, he isn't."

"And do you have any fresh suspects now?"

"We have a number of fresh leads we're pursuing. But nobody currently as a firm suspect. No."

"But how much longer might it take? How many more fine girls might be murdered before he's apprehended?"

A murmur ran round the theatre hall, a few voices of support. The first questions had batted back and forth between Argenti and a *New York Times* and a *Herald* journalist in the first rows. This comment now had come from a businessman in top hat and tails midway back. Argenti doubted the term "fine" would have been used if it were still East Riverside girls like Camille Green and Laura Dunne being murdered.

"We feel confident we're aimed in the right direction with these leads. But as can be seen from his letters, he follows our investigation progress closely. So it prevails upon us not to show *all* our hand, that would lend him more advantage. As a result, we're closer than you might think."

"Yes. Only a few yards away at one stage, it appears."

A ripple of laughter ran through the audience, some guffaws.

"I'm glad to see that some can still find humour in the brutal murder of these girls." Argenti fixed his gaze on the *Herald* reporter who'd made the comment. "But you haven't just had the task of telling her parents about her death as I have."

The laughter ripple quickly died, a more sombre mood returning. The *Herald* man looked down, sought refuge in his notes. A *Post* reporter four along in the front row held up his pen.

"And you have the victim's name confirmed as Olivia de Vries, I believe?"

"Yes. Olivia Danielle de Vries. 'Olandra' to her friends. Twenty-five years-old."

Olivia had been the second eldest of three girls and a boy in the de Vries family, who lived in a humble but respectable Queen Anne style boardframe in Washington Heights. Her father worked as a bookkeeper in a nearby tannery while her mother kept the house. Argenti recalled the moment he'd told them about her death. Not a sound, the ticking of a grandfather clock from the hallway had suddenly seemed deafeningly loud. He'd asked them if they'd like to be present at the press conference; seeing the circus it had become, he was glad they'd declined.

Revelling in that circus at the end of the front row was Inspector McCluskey, poker-face concealing his glee at the press ribbing and the dance the Ripper was leading them. Just deserts for Watkins having pulled the case from him.

"Has this girl been confirmed as a lady of the night? And also his choosing a Broadway location now is different to the others."

Argenti picked out the man third of the way back. Probably a local theatre-owner, from the edge in his voice eager to try and separate this killing now. "RIPPER STRIKES ON BROADWAY" had been that morning's *New York Times* headline.

"Her status hasn't been fully confirmed, no. And despite the change in location it has the same trademarks as the three previous murders."

"So you believe it to be another Ripper killing?" the *Times* reporter pressed.

Argenti looked to his side towards Jameson and Colby. Jameson answered.

"The mode of attack and injuries received are consistent with the past three attacks in New York, and at least five others in London." Jameson looked briefly towards Colby, who nodded his accord. "Along with, of course, the declaration in his letter. So, yes, our conclusion is that it *is* the Ripper."

A more unsettled murmur and hubbub ran through the audience.

The *Herald* reporter had his notepad raised, had obviously recovered from his earlier chiding. "And this policy now of not showing all your hand. Is that why details about Miss de Vries's companion that night, noted industrialist Nathan Galen, were not reported?"

"No, not at all," Mayor Watkins answered, slightly flushed. "Might I remind you too that's little more than an unconfirmed rumour."

Colby interjected. "That would in fact relate more to withholding forensic and investigative details that might give away – as Detective Argenti suggested earlier – just how close on his trail we might be."

"Such as these marks found on some of the victims?"

Colby smiled gently. "Now if I confirmed that one

way or the other, that would be defeating the previously stated objective, wouldn't it?"

The reporter's brow knitted, trying to fully fathom what Colby had just said.

"And has a mark been found on this particular victim?"

It took a second for Jameson to realize that Colby was looking his way and to respond. "Yes... yes, it was. A mark was found on her pancreas."

Due to the time restraints, the Ripper had obviously removed the pancreas to mark later. It had arrived at The *New York Times* offices along with the letter.

The journalist enquired the nature of the mark, and Jameson answered that would come under the "necessary secrecy" already covered by his colleague, Doctor Colby.

As local businessmen started asking what extra policing and security would be put in place to protect Broadway theatre patrons, it was clear the session was losing steam. The journalists in the front row started to look impatient. They already had the bones of what looked like another juicy Ripper front page, and had little interest in the cash-register concerns of local theatre owners.

Jameson surveyed the departing crowd and the unsettled hubbub as minutes later the conference wound up.

"Everything okay?" Argenti enquired. Earlier also he'd noticed Jameson staring vacantly into the crowd, thoughts seemingly elsewhere.

"Under the circumstances." Jameson grimaced tautly and finished packing up his papers. "Just I was thinking, you recall when you asked me earlier how it was in London; what became termed there 'Ripper Fever'? And I told you at the time that it simply wasn't the same here. Hadn't arrived yet."

"Yes."

"It has now."

••••

What had made Jameson lapse into contemplation at the press conference was being suddenly struck with the thought that the Ripper might be there too. "I was standing just yards away from you all at one point." And as at the opera, he'd found himself desperately scouring the audience for a face that might strike a chord.

The thought preyed on his mind as Lawrence took him home in the hansom, Colby and Argenti having gone their separate ways. It was Colby's last day in New York, so he had some last minute shopping planned with Emilia, and Argenti had some other case work to catch up on.

"You all but killed her yourself." The thought that he might have been responsible for the girl's death sat heavy on Jameson's shoulders. His eyes had settled on the red ruby in her tiara a second longer than need be, and in that instant the Ripper had followed his gaze and seen it too. Paradoxically, his own pinpointing of the Ripper's likely obsession had sealed her fate.

When he'd initially read the letter along with Argenti and Colby, they'd tried desperately to recall who'd been nearby possibly observing them, but nobody had come to mind. He wished that Lawrence had been with them in the opera hall; he'd have no doubt been able to match a face from the press meeting.

Conversation was stilted over dinner, and Lawrence sensed that he was preoccupied and would prefer to be alone with his thoughts.

"I'll be in my room if you need me."

"Yes... yes. Certainly." Strange that while labelled mentally unstable by many, Lawrence was so in tune with the mental sensitivities of others.

Less intuitive, or perhaps because she was the only one in earshot, his maid Alice got the brunt of his edgy mood. First he complained that she was being too noisy clearing up from dinner, he couldn't concentrate on his work. Next he shouted out where had some papers gone – almost a regular pantomime between them now – had she moved them?

Flustered, she came from the kitchen and nodded towards the papers now spread in disarray across his desk. "I didn't move anything there, Mr Jameson. When I saw them, they were in three neat piles. I left them as be, simply dusted round them."

Then some time later he demanded where was his tea? "I requested one ages ago."

Red-faced, Alice was back in the doorway. She pointed to the silver tray on a side table. "I brought it through almost twenty minutes ago, sir."

Jameson looked at it as if it was a strange apparition. He hadn't noticed her come back in the room, let alone set the tray down. Had he been that absorbed?

"Yes... sorry. Thank you."

He felt his cup. It was already cold. Perhaps he'd had another blackout, as at the opera. How many minutes had he lost then? The lapses were getting worse, and he didn't even know who he could talk to about them. The only one he was close to was Lawrence, and it would be too painful a reminder to Lawrence of his own disorder. His aunt's old doctor he didn't know well enough to trust, and if he told Colby conclusions might be hastily drawn.

He recalled an old colleague at St Thomas's who'd complained to colleagues about memory lapses. They'd recommended a long holiday; when he returned after two months, they said he still wasn't well enough and signed him off on a leave of absence for a year. That became two years, then three. They might as well have told him at the outset that he'd never be fit to work again.

Jameson looked back at the papers strewn across his desk. Still the sense that they were missing something, some small but vital detail, and it was buried somewhere in his file papers. To one side were his copied handwriting samples of the Ripper letters. What a fiasco that had turned out to be. All their efforts to get closer to him, get into his mind, and they'd ended up the ones being observed... "Don't forget, I'm watching you." The Ripper could get close to them at will, only yards away at one point, but was still little more than a shadow to them, as out of their reach now as the first day.

He felt suddenly claustrophobic. He needed some air. He grabbed his coat and cane and called out to Lawrence and Alice that he wouldn't be long.

No answer returned from the house.

The walk was invigorating for the first few blocks, settled his mood, but as he entered 14th Street it was busier and he started to feel conspicuous; as if, with more people observing him, his private thoughts were also under scrutiny.

At the junction with Fifth Avenue, he saw an electric tram approaching and decided on impulse to catch it. They were still a novelty and he hadn't yet been on one.

"Where to, sir?" the conductor enquired.

"Uh, Grand Central, please." He was sure he'd seen that as one of its destinations as it had pulled in.

"Twelve cents. Thank you."

He found the sensation odd at first. A steady gliding motion as it pulled off, rather than the muscular pull of a horse drawn carriage or the piston turned wheels on a steam train. There were only five other people in the saloon carriage and after a while he relaxed and started to enjoy the ride.

Close to 10 pm, but the streets were still busy. This uptown section was far better lit than lower dock areas such as the Fourth Ward, though sometimes that had its disadvantages he considered as he observed the garish billboards at the intersection with Broadway. A soap advert with Lillie Langtry in a diaphanous dress jousted for prominence with a billboard for the Barnum & Bailey Circus.

Electric trams had been in operation less than a year on New York streets and already most people paid little attention to them. Staying seemingly remote as the tram rolled past sat well with Jameson. He could play the role of detached observer rather than feeling like the object of attention... "Don't forget, I'm watching you."

Although he noticed that on some of the darker street sections, electric flashes from the overhead wires would briefly illuminate people and their faces would turn towards the tram, startled by that sudden glare. He found himself studying intently a number of the middle-aged men they passed. Just one small detail that might make him stand out from the pack. But after a while the faces and dress of the men all merged together.

He recalled an audacious bank robbery in St Louis he'd read about recently. Three men, all dressed in black suits and top hats, had robbed the bank on one of St Louis's main streets in broad daylight. But they hadn't run out or galloped away on fast horses, they'd simply walked out and merged with others on the busy sidewalk. When a teller and the manager had run out a moment later, they found themselves looking at a sea of similar black suits and top hats. It was impossible to pick the robbers out.

The tram picked up more people at each stop, with another nine getting on at the 34th Street junction. Suddenly it was busy, people sitting each side and opposite him, and Jameson didn't feel so comfortable, that sense that he was being observed again. As the gaze of a man opposite settled on him a moment too long, he got up and pulled the cord to be let off at the next stop.

He hadn't intended to go to Ling's, but after walking aimlessly for two blocks from the tram stop, he still felt unsettled. It had been a tough day and perhaps one of Sulee's massages and a quick pipe would help ease the tension knotted at the back of his neck.

He hailed a hansom to go there and took the massage first, then retired to the general lounge area for a pipe. He started to mellow, feel more at ease than he had in the days since the murder at the opera. Not only due to it happening so close to them or another of his worrying blackouts, but the fact that such a special night for Ellie had been marred and cut short.

Argenti's comments just before the press conference stuck in his mind:

"I think with this last murder so close, as with Lucia Bonina on a boat only a hundred yards away from us, it's gone beyond mere taunting. I think he's trying to prove a point."

"What's that?"

"I think he's trying to say, 'If you can't catch me when I kill a girl right under your noses – you'll never catch me!'"

So close. Only a hundred yards away. Right under their noses. The clues were all there somewhere, if only...

Jameson's thoughts were broken as he noticed a man opposite, mid-forties with a thick, dark beard, staring at him. The man was with two others and was also, like Jameson, sucking distractedly at a pipe. His gaze though was far from distracted, it appeared to be fixed directly on him.

Jameson looked away. But looking back a moment later, the man was still staring at him. Jameson felt compelled to say something.

"May I ask, sir, what it is about me that so holds your fascination?"

The man looked more intently at Jameson, as if he'd only just noticed him or was trying to focus beyond his own personal opium haze.

"I'm sorry. I thought for a moment I'd seen you somewhere before, and then my thoughts drifted. I didn't realize I was still staring."

"I understand."

But Jameson wasn't sure if he did. Yes, his picture had been in the newspapers a few times with the Ripper investigation, but what if this was the ultimate Ripper test? Having watched them, he moves to the next stage of direct confrontation?

Then as quickly he discarded the thought; too bold and clumsy. And that had probably been the Ripper's intention with the taunting all along, telling them he was close and watching them so that they started to see his face on every other street corner and every other man. Drive them half-mad with it.

Still, the thought that someone here might recognise him from his pictures in the press was in itself unsettling. And if they told a newspaper that they'd seen one of the leading Ripper investigators in a lowly opium den and a reporter was sent to ask questions?

On the way out, he took Ling to one side and told him that if anyone came by asking about him, he'd never been there. "And I mean *anyone*. Understand?"

"I understand." Ling blinked slowly, the message dawning. "If anyone comes here asking about you – you've *never* been here."

From his room, Lawrence had still been able to hear Jameson's voice as he shouted out to Alice, the main reminder that his dark mood was still raging. Though Lawrence knew of old that, like a storm, it would last a few hours before finally blowing over.

Lawrence's escape from those stormy moods was reading. A prolific reader, he'd often consume an entire book in only five or six hours. He recalled once Jameson asking him to read two chapters in a reference book. As Jameson watched him turn a fresh page every seven seconds, looking up finally after only a few minutes, Jameson raised a brow.

"No, I meant read it properly. Not just skim through."

"I have."

"Okay. Let us see."

Jameson posed a number of questions about those two chapters, surprise mounting as he answered each one correctly; though Lawrence's surprise had been that Jameson had ever doubted. Didn't others have the same reading and recall ability?

So when Jameson's moods raged, Lawrence would escape to Lilliput, Monte Cristo, *The Old Curiosity Shop* or the equally raging seas of Melville's *Moby Dick*.

Although tonight was different. And as Jameson shouted out for a second time, he found himself looking up from his book. He reminded himself that it was Alice on the receiving end and how upset she'd been at Jameson's last outburst. She simply didn't understand Jameson's changing moods the way he did.

As Jameson's third bout of shouting rose up the stairs, Lawrence closed his eyes, muttering, "Please stop... Please, dear God, stop." And when half an hour later he heard Jameson call out that he was going out and the front door slam, he went down to console Alice again, and this time he told her the rest of the background with Jameson.

It was a difficult subject to broach, so he helped her prepare some tea before he started to relate how Jameson's mother had been committed to London's Bedlam and that was why he'd been sent to stay with his aunt and uncle.

"And that's where he met me for the first time." He noticed Alice look at him differently then, quizzical more than concerned. "It's okay. I'm not a danger to anyone. Probably never was."

As he went on to explain about Jameson's efforts to get him out of Bedlam and gain approval to be his ward, he realized it was the first time he'd shared the account with anyone. "Without his help, I might still have been there."

Alice was silent for a moment as he finished. She looked up, shadows heavy in her eyes. "So you think that's why Jameson took pity on you? Because of what happened with his mother?"

"Yes, I do. And probably too why I'm so forgiving of his worst traits."

He saw an acceptance of sorts settle on Alice's face; at the very least it might give her some extra understanding and guard against Jameson's dark moods in future, so he was glad that he'd finally shared the account with someone.

But what he hadn't shared, and probably never would, was the other factor which inextricably bound himself and Jameson, made them kindred spirits; that Jameson's mind too was at times troubled, though unlike himself he'd never accepted or faced that, and probably never would.

26

Inspector McCluskey watched out of his office window as two floors below Brendan Mann and two others headed away in a police wagon, then took the stairs down to the street and went round the corner to meet the girl in the café.

There was a café directly opposite the police station, but it was a regular gathering place for detectives and Mulberry Street staff. He didn't want to be seen with the girl, so he'd chosen a café a block away.

Her name was Dora Clarke, a twenty-two year-old coiffeured blonde recommended by Mike Tierney. She was green-eyed, soft-skinned and beautiful, marred by an egg-sized bruise on her left cheek.

"I rouged it up a little," she said, turning her cheek. "Does it look good?"

"Perfect." McCluskey grimaced. "But there's a real bruise beneath that, I take it? In case they wipe it clean."

"Yes, surely. A real corker." She smiled hesitantly. "And those here too. Couldn't make 'em look any worse, so let them be."

McCluskey nodded, studying the purple-blue bruises on her neck. He didn't know whether Tierney perchance had found a girl with just the right bruising in the right places, or had someone put them there to fit the bill; and he didn't want to know.

"And you've got your story straight?"

"Every line well rehearsed." She took a sip of coffee and gave a prim smile. "I wasn't an understudy on Broadway for a year for nothing."

McCluskey checked his watch. "You proceed there. I'll follow a minute later. We shouldn't be seen together."

Since Camille Green's murder at the Riverway Hotel, there had been a dozen "I thought I saw the Ripper" leads, and Jameson had remarked that there'd been three times as many again in London.

Most of them faded to nothing before they'd hardly started, but Argenti reminded himself that each one nevertheless needed to be thoroughly checked out.

Argenti conducted the interview with John Whelan alongside taking notes. The interview rooms were in the basement at Mulberry Street, because most of those interviewed were suspects being held in the nearby cells. Certainly the girl's injuries looked real enough, and very recent. And the club where she'd met this man seemed to fit with the Ripper's stomping ground so far in New York.

"So you say you met this man in a club in the lower part of the Bowery?"

"Yes, that's right."

"Have you seen him in the club before, or anywhere else?"

"No, I haven't. It was the first time I've seen him." She shrugged. "Or, at least, if he has been in there before, I never noticed him."

"And what does he look like?"

Dora thought for a second. "Medium height, only a few inches taller than me. Quite stocky."

"Hair colour? Beard, moustache?"

"Dark brown hair, small beard and moustache. Quite neat and dapper." She traced a finger on her forehead. "And he had a small scar just here on the right-hand side of his head."

"You must have been quite close to him to notice that."

"Yes. At the point he gripped my throat, only inches away." She slid one hand down her throat almost sensuously. "Feared it might be the last thing I saw, I tell you."

She glanced at Whelan making notes to one side, then quickly past him to the clock on the wall and back again.

Argenti paused a moment for her to contain herself before continuing. "You say also that this didn't take place inside the club itself."

"That's right. He said he didn't feel comfortable in there and needed a breath of air. So we went to the service alley at the back."

"And did any of the other club girls see him?"

Dora pondered briefly. "Don't think so. It was very dark in the corner where we were, see. I got the impression that he didn't want to be seen. Get the same with a lot of city gent types. Almost ashamed to be where they are, so why do they come in the first place?" She held a hand out. "That's why I wasn't too surprised when he suggested going outside."

Argenti nodded in understanding. Most elements in her account matched well, the dark corners, the insistence on secrecy, the side alley, the neck bruising. But as he paused then, he noticed her glance again towards the wall clock, the second or third time now she'd done so. She seemed agitated, as if she had to be somewhere else, yet the way she was relating her account was quite leisurely and detailed.

"What did he say, if anything, prior to gripping your neck? What led up to that?"

"I... I said I wasn't comfortable staying in the alley. I said I wanted to go back inside the club or to a hotel somewhere. We started arguing. I turned to walk away, and he suddenly spun me round and gripped me by the throat." She gasped faintly and her eyes glassed over with tears, as if she was reliving the moment. "Then he said, if... if I tried to move he'd do me right there and then."

"Anything else you can recall him saying?"

"No, that was it." Her eyes flickered; sudden afterthought. "But that's when I thought I saw the blade."

"Thought you saw a blade, or actually saw one?"

"Just the handle, like, and part of the blade as he went to pull it out. But we were disturbed then by two gentlemen walking down the alley towards us."

"That's what finally disturbed him? Why you believe he didn't go through with anything?"

"Yes, I think so."

Argenti nodded again, more sombrely this time. Without doubt it was the most convincing near-miss account so far. Yes, she was agitated, but then that was probably understandable given her close brush with death and now having to retell the events. But as he saw her glance towards the clock again, he thought he should ask.

"Do you have somewhere else you should be Miss Clarke?"

"No, no... I'm fine. I have the time free." She smiled tightly, patting the breast pocket of her jacket. "Just realized my own watch is probably running slow."

Argenti smiled back with equal grace. In that brief moment she'd appeared like a child with her hand caught in a candy jar. "Glad to know that you're all right for time. Because I have something myself to check for a moment. Excuse me." He nodded to Whelan. "And arrange some tea or coffee meanwhile for Miss Clarke. I won't be long."

He might well be wrong; but it suddenly struck him that with Brendan Mann and the others out on an investigation and himself and Whelan in the interview room, his office was left unmanned.

Argenti took the first yards from the room at normal stride, then started running, taking the stairs two and three steps at a time up the three flights towards his office.

Bill Griffin looked at the wall clock. The third time he'd done so in the last five minutes. McCluskey had said that Argenti and Whelan would be at least fifteen minutes, but he'd already taken up twelve of those frantically searching and found nothing.

He tensed as he heard another set of footsteps and voices from the corridor. He had the door to Argenti's office a few inches open, so he could hear activity from the corridor but couldn't be seen. No McCluskey shouting out, which had been the agreed signal, and after a second the voices drifted past.

Griffin looked frantically around, eight filing drawers in two cabinets already searched. Nothing. One more cabinet to search and Argenti's desk. But for the desk he'd need a key, which should be readily available because it also contained his department's gun drawer. He kept scanning, finally spying a bunch of keys on a hook by the hatstand.

He went across, grabbed them, and found a match on the third key tried. The top drawer was just assorted loose papers awaiting filing. Nothing there. The second was the gun drawer, and the last two contained more files.

At first he almost missed the notes relating to a rabbi in the fourth file down, thought it was an unrelated case. But the sentence, "Consulted Rabbi Sabato Morais regarding identification of Ripper markings" leapt out at him. He started reading.

He became so absorbed in the following few sentences, grappling with their significance and whether he'd memorized them accurately, that he was a moment late becoming aware of McCluskey's voice drifting along the corridor outside.

"So when do you expect Brendan Mann to return? My man Griffin was looking for him. The Proctor case."

The signal! McCluskey had kept his office door half-open so that he'd see Argenti or Whelan passing as they came up from the basement interview room. Griffin closed the file and locked the drawer.

"Could be an hour or more. They left only recently."

Griffin ran across and put the keys back on the hook. He could hear Argenti continuing to pace rapidly towards him as he'd answered McCluskey.

"Fair enough. No doubt he'll catch up with him later." McCluskey's gaze shifted past Argenti's shoulder as he saw Griffin come out of Argenti's office. "Ah, there he is now." Then, to Griffin, "Apparently, Mann won't be back for a while."

"I see." Griffin smiled meekly at Argenti as he passed him only two yards from his office door. "Little point in waiting for him, then."

He could feel Argenti's eyes on his back as he paced away. Had Argenti suspected anything?

"We'll see him later," McCluskey said to Argenti; then as he pulled Griffin into his office and shut the door behind him: "Well? Did you find anything?"

"I'm not sure."

27

Jameson's mood was entirely different the next morning. It was a fresh, sunny day. Perhaps that was partly the cause, Lawrence thought, checking the barometer rising in the hallway; or possibly one of the letters he'd handed Jameson moments ago along with that morning's newspapers.

"Excellent... excellent!" Jameson called out from the dining room. "An invitation to this year's Hampden-Robb ball. Does that represent acceptance into New York society?"

Lawrence shrugged. "They're certainly one of the city's more notable families, and their society balls the past few years have gained a certain notoriety."

"This will be a marvellous way to make things up to Ellie after the disaster at the opera." Jameson lapsed into thought for a moment. He recalled Ellie's comment when he'd complimented her on her evening dress at the opera that it was the only one she had. "But she'll need a new dress. Come on, let's go."

Jameson knocked back the last of his breakfast tea, and it took Lawrence a moment to catch on that Jameson meant buying the dress there and then. He grabbed his hat and followed Jameson out.

"Fifth Avenue offers a good choice," Lawrence commented.

"Yes. Or possibly Bloomingdale's. I recall her mentioning Bloomingdale's."

••••

McCluskey was apprehensive when he received Michael Tierney's message to meet him at the Saratoga Springs Race Course. They'd only just met three days ago and during April it was still closed, its first race meetings not until the end of July. Why would Tierney want to meet him at a deserted race course?

Only a few answers to that, none of them good. It was important for their meetings to be discreet, but the race course was a three-hour journey away; there must be a hundred places closer they could meet. He'd heard that Tierney had an upstate farm not far from the race course where a number of his enemies were buried. Perhaps Tierney had decided he was no longer in favour, and this was his way of ending their association.

So as a precaution he took Bill Griffin on the train with him to Saratoga, then had Griffin stay with the hansom they took from the station while he met with Tierney.

"Keep me in clear view. And if you see anything untoward happen while I'm there, head straight to the Saratoga police station in the hansom."

McCluskey doubted that Tierney would try anything with both Griffin and the cab driver observing, but still his mouth felt dry as he approached Tierney and the group with him.

A dozen or so, all dressed in top hat and tails, looked like gentry. He relaxed a bit. But then he could see that Tom Brogan was also amongst them and dressed the same, and he reminded himself that Bill the Butcher had also been an elegant dresser, it was no indication of genuine respectability. Perhaps this was one of Tierney's macabre scenarios, for certain ritual killings, the participants should already be dressed in funeral garb.

It was bright and breezy. Occasionally a hand would go to a top hat to hold it in place. All the men were

looking towards the racetrack, and following their gaze
McCluskey saw five horses racing round it. As Tierney
noticed him approaching, he pulled away from the group
to greet him.

"Glad you could come." Tierney nodded towards the
track. "If you wanna pick the right horse to enter for
one of the big races in August, now's the last chance to
do it. Lot of horse tradin' takes place over these days, so
meantime I stay at my farm."

"Your message said it was urgent."

"That would depend." Tierney smiled tightly. "Last talk
we had, didn't look like Argenti an' the toff were getting
that smooth a run of it with the press, yet at the same
time were crowing they were near breakin' the case.
That little set-up I helped you with the other day shine
any light on that?"

"My man managed to find something, but not sure
yet how significant it might be." McCluskey went on to
explain about the references to Hebrew markings on the
body Griffin had unearthed amongst Argenti's private
files.

"And d' yer think that might be the thing to have put
them closer to breakin' the case, as they claim?"

"Your guess is as good as mine." McCluskey shrugged.
"If there's an explanation to just how these body markings
might lead to a breakthrough, it certainly wasn't in the
file my man viewed."

Some cheering arose for the horses running from the
group ten yards away.

Tierney nodded towards the group. "Yer see that man
in the grey top hat on the right?"

"Yes."

"That's Freddie Gebhard, one of the city's top thorough-
bred owners. An' the man he's talking to is Louis Sullivan,

the renowned architect. I've got a project I'm doing with him now – that's why he's here."

McCluskey looked their way. The other side of them, a table had been set up under an open gazebo tent from which two negro waiters in red livery served drinks. An ornate white cage with Tierney's pet canary was at the end of the table.

Tierney brought his attention back to the subject at hand. "That's the rub, isn' it? Are they all at sea with the case and jus' bluffing – so you can rest easy? Or are they indeed close to glory with it? An' are yer prepared to flip a coin and take the risk on which one it is?"

McCluskey nodded, thoughtful. "The dependent factor you mentioned earlier?"

"*Exactly.*" Tierney grimaced. "But then it's not my neck on the line and I could settle my score with Argenti in other ways."

Other ways? McCluskey looked at Tierney sharply. He obviously hadn't invited him out here simply for a casual exchange of information or to show off that he rubbed shoulders with the city's elite as much as he did low-lives.

"You have something in mind?"

"I might at that."

As Tierney explained his idea, McCluskey raised an eyebrow. "That's quite a plan. I'm impressed."

"As much as I'm flattered, it's obvious when yer think about it. I'm surprised you didn't work it out before."

"Why's that?"

"What with you being the detective an' all." Tierney smiled, enjoying the tease. "But to make this work, we're probably gonna need a tame journalist."

McCluskey nodded. "I think I might know someone."

"Thought you might." Tierney grimaced, took a fresh breath. "The question remains, though, do yer think you can take th' risk that they might not get far with the investigation?"

McCluskey considered for a moment, Tierney's eyes on him keenly, relishing the discomfort of his decision. "No. No, I don't think the risk can be taken."

Tierney looked towards the horses ahead, a sly smile rising as something struck him about the information from Argenti's file McCluskey had just shared.

The horse running second had suddenly put on an extra spurt and to mounting cheers and encouragement from the group by the marquee eventually pulled ahead of the front runner.

"That's the thing about life. Full of little surprises. Now that filly there, a year ago she'd have jus' stayed a half length behind all th' way. This year, she's got it in her to be a winner. The time is right for her." Tierney looked at McCluskey. "An' who would have thought that this information you jus' brought me would put the final embellishment to my little plan. The icing on the cake, if yer will."

"In what way?"

"Like I said, you're the detective, you can work it out for yerself."

Tierney turned away from McCluskey and rejoined his guests.

28

"So do you think she'll like it?" Jameson asked Lawrence as they walked along the alley towards Ellie's.

With the notoriety of the streets around Ellie's and the dusk light fast fading, it was arranged that Lawrence would run him in the hansom and accompany him to her door before heading away, too long to wait out the three-hour lesson. Lawrence examined the dress draped over Jameson's shoulder, emerald green satin with an elaborate burgundy brocade trim.

"I think it's wonderful, and she'll love it."

"And the colour's all right? It's not too bright?"

"No, it's not." Lawrence sighed. "I'm sure she'll think it's perfect."

"Yes, I suppose. Just that dress choosing isn't my forte." Not long after buying it, he'd had a brief concern about taking Ellie to the ball. While furthest from his mind was trying to turn Ellie into a lady, if it was purely to make up for the disastrous opera evening or brighten up her drab life, it was poor recompense if she'd just feel awkward there. Jameson paused for second by her door before reaching out with his cane to rap twice on it. "I should be fine on my own now."

"Very well, yes." Lawrence paused, as if something had made him suddenly hesitant, took one last look along the alley before turning away.

One of the children at Ellie's, nine year-old Sarah, peered through the window, her voice ringing out: "It's Finley... it's Finley!"

Martin quickly ducked back into the shadows, was sure he hadn't been spotted. Although this time it had been the man with the toff – who he hadn't seen before – looking round to check who might be watching.

Martin waited a few minutes after the toff had gone inside Ellie's, then ran the two blocks to pass the message to Jed McCabe.

"Are yer sure it was the toff?" McCabe pressed.

"Course I'm sure. Bold as day he was. An' carryin' a bright green dress with 'im."

McCabe nodded slowly. With the last muck-up and what it had cost him, he couldn't risk another. But it sounded altogether too much detail for Martin to be mistaken.

"Okay. Yer head back there. I'll go tell Mike."

Tierney was about to hand over to the night shift when McCabe ran into the brewery yard. He took McCabe and Tom Brogan into his private office and left his night foreman waiting outside while McCabe, still breathless, told him about the toff arriving at Ellie Cullen's.

"Just now, yer say?" Tierney quizzed.

"Tha's right. With th' time fer Mike to tell me and me to run 'ere, ten minutes, no more."

Tierney checked his pocket watch, his expression thoughtful as he stood. He swore he saw McCabe flinch as he reached a hand towards him, and he fed on that fear for a moment before smiling. He patted McCabe's shoulder.

"Yer did well. Good work."

McCabe's smile in return rose above its initial hesitancy, and Tierney knew then that keeping McCabe sweet had been the right ploy. Truth was he didn't want Martin breaking off too long from watching Ellie Cullen's door, and McCabe's new collection area had been the closest.

"And yer got clear what you gotta to do later?"

"Sure. Worked out every las' detail and the timin' already wit' Martin."

"Glad to hear it. Treat yourself to a pie and pint at Fennelly's meanwhile." Tierney handed McCabe two silver dollars.

"Much appreciated, Mike. An' don't worry – I won't let yer down."

"I'm sure you won't."

"Oh my, Finley... Oh, my. You've outdone yerself. It's beautiful." Ellie admired the dress again as Jameson held it up, then leant forward and planted a kiss on his cheek.

Jameson smiled awkwardly. Perhaps he wouldn't have felt so embarrassed if it wasn't for her friend Anna and little Sarah looking on from the side of the room, faces beaming.

"I never seen such a beautiful dress," Anna remarked. "Try it on."

Ellie was distracted for a moment by a face at the front window looking in at them. Josh Rawlings, one of the policemen on patrol, with his usual check up and acknowledgment that they'd returned. She gave him a tight smile to let him know that everything was fine before looking back at Anna.

"No, no. Not now." She shook her head. "It'll get all creased while I'm havin' my lesson."

Anna looked crestfallen. "Jus' for a minute, like – so we can see how it looks on yer."

Ellie appeared to sway for a second, but then her resolve returned. "I'll try it on later, at the end of the lesson, I promise – so yer can see it then." Ellie shooed her hands at Anna and Sarah. "Now away with yer all, so we can get on. Mr Jameson's here to teach me how t' read and write, not to be a dressmaker's assistant."

The arrangement was the same each time Jameson visited. The other girls would take the children out so that they were left undisturbed. Jessie had left ten minutes before with the other children, leaving Anna to follow on with Sarah and Ellie's baby, Sean, asleep in his carrycot.

"Okay, we're goin', we're goin'," Anna said with a dry smile as she grabbed her hat. She wagged a finger back at Ellie as she lifted Sean and nestled him on to her shoulder. "But that's a date mind to see that dress on yer later. Don't let me down now."

"I won't." A moment later Ellie heard the back door close and eased a sigh of relief. "Peace at last. We can get on."

"Chapter twelve of *Dombey and Son*, if I remember correctly."

"Yes." Ellie reached for the book already on the table. But as she opened it at its bookmarked place, she slid her fingers across and lightly touched Jameson's hand. "Are you sure you feel all right about takin' me to this society ball, Finley? That I won't let yer down or show you up?"

"You'll be fine." He pressed her hand back reassuringly. "You'll be fine."

Running full pelt, Martin approached the two policemen as they were only a few hundreds yards from the Riverway on Catherine Street.

"My pal, he's hurt bad… some robbers done him good," he exclaimed breathlessly.

"Where is he?" Josh Rawlings asked.

"Jus' a block away. I'll show yer."

Rawlings turned to Bill Payne. "Look – you go with him. One of us at least should stay on the beat."

"I… I suppose."

"It's not far," Martin pressed, sensing his uncertainty. "I'll go with yer."

"If you end up needing help," Rawlings said, "alert the patrols up on Madison."

Payne looked from one to the other, the boy already a few paces away, looking back expectantly, as if to remind him that his friend was hurt and vital time was being lost.

"Okay. Lead the way."

How much time had passed? Two minutes, three?

He could see she was still wearing the same bright green dress as he glimpsed through the window.

She was half-turned away from him as he burst into the room, and the surprise hardly registered in her eyes before he was upon her. He swept his cape swiftly across the two candles between them, snuffing them out – he didn't want to risk being viewed from outside. Only a single candle in the corner gave a weak, guttering glow as he pinned her against the back wall.

She'd only been able to make one stumbling step back as he'd advanced, gripping her hard by the throat as he made his first knife lunge. He made four more in swift succession before letting her slump down, watching her eyes flicker rapidly in her final death throes.

He sliced through her carotid artery, its blood spray weak with the main pressure having already dissipated. He ran the blade up to her earlobe, then sliced across her cheek before cutting off her nose.

Her eyes were stark and frozen now, seemed to be staring up at him – but the blood from her severed nose quickly spread into her eye-sockets, obscuring her gaze.

He was sweating for the first time with the exertion of cutting through her septum. How long had his butchery taken so far? Forty seconds, fifty? He paused for a second, listening out, no sound from the alleyway. No movement. Nobody passing.

Slicing across and up the soft flesh of her abdomen was easier, and he pulled out a yard of her intestines and laid them to one side. Then he removed the most visible organ, the liver.

He continued with more straight lunges, and for a moment got caught up in the frenzy of them. He was sweating and breathless again as he came to his final task.

Ripping open her green dress to expose her left breast, he leant in close to carve the symbol. And he was just on the final loop when he heard the sound: faint rustling from the next room.

He looked up sharply. Someone was in the kitchen.

At first, peering through an inch gap in the kitchen door, little Sarah wasn't sure what she was looking at. Then as the full horror dawned on her, she was frozen in shock. It took her a second to realize the man was looking at her.

She looked round frantically, too far to grab Sean in his carrycot at the far end of the kitchen – already she could hear footsteps approaching – and the larder half-way down was locked. She scampered quickly to underneath the sink, where an old ragged curtain was pulled across to hide the trash bin beneath. She wedged in tight at the side of the trash bin, holding her breath.

The kitchen door swung open and she heard the shuffle of his feet before she saw them from beneath a small gap at the bottom of the curtain. She was suddenly gripped with fear that if he bent down he might see her feet too.

She kept perfectly still, not daring to breathe, and prayed that the heavy, rapid pounding of her heart couldn't be heard beyond her own eardrums.

It took a moment for the man's eyes to adjust to the dark, make anything out from the faint candlelight flickering in from the lounge. The back door at the end was closed, he'd have probably heard someone going out there. He went to the larder halfway down. Tried its handle; locked. He hacked at the lock with his blade, gave two heavy kicks and it opened. A sack of potatoes, some onions, two butcher's bones on a plate and a few cans of bully beef and peas. Nobody there.

Then he heard a faint rustle close to the back door, and spotted the carrycot on the counter-top for the first time. He went across and looked down at the baby, barely six months old, blinking as it stirred from sleep, it hadn't even focused on him properly yet.

Suddenly another sound made his head turn, shuffling and movement from the alley outside. He did one last rapid scan of the kitchen. Probably just the baby stirring or a rat somewhere. On his way to the front window, he snuffed out the last candle at the back of the room.

He looked out to see the back of a drunkard ten yards away shuffling towards the road. The drunkard hadn't stopped or seemed to have noticed anything. But a moment later he saw one of the policemen emerge from the other direction at the end of the alleyway. He'd only have seconds to get away.

He watched the drunkard teeter uncertainly away, and timed the gap between them, running out before the policeman got too close.

Josh Rawlings saw the man emerge from Ellie Cullen's and throw his cape to one side as he went. A frozen moment, as if the shadowy apparition didn't immediately register, then he shouted.

"Hey... hey you! Stop!" He took out his whistle and blew it. "Police! *Stop!*"

The man didn't stop, he ran at full pelt out of the alley and took a sharp left turn.

Rawlings gave pursuit, but the man was a full thirty yards clear and swallowed up in the darkness as Rawlings came to the end of the alley and looked along the road.

"Police... *stop!*" One last shout and another blow of his whistle, then he turned back towards Ellie Cullen's house.

Only one door had opened with the disturbance, a woman forty yards along standing in her doorway with a shawl round her shoulders. Rawlings didn't acknowledge her, his eyes fixed solemnly on Ellie Cullen's door ahead.

He lit his kerosene lamp and looked at the bloodied cape on the ground first, then he went over and pushed Ellie Cullen's front door wider ajar, shining his lamp on the carnage inside.

Bill Payne approached then and Rawlings looked towards him gravely. Rawlings briefly closed his eyes and shook his head.

"What is it?" Payne's brow knitted sharply.

Rawlings didn't answer, simply waited for Payne to come alongside him and view the gruesome scene within. Payne's hand went to his mouth and he looked suddenly pale.

"Oh, God. Oh, dear God."

"I got here just a moment too late," Rawlings said, sighing. "And when he spotted me, he ran off sharpish."

"What? You actually saw him?"

"Yeah. Clear as day. Clear as I'm looking at you now. It was that Jameson fellow. Finley Jameson."

29

There was a faint early morning mist at Manor Park Cemetery as Thomas Colby watched the grave diggers do their work.

Beyond the cemetery gates, a trader with a handcart had joined the group of five looking their way the past twenty minutes. Colby wished now the mist had been heavier to obscure them. A weak sun had started to break through, burning it off.

To their side was a mortuary wagon, a driver and porter by its horse. The approval for Annie Chapman's exhumation had come through the day before Colby returned to Southampton on the *Britannic*.

They'd started digging at 5.45 am, hoping to get finished before the streets became busy. But those first pickaxe and spade strikes had seemed deafeningly loud on the pre-dawn silence, and Colby began to wonder whether it might have been better later; the sound of their digging would have been obscured by the rattle and clatter of passing carts and carriages.

Colby grimaced as with a few last grunts and exhalations the two gravediggers lifted the coffin out the last foot and hoisted it to one side. The foreman, jemmy in hand, leant over and brushed the remaining earth off the coffin.

"Do you want us to open it here for you?"

"No, it's okay, thank you. We'll do that back at the mortuary." The last thing Colby wanted was an open coffin for the ride back. "If your men just help load up."

Colby nodded towards the porter, who stepped lively to help the gravediggers. As they were sliding it into the back of the mortuary wagon, they were disturbed by a man in a brown suit running towards them.

At first, Colby thought someone had broken free from the group by the gate, but then he recognized it to be Grayling's assistant, Detective Inspector Palmer.

"There's some news from New York," Palmer announced as he approached. He caught his breath for a second. "An arrest has been made."

"I see." Colby's brow furrowed. Palmer's solemn countenance seemed at odds with his news. As Palmer's gaze shifted towards the others there, Colby got the message and they moved to one side out of earshot. "Tell me."

"It's our man Jameson they've arrested over there."

The Tombs. Its original, formal name was The New York Halls of Justice and House of Detention, and nobody was entirely sure how it gained its more commonly employed moniker.

Some said it was because its Egyptian inspired façade gave it the appearance of a Pharaoh's tomb or due to its structure sinking three floors below Manhattan's pavements; whereas others asserted it was because once sentenced there for serious crimes you'd never leave the place, it would become your tomb.

For ease of processing and transporting felons, the Tombs was only two blocks from Mulberry Street police station. Many a prisoner would simply be handcuffed and walked by two or three flanking policemen.

A two-mile journey to his Greenwich Street home, Finley Jameson had been picked up in a wagon. It arrived with Bill Griffin and two night-duty sergeants only forty minutes after he arrived back from Ellie Cullen's.

Griffin duly informed him that he was being arrested in connection with the murder of Ellie Cullen "... and other possible Ripper victims."

"Don't be ridiculous," Jameson snapped. "I just left Miss Cullen's place."

"That's right," Griffin said flatly. "You left her for dead. That's why we're here."

Jameson faltered for a moment with shock, unable to make sense of it all. Then he said, "And where's Inspector Argenti?"

"Don't fuss yourself. He's getting notice of what happened right now. You'll get to see him soon enough."

Jameson was silent for most of the ride down to the Tombs. Surely they must be mistaken about Ellie dying? Some sort of grotesque error. The mention of other Ripper victims was equally daunting, but he'd never fully satisfied in his own mind why his brief blackouts coincided with the death of some of the girls.

The thoughts spun in his mind and sat heavier on his shoulders with each passing hour in the Tombs.

Jameson's gaze fixed on a faint light on the raised vestibule opposite. In contrast to the Tomb's palatial front steps, a rough iron flight of steps sunk sharply down into a courtyard pit, from which four floors of cells rose. Jameson's cell was on the first floor, almost two floors below street level. He could see now first-hand how the prison had gained its nickname.

Sleep was impossible. An incessant faint murmur from other prisoners punctuated by coughing or distressed crying, wailing or wild cackling. The hours dragged.

Where was Argenti? Lawrence too said when they'd parted that he'd call by with his washbag and a fresh change of clothes. He hadn't seen anything of either of them.

At first light a jailer opened up his cell and shoved in a tin dish containing some grey slop, which could have been either porridge or semolina.

Jameson shook his head. "I'm not hungry."

The jailer turned away with a grunt, totally uninterested in anyone's food preferences.

There was more noise now. More persistent talking and murmurs, the clatter and rattle of cell doors being opened and closed, footsteps on the iron corridors. The Tombs coming to life. It had a certain rhythm to it, and after a while Jameson felt himself finally drifting off.

He suddenly snapped to. Heavier boot steps approached. How long had he dozed for? Probably no more than an hour.

"Got visitors for yer," the jailer said.

At last, Jameson thought, Lawrence or Argenti had come to see him. Though both at the same time? He sat up, rubbing his eyes as he pulled himself together.

"Thank you." His expression quickly fell as he saw who had come to visit him. For the second time in the past twenty-four hours, he asked, "And where is Detective Argenti?"

Argenti was off duty when news of the murder came into Mulberry Street, so Inspector McCluskey quickly took control of the situation. After dispatching Bill Griffin with two others to arrest Jameson, he sent another detective with a brief letter explaining what had happened to Argenti's house, with the footnote:

"I hope you don't mind me intervening as I have, but there were some time sensitivities involved and you were off duty when it happened. Also, given your close association with Jameson, you might have felt uncomfortable making the arrest personally, and I'm sure in any case the first thing you'd like to do is study the crime scene. Rawlings and Payne have stayed there and I'll leave it to you to call in a mortuary wagon when you've finished your inspection."

As soon as Argenti received the note he took a hansom cab to Mulberry Street to pick up Brendan Mann and some kerosene lamps before proceeding to the murder scene.

Argenti spent the first fifteen minutes with a summary inspection and clarifying with Rawlings and Payne exactly what they'd seen. He then asked Rawlings the main question on his mind since getting McCluskey's note.

"And are you sure it was Finley Jameson you saw leaving Miss Cullen's?"

"Yes. As clear as you're standing in front of me now."

Argenti held his gaze for a second. Rawlings seemed sure, little shadow of doubt, then he nodded towards the alley outside.

"You say he dropped the cape outside as he ran?"

"Yes. Just two yards away from the door he was then."

"And how far away were you at that point?"

Rawlings shrugged. "No more than seven yards."

"But not close enough to catch him?"

"He... he was in full flight by then. It took me a moment to realize what had happened."

Argenti looked back towards the body. The three kerosene lamps they'd set up brightly illuminated the area.

"And she was alone with Jameson, you say. There was nobody else here?"

It was Payne who answered this time. "That's right. There was another woman and a young girl here when Jameson first arrived. But they left soon after."

Argenti looked towards the window as the hubbub in the alley outside rose. A small crowd had gathered outside, including two women and three children from Ellie's house who'd since returned. Two extra constables had come down from Madison Street to hold them at bay. Argenti brought his attention back.

"The dress? Did you actually see Mr Jameson arrive with it to give to Miss Cullen?"

Rawlings and Payne looked at each other.

"No, we didn't," Rawlings said. "But I looked through the window soon after we returned and saw Mr Jameson holding the dress up for Miss Cullen to admire."

Argenti nodded. No doubt more would be ascertained about the dress once he'd questioned Jameson and Lawrence. The original green of the dress could now only be picked out below the knee and on one shoulder. The rest was saturated in blood, the only relief in that dark crimson swathe where the intestines had been pulled out, glistening pearly-white. Her nose had been cut off and one cheek heavily sliced through; Ellie's face was a mask of blood, unrecognizable.

One benefit of the stench of the area, Argenti thought sourly, the smell of her body waste hadn't yet risen above it. Argenti was suddenly struck with a thought. He looked at Ellie's neck and at her hands, no jewellery visible.

"Did either of you see Jameson bring her any jewellery? Particularly anything with red in it – a ruby or garnet?"

Payne: "Not that I saw."

Rawlings shrugged. "No."

They were silent for a second, then Rawlings offered, "But her dress had a burgundy lace trim to it. Why?"

"No reason." No point in sharing Jameson's pet theory. After all, if it was Jameson's personal obsession, no wonder he'd been first to pinpoint it.

Mann's voice from the kitchen disturbed him. "Sir! I think you should see this."

As he made his way through, Argenti kept to one side of the bloodied footprints he'd studied earlier with Mann. Mann was pointing to just beyond where the footprints appeared to peter out.

"We appear to have missed a few footprints here."

Mann shone his kerosene lamp closer to the floor. Argenti could see now why they'd missed them earlier. Apart from being extremely faint, the last close to the back door, they were half the size of the others.

"Looks like somebody young."

"Or a woman with very small feet."

"Yes, possibly."

Argenti followed the small footsteps back and saw that they stopped three yards short of the body before returning through the kitchen. The blood imprint faded as they went – the last few by the back door barely discernible. At first he'd thought that the larger footprints had become indistinct from rapid motion due to the frenzy of the attack. Now as he looked closer part of that lack of clarity was where the smaller and larger bloodied footprints had merged.

Argenti looked up at Rawlings. "Did you see anyone else here when you first arrived back on the scene?"

"No." Rawlings shook his head. "No, I didn't."

"Because it certainly appears as if someone else was here shortly after the murder." Argenti crouched down, studying the small footprints closer. "If only briefly."

••••

After checking some final details at the scene, Argenti spent a few minutes outside talking with the two women who'd since returned to the house. They hadn't seen anything either.

"Only jus' came back twenny minutes ago," said one of them, Milly, a brassy blonde in a floral pinafore.

"Anyone still not accounted for?"

The two women indulged in a brief discussion over the roster of who was working where and when. Milly answered.

"Haven't seen either Sheila or Anna – though they could show later. Oh, and little Sarah and Ellie's baby, Sean. Haven't seen them either."

He thanked them and headed away, Brendan Mann half a step behind. Argenti scribbled a quick note for Mann to take to Jacob Bryce.

"You get the autopsy in motion, tell Bryce to get a mortuary wagon here sharpish. I've got to go to the Tombs for something."

It turned out to be a long night. After making arrangements for that something with Warden Simmons at the Tombs, Argenti spent over an hour after he returned home making notes, then sleep was fitful, ghostly images of Ellie Cullen's torn body and too many conflicting thoughts revolving in his mind.

At first light he went to the Western Union offices to send a telegram to Colby in London, then convened a meeting with Brendan Mann and John Whelan at Mulberry Street, going over his notes and priming them for their interview with Jameson.

Mann raised a brow. "Our interview?"

"Yes. You'll be doing the questioning. I'll be present at the interview, but not visible."

30

"What time did you arrive at Miss Cullen's?"

"Just after six thirty in the evening."

"And what time did you leave?"

"8.40 pm."

Argenti looked through the one way glass screen at the ten-foot square, spartan room. Jameson sat in a straight-backed wooden chair one side, two chairs the other side with Brendan Mann and John Whelan. A small table in between with a water jug and three glasses. No other furniture. Their voices had a strange, high-pitched timbre as they came through a grill in the wall below the glass screen.

When Argenti had made his request, Warden Simmons had informed him that they had two such rooms, "Usually used for psychiatrists or doctors wishing to observe unseen the behaviour of suspects. But suitable for your purpose I think you'll find."

Argenti wanted to avoid handling the initial questioning; his close association with Jameson could present an obstacle. Argenti thought Mann would be a tougher questioning taskmaster than Whelan, so he assigned Whelan to assist and take notes. The first minutes were taken up with Jameson giving his name and personal details before they focused on his recent visit to Ellie Cullen's. Mann paused in contemplation.

"Are you sure it wasn't eight forty-three? Because that was the time you were seen leaving by Sergeant Rawlings."

"No. It was eight-forty. I checked my watch as I left. My maid and Lawrence were preparing supper and I didn't want to be late for it." He gestured with one hand. "And Rawlings and Payne hadn't returned on duty when I left. I didn't see either of them then."

"I see. But even if we are to accept your claimed leaving time of eight-forty, are you really trying to tell us that someone else arrived and butchered Miss Cullen in only three minutes? You can see how unlikely that would be."

A sly leer rose in Jameson's face. "But don't you see. That's exactly the Ripper's modus operandi. Some of his past victims we estimate he killed and ripped apart in only a minute."

Silence settled for a moment, only the sound of Whelan's pen scratching across paper. Then, as if realizing his exuberance in sharing such insight was out of keeping with the horror of what had happened, Jameson's expression quickly fell.

"I didn't kill her, detective Mann. I could never do such a thing to *any* woman, let alone Ellie Cullen. I… I liked Miss Cullen, had become extremely fond of her."

"Yes. So you say." Mann held Jameson's gaze levelly for a second before looking back at his notes. He flicked back a page. "On which subject, did you bring Miss Cullen something that day? A gift?"

"Yes. I brought her a dress."

"Could you describe it for me?"

"It…. it was a ball gown. Emerald satin with a burgundy lace trim."

"And did you bring her any jewellery?"

Jameson's brow knitted. Obviously he found the question odd. "No. No, I didn't."

"Did Miss Cullen put on the dress while you were there?"

"Yes. Yes, she did."

"When would that have been?"

"Towards the end of the lesson. Not long before I left."

"And was she still wearing the same dress when you *claim* you left her?"

Argenti observed Jameson flinch with the emphasis, bristling that anyone would dare question his word. He quickly regained composure.

"Yes, she was," he said.

Again Mann briefly referred to his notes. "Now was there anything different about your meeting with Miss Cullen that evening?"

"In what way?"

"Some words out of place between you. Something she perhaps said to upset you. Did you have an argument?"

"No, no. Nothing like that. The lesson went very well. And she was very pleased with the dress I'd brought her. She was looking forward to wearing it at the Hamden ball the coming weekend. I'd rarely seen her so happy."

Argenti saw Jameson bring one hand up to cradle his forehead then run it through his hair. But for an instant he swore he saw Jameson's eyes glisten with the reminder of Ellie and what had happened to her; and, embarrassed at showing his emotions so openly, he'd brought one hand up as a shield.

Or was it sudden guilt and shame at what he'd done? Argenti's first thought upon receiving the news had been that it couldn't possibly be Jameson. But Rawlings's eye-witness account was firm and the timing damning. As for the other murders, he'd actually been with Jameson when a couple of them occurred. Then his thoughts stopped mid-track, reminding himself that Jameson had in fact been away vital minutes during those murders and how close they'd taken place. Now Jameson had all but answered that himself; the Ripper could kill in only a minute or two.

Argenti jolted, sat back in his seat. Jameson had stood up, was moving towards him – seemed to be staring straight at him. As Jameson got closer, Argenti could see that his point of focus was actually on the mirror.

Jameson sighed and closed his eyes briefly. Then he studied himself more keenly in the mirror, rubbed one hand over his unkempt beard and fresh stubble, adjusted his skewed cravat. He grimaced, as if displeased at how worn and dishevelled he looked after only one night in the cells.

"Would you please sit down again, Mr Jameson?" Mann said. "So that we can continue with the questioning."

"I'll sit down when I like, thank you. Continue with your questions meanwhile, or wait. It's up to you."

Argenti smiled to himself. Trademark Jameson. Despite his obvious upset, appearing perfectly in control.

Silence for a moment. Mann checked his notes again before continuing. "Now you say Lawrence was with you when you arrived at Miss Cullen's, but did he pick you up for your return?"

"No. No, he didn't."

"Why was that?"

"As I said before, he and my maid Alice were preparing something for dinner."

"And what time did you arrive back at your house on Greenwich Street?"

"Not long before nine-fifteen."

"That's rather a long time to get there from the Fourth Ward."

"It took me four minutes to hail a cab, and traffic was appalling in between."

Mann nodded slowly. "Rather a convenient way to lose the few minutes that you *claim* you weren't at Miss Cullen's, wouldn't you say?"

"If you say so."

Offhand, disdainful – but inches away through the screen, Argenti saw the flinch in Jameson's face.

Mann waited a second for Whelan's note taking to catch up. Then, "You said 'Not long before' nine-fifteen. What was that precisely, nine-twelve, nine-thirteen?"

"I don't recall exactly. Around then."

"Ah, I see. But you were sure of the precise time you left Miss Cullen's at eight-forty. Why aren't you similarly sure of the time you arrived home?"

Jameson closed his eyes again briefly. Some of the questions and angles Argenti had prepared for Mann were starting to hit their mark. Jameson was getting rattled, off balance.

"Because the timing wasn't so important then. Dinner was planned for nine-fifteen – so as long as I made it back by then. Which I could see was going to be the case as my cab approached. With a few minutes to spare."

"A few minutes? Or two or four... or indeed five? Nine-fifteen or nine-ten? You can see the vital difference it would make – as it did when you left Miss Cullen's."

No answer from Jameson, only a slight headshake. And from his expression, Argenti saw that his mood appeared to have shifted as quickly again from unnerved to tired indifference.

"I put it to you again, sir, that you've purposely adjusted the time you left Miss Cullen's to cover up what you did to her."

"Don't be ridiculous."

"And that in fact you left her place at eight forty-three, as Sergeant Rawlings witnessed, having only minutes previous brutally butchered and killed her."

No answer, but through the glass Argenti could see Jameson's jaw setting tight.

Mann gave a slow smile, which Jameson could see clearly reflected in the mirror.

"Mind you," Mann said. "Given the mess you left her in, I can quite easily see why you might wish to lose those minutes, blot out what you'd done to her."

Jameson had kept his back resolutely to Mann since he'd stood up, but now he wheeled round sharply, his anger flaring. "I didn't lose or blot out anything, detective. I was perfectly lucid then, didn't have a bl..." He cut off sharply, and turned back to face the mirror equally as sharply, as if only then realizing what he'd been about to say.

"Didn't have a *what*?"

"Nothing, detective... it doesn't matter." He gently shook his head, and Argenti observed Jameson's calm, placid persona instantly return again. "Suffice to say that you're barking up the wrong tree with your theories."

Argenti told Sophia the news about Jameson that night when she brought a coffee into his study an hour before dinner.

One hand went to the side of her jaw in shock, as if she had sudden toothache.

"Oh my. Surely not? He seemed such a nice man, genteel in the true sense of the word. I know you had some initial differences with him, but you said you'd started to see that side of him yourself."

"Yes, I did."

"Surely you've seen the signs of something like this, working so closely with him?"

"You'd have thought so."

Sophia studied him more intently then, saw the battling emotions in his face.

"You're not beginning to believe it, are you? Surely it's some terrible mistake."

"There are some things which don't quite add up. Some inconsistencies." Argenti tapped his pen on the writing pad where he'd been making notes. "And it's essential that I keep an open mind on the matter, not let my close association with Jameson colour my judgement." Indeed, if he couldn't make that separation he might have to step aside from the case, but he left that unsaid.

Sophia contemplated him a moment longer before slowly nodding. A look that said, I accept what you say, but don't expect me to understand it. "Dinner will be served in an hour," she said, and turned away.

He could tell that she was disturbed by the news. The rhythm of her handling the kitchen pots was stilted, and there was no gentle humming or singing in accompaniment.

Argenti looked back at his notes. Not only had Jameson been away vital minutes during the two murders close to them, but Argenti reminded himself that the New York murders had commenced only months after Jameson had arrived in New York from London. Could that be the reason why he'd been Colby's star pupil, seemed to get closer to the psyche of the Ripper than any others?

Other factors had then rapidly struck Argenti. Jameson's swordstick being just the right length to butcher victims; his competence with that weapon combined with his medical knowledge; the blood on his hand at the opera; his close association with Ellie Cullen.

All of those could be purely coincidental, but as a whole, especially combined with Rawlings' eyewitness testimony, they were damning.

But what had disturbed Argenti most had been Jameson's fast-shifting emotions in the earlier interview.

In the blink of an eye he'd seen him go from sullen and sad to disdainful and smirking; placid to fiery and angry. Then as quickly back again.

Were those the sort of emotions which would serve a killer well? Able to butcher and kill a girl in a fiery frenzy one minute, then the next appear as a calm and placid city gent out for an evening stroll. What better way to merge unnoticed with the crowds?

Argenti reminded himself of his own initial discomfort with Jameson, the thought that they wouldn't be able to work together. Was that the thing he hadn't quite been able to put his finger on? Not just their differences, but an imbalance in Jameson which hinted at something deeper and darker? And he'd then buried that concern in order to further his own advancement.

When he'd visited Jameson's house at Greenwich Street earlier that day, his maid Alice had similarly complained about Jameson's moods.

"Yes, at times Mr Jameson was pointed with me; un reasonable, you might even say. But I'd have never dreamt for a moment that... Oh my." She'd suddenly broken off with a gasp, wide-eyed as she held one hand to her mouth.

"What is it?"

Alice related to Argenti how one day she'd seen Jameson in the kitchen handling a bloodied heart and raw liver and kidneys. "I wasn't even sure if they were human innards or not, but his hands were covered in blood. And Lawrence was there too, assisting him. Said later it was some sort of test."

Though when he'd questioned Lawrence over the issue, Lawrence had smiled, confirming they had indeed been testing which body organs could or couldn't be marked easily, "And on which organs they might show up best. Be more visible."

"Or indeed a good trial run for that practice in real life?"

Lawrence had fired back a quizzical frown. Jameson had warned him that Lawrence's condition precluded him from dealing with oblique assumptions. "A fact was a fact was a fact."

But by that same token, it was the rest of Lawrence's account which was particularly damaging. Along with the letters they found amongst Jameson's files and papers when they searched his house at Greenwich Street.

And what had Jameson been about to say in his interview, was so keen to bite his tongue on?

"In your interview with detective Mann you mentioned being perfectly lucid, as if suggesting there were times when you were not so lucid. You were about to say that you didn't have a blackout, weren't you?"

"You deduced this from the transcript?"

"No, I was watching, from behind the glass there."

They were in the same interview room as the day before, with Argenti now on Jameson's side of the glass while John Whelan took notes.

"You were keen to keep your emotions hidden from Detective Mann, but I saw them clearly. And I saw not only a man saddened by what had happened to Ellie Cullen, but at the end one desperately afraid that he might have said too much." Argenti leant forward on the table. "What was it that worried you so about mentioning blackouts, Finley? Did you think it might incriminate you?"

"Well obviously with Ellie Cullen, quite the opposite." Jameson smiled crookedly, shrugging. "Because I didn't have one then, so I was quite clear and certain I didn't kill her."

"Some other occasions, then? Some of the other girls perhaps?"

Jameson said nothing, but Argenti saw the troubled shadows in Jameson's eyes before he quickly averted them. Argenti knew he'd struck a nerve.

Jameson looked towards the wall mirror. "And is there someone watching behind the glass now?"

"No, there's not."

Jameson nodded, applying more thought for a moment. "Even if, as you suggest, and purely hypothetically you understand, I did have some blackouts coinciding with the murders of some of the other girls, where would that lead us? On one hand you'd simply have a collection of coincidences, but on the main murder you're investigating now – that of Ellie Cullen – that key factor would be missing."

A valid point, but if Argenti gave any concession Jameson would no doubt steer him into a dead end. Argenti noted that Jameson was still trying to act as a detached observer, as if he weren't the central focus of the investigation.

"In the case of Miss Cullen that's one murder where thankfully we don't need to depend on coincidence. We have a firm eye witness."

"He's mistaken or he's lying."

Argenti continued unabashed. "On the others, as you rightly say, we'd mainly be left with a number of coincidences. But as you know from your own experience, when you have too many such coincidences, invariably they add up to something else."

Argenti paused for emphasis, then confronted Jameson with the various coincidences in quick succession: his swordstick blade being the right length, his bloodied hand at the opera, his disappearance for vital minutes during two of the murders, the fact that the fresh murders commenced soon after his arrival in New York.

Jameson attempted a challenging smile, but it was uncertain. Perhaps the two nights in the cells had worn him down, or possibly it was from being confronted with so many things to defend all at once.

"I can see you've been doing your homework."

"As you'd expect me to. And I too would expect from you if the situation was reversed."

Jameson nodded curtly. Mutual acceptance; mutual respect.

"Regarding my hand, I believe I told you at the time that when I fell I cut it on some glass. My swordstick blade many pathologists might argue is too long. As for the body parts, no doubt Lawrence will tell you if you ask him. We were testing which organs would be easier marked. And there were probably twenty thousand or more coming through immigration around that same time."

"But how many from the same London hunting ground and with such intimate knowledge of the Ripper's modus operandi?" Argenti held a palm out. "You have to admit, what better way to know so much about the Ripper's inner thoughts and habits than if you were the Ripper himself? And staying at Colby's right hand you'd have not only got forewarned if he was getting too close, but would be able to steer him in the wrong direction if necessary."

Jameson's wry smile in acknowledgment, as if impressed by the ingenuity of Argenti's thinking, overlaid his initial unease. Argenti continued.

"And yes, Lawrence *did* mention you testing organs early one morning. But that wasn't all he mentioned." Argenti took a fresh breath. "He said that you were absent from the house for all the pertinent nights in question, couldn't be accounted for. Including those in London."

"Ah, trusty, reliable Lawrence. I did warn you that his condition precluded him from any subterfuge. Ask him a question and you'll get the cold, hard truth."

Argenti was nonplussed by the diversion. He waited for Jameson to answer his main question.

"The various murders in London, I don't recall that far back." Jameson waved one hand. "If Lawrence says that I was not present in the house during those, then I daresay he's right. But I know where I was when away from the house for the murders in New York. I was at a place called Ling's, in the north part of the Bowery."

"You have an address?"

Jameson told him and Argenti wrote it down. "And you were at this Ling's all the time on the nights of the murders in question?"

"I believe so."

"What do you mean, you *believe* so?"

Jameson smiled crookedly. "That's the whole point of Ling's, to forget where you are for a while. It's an opium den. So I'd have little recall of those hours. But Ling or his assistant Sulee can vouch for the fact that I was there."

"So, as with the blackouts, you'd still have no direct recall of what you did during those hours?"

Jameson shrugged. "I suppose you could look at it that way."

"Which brings us again to those vital minutes you were away during the two murders close by, and the blackouts?"

"They're one and the same. Both ends of the same equation."

"In what way?"

"Because I know more or less when the blackouts are impending. That's why I disappeared for a while at the opera, to go to the washroom. Nearly all of my blackouts occur unseen for that reason." Jameson grimaced. "Though in the case of the cattle steamer, it was brought on from my bashing my head during the stampede."

Argenti reminded himself that on that occasion Jameson had been gone from view for almost twenty minutes. He glanced at the folder to one side, weighing up if the timing was right.

"We've talked much here about coincidences. But I fear that some things will be considered beyond sheer coincidence." Argenti opened the folder and passed across its contents, seven draft letters they'd found amongst Jameson's files at his Greenwich Street home. In the first letter the writing was clearly Jameson's, though the wording was the same as one of the Ripper's letters to the newspapers. Then on successive letters the writing became more like the Ripper's until on the last it was practically identical.

Jameson's face dropped as he viewed them. "I... I can explain."

"I'm sure you can. Another 'coincidence' no doubt."

Jameson appeared momentarily put off step by Argenti's mocking tone. "I... I was trying to get inside the Ripper's mind, don't you see? Try and tell what kind of mind might produce such a letter. And I felt I could only accurately do that by not only copying his wording, but his writing style as well."

"Or indeed practice a different style of writing so that when your letters were received by the newspapers, it wouldn't be recognized as yours."

"No... no. That's not it at all." Jameson shook his head.

"Is that why you were so quick to pick up on the issue of proximal scribe dexterity, when we questioned Jack Taylor, because indeed you'd practiced the very same thing yourself?"

"No, no. You've got it wrong." Jameson clutched at his hair, clearly daunted. "You believe me, don't you?" Silence for a second, and Jameson added, "Particularly with Ellie Cullen. Surely you must know that I couldn't possibly have harmed her?"

Argenti had suspected the personal plea would come at some stage. "Even if I did believe you, how would that help us? Many would say that was mainly because of our past association, which would then render me ineffective on the case. They'd simply appoint somebody new." Argenti shrugged. "Besides, it's not me you have to convince, it's a judge and jury. And I think you can see how bad all of this would look."

Argenti watched Jameson close his eyes and gently shudder, as if his tiredness from his nights in the cells, the repetitive jabbing of the questioning and what he was potentially facing was all catching up with him at the same time. Jameson sighed.

"What would you suggest?"

Argenti paused, in turn put off step by the open question. "You could start by explaining more about the blackouts. At present you only offer an explanation that you didn't have a blackout at the time of Ellie Cullen's murder, as if that alone might exonerate you. But that still leaves a number of other murders where you've yet to explain the blackouts."

"I... I can't." Jameson shook his head again.

"Because you fear you might incriminate yourself?"

"No, it's not that. It's because the history behind them is personal; more to do with my family. In particular my mother. It has little to do with–" Jameson broke off, suddenly struck with a thought. He took a fresh breath after a second. "Look, I'll agree to talk about them, but only if it's in private. Off the record."

Jameson glanced at Whelan, but Argenti held his gaze steady on Jameson.

"You appreciate that's unethical? In a murder investigation like this, all related information has to be recorded."

"Yes, *if* it's relevant. As I've said, much of it is personal and unrelated to this case now." Jameson held out a palm. "Besides, if at any stage you feel I'm returning to details germane to the case, you can always ask Whelan back in to start taking notes again."

Argenti's gaze shifted to Whelan for a second. "I don't know."

"Really, it's up to you, but it's the *only* way I'll talk about it."

"And is there someone watching behind the glass now?"

"No, there's not."

It had taken all of McCluskey's willpower not to let out a hearty chuckle as he'd heard those words, reminding himself that any sharp sounds his side would also be picked up through the grille. And as Argenti and Jameson had looked his way towards the glass, he'd leant back on reflex.

McCluskey had arrived at the Tombs in a separate hansom shortly after Argenti. He'd already learned about the observation room back at Mulberry Street and got hold of Warden Simmons two minutes after Argenti and Whelan had gone to the interview room. Upon asking where to go to join them, Simmons gave him directions.

"And if I wish to sit in simply as an observer, which door is that?"

"Door on the left just beforehand."

McCluskey took his seat in the small room just as Argenti was finishing his preamble. He made notes at intervals and quickly became absorbed in the drama being played out only yards from him, the back and forth question and answer dynamics. It was like watching two experienced verbal swordsmen.

But then as it took the dramatic turn of Jameson's requested privacy, McCluskey tensed as Argenti acquiesced and Whelan stood up. Whelan might come and discover him in the observation room!

He looked sharply at the door. He knew he should leave before Whelan came out, but it looked like Jameson was about to impart some dramatic secret. Something he didn't wish anyone else to hear.

He felt torn, and with the moment's pause he was already too late. He could hear Whelan's footsteps shuffling outside the door. He grabbed a wooden chair and rushed over, wedging it under the door handle.

McCluskey stood for a moment, perfectly still, breathless, listening out for Whelan's movements, concerned too that his own rush towards the door might have been heard.

He watched the door handle expectantly. Nothing. Stone silence. Then after a moment he heard the footsteps turn and slowly recede.

McCluskey let out his held breath and returned to his seat.

31

"You might remember my mentioning that I lived with my aunt and uncle from quite a young age? It's their house in Greenwich Street which I've inherited, and indeed what brought me over to New York six months ago, my aunt dying."

"Yes, I recall you mentioning that."

"Well, if you'd heard the full background, the story I've been relating to everyone for the past two decades, it was that I went to live with my aunt Claris and uncle Gregory at the age of nine when my mother and father died." From Argenti's brief nod, Jameson could see he had Argenti's full attention. He took a fresh breath. "The age that I went to stay with them is correct. I was nine at the time. But my father was very much alive. And so was my mother apparently."

Argenti knitted his brow. *"Apparently?"*

"Yes. She was no longer in the house, and I only had my father's word for it at the time, but he claimed that she'd gone away and left us. Also, that she'd cut off all contact, didn't wish to see us any more. Myself or my father."

"You say that as if you doubted your father's word on the matter?"

"Yes, I did. Very much so. Of course, much of that was to do with a nine year-old not wishing to accept that his mother had run out on him, abandoned him. In the case of my father, I could perfectly understand it, given how he'd abused her."

"In which way? Verbally, or did he strike her?"

"Both." Jameson shrugged. "Oh, at first it was mostly verbal. The beatings started in earnest when I was about four, and became steadily worse. My mother was a frail woman, barely five-foot high, and she appeared to get frailer and weaker with every beating. It was as if my father derived some extra power from her weakness, so beat her all the more."

"And what excuses did your father give for these beatings, if any?" Argenti knew that most people tried to rationalize their behaviour, however unreasonable. "What was his side of the story?"

"He said that my mother was mad, used to provoke him. But personally I couldn't see it. All I saw was a frail, broken woman at the end of her tether, fearful of my father's increasingly unpredictable moods." Jameson paused for a moment, the memory still painful. "I used to take more my mother's side, and so my father ended up hating me for it. A gulf grew between us."

Jameson sighed, ran one hand through his hair. "That was why only two months after my mother left my father packed me out of the house. He said that the atmosphere was insufferable between us, facing me every day was too painful a reminder of my mother. And possibly he was right. I *did* blame him for her leaving, and he could see it in my eyes.

"Of course, that wasn't the excuse he gave to my aunt and uncle to take me in. He said I needed a stable household with both a mother and father figure, which he could no longer provide. And that he was too much of a broken man to cope with me on his own." Jameson broke off.

"Are you saying that this violence was brought on by your father being unbalanced, possibly mad?"

"No, I'm saying that my mother was in fact the mad one, that my father had probably been right all along. But I wasn't to discover that until many years later."

Jameson watched Argenti grapple with incomprehension for a second, his forehead creasing. Jameson took a sip of water.

"One of the thoughts to hit me when my mother first left was that she'd died. And that my father was covering up to protect my sensitivities; or perhaps also to shield his own guilt because he felt responsible for her death. Though it wasn't in fact until my father's death that I finally discovered the truth."

Jameson recalled how cold the house had been the morning when he'd visited with his father's probate clerk. There had been no fire burning or heating in the house for five days, but perhaps it was the chill too of all those old memories. He hadn't been back to the house since he'd left as a child, and all he could see were the ghost images of his father beating his mother. Her frightened screams seemed to sail at him down the empty corridors past the dustsheet covered furniture.

"I found the papers of the committal proceedings in my father's desk. He'd had my mother committed to Bedlam that fateful day. I went to see her immediately." Thirty degrees Fahrenheit warmer in Bedlam, and crammed full of people gibbering and screaming, it had felt like hell in contrast. "I was twenty-three then, my second year of medical college, and I hadn't seen my mother in fourteen years." A grey, frail woman, even smaller than he remembered, skin like porcelain and a distant, lost look. "She was a shadow of the woman I remembered, and I'm ashamed to say I hardly recognized her." Then, against all odds, a glimmer of recognition in her eyes as she reached a bony hand his way. "But she recognized me, it appeared, despite the years in between and what she must have endured." Jameson flinched, as if he still could feel the gentle touch of her hand against his cheek now.

"God knows how she survived it." Tears welled in Jameson's eyes. He looked around. "I've been in here only two nights, and already I can feel myself on the edge. She'd been in Bedlam fourteen long years. And the noise in there, constant wailing and screaming day and night." He shook his head. "If she wasn't mad the day my father had her committed, she certainly was by the end."

Jameson wiped back his tears, took a fresh breath. "I got her transferred to a softer, kinder care home – the polite term for a sanatorium – but it was too late. She died only four months later, though it was probably the most heartfelt four months of my life. Four months of catching up on fourteen years with the person who'd loved me most in my life, and I her."

Stone silence. Argenti nodded solemnly, said nothing; any comment would have seemed lame and inappropriate at that moment. He understood now why Jameson had insisted on privacy and no notes being made. It was an intensely personal story, only part of which linked to the investigation now. Jameson continued.

"And it was in Bedlam too that I first met Lawrence, appreciated that he was far from mad. I had him moved to that same care home while I got the papers prepared to become his official ward." Jameson smiled crookedly. "Perhaps I thought, if I couldn't save my mother, I could at least save Lawrence."

Jameson gestured. "That was another reason why I requested talking privately. Lawrence is still officially certified as insane, so it was a continuing condition of his release that I remain his ward. If it reached the attention of the authorities, including immigration here, Lawrence could end up in some Godforsaken place like Bedlam again. I'd never forgive myself if that happened."

"I understand." Argenti tied the remaining threads together. "So your main concern with this background is that you might have inherited your mother's condition? Her madness?"

Jameson shook his head. "Fact is, I simply don't know. Blackouts were mentioned in her papers from Bedlam. She apparently had fits of madness yet would have no memory of them afterwards."

"And was she violent during these spells?"

"Apparently not. Just bouts of extreme catatonia, sometimes her speech frozen and simply shaking, other times writhing and screaming. That's one of the reasons I don't think the blackouts are significant in my case, because she was *not* violent. So my not mentioning them is not because of possible self-incrimination; it's simply because it's an unsettling reminder of what happened to my mother."

Argenti nodded his understanding. But then was struck with the thought, "But what if you've also inherited your father's violent streak? Your mother's madness and your father's violence; a volatile combination!"

Argenti watched Jameson give a smile of acknowledgment, but it was too readily, as if he'd already considered the possibility.

"Highly unlikely. I hated my father. The last thing I'd want to do is emulate him in any fashion."

"But if this was in your subconscious or 'other' consciousness you'd have little way of knowing; little control over it."

Jameson's expression darkened for a second, as if a more uncomfortable nerve had been struck. He sighed, stroking his forehead.

"Thing is, Joseph, I can't know for sure. But if the blackouts *are* the link, and I only had those on a few occasions coinciding with Ripper murders, and on the others in New York my presence can be vouched for at Ling's, then that would exonerate me."

"Why is that?"

"Because one thing we know for sure – from Colby and everyone else who has ever examined this case – it has been the *same* murderer throughout."

As the horse pulled the police wagon along Walker Street, John Whelan read from his notes.

"The suspect admits to brief blackouts coinciding with the murders of Lucia Bonina and Olivia de Vries, and admits being in proximity of both victims at the time. However, the medical history of these blackouts concerns more the suspect's family, unrelated to the case at hand. That background has therefore been made off-record." Whelan looked up from his notes at Argenti. "Does that accurately convey what Jameson related?"

"Yes, I believe that covers it."

Argenti had advised Jameson that elements pertinent to the case would have to be noted, and they'd agreed the wording at the close of the interview.

"Nothing else?" Whelan enquired. "You were in there alone with him quite a while."

"It was quite a long background. Involving not only his family, but also his assistant, Lawrence, equally unrelated to the case now."

Whelan nodded after a second and put away his notepad.

Argenti looked out thoughtfully at the passing street. Next to a large piano showroom was a shop displaying harps, then on the corner a queue of men seeking work in a newly opened foundry. Top hats and tails became derbies and cloth caps.

"Apart from Lawrence, you're the only one I've ever told about my mother," Jameson had commented as they'd parted. It suddenly struck Argenti that he hadn't shared with anyone what had happened with his sister. He had a better grasp now of why Jameson had taken Lawrence under his wing and tried to help Ellie Cullen; his caring for those less fortunate who'd fallen from grace. Jameson had failed to save his mother, so attempted to make up for that where he could.

But he still wondered whether Jameson had cleverly steered him into a dead end. Jameson had admitted no recall or alibi for two of the murders, but then the fact that the murders were all meant to be by the same hand and he had an alibi for others would exonerate him.

Yet there was another theory, what if Jameson had latched on to Colby's team at the time of the first Ripper murders, then had committed a few murders of his own under the cover of that? Or perhaps his other psyche, as he got close with his analysis of the Ripper, had been responsible for those murders without his core consciousness being aware?

Who better would know how to copy those murders than a trained pathologist and criminal analyst studying the Ripper case? Then the letters. Again those were all in the same hand and so pointed to only *one* killer. But what if the real Ripper had never written any letters at all, and these had been Jameson's creation all along? He would know just how to taunt Colby and himself – his other psyche. And while committing those other murders under that "Ripper" cover, the letters would also have reinforced the *one* murderer stance.

Argenti's thoughts were broken by Whelan talking to the wagon driver. Whelan turned to Argenti.

"We're almost there now. Next on the right."

There was the tendency to duck as they passed under the double-decked train parapet running alongside that side of the Bowery. The other side, the driver started counting numbers. The doorway to Ling's was small, wedged between a haberdashers and a groggery, and could easily have been missed.

A full minute after rapping the door knocker, a hatch in the door opened and an elderly Chinaman surveyed them. The wagon driver was in uniform and Argenti held up his badge. The hatch closed, a bolt was released, and they were let in.

Whelan said that they wished to talk to the proprietor, "A certain Huang Ling."

The Chinaman nodded. "That is me. What can I do to help you gentlemen?"

To Argenti, Ling appeared to be approaching seventy and had a slight stoop. He peered anxiously past their shoulders, as if he was expecting more policemen to arrive. Behind Ling, Argenti saw that the establishment widened out from its narrow reception vestibule. In one corner were some bench seats, a sofa and a potted palm by a frosted glass window. An attractive young Chinese girl approached from the back room. She nodded with a courteous smile but held back just behind Ling.

"We're looking for this man." Argenti took a photo from his folder that he'd collected from Greenwich Street the day before, Jameson and Lawrence standing proudly on the front steps of his aunt's old house. "He's the one on the left with the lighter-shaded waistcoat. We wondered if you might have seen him?"

Ling studied it for a moment, squinting. He shook his head. "No, sorry. I don't recall ever seeing him here." Jameson's instructions were still fresh in his mind, and he'd also dutifully informed Sulee. He turned to her. "Sulee? Have you seen this man? Perhaps some time while I wasn't here?"

Sulee stepped forward and studied the photo. She shook her head and shrugged.

"No, sorry. Never seen him before."

32

"Mr Lawrence... Mr Lawrence!"

Alice's voice, combined with the heavy rapping on the front door, awoke Lawrence.

He glanced at the bedroom clock, 7.08 am, then went over to the front window and looked out: Bill Griffin along with two uniformed policemen and three men in suits and derbies he hadn't seen before. Probably more file papers or something else they wanted from the house. Hadn't they collected enough the past two days?

Lawrence opened the window and called out. "I'll be down in a minute, gentlemen."

Bill Griffin and one of the policemen looked up at him, but the others were distracted by Alice opening the front door.

It took Lawrence two minutes to freshen up and get dressed, by which time Alice had invited the men in and they were grouped in the hallway. One of the suited men stepped forward.

"Mr Lawrence Bidell?"

"Yes."

"My name is Edward Hicks. I'm attached to United States Immigration Authorities. It is my duty to inform you that it appears the terms of your ward and care with Mr Jameson have been breached."

Lawrence looked at Hicks, then at Griffin. "Is this some manner of joke?"

"No, it's no joke," Griffin said flatly. "These men are here to escort you to a secure establishment such as Bellevue where you'll be taken care of."

"I believe in this instance it will be Blackwell's Island," Hicks commented. He looked at one of the men behind him, who nodded. "That's where it was agreed would be more suitable given his condition."

Blackwell's Island? Nineteen hundred inmates with another five thousand plus assorted convicts and patients spread between the adjoining penitentiary, almshouse and hospitals for smallpox and incurables. Lawrence recalled the statistics and the comparisons to London's Bedlam, and was still lost in that contemplation as Griffin yanked his arms behind him and snapped on the handcuffs.

Lawrence half-turned, straining against the restraint. "This is outrageous."

"That as may be," Griffin said. "I suggest you take that up with your master. He's the one who signed the papers that in order to maintain your ward he wouldn't be involved with any criminal activity."

Lawrence was hustled outside to the waiting police wagon. Two yards from the wagon a photographer had set up his camera on a tripod, and at his side was a reporter with his notebook.

The camera flashed as Lawrence approached. He was bundled into the back by the two uniformed men while Griffin hung back a moment to talk to the reporter.

The reporter was a twenty-seven year-old called Theobold Behrens, eager to rise up the ranks at the *New York Post* by attaching to a bold story.

So he'd been first on the scene when Jameson had been arrested and first to file a story. One story or two? Or a main feature with the second story riding on the same page in a side column?

He chewed at the end of his pencil for a moment as he deliberated. Then he started hitting the iron keys on his typewriter again.

Behrens's first story in the *Post* had been picked up by Reuters in London.

Julius Reuter had switched from homing pigeons to telegraph some twenty years before and was one of the first to subscribe to the Trans-Atlantic wire established in 1890. American news stories were then fed to every major newspaper between London and Berlin.

One of those was a provincial newspaper in Guildford, Surrey. To a young reporter there, the name Finley Jameson attached to attacks on prostitutes struck an uncomfortable chord – though it took him most of the day searching through back issues to uncover why.

Reading the article, he could see why it had been picked up locally rather than by the London press. He headed up to the first floor to see his editor, taking the steps two at a time.

As the newspaper presses churned either side of the Atlantic, the engine churned on the small steamboat carrying Lawrence to Blackwell's Island.

Only half a mile from the East River docks, its cluster of brown granite buildings with castle turret roofs made it look more like a fortress. An early morning mist shrouded the island as the steamboat approached, lending it an ominous, mysterious aura.

But there was little mystery in Lawrence's mind. Images

of Bedlam were still embedded in his mind as if it was only yesterday. He could practically picture every yawning scream and spasm-wracked body; the straitjackets and leather-strapped chairs, the cloths wedged between teeth and icy water thrown to break fits.

And as those images gripped him he started gently rocking back and forth in time with the churning rhythm of the steamboat's engine.

33

Commissioner Grayling slapped the *Guildford Mercury* down on the desktop, prodding at its headline.

"What on earth is the meaning of this?" As Colby looked at it, dumbstruck, Grayling also slapped down a copy of *The Times*. "And much the same story now running in the London newspapers as well."

Grayling had convened the meeting in his private office. While normally he'd arrange a meeting with someone of Colby's standing more on neutral ground – a restaurant or hotel tea parlour – the urgency of the situation swept aside all such protocol and, besides, they couldn't risk being overheard.

"Did you know anything of this beforehand?" Grayling pressed.

Colby cast his eyes over the two stories. *The Times* account looked merely to be an embellishment on the earlier *Guildford Mercury* story. He didn't need to read them in detail, he knew all too well what they said.

"Yes, I did." Flat, matter of fact, no tone of apology.

"Then why didn't you say anything earlier?"

"There was little point. It simply wasn't relevant."

"Not relevant?" Grayling arched an eyebrow sharply. "A criminal analyst as main suspect in the most sensational murder case of the century, compounded now with the exposure of a past proven case of him assaulting a prostitute?"

"It was never proven," Colby defended. "The charge was made, but the case failed on insufficient evidence."

"As you well know, there's no smoke without fire." Grayling's lips pursed tightly. "And now we have a fire of gargantuan proportions. Didn't you realize that something like this might come out when you allowed him on the Ripper case?"

"No. I didn't know he might get charged with the Ripper murders, if that's what you mean." Colby realized that sounded flippant. He sighed, adding, "As I said, it was never proven, and who would have dreamt it would come back linked in this manner years after the event." He shrugged. "Besides, how many young medical students get involved in minor affrays with club girls or wake up where they shouldn't?"

"Minor affrays?"

"Apparently it was a club girl he accused of charging him too much for champagne. An argument ensued and she struck out with her fan. He claimed he simply fended her off. She boasted a bruise on one cheek, but Jameson's defence demonstrated that she in fact manufactured most of that with rouge and eyeshadow. That's largely why he was acquitted, and why in turn I didn't consider the matter of much significance."

Grayling ruminated for a moment. "Is that why it only appeared in a provincial newspaper?"

"Probably. If it had been a more serious incident, it would have appeared in the London papers. But this was big news to them in Guildford, a local lad from a prominent Guildford family possibly fallen from grace."

Grayling glanced at the papers again. "Still, now that connection has been made, it would simply make matters worse attempting to trivialize that background to any degree." Grayling cradled his fingers. "My advice, if anyone asks if you knew previously of that background with Jameson, deny any knowledge."

Colby immediately felt uncomfortable. "But Jameson openly told me the entire background. If I now deny that, it would make matters worse for him. It will look like he lied."

Grayling grimaced dryly. "In case you hadn't noticed, things are already looking bad for him, a police eyewitness, claims of madness against both him and his assistant, blackouts, and now a failed alibi. There's little we could say that might stem that tide." Grayling steepled his hands sharper. "And if we lend any voice of support, we risk our reputations being dragged down with him. I think we need to distance ourselves from him as much as possible."

Jameson slapped the newspaper down on the table.

"What in the hell is happening? I thought we had an understanding."

Jameson saw that Argenti glanced only fleetingly at the two stories side by side; he'd obviously seen them before.

Jameson himself might not have seen the headlines if it hadn't been for Donovan – nobody knew if it was his first name or last – who fancied he ruled the roost in the Tombs. The guards on duty on the end of his cell row would sometimes read the newspapers, but Jameson had been in a daze the past two days and had hardly paid them any attention.

Donovan, charged with robbery and a double murder in Brooklyn, took to ridiculing and teasing other prisoners when they were let out on exercise, and that morning had decided to target Jameson's fancy waistcoat and cravat.

"My, my. Isn't it always the way that those fancying themselves as ladies' men dress like women?"

A few guffaws from Donovan's supporters. Jameson looked at Donovan disdainfully. He was almost as broad as he was tall, with leather braces stretched over a prodigious beer belly.

"Well, at least I don't look pregnant," Jameson retorted.

A few tentative chuckles fell quickly to silence with Donovan's stony glare.

Donovan moved in, swinging a wild haymaker which Jameson sidestepped with ease. The two guards on duty decided to let the conflict ride for a moment for the sport of it, intervening only after the third haymaker missed its mark and Jameson responded with a swift jab, catching Donovan on one cheek.

"I don't think he likes women as much as you think," one of the guards called out, waggling that morning's newspaper. "Upset him too much and no doubt he'll rip your gizzards out like the rest of 'em."

Donovan glanced towards the newspaper, confused. He couldn't read, so the comment meant little to him.

"They got him down as The Ripper," the other guard prompted.

Donovan looked at Jameson afresh, incredulity giving way to reluctant respect.

But Jameson was no longer paying any attention to Donovan as his eyes fixed on the newspaper, in particular the column about Lawrence.

He prodded at it now as he observed Argenti's reaction. "You promised that the matter would stay between the two of us."

Argenti closed his eyes briefly in supplication and shook his head. "I know. I know. And I kept that promise. I didn't tell anyone."

Jameson held Argenti's gaze for a moment before looking to one side, as if in search of an alternate explanation. "What about the policeman with you? Might he have said something?"

"John Whelan? No. He's one of my most trusted officers."

"Or possibly he went to the room next door to watch and listen. As you mentioned, that last room we were in had one-way glass."

"No, I strongly doubt it. My instruction to leave us in private was very clear. He wouldn't have disobeyed that."

Jameson nodded after a second. Argenti was telling the truth, or at least believed he was. "If not Whelan, then certainly someone else was in there." Jameson prodded the newspaper again. "Unless you can work out how else they got hold of this information."

Argenti looked down into the water over the deck rail of the ferry as it chugged towards Blackwell Island. Dusk light, it would no doubt be fully dark by the time he returned.

He'd felt obliged to leave a coffee break between his first session with Jameson and dropping the bombshell news that his alibi had failed. Not only because following one with the other might have seemed insensitive, but because by necessity he needed John Whelan there to take notes for the second session.

Jameson had cradled his head in his hands as he'd told him about Ling not vouching for him.

"Oh *no*." Though he'd been quick to come up with a credible explanation. "I recall being concerned about being seen there – what with my photo in the newspapers having taken on the Ripper investigation. I told Ling that if anyone came asking about me to deny I'd been there."

Argenti reminded himself that given Jameson's background that was to be partly expected, he'd be adept with off the cuff explanations. Though as he'd voiced that thought, Jameson had shaken his head with incredulity.

"Then why on earth would I send you to such a place – knowing full well my alibi would fall flat?"

Argenti had no ready answer to that, and so they were back to square one: Jameson the enigma, the mystery. Was he a killer, or wasn't he?

"Almost there." John Whelan's voice broke into his thoughts.

"Yes." He looked up as the ferry passed Blackwell's Island's gothic lighthouse and approached its jetty.

Regardless of his thoughts, he didn't feel he could refuse this duty now. Lawrence was an innocent in all of this, swept along on the cruel tide of due process washing over Jameson. The irony was that if convicted, in the months waiting for the gallows Jameson would likely end up in the island's penitentiary only a hundred yards from Lawrence.

"You'll go along and see Lawrence, won't you?" Jameson had pleaded towards the end of their meeting. "Assure him everything will be okay."

"Yes... yes, I will." Argenti had faltered as he'd said it, uneasy as Jameson had reached out and clasped his hand, the first physical touch between them.

"Thank you. *Thank you.*"

"Is there anything in particular to look out for with Lawrence?" Argenti had enquired. "Any warning signs?"

"Any repetitive movement. Sometimes just a rocking motion or stamping of one foot. Another time I found Lawrence cleaning a silver pot – except that he simply wouldn't stop. The danger is it can bring on a fit, which could cause brain damage. So he should be distracted as quickly as possible to break him out of it."

"I'll tell his ward matron or one of the orderlies to watch out for that. But hopefully he won't be in there long."

"Yes. And thank you again, Joseph. At least try and save the one of us who isn't mad."

But as they approached the Blackwell's Island jetty and even from there he could hear the keening wails of its inmates, it wasn't recall of that touch or Jameson's last words that gave him pause for thought. It was the fact that he'd be lying.

So while he'd do as promised and assure Lawrence that everything would be okay, he'd avoid the stark reality he hadn't had the stomach to share in that moment with Jameson, that the evidence against him was so overwhelming that nothing short of a miracle would save him from the gallows.

A Warden's assistant called Perigree had been one of the men to escort Lawrence to Blackwell's Island the day before.

A compact, insignificant man with mousy hair and a trim moustache, he'd have rapidly become lost in most crowds. Amongst the seething, wailing melee of eighty human dregs in Lawrence's ward, he was all but invisible.

He recognized Argenti from his newspaper photos as soon as he walked into the ward accompanied by another detective and a ward matron.

A Rasputin lookalike with wild, black bushy hair and beard close to the door seemed to take a special interest in them. As he moved closer, Argenti's assistant held out his detective's badge to fend him off. The man looked curiously at the badge for a moment before leaning in closer to sniff it. Then his tongue snaked out to slowly lick it.

The detective recoiled and pulled the badge back. A few sharp words from the matron and a shooing motion and the man retreated with a challenging leer.

Welcome to Blackwell's Island. Perigree allowed himself a dry smile as he watched them make their way through the crowd towards Lawrence on the far side.

Lawrence was half-crouched as he rocked slowly back and forth, and it took him a moment to register their presence. Lawrence stopped rocking, and Perigree observed Argenti stoop down as he talked to Lawrence. His assisting detective and the matron stayed a couple of paces behind.

Argenti spoke for several minutes while Lawrence said little, merely nodded his understanding at intervals, although something was said at one point which lifted his sombre, lost countenance, brought the trace of a smile to his face.

That smile remained as Argenti finally finished and tipped his derby in parting, and indeed was still there a full minute later. Then, as the noise of the surroundings once again impinged, Lawrence started gently rocking again.

When the telephone rang the next morning in Argenti's squad room, the four detectives present looked at it for a moment.

Telephones were still a novelty and only the rich and key public offices had them. So the telephone rarely rang, and when it did it was either the Mayor, Police Commissioner Latham, the Morgue, *New York Times*, Western Union or the Vanderbilts.

Brendan Mann answered it, listening for a minute

before looking towards Argenti as he put one hand over the mouthpiece.

"It's Jacob Bryce. He's asking whether you've got the photographs and report he sent?"

Argenti acknowledged with a half-raised hand and went over to the side table to sift through that morning's post. He'd been busy with the first interview with Jameson when the autopsy had been done.

Having cleaned the excess blood from the body and examined the internal organs, Bryce had phoned the day before to say he'd found a mark on the body which required identifying. Argenti had asked where.

"On her left breast."

"Nothing on her internal organs?"

"No, that was the only mark."

Argenti had asked Bryce to have the mark photographed and sent over with his report. He found the envelope fifth down in the post pile.

He waved it in the air, went over and took the phone from Mann. "Yes, I have it here. I'll have a look and phone you back within the hour."

"If you could. I should sign off the report internally by tomorrow at the latest. Also, have a look at the other details in the report, see whether you feel they're consistent with past attacks."

Argenti's first ironic thought was that the best person to determine that was now languishing in the Tombs. But from Bryce's tone he obviously had something specific in mind.

"In what way?"

Bryce took a fresh breath. "It might be nothing, but I noticed some wounds were very heavy and deliberate, while others – those invariably not as deep – appeared to have been done in more of a hurried frenzy. I don't recall that contrast before."

"I see." Argenti slid out the report and the photos. Six in total, two close up, four from further away at varying angles to show the mark in relation to the overall body. It looked like *"Daleth"*, the Hebrew for D or Da, but until he compared it against Morais's alphabet list he couldn't... Argenti's thoughts suddenly froze.

Something about the contour of the left jaw-bone struck him as odd. He tilted it for a better perspective but it didn't help, the photo edge ended at her eye line. He couldn't be sure. He quickly leafed through the others. He found one which showed up to the hairline, but it was more distant and her face was partly in shadow and tilted away.

With the pause, Bryce asked, "Is something wrong?"

"I don't know. I'm not sure. Do you still have the cadaver readily accessible?"

"Well, it's back in the storage rows, but, yes."

"Okay. Get the body back on a morgue table ready for my inspection. I'm on my way down to you right now."

"There's been a small problem. A possible witness at the scene." McCluskey held out a palm as he saw Tierney's expression darken. "Though we can't be sure as yet..."

McCluskey had taken a deep breath as he walked into Fennelly's. Stark contrast to his last meeting with Tierney when he'd imparted what he'd learnt from behind the glass screen, Jameson's family history with madness and in turn Lawrence. The final laying of their master plan through his journalist contact, if Lawrence was incarcerated too, it would paint the last part of the picture for the press, "Madman killer and his madman apprentice."

Now all of that was at risk if there was a witness who might have seen Tom Brogan that night.

In the corner of the bar a man played *Toss the Feathers* on the fiddle while another accompanied with a steady beat on a bodhrán. The floor was rough flagstone covered with sawdust, heavy with the smell of stale beer and urine.

As he'd slid into the table's bench seat alongside Tom Brogan, Tierney had asked him to join them in Fennelly's speciality of steak and ale pie and one of his brewery ales. He'd have preferred sirloin and wine, but with the news he had to impart he didn't want to further ruffle Tierney.

The steady bodhrán drumbeat weighed heavy on McCluskey's heart as he explained about the small blood-stained footprints and how they'd been picked up close to the body and again approaching the back door.

Tierney looked to one side as he took in the information. A drunken tramp had got up to jig to the music, his torn and soiled brown coat twirling. Fennelly's owner, Padraig, kept a keen eye on the tramp, but while a few around were laughing and clapping beat with his drunken dancing and he remained part of the entertainment, he wouldn't throw him out.

Tierney's brow furrowed. "But it might be someone come in afterwards, right? Doesna mean they were there at the time."

"Yes. There is that possibility."

Tierney looked sharply at Brogan. "You didn't see or hear anyone else there at the time, did yer?"

"No," Brogan said quickly, on reflex. But then he recalled that rustling sound from the kitchen and the baby on the side counter. He decided not to mention them.

Tierney looked back at McCluskey. "You know what it means if there *is* a witness and this all goes the wrong way?"

"Of course I do. Why do you think I told you?"

Tierney held McCluskey's gaze, nodded slowly. Every part of his plan had been carefully thought out. The toff's closeness with Ellie Cullen; only Rawlings in their pay, so Martin distracting Payne those vital moments with his "friend", McCabe, apparently attacked by footpads, the inside information from McCluskey about the Hebrew symbols for Brogan to mark on her breast. There was too much at stake for it all to go wrong.

"I don't like being let down."

Tierney's signal was barely perceptible, but the response was instant. Tom Brogan smashed his beer bottle on the table edge and held its jagged edge against McCluskey's throat.

"So you make sure now, if indeed a witness is found, to let me know who and where they are before anyone at Mulberry Street."

"Of course."

"I mean. Wouldn't wanna see you go the way of some others at this fair establishment."

"Don't be ridiculous." McCluskey said, but his eyes fell anxiously to the jagged bottle. He forced an incredulous smile. "And you say it as if you've done that here before."

"Oh, you wouldn't like to guess how many times – but that would be telling." Tierney smiled crookedly. "Crowded place like this, my own turf. Ideal. If it's someone that won't be missed, Tom and Padraig will drag them out back and take care of 'em. Chop 'em up and feed them to the alley dogs or throw 'em down the sewers. Nothing to say they were even here, and nobody here's likely t' tell."

McCluskey swallowed, his Adam's apple pulsing against the glass. "That as may be. But someone like me... you wouldn't dare."

"Someone like yourself? I grant you, mo' of a fuss would need t' made. The blame pinned on someone else." Tierney's eyes scanned the bar and fixed on the tramp dancing to the music. *"Him,* for instance. Padraig would say you bumped into the fella, there was an argument and he jabbed you with a bottle. Everyone here would back him up, and if the key question came, "Was Mike Tierney or Tom Brogan here at the time," there'd be nothing but headshakes. Nobody here would say any different." Tierney smiled. "Yer see now how it might be more ideal than yer think."

McCluskey's unease settled deeper, his wry smile slow in rising. "You forget one thing. I know you too well. And one thing's for sure, you're not stupid or suicidal. Get rid of me and you've lost your main protection at Mulberry Street." McCluskey raised an eyebrow. "Or had you forgotten what all this was about in the first place?"

Tierney stared at McCluskey levelly for a moment, his jaw set tight. The atmosphere was tense, the message clear; another small signal from Tierney and Brogan would plunge the bottle into his neck.

"That's the rub though, isn't it? If this goes wrong and Tom goes down, then not only am I then threatened, you're on the way out too." He shrugged. "In fact, that happens, given that you know far too much about my operations for comfort, I'd feel a whole lot easier if yer were *not* around."

McCluskey stared back at Tierney, but he sensed no bluff this time. "I see."

Tierney nodded and Brogan lowered the bottle. "That's all right. Nothin' personal, you understand. I jus' thought it only fair you should know where you stand." Tierney looked up as Padraig approached with a silver tray. "Ah, our pies."

••••

New York Police Commissioner Bartholomew Latham's office was dark. The curtains were invariably drawn and walnut wall panelling and mahogany furniture sucked most of the remaining light from the room. Only a gas lamp on his desk cast an eerie glow, and it had taken McCluskey's eyes a moment to adjust to the darkness as he walked in.

McCluskey had received the news from Perigree soon after his return from seeing Tierney, and immediately requested the meeting, hopefully the final touch to his game plan. Latham avoided leaving his office as much as possible, so ran affairs in the four floors below his office sanctum at Mulberry Street largely through a series of sharp memos delivered by his secretary, Marsha Talbot, who sat now to one side taking stenographic notes.

Latham perused the latest newspaper offering that McCluskey had brought to his attention as he sucked on a small clay pipe.

"Indeed, I can see how this might cause a problem. And you say a more damning problem is about to emerge?"

"Yes. It always helps to keep an ear to the ground with the press. And one of my contacts at the *New York Post* says he's been informed by one of the senior staff at Blackwell's Island that Inspector Argenti has visited there and passed a message from Finley Jameson to his assistant, Lawrence." McCluskey had transposed events to suggest that Behren's was feeding him with information rather than the reverse.

"I see." Latham tugged sharper at his pipe. "And when might this second story appear?"

"Tomorrow morning, I believe."

McCluskey watched Latham deliberate. One article to date about Argenti's collusion and withholding crucial information on the mental history of Jameson and his assistant; another to follow the next morning. It wasn't looking good.

Latham tapped the newspaper. "Has Inspector Argenti seen this article?"

"I don't know. I don't believe so. I only picked up this edition half an hour ago, and when I went by his office they said he'd gone urgently to the morgue."

"Is that where he is now?"

"Possibly. I can get one of my men to check."

"It's not her. It's *not* her!"

Argenti had to reach out and shake Jameson by one shoulder to break him out of his stupor.

"I... I don't understand." Jameson's eyes darted haphazardly for possible explanations. "Are you sure?"

"Of course I'm sure. I've just come straight from the morgue. I spent almost an hour there with Jacob Bryce looking at the body from every possible angle."

He'd asked Bryce to put the gas lamps on maximum brightness above the slab. He'd felt sure within the first minutes that it wasn't Ellie Cullen, but he also wanted to go over Bryce's report while there and make one hundred per cent sure the cadaver was who he suspected. They couldn't afford a second mistake.

"How... how could this possibly have happened?" Jameson held one hand out in a plea.

They were sat side by side on his prison bed. Argenti had wanted to break the news to him straightaway and there seemed little point in delaying for the formality of an interview room. Brendan Mann waited at the end of the cell row with the guards.

"There was so much blood when I saw her initially. Her nose had been cut off and one ear removed, her face was a complete mask of blood and even her hair colour couldn't be discerned as a result. The main point of identification had been the emerald ball gown you bought for her. And only the bottom part of that was recognizable beyond the swathe of blood."

"You weren't present at the autopsy then?"

"No, I wasn't. I felt I'd already spent sufficient time with the body at the crime scene. Also the factor that you'd already been arrested and there was intense pressure that you should be questioned as quickly as possible." Argenti grimaced awkwardly. "I asked Jacob Bryce to send me photographs along with his report, which in fact I only saw this morning."

Jameson nodded slowly as the pieces fell into place. "So who do you think is the victim?"

"I believe it to be Anna Walcott, the only other person not accounted for aside from the young girl."

"Young girl?"

"Yes. Sarah Tomkins. Only nine years old. I think it's her footprints we've found on the scene, so she might have been a witness to what happened. She hasn't been seen either since the night of the murder."

"So both Ellie and this little Sarah are missing?"

"Yes. And indeed Ellie's baby, Sean. It was always assumed that Anna Walcott had her baby somewhere, because she was the last one taking care of him."

"Could they all be together?"

"Possibly. Certainly roaming the streets on your own is a tough proposition for a nine year-old."

Jameson lapsed into thought again for a moment, a wry smile curling his mouth as the full implications hit him.

"I knew it. I somehow always *knew* she was alive. One thing that never made sense to me is why she didn't use the revolver I left her."

"Revolver?"

"It doesn't matter." Jameson shook his head, his face clouding again. "Though how on earth is it possible, the dress being on Anna? Surely there wasn't the time? Ellie tried on the ball gown at the end of our lesson and was still wearing it when I left."

"Perhaps there was more of a time gap between you leaving and the murder than Rawlings has suggested?" Argenti watched Jameson wrestle with that thought, then asked, "Was Anna Walcott there at any time while you were there that evening with Ellie?"

Jameson took a second to detach himself from his thoughts. "Yes. Yes, she was. She was there initially when I arrived, then she took Sean and little Sarah to the shops to leave us alone for the lesson. She came back in through the back door with them just a moment before I left."

"And you say that was when Ellie tried the dress on for you?"

"Yes, at the end of the lesson. Indeed, she'd promised to show it to Anna when she returned from the shops, so she probably kept it on for that. Anna had earlier admired the dress."

A confusion of voices and clatter of urgent footsteps heading their way along the iron walkway outside the cell reached them, but Argenti looked up only fleetingly towards the noise before bringing his attention back to Jameson. No doubt a group headed towards another cell.

"And Ellie was still wearing the dress as you left?"

"Yes. Yes, she was."

"Had Anna at any time asked if she could—"

Argenti broke off as the entourage came alongside Jameson's cell and he saw Commissioner Latham. In his shadow was McCluskey, Warden Simmons and one of the cell row guards. The guard stepped forward and opened the cell door.

Argenti stood up sharply and nodded in respect. "Sir?"

It was obvious from Warden Simmons's countenance that visits from Latham to the Tombs were rare, and Argenti was also in something of a daze as Latham announced that due to information recently come to his attention, he no longer thought it provident that Argenti continue with the investigation into Finley Jameson. "I'm sorry it has come to this."

Argenti felt the blood rush to his face. He glared at McCluskey, who looked away uncomfortably, before bringing his attention back to Latham.

"But with all due respect, sir, there has been a crucial development. The girl murdered appears to be one Anna Walcott, not Ellie Cullen as first thought."

Latham nodded thoughtfully. "As may be. But don't you think the first people you should be sharing this with are Inspector McCluskey and myself, *not* the main suspect in the case?"

"I fully appreciate that, sir. But the only reason I did so was because the suspect and Ellie Cullen had a special relationship. Indeed it was part of the rationale argued for his guilt that he'd only got close to her so that–"

Latham held a hand up. "*Enough!* To me this underlines all the more the uncomfortable issue of your own closeness with the suspect. Along with incidences of possible collusion which have been brought to my attention. Combined, they render you no longer fit to conduct the case. I'm sure even you can see that."

"Yes, I daresay I can, sir." Argenti cast his eyes down in submission. There was little point in arguing. Though it seemed cruel fate that at the moment he'd finally believed in Jameson's innocence – Jameson's surprise and elation upon hearing that Ellie was still alive had been real – the case was being yanked away from him. "May I have a final moment, sir? In respect of that past closeness?"

"I suppose so." Latham turned away reluctantly. "But make it quick."

Argenti reached a hand out to Jameson. They shook. Jameson grimaced awkwardly.

"I was going to say, you should try and find Ellie. She probably holds the key to what happened that night." Jameson's expression was suddenly lost, distant again, a man that had given up all last hope with the tide of events against him. "But it looks as if you won't get that opportunity now."

"Don't worry. I'll find a way." Argenti kept his voice low, conscious of Latham and McCluskey only a few paces behind. They embraced. "And I'm sorry if at times it seemed I doubted you, my friend."

34

Four nights earlier.
Sarah feared that if she held her breath any longer she might burst. It would all come out in one gasp and the man would hear her and find her behind the curtain underneath the sink.

She could no longer see his feet through the gap below the curtain, but she could hear him moving around only a few paces away. The sound of the larder door opening, then the sound of Sean stirring in his cot and the footsteps moving towards it; her heart in her mouth for a moment that the man might harm Sean.

A voice from the alley outside, then the footsteps were moving back towards her again. She feared he'd suddenly yank the curtain back and find her, but they continued past, back into the front parlour.

A frozen moment with no sound. Was he pausing in thought and would come back? She was shaking uncontrollably, the sweat cold on her skin. But then she heard the front door opening and his footsteps moving rapidly away.

Still she waited, frozen, and it wasn't until she heard the first shout from the alley and the sound of a whistle that she let out her held breath in a burst, leapt up, grabbed Sean from his cot, and ran out.

Through the back door, along the back alley past piles of rotting garbage, a couple of rats scurrying as she disturbed them, through a dogleg into another alley. She collided with the figure in front of her so hard that it took another burst of breath from her.

In the pitch blackness she feared for a moment she'd run straight into the man, but as she felt arms wrap round her and heard a familiar, soothing voice, she realized it was Ellie.

"Shush. Calm now, Sarah... *calm now*. What is it?" Ellie took Sean from her and hoisted him on to her shoulder. He was coughing and had started to cry, and Ellie gently patted his back.

"A... a man with a long knife. He... he's killed Anna. She was wearing your dress and... and..." Spitting the words out between gasped breath, she suddenly was at a loss to say more.

Ellie looked at her sharply. "My dress? Are you sure?"

Sarah nodded numbly, her eyes wide orbs of fear.

As promised, Ellie had given Anna a quick twirl in the dress when Jameson left. Anna had cooed with delight.

"My, my. I've hardly seen a finer dress. You'll be the belle o' the ball alright."

Then Ellie noticed that Anna had forgotten to get carrots for that night's stew. "S'alright. I'll go get 'em. Always like a break after being cooped up for a lesson. Better change out o' this, though. Don't want it g'tting messed up."

Obviously Anna had tried it on while she was out, imagining herself as the belle of the Hamden Ball for a moment. Her last moment.

So the Ripper had returned for another of them. Finley and Detective Argenti had reassured them that was unlikely, but they'd been wrong.

Ellie's first inclination was to go back to the scene to see for herself. Her free hand went to Sarah's shoulder to guide her, but the girl was rooted to the spot, her eyes fixed that direction in abject terror. Whatever she'd seen, there was no way of getting her back there. And Sean had started to cry again, as if he could sense the tension in her body.

Then another thought hit Ellie about the green dress? What if the killer had expected her to be wearing it? She might have been the target all along.

She needed more time to gather her thoughts. She gave Sarah a reassuring hug as they headed away along the alley.

"Come on. Let's get you somewhere safe for the night."

The rhythms of the house were wrong again. The clatter of dishes from the kitchen as Sophia prepared dinner was irregular, as if she was pausing for thought at intervals. Marco and Pascal's playing was subdued, and Oriana had hit false notes on Chopin's *Heroic Polonaise* and had to restart three times now, when Argenti thought she knew the tune quite well. Argenti had said nothing about the events of the day, but it was as if his family could sense something was wrong.

Hadn't he smiled in acknowledgment at all the right moments? Picked up and hugged Marco and Pascal as he'd come in from work? Was it that transparent that inside he felt destroyed?

The mood continued over dinner, and halfway through Sophia ventured:

"Is everything okay at work?"

"Some changes, that's all." He grimaced tightly. "I'll just have to get used to them."

Sophia no doubt sensed it was troubling him more than he was letting on, but she waited until after dinner and the children were in bed before she asked, "So, these changes. You want to talk about them? Or would it be best left for another night?"

Another night? It was tempting to simply put it off. Another night, another week, maybe never. But then it would become just like the other secret he'd never shared with Sophia, weighing all the heavier now with what had happened with Jameson.

He took another sip of after-dinner wine and with a fresh breath told her about being taken off the Ripper case and what had led up to it.

She was thoughtful for a moment. "How do you think they found out about Jameson's background? You said you were alone with him when he shared that."

"I think someone was behind the one-way interview room glass, watching and listening."

"Who?"

"I don't know. John Whelan was one suggestion, he was in the earlier part of the interview, taking notes. But he wouldn't do something like that." Argenti held a palm out. "I suspect someone connected with McCluskey. He was never happy with me replacing him on the Ripper case."

"And is he back running the case now?"

"Yes. At least in the interim until someone else is appointed." What he left unsaid was that McCluskey could spin that "interim" out for months; it looked unlikely that anyone new would get appointed in time to save Jameson's neck. "The damndest thing too is the timing. Just when I've finally become convinced of Finley's innocence, my hands are tied. I feel I've let him down when he needs me most."

Sophia sunk into thought again for a second, took a sip of her own wine. "But surely you've done all you can. And isn't it more the case that through trying too hard, going a step further than you should have in the eyes of some at Mulberry Street, that has led to you now being taken off the investigation?"

He nodded after a second. "Yes. I suppose you have a point. Still, doesn't stop Finley from feeling it's a pretty poor repayment. He bares his soul to me in confidence, and next day half the world knows about it. Not only that, it's used to further ensure his position on the gallows platform."

"Are things that bad?"

"Could hardly be worse." Argenti nodded solemnly. "Much of it's circumstantial, but as a whole it paints a grim picture. And with none of his alibis standing up and a police eyewitness, the conclusion for a jury would be all but inescapable." Silence as Sophia took it in. "You know, it's strange, all the time I was thinking how different Finley was to me, but in the end we were much the same."

Sophia's brow furrowed. "In what way?"

But having kept the secret from Sophia for half a lifetime, it seemed suddenly wrong blurting it all out now. What would he do? Withhold it for another week, another month, another half a lifetime? He ran one hand through his hair as he felt the weight of the decision.

"What led to Finley wishing to help Ellie in the first place derives from what happened with his mother. He felt he'd failed her and so he tries to make amends with others." Argenti exhaled tiredly. "And I feel much the same about my sister, Marella."

"Marella, the dancer? But that was years ago, Joseph," Sophia shook her head, "And why on earth should you feel responsible for a careless coal wagon driver?"

"That was the account my mother invented for friends and neighbours, that Marella was hit by a runaway team of horses as she left a Broadway show. Her daughter the beautiful dancer, cut down in her prime. And I kept to that same story over the years." Argenti sighed. "But Marella was a prostitute, and she ended up hanging herself in her jail cell."

Stony silence. Sophia's intake of breath broke it after a second.

"Did your mother get to know that Marella was a prostitute before she died?"

"Only during Marella's final months when her pimp was beating her and it became impossible for me to cover up any more. Marella herself kept up the pretence that she was a showgirl. She wanted her mother to be proud of her and knew she'd never accept her real work. Through working in the police department I found out the truth soon enough, but promised Marella her secret would always be safe with me." Argenti shrugged helplessly. "Thing is my mother never forgave me for withholding that secret for so long. She felt that if I'd said something earlier, we might have been able to save Marella. So she partly blamed me for her death, and possibly my mother was right, although not in the way she thought."

Sophia nodded, said nothing; perhaps sensed that he needed to unburden himself of this story in his own way, at his own pace. He took a quick swill of wine.

"When Marella's pimp started beating her, a fellow Italian, Georgio Furrello, she finally came to me for help. But new to the force and hopelessly naive about corruption at Mulberry Street, I simply went to the head of vice and lodged a complaint about Furrello. Little did I know that the vice captain was in the pay of the pimp." Argenti shook his head. "The account of him beating Marella was completely switched round. Furrello claimed he was a respectable club owner and her bruising was simply from where he'd defended himself when she lunged at him with a knife. He even inflicted a skin wound on his own stomach to back up his claim. Marella was arrested and held without bail. Three days later, she hanged herself in her cell."

The silence was stifling as he finished. Sophia reached out and gently touched his arm.

"You did what you felt was right at the time. You weren't to know how things worked back then. You can't blame yourself for her death, Joseph."

"Can't I? In trying to help, I made the situation far worse. I might as well have signed her death warrant myself." As he remembered Marella laid out on a cold slab, rope marks round her neck – his mother had refused to visit the morgue, didn't wish that to be the last memory of her daughter – he felt the first tears sting his eyes. But suddenly the memory changed to the image of Lucia Bonina laid out on the mortuary slab. "When I see these girls, like that *Showboat* girl only a few weeks back, all I get is a picture of Marella haunting me again."

"I recall you being particularly disturbed by that murder. I thought it was just because of her Italian background."

Argenti grimaced tautly, bit back the tears. "So, you see, I'm not the only one with a soft spot for the city's waifs and strays. But then I'm not the one right now with a hangman's noose halfway round his neck."

Sophia looked down for a second before looking back at him directly. "What can be done to help Finley?"

"I don't know. I don't know. I told him that I'd find a way of helping him, but it was mainly to lift his spirits. He looked so defeated." Argenti shrugged. "In truth, now that I've been taken off the case, I don't have the first idea how to help him."

Sophia tapped one finger thoughtfully against her wine glass. "You feel somehow responsible for both? What happened with Marella and now Finley?"

"I suppose I do."

"Ever thought that the main link between the two is that you did your best?"

"You're being very gracious." Sophia in turn now trying to make *him* feel better, possibly because he felt as equally dejected as Jameson. Defeated. "But perhaps one day I'd like to be known for more than just the man who did everything he could, but it still wasn't good enough."

35

"Husband, father, whatsoever your lot, be your heart pure, your life honest. For the sake of those who bear your name, let no bad action sully it. As you look at those innocent faces, whichever tenderly greet you, be yours, too, innocent, and your conscience without reproach..."

"What's that?"

"It's from Thackeray's *The Virginians*."

The only friend Lawrence had made at Blackwell's Island had been Gerald, an affectionate thirty-two year-old mongoloid* who'd watch with gaped-mouth wonder as Lawrence recited one passage after another.

For Lawrence the recitals, often coupled with a gentle rocking motion, were his form of protection, his way of blotting out with his voice and the motion exactly where he was. And so he'd recite Thackeray or Milton's *Paradise Lost*, or Mendeleev's Periodic table, and those mantras would drown out the keening wails, shouts and screams around him.

He could believe, at least for the hours he could keep up the recitals before he became exhausted, when hopefully sleep would take over, that he was somewhere else, Jules Verne's Nautilus, Stevenson's Treasure Island, or in pursuit of Dumas' Monte Cristo treasure.

---

* *The term commonly used prior to 1938 for Down's Syndrome.*

He suddenly stopped his gently swaying recital and studied Gerald's shoes. "Those are quite dirty."

Gerald looked down at them as if he'd never seen his feet. "I never noticed before. Do you really think they are?"

"Yes, I do." Lawrence's lips curled disdainfully as he took in the dirt, scuff marks and dried food stains. He doubted they'd ever been cleaned. "Give them to me, I'll clean them for you. I'm an expert polisher."

Gerald looked at them again for a moment. "Oh, okay." He squatted down to untie the laces and handed them to Lawrence.

Lawrence studied the shoes again, turning them to different angles as he took out his handkerchief. He wiped away some loose dirt, then spat on them and started polishing. And polishing.

After a few moments, Gerald smiled brightly at how clean they'd become. "That's lovely. Look how clean you've got them." He held out a hand to get them back, but Lawrence turned away.

"No. They're not clean enough yet."

Lawrence hit a more strident, frenzied rhythm, and Gerald's smile slowly faded.

"No, that's enough. You might damage them."

"No, *no*. Not enough yet." Lawrence continued the polishing.

"Yes, yes it is." Gerald reached a hand out desperately and hooked a finger inside one shoe, tugging it his way. "Look, I can see my face in them." He beamed brightly again for a second.

"They're not perfect. Not perfect!" Lawrence tugged back. "Leave them with me a few minutes more and they will be."

The back and forth tug of war between them continued, and as Gerald saw the wild determination in Lawrence's eyes it was as if something dawned on him for the first time.

"You know you're mad, Lawrence. Quite mad."

Lawrence suddenly froze, glaring blankly at Gerald, as if unsure how to compute the comment.

But then Gerald noticed that Lawrence was staring at something past his shoulder. He turned to see the Warden approaching with another man.

"I think your friend's perfectly correct, Lawrence," Argenti said. "I think the shoes *are* clean enough. Now let's get you out of here."

As Vera Maynard opened the door of her back office, she saw Mike Tierney and Tom Brogan over at the far end of the club talking to a couple of her girls. She swiftly shut it again.

She turned to Ellie, hissing, "It's Tierney with Tom Brogan. *They're here*! Lock the door after me and slip out the back!"

She'd had Ellie, little Sarah and baby Sean staying at her place since that first night Ellie had come to her for help. She kept them there except on days when her landlord might come round to check, then would take them with her to the club and sneak in the back door unseen. The only other person in on her secret was her bar manager, Jeremy, busy the other side of her desk counting last night's take.

Ellie looked anxiously at the back door. "What if he already suspects we're here and has someone watchin' the alley?"

"Fair point. Check it's clear first. And, Jeremy – lock the door straight after me. If I knock twice, Tierney and Brogan are with me. Three times means it's all clear."

Jeremy, in his trademark green and red paisley waistcoat, came over as she opened the door again. She took a fresh breath as she heard the lock click behind her and started her way towards Tierney and Brogan. Tierney was pointing to a newspaper as he talked to the two girls.

Tierney broke off as he saw her approach and walked towards her, Brogan a step behind.

"Always good t' see you, Vera," he greeted. "Jus' asking a coupla yer girls here the same as one of my men when he came by the other day."

"Liam? Yes, I spoke to him myself. Told him I hadn't seen Anna since the murder."

"An' this would explain why." Tierney passed her the newspaper, stabbing a finger at the headline. "It appears we were looking for the wrong girl. So now we're asking the same set o' questions, but with Ellie Cullen in the frame. Looks like she's the girl gone missin' since then."

Vera felt the blood rush to her head as she read the report about the police getting the girls' identities mixed up. Anna Walcott had been the recent Ripper victim, not Ellie Cullen as previously reported. Ellie had hoped to keep playing dead because meanwhile nobody would come looking for her.

"No, sorry." She hoped she'd remained poker-faced. She handed back the newspaper. "I haven't seen Ellie either."

Tierney squinted uncertainly, as if unsure how to take that. "You recall Ellie, don't yer? She's the girl we spoke about last time I was here. The girl the toff now down as the Ripper had a run-in over with one of my men."

"Yes, of course I do." Vera looked towards a noisy group of men on the far side, the distraction also hopefully hiding any telltale reactions on her face.

But Tierney seemed to misread that she was half-checking out her office door behind. He glanced past her shoulder towards her office.

328
        LETTERS FROM A MURDERER

"Some of this could be a touch delicate," Tierney said. "So maybe best done in private."

"Ah – Jeremy's in there right now. Counting last night's take." Vera knew Tierney's idea of "delicate". It meant he'd rather be somewhere private when he ripped off her earlobe.

"Thas alright. We'll only be a few minutes."

Vera nodded. The more she made excuses, the more suspicious and insistent Tierney would become. It would just make matters worse.

Her heart pounded as she led the way towards her office. Would Ellie have left yet with Sarah and Sean? Or, if Ellie had seen someone watching the back alley, where else would they have found to hide?

Vera paused for a second by the door, knocked twice firmly, and waited.

"What's wrong?" Tierney pressed impatiently after a second.

"Jeremy always keeps the door locked while he's doing the take." She grimaced. "I have to knock to get back in my own office."

A shuffling sound the other side of the door, then after a second the lock turned.

Jeremy opened the door looking flustered, as if he'd been distracted in the middle of something. "I'm sorry. It's taking me longer than I expected. Do you want to be left alone for a while and I'll return later?"

As the view of the room widened with the opening door, Vera was relieved to see that aside from Jeremy it was empty. She caught Tierney in her peripheral vision scanning the room too, eyes cannoning from the ten-dollar bills stacked on her desk to each corner.

"I think that would be a good idea," Tierney answered for her.

As they sat down by her desk, Tierney couldn't help noticing her earrings, pearl drops in an elaborate miniature candelabra. Pearls for tears, he thought.

The man looked up from his newspaper at the farm fields of Alabama rolling by his train window.

Another front page sidebar in that morning's newspapers, and the papers had been full of little else the past few days, "British Forensic Analyst the Ripper." He laid the newspaper to one side, tapping one finger on it pensively. He wondered whether he should end the circus or let it run its course? Perhaps wait until they hanged Jameson and then emerge? Certainly letting the criminyst hunting you hang for your crimes held a satisfying irony.

Should he, shouldn't he? If only he could get a clear signal of whether he was making the right decision with this journey now.

A faint glint caught his eye and his gaze drifted down the train aisle to its source, a middle-aged woman five rows down in a lavender dress; the sunlight caught the ring on her finger as she gesticulated while talking to a young girl at her side. The stone at the ring's centre was red, encircled by small diamonds. The right colour, so could that be the signal he was seeking?

His eyes fixed on the ring. The stone wasn't large or significant enough, only a mid-sized garnet. Also the complication of the girl with her and the fact that he'd been on the train a full day already, people might remember him. No, he'd bide his time and wait until he got to New Orleans, as originally planned. But what if he didn't see the right ring or the right victim there, either?

What other way could he know whether he was doing the right thing? His thoughts churned to the chug-chug of the steam engine, then he suddenly sat up sharper. He reached into his waistcoat pocket and contemplated the coin in his hand; a lucky sovereign, it had guided him well in the past.

"Excuse me... what is that?"

He looked across the train aisle towards the voice, a man in his early forties in suit and derby with a woman of similar age, presumably his wife, and a young boy. "An English sovereign," he said.

"Oh, I see." He indicated the boy. "Just that my young one here collects coins, and I haven't seen one of those before. He's got a great dollar collection, two Mexican pesos and some French francs, but nothing from England."

"This one's early Victorian, so not as many of them around." Seeing the young boy's eyes gleam as he held the coin out and twirled it, he was suddenly struck with an idea. "Look, I've got a decision to make. And if your boy wants to call the coin toss at the same time and gets it right, I'll let him have the sovereign to add to his collection."

"That's very kind of you – but you don't have to," the father said.

"I insist. It would be my pleasure to give the coin to him."

"My goodness." The father ruffled the boy's hair. "Have you ever heard such a generous offer?"

The boy beamed in delight, though his mother looked more circumspect, she knew she'd be the one to have to console him if he called it wrong.

"So, what will it be?" he said, poising the coin to flip.

"Heads," the boy said, and they both watched the coin expectantly as it twirled in the air.

••••

"I've got to say something. I've *got* to. If I don't come forward and say something, he could hang."

Vera ruminated for a moment, shook her head. "Not a good idea. With McCluskey back on the case, I don't see it doing much good. You'd just make yourself a target for Tierney, and besides, what could you say that you saw?"

"I could say that Finley left jus' a moment before I did. That he simply wasn't there any longer to kill Anna."

Vera mulled over the proposition. "And they'd no doubt come back with the fact that since you were no longer there, you couldn't say whether he came back or not moments later to kill Anna." She shrugged. "Maybe too they'd suggest he was enraged that she dared try on your dress, and that's why he killed her."

"No, no he didn't." Ellie shook her head. "I know he didn't. I *know* him. And little Sarah was there, she saw..."

Ellie broke off as she reminded herself that Sarah hadn't seen much at all. Twice now she'd sat down with the girl to try and gently coax from her what she'd seen that night, what the man had looked like?

"I... I don't recall clearly. It was very dark."

"Was he big, small, heavyset? What was he wearing?"

"Quite big, and he was wearing a black cape."

"And his face? What did he look like? Was it Finley, the man who brought me the green dress earlier?"

"I... I couldn't see. It was very dark."

Sarah had been wide-eyed and fearful as her mind drifted back to what she'd seen that night, so Ellie didn't like to push her too hard.

Vera reached out and gently touched Ellie's arm. "Maybe at some stage the poor girl's mind will unlock the horrors of what she saw and she'll get a clearer picture. But not right now. It won't help Finley, and all you'll end up doing is getting yourself and the girl killed." She sighed as she recalled the day's events. "And probably me along with you."

They were back at Vera's room five blocks from the club. She'd headed there soon after Tierney and Brogan left, but still had to anxiously wait another three hours for Ellie and Sarah to appear. On closer inspection of her earrings, Tierney had noticed they were clip-on rather than wire-loop.

"Ear still sore after the last time, is it? Or is it jus' a precaution in case I paid you a visit again?"

"Maybe I just like the variety." She'd aimed for an enigmatic smile, but perhaps Tierney had sensed some challenge in it because he'd nodded to Brogan at that moment. Brogan slipped out a razor sharp knife. Tierney's smile dropped.

"Mind you, doesn't help much either way if you've got no ears to hang 'em on."

She'd stood up and backed away a step, eyes wide in alarm, and as Brogan moved closer Jeremy had burst in.

"Looks like we've got company," Jeremy announced.

All eyes shifted to the door Jeremy had left half-open and the uniformed policeman by the bar. Brogan backed off and tucked away his knife and Tierney waggled a finger in warning as they left.

"We'll continue our little discussion later, my dear Vera. Later..."

Jeremy had sensed there was a problem from the look she'd fired him as they went in the office. He'd run straight out and grabbed the first uniformed policeman, telling him they had a problem with a drunkard starting a fight at the bar. There was no drunkard or fight; though Vera knew that next time there might not be a possible invented diversion. She looked at Ellie.

"It's not safe any longer for you to stay here or at the club. Or me, for that matter. We'll have to go somewhere."

Ellie's eyes darted uncertainly. "But where? Tierney's got eyes an' ears in every corner of the city."

"I know. I know. I'll think of something."

The faint drone of Lawrence reciting to Marco and Pascal drifted down to the dining room from upstairs. Sophia put an ear to it, but still couldn't pick up the words.

"What's that he's reading to them?"

"It's from Rudyard Kipling's *The Man Who Would Be King*," Argenti said.

Sophia nodded, then after a second said, "I didn't know we had that book."

"We don't. He's telling the story from memory."

"Oh, I see." Her eyebrows lifted; she was clearly impressed. But then her earlier concerns when Lawrence had first arrived drifted back. "Are you sure it's safe having him here?"

"Of course it is. Look how many years he's been with Finley without any problem." Though it made him suddenly ponder just how long he could extend the ward he'd signed for. Certainly he couldn't let Lawrence go back to Blackwell's Island. "One thing they no doubt didn't consider when they took me off the case. They can't exactly dictate what I do with Lawrence. Especially as I've now taken a few days leave."

"You have reason to believe they're unsettled about it, though?"

"You could say." Argenti puffed out a gentle plume from his after-dinner cigar. One event he'd ensured Lawrence was present for had been Jameson's arraignment, with the hope of lifting his spirits. But Jameson had appeared so dejected, ankles shackled and handcuffed to a bailiff, head down and giving only one-word answers as the charges were read out – far removed from the full-of-verve Jameson of only a week ago – at first Jameson hadn't noticed them in the public gallery.

At the other end of the gallery, relishing Jameson's showcase demise, had been McCluskey. That had been the only small victory of the day, viewing McCluskey flinch as he'd looked across and seen Lawrence by his side. And a moment later, as if McCluskey's glare had telegraphed it, Finley saw them too, and his countenance instantly lifted. Finley smiled and nodded at them as he silently mouthed, "Thank you, my friend."

Argenti gestured with his cigar towards Sophia. "And who better to try and get Finley out of this predicament now than Lawrence? Nobody knows him better than Lawrence."

Sophia nodded. "Did you have much success today?"

"No, I'm afraid not. But it's early days, *someone* must have seen her since that night." Straight after the arraignment, he'd started doing the rounds of Ellie's regular haunts. At one point, halfway through jotting down a fresh address in his notebook, Lawrence had held a hand up. "There's no need for that. I'll recall it, as with the other addresses."

Argenti took a brief tug at his cigar. "If she's with this young girl, Sarah, while that might make Sarah less visible, it should pinpoint Ellie easier, woman with a baby and nine year-old girl should be easier to find than just a woman and baby. They can't have simply disappeared off the earth."

36

She was perfect. He knew as soon as he saw the ring on her finger. It didn't glint as much as the ring of the woman on the train, probably because the light in the club was more subdued, but even at a distance he could see that the ruby at its centre was far larger, prouder.

He'd chosen a hotel on the other side of the French Quarter on Canal Street, because he knew the area he'd be searching would be closer to the docks. He wanted as much separation as possible.

Separation. He'd heard that Jim Crow laws had segregated the city, but he couldn't see it evident on the streets. All races and colours intermingled, with many of the women on offer, openly hawking from verandas and doorways, an exotic blend.

He looked back at the girl at the far end of the club, café-au-lait skin and warm brown eyes with an enticing slant. He was sure he'd seen her smile slyly as he'd caught her eye momentarily.

He focused again on her ring. Its small surrounding diamond clusters formed a pattern which he couldn't quite make out in the dim light. He went across.

"Excuse me, but I couldn't help admiring your ring. My brother's a jeweller, you see. And I wondered what that pattern might be?"

"It's a fleur-de-lis. Originally from France."

"Do you mind?" He gestured to the chair closest to her.

"Of course not. It's my job to entertain the gentlemen here."

Again that sly smile. Within only minutes he had a potted history of the ring, and her, her mother was French and her father a mulatto who used to ship spices from the Windward Islands. The ring was originally her grandmother's, but was given to her by her mother when she died.

"It's superb. Quite unique," he said. Something that others would readily remember, he thought; especially if she'd shared that same history with them.

She nodded, bright-eyed at the appreciation as she took another sip of her champagne. Then, noticing his glass of red wine was two-thirds down, she said, "Would you like another drink?"

"No," he said hastily; possibly too hastily. As she'd lifted her hand, a waiter had looked their way. The lights were subdued in their corner, shadows heavy; but if the waiter came closer, he'd see him more clearly and might later remember him.

But looking at her champagne glass, he noticed it was under half full. Pretty soon she'd expect him to buy her a drink.

"You said something about 'entertaining'. Where would that happen, if I might ask?"

"Upstairs. The club has some rooms."

"Ah. I was thinking of somewhere more private." He recalled the background of the man at the opera. "I'm a noted industrialist who some might recognize, you see. And the lights by those stairs do appear somewhat bright."

She nodded, pensive. "Your hotel?"

"I fear they're a touch too intrusive as well. Do you have your own room nearby, perhaps?"

He thought he saw the first shadow of doubt cross her face. "I do. But it's shared with a friend and I'm not sure if she's working tonight." Her expression as quickly lifted again. "Though even if she's there, she should leave us be."

"I see." He'd just have to take the risk. It was as close to a perfect situation as he'd get, especially with the factor of the ring. If her friend were there, he'd simply make an excuse and leave. He'd take that as the signal he'd been seeking. "Okay."

She held up three fingers to indicate the fee. He handed her three silver dollar coins and they finished their drinks.

Outside, Decatur Street was still bustling with activity. But he welcomed it, the sort of vibrant throng that quickly swallowed them up. Nobody would notice them.

Each city had its own smells, he considered. New Orleans smelled of fish. The smell of it was even stronger here, even away from the dockside; but it was suffused with aromas of wood-smoke and pungent spices rather than the prevalent coal smoke of New York.

Across the street an elderly Creole man played a clarinet, while on the corner a man was hawking and handing out pamphlets for the nearby West End Fair. "Come see its giant Ferris wheel. The eighth wonder of the world."

Her room was on a first floor up a side alley eighty yards along, approached by a rickety wooden outside staircase.

As she got to the top and opened the door, she called out, "Bernice... Bernice." No answer. "Looks like it is one of her working nights, after all. We got the place to ourselves."

"Yes."

She lit a candle in the sitting room and another in the bedroom. It cast a flickering glow on a patchwork bedspread as she started to undress.

"Aren't you taking off your own clothes?" She arched a teasing eyebrow.

"I want to admire you for a moment first."

He knew he had to be swift and already he had one hand on the blade handle inside his jacket. But as she unhooked her Basque, he feared getting entangled with her arms and the first thrusts wouldn't be clean.

He suddenly tensed. There was a voice close by. Had her friend come back early? But then he heard the same voice, slightly more distant, and realized it was rising from the alley below.

She'd left a window open in the bedroom. A floral curtain billowed slightly on a gentle breeze drifting from the nearby harbour.

Stripped to the waist, she turned to face him, her smile mellowed by something warmer, softer. And taking in her beauty, he felt a sudden pang of regret. If someone hadn't started playing these games, I wouldn't have to do this now, he thought.

She reached a hand towards him, as if to help him undress, and he made his move before his resolve went.

He lunged hard and they fell back against the patchwork spread, breathless. He held her pinned down, his face only inches from hers as he worked the blade deep inside her. And as he felt her warm blood seep against him and saw the flickering shock in her eyes, almost in rhythm with the nearby candlelight, he ejaculated.

He paused for a second, gathering his thoughts. He should deal with her ring first before continuing. If rigor mortis set in, her fingers might curl awkwardly.

He leant across and pulled her ring finger straight. But as he pressed his blade against it, he heard her mumble something, muffled by the first blood trickling from her mouth. Her eyes were fixed in consternation on her ring hand. He leant closer to hear.

"Not my ring," she murmured. "Please... not my ring. It was my grandmother's."

"It's okay," he said placatingly. "Where it's going, it will save a man's life. It's going to a good cause."

37

I suppose could have just let things be. Let you hang for the murders I committed. There would have been a certain satisfaction in that.

But my thoughts on the matter were divided, you see. To all intents and purposes, it could have meant my freedom. No shadow of those murders hanging over me, no policemen continuing to hunt me down. Though to keep up that pretence, I would have had to cease any further murders. My message to you and Colby would have remained unfinished. Worse still, it would have ended on a false note, the last letter marked on the body the invention of an impostor.

I couldn't stand for that. An impostor not only passing themselves off as me, but changing the nature of the game between us.

Ah, but the trouble I've had to go to. Travelling all the way to New Orleans and finding a girl with a special ring so that there could be no possible confusion or alternate explanation.

What a beauty she was too, and she so loved that ring. That's three girls now you've been responsible for, the first because you and Argenti lied about the body markings; that girl at the opera you picked out for me with your eyes. And this one now to save your neck.

Don't ever forget that. The lengths I've had to go to in order to save your life, the debt you owe me. How can you ever repay me?

The package containing the girl's finger wrapped in cloth with its ring still in place and an accompanying letter arrived at the *New York Times* five days after it had been posted in New Orleans.

By that time, The New Orleans Police Department had identified her: Celia Benton-Roux, age 22, her only living relatives a brother who'd followed her father into merchant seamanship and an aunt in Bordeaux. But it was her roommate Bernice and two other close friends who identified her body and spoke about the distinctive ring missing where her finger had been cut off.

Upon autopsy, the New Orleans coroner had sent a message to New York saying he believed he had a Ripper-style murder. McCluskey answered it directly, claiming it was impossible. They had the Ripper in custody in New York. "I suspect it's nothing more than a copycat murder," he insisted.

Two days later the letter and severed finger arrived at the *New York Times*.

McCluskey tried to drag matters out with the New Orleans Police Department, still in disarray after the Captain Hennessey outcry, but Argenti meanwhile mounted his own campaign. He sent a letter to Mayor Watkins along with an ink-press copy internally to Commissioner Latham.

"It's time this travesty of justice was ended. Not only have we clearly imprisoned the wrong man, he also happens to be probably the only one capable of helping us catch the Ripper. With the mood I see mounting in the Press, the longer we keep him behind bars, the more we will be seen as incompetents.

"I also respectfully request that I be reinstated to head the Ripper case so that with Mr Jameson's assistance we may conclude our investigation and pursuit of the man guilty of these heinous crimes."

The next day Huang Ling walked into Mulberry Street to amend his alibi account and Rawlings took a hasty step back and said he suddenly wasn't so sure. "It was very dark at the time," he said. With the growing Press furore, within forty-eight hours the situation was untenable. Latham signed an order for Jameson's release and reinstated Argenti to head the case. At the same time he put McCluskey on a week's official leave, so that he simply wasn't available to answer any awkward questions about the debacle. With two watch changes already on the investigation, the last thing Latham wanted was any conflicting voices at this delicate juncture.

They celebrated with a dinner at Brown's Hotel. They served the largest steaks and pies that Argenti knew of in the city.

"I thought you might like something substantial after the slops at the Tombs."

"Much appreciated. You know me and the Tombs well." Jameson finished studying the menu, and when the waiter returned ordered a prime Sirloin.

They were mostly silent at the start of the meal, just brief small talk, and Jameson ate slowly, either he was relishing his first fine food in twelve days or was having to pace himself digesting something so substantial.

Jameson looked gaunt and tired from his spell in prison. Finally, easing a satisfied sigh after downing a heavy swig of red wine, he appeared to have regained some equilibrium.

"So. You've both been busy, I understand?" Lawrence had visited him in the Tombs two days back to tell him how their search for Ellie was progressing, and now

Argenti brought him up to date on the places they'd visited since.

"Not that it's helped much," Argenti commented. "Nobody appears to have seen her."

Jameson nodded, thoughtful. "Or if someone *has* seen her, they're not admitting to it." He took another mouthful of steak, waggled his fork. "None of the other girls she shared the house with have seen her?"

"No," Argenti said. "With Anna dead, there are only three of them now left in the house. Milly, Sheila and–"

"Josie." Lawrence filled the gap as Argenti searched the air for the name. "And a new girl just joined them, Patricia."

Jameson took the last couple of mouthfuls and dabbed his mouth with his napkin. "Yes. I recall Ellie telling me they needed a certain quota of girls there to take care of the children while the others were working." Jameson embarked on a series of questions to get clear in his mind who and where had been checked, and at one point Argenti found himself smiling. "What is it?"

"Just that it's good to have you back, Finley. That's all."

Argenti meant in mind and spirit, not just in body, though it wasn't until halfway through Jameson's blueberry buckle pie dessert that he finally struck on some inconsistencies. He lifted his spoon.

"This Vera Maynard. I recall Ellie mentioning how she'd taken a few club girls under her wing. You say that she wasn't there when you visited?"

"That's right. She'd gone on holiday just the day before."

"And that according to a couple of girls there, Michael Tierney and his henchman had called by the club a couple of days before you?"

Lawrence offered, "Yes. We spoke to a certain Vicky and another girl, Joyce."

The clatter and bustle of the restaurant imposed itself as Jameson was lost in thought for a moment.

"Curious timing," Jameson said. "She disappears on holiday straight after a visit from Tierney. Might just be a coincidence, but that's one place I'd like to pay a visit along with the girl you mentioned was somewhat circumspect at the Flamboyan Club."

"Rebecca Brydon," Lawrence said.

"Yes."

As Argenti paid and Lawrence went ahead of them to bring the hansom out front, Jameson commented, "Thank you for what you did with Lawrence. I owe you a hearty debt of gratitude for that. I hope he wasn't too much trouble and didn't drive you to distraction reciting Milton or the *Charge of the Light Brigade*?"

Argenti smiled. "Not at all. The children loved his company. I've never seen them so wide-eyed in wonder at storytelling." As they left and the cloakroom attendant helped him on with his hat and coat, he added, "From that letter, it appears someone else believes you owe him a debt of gratitude."

"Yes. I shall have to see just how I repay that."

But from Jameson's wry smile, Argenti could tell Jameson's thanks would not be the kind the Ripper had in mind.

38

"Light...."

"Brush..."

"Loop..."

A twenty to thirty second pause with nothing but silence in between each being passed to Thomas Colby by his assistant, Christopher Atkinson. A departure from the normal calls of "scalpel... probe... retractor". With just a skeleton left to examine, there was no flesh to slice or hold apart.

When Annie Chapman's body had first been exhumed, the only trace of the flesh once there had been some maggot chrysalises still in the coffin. But the stench of that past rotting flesh had permeated her bones.

Colby had ordered Atkinson to brush her skeleton down with a bleach-water solution, then upon hearing Jameson had been cleared immediately commenced also with the exhumation of Mary Anne Nichol's and Mary Kelly's bodies. Their skeletons awaited his and Atkinson's attention on adjoining slabs.

He'd felt guilty though at his lack of contact during Jameson's incarceration and had sent a telegram the previous day.

PLEASED TO HEAR OF YOUR RELEASE. NEVER DOUBTED YOUR INNOCENCE FOR A MOMENT. SOME HERE THOUGH FELT CONTACT WAS

INAPPROPRIATE WHILE THE MATTER WAS STILL IN PROGRESS. INTERNAL POLITICS – WHICH AS YOU KNOW I'VE NEVER BEEN KEEN ON. EXAMINATION CONCLUSIONS FOR ANNIE CHAPMAN, MARY KELLY AND MARY ANNE NICHOLS WITH YOU SHORTLY.

Despite the bleach-mix washes there was still residual dust in some areas, and he'd brushed it from the bones before inspecting closer with his loop.

It took Colby only seven minutes to find the mark on the outer rim of the left pelvis, though he spent another twenty minutes checking for others. The symbol left on Mary Anne Nichols' body, on the inside of the right sternum, took him twice as long to find, but Mary Kelly posed more of a problem. He searched thoroughly for over an hour without finding anything before finally giving up.

"Okay. Let's call it a day." He ran one hand through his hair, sighing. Two further markings to support Jameson's theory; it looked like the best they were going to get. "Arrange for those markings to be photographed, and I'll make my report and send it off."

"Do you want me to also request a reburial of the bodies?" Atkinson asked.

"No. Not yet. There might be requests for further examination or photos. Let's wait until we've heard back from New York."

He lifted his eyes towards the auditorium tiers as the applause rose, many people now on their feet. A lot of attractive women with their finery and jewellery, he considered, though right now all eyes were only on one woman, Lillian Russell, as she bowed repeatedly amidst rousing cheers and shouts of, "Encore!"

Currently drawing one of the largest audiences on Broadway, she'd already responded to earlier encores with two further songs. As he watched her smile appreciatively and start to exit, gathering some of the flower garlands that had been thrown on stage as she went, it looked doubtful that she'd do another.

He'd stayed in New Orleans for another two days, not only to take in the sights but because the police presence at rail stations in and out of the city might have been heavier straight after the murder.

The lights dimmed as she left the stage. The auditorium started to empty, the hubbub merging with the rumble of equipment and scenery being shifted behind the curtains. Over a quarter of the audience left their seats to get refreshments, but some he knew wouldn't return, had no interest in the supporting act.

He looked at the programme in his hand. "THE GREAT BELLINI – SEE THE DEAD COME ALIVE!"

He was as intrigued by the promise of the act as he was by Lillian Russell's lark-song voice.

A drum roll announced the curtain opening again, and on stage was a solitary man in a black coat and top hat. He had a long, waxed moustache, which he preened as he leered at the audience, as if to dispel any doubt he was a villain.

From the wings appeared a woman in a long, flowing white dress. She had long auburn hair curled in tresses each side and gently fluttered her eyelids; the epitome of soft, vulnerable femininity. She put one hand suddenly to her mouth in a mock gasp at something the man had said, clearly offended.

They started to argue and tussle, and the piano and violin trio in the orchestra pit hit a more strident rhythm to underscore the tension between them.

Finally the man threw her back, reached inside his coat and took out a pistol. Her hand raised in horror and a second later he fired, a gout of red blood appearing on her dress as she clutched her breast. The piano and violins hit a crescendo.

The man in the audience seemed more enrapt with that splash of red on her dress than anyone else observing. His pulse quickened, fingers tightening on the programme in his grip. She was a fine actress, and he felt himself swept up in the drama as she slumped to the stage floor, apparently dead.

The man in black beckoned to the side curtains and another man in a long brown coat and derby emerged. They embarked on a frantic animated conversation, pointing to the body and then behind them. And, as they gesticulated, a curtain behind slowly slid back to reveal a large glass vat, ten feet high and as wide with an iron staircase up one side. In front of the vat was a large cabin trunk.

Reaching agreement on what should be done, the two men picked up the body and dropped it into the trunk, then secured its lid with two large padlocks. As the piano and violins picked up their staccato rhythm again, the two men hoisted the trunk up the steps and then dropped it into the water.

The music suddenly stopped, catching the gasps of the audience as they watched the trunk slowly sink.

Another drum roll as the trunk hit the bottom, but the two men were barely paying attention. The man in the top hat was handing his dastardly accomplice a succession of silver coins, when suddenly the accomplice looked over his shoulder, startled. At the other end of the stage mist rose and a figure in white emerged.

The man in black too turned sharply towards the apparition. Clearly the woman they'd buried in the trunk only seconds ago, she wore a white diaphanous gown, as if she was a ghost come back to haunt them. The two men gasped in horror and fled from the stage.

The applause rose. The audience couldn't work out how they'd done it. The mist, now rapidly clearing, had at no time spread much beyond her body, with five yards fully visible between her and the glass vat. And the trunk was still at the bottom of the vat, undisturbed.

He was slow in joining the applause, his hand still gripped tight to the programme, the image of that gout of blood against her white dress hard to shift from his mind.

The two men returned from the wings and joined the woman for a bow to the audience. He waited a moment before leaving his seat to go backstage.

Most of the audience who'd ventured backstage were in a queue for Lillian Russell's autograph. As the Bellini-act girl saw him approaching, she glanced towards the queue, as if he'd surely got confused. Nobody ever bothered to come and see her.

"No, it's you whom I wish to see and offer my praise," he said as got closer. "A marvellous act. Truly spellbinding."

"Why, thank you." She shrugged, blushing faintly. "But shouldn't you be offering your praise to Mr Bellini? After all, the act is his creation. I'm merely his assistant."

Some dancers ran past them, going on stage for the next act. And as the last one passed, she pulled the curtain back behind her, separating them from the Lillian Russell queue.

He looked to each side. They were all but alone, out of view. Nobody looking on. His pulse pounded hard at his temples, and as he looked back at her it was as if the red stain was back on her white dress.

"Ah. You shouldn't make light of what you do," he said. "After all, how many people get to die every night and live to tell the tale the next day?"

••••

"Vicky. This is my colleague, Mr Jameson. He'd like to ask you some questions."

As they'd walked into the club, Jameson had noticed the door at the back of the room open a few inches, a shadow of movement in the room beyond. Then it had hastily closed.

Jameson smiled ingratiatingly at Vicky, an amiable looking redhead in her mid-twenties, already in an evening dress for pre-supper visitors.

"Yes, I'm sorry to trouble you. But you mentioned previously to detective Argenti that just before Mrs Maynard left for her holiday, Mr Tierney and another man visited the club to see her."

Her eyes shifted between Argenti and Jameson before she answered. "Yes. That's correct."

"And has Mr Tierney and this other man revisited to see her since then?"

A more pronounced pause this time, as if she was already trying to fathom where the questioning was heading. "Uh, yes. They did. They returned just yesterday."

"As I thought." He glanced at Argenti knowingly. "And tell me, with Mrs Maynard having already left for her holidays, who did they request to see?"

"Uh, Jeremy Lane. The bar manager."

"And did Mr Lane see them?"

"No, uh... he wasn't here at the time. He'd gone out for a few hours."

"I see. But he's here now?" Jameson looked towards the door at the back.

"No, no. He's not. He's gone out on an appointment."

Jameson held his eyes on the door for a moment. The rest of her answers had been faltering. Uncertain ground. Whereas this response had been speedy. Clearly she'd been prompted. "If anyone comes asking for me, I'm not here."

They'd come straight from seeing Rebecca Brydon at the Flamboyan Club. While she'd certainly been blunt and offhand, in contrast she'd showed little hesitation with her answers. Jameson didn't think Brydon was harbouring any secrets.

"And did Mrs Maynard say where she was going on holiday? Leave a contact address with Mr Lane, or indeed anyone else here?"

"No. As I told detective Argenti before, she said she wanted a complete rest. Didn't want any contact or disturbances."

Jameson nodded. He reached into his pocket and took out some coins.

"Look. It's our assertion that Mrs Maynard is also with another woman, Ellie Cullen, and they could both be in grave danger from Mr Tierney. So it's in their interests that we find them first so that we can offer them protection." He held out four silver dollars. "This is for your trouble. And if you hear from Mrs Maynard and she has a change of heart and wishes to make contact, there'll be another four dollars and the cab fare waiting for you at this address." He handed her his business card.

She paused a second before taking the coins. "I'll keep it in mind."

As Lawrence cantered the hansom down Lafayette Street, Argenti commented, "Looks like you were right with your earlier assumption. I think she does know something and is covering up."

"Yes. I think she was lying too about her bar manager, Jeremy Lane. I think he was there all the time. But no point in barging through to the back office. There's a back door for him to slip out, and even if we caught him in his office he'd have just repeated the same, that Vera Maynard left him no contact address, he has no idea where she is. Let's just pray our 'leading the horse to water' approach works."

Argenti was pensive, and didn't speak again until they reached the start of Centre Street. "You mentioned to Vicky the threat from Tierney. You believe Tierney's somehow involved with Anna's murder?"

"Yes, I do." Jameson sighed. "Obviously while in the Tombs I had a lot of time to reflect on what might have happened. Tierney's eagerness to find Ellie, my private family background sneaked from the interview room through McCluskey, all of it points to some form of conspiracy. Also you mentioned that Bryce thought the wounds on Anna were inconsistent with past victims."

"Yes. He thought they were irregular. Some wounds were quite shallow, superficial, while others were particularly deep. Deeper than he'd witnessed on the other autopsies."

Jameson nodded. "I'll go through that with Bryce when I see him tomorrow. The one thing I haven't been able to work out is the Daleth mark on her breast. After all, we kept the exact nature of those marks under wraps, nobody would–" Jameson broke off as he saw Argenti's expression change. "What is it?"

Argenti recalled being diverted by the bogus interview with Dora Clarke and seeing Bill Griffin come out of his office. He told Jameson about it. "That might explain why they set that up, so that Griffin could go through my desk. My other men were out on another investigation at the time."

Argenti watched Jameson's right hand manipulate the silver head of his cane as he slotted together the pieces of the puzzle in his mind.

"Yes, I daresay you could be right, though we might never know unless we can get to Ellie before Tierney."

••••

"Leading horses to water" was far from Michael Tierney's style, and he hadn't hesitated before barging through to the back office the day before.

Empty. No Jeremy Lane. But he sensed that Lane had left in a hurry. A half-counted stack of silver dollars was still on his desk and a coffee cup half full, unfinished. Lane had probably leapt out the back as soon as he saw him and Brogan enter the club, or had arranged a door-knock warning signal with one of the girls. They weren't likely to ever find him here.

They'd waited almost an hour for Lane to return while Tierney supped at their best malt whisky, but no show. He'd gripped Vicky's arm and wrenched it hard enough to leave a bruise.

"Yer tell Jem Lane we called, and if he's not here next time we'll start hurting his girls. Maybe starting with you."

Vera was still protective of all her girls, so if Jem was in touch with her it should be an effective ploy. But when he called back the next night only a few hours after Jameson's visit and neither Jem Lane nor Vicky were there, he sensed he might have to change his plans. What was he going to do, threaten a fresh girl each time, who probably wouldn't even have a clue of what was going on?

"He's gotta be making his way in and out somehow," he said to Brogan as they left the club. He now knew what was required, but his patience was already worn even if he had the time personally for such a vigil. "My guess is through the back, so the only points you're gonna see him are the alley exits each side. Come back at different times over the next couple of days with Martin. Park a discreet distance away by one alley and have Martin watch the other. He's bound to show at some stage."

39

"Is the fresh murder in New Orleans another Ripper murder, as the letter claims?"

"From the autopsy details we've received, it would appear so."

"And the last murder in New York of Anna Walcott, do you now have doubts about that also being a Ripper murder? The other claim of that same letter?"

"We had started to have doubts about that even before the letter's arrival."

A small group of city officials and newspaper reporters in the conference room at Mulberry Street, most of the questioning so far had been between Argenti and a *New York Times* and *Herald* reporter.

Alongside Argenti on the conference table was Jameson, Mayor Watkins and Commissioner Latham. A show of solidarity to leave no doubt about their reinstatement to lead the investigation.

The *Times* reporter glanced along the row to his colleague, as if wondering if the same anomaly had struck him.

"If you don't mind me venturing, Detective Argenti, that wasn't exactly what we in the Press were led to believe at the time."

"I appreciate. But sometimes wheels in motion in the back rooms here at Mulberry Street take a while to become visible at the front." He smiled tightly. "And you might recall I was on leave and not directly involved in the investigation for much of this past week."

"And slightly longer for myself," Jameson interjected, raising wry smiles and an uneasy chuckle from some in the room. His first words after an initial perfunctory greeting as they'd taken their seats. "So may I take this opportunity of saying it's good to be back on the investigation."

An awkward silence settled, as if everyone was suddenly reminded what had happened to Jameson but didn't wish to comment on it. The main reason why Argenti had fielded the early questions, to allow time for Jameson to settle in. Argenti was the first to break the silence.

"And may I be first to welcome Finley Jameson back. If anyone knows the Ripper well and can aid his apprehension, it's Mr Jameson, which is why I insisted on his return to the case."

A sotto-voce "Hear, hear," from Watkins, which set off a murmur of accord from a couple of others in the room. Latham simply nodded, eyes fixed just above the heads of the gathering.

"And my first announcement now that I've returned," Jameson said, "is that from information recently received from London, I believe we're now far closer to catching the Ripper."

The murmur ran stronger this time through the audience.

"Can you elaborate?" the *Herald* man enquired.

"Certainly. As indicated at an earlier conference, for a while now we've been identifying marks left on the victims, the exact nature of which we've kept secret to preclude copycat murders. Sir Thomas Colby has just sent me details of two further body markings from London, and, combined with the mark identified in New Orleans and my recent meeting with a relevant expert, we've had a significant breakthrough."

It was partly a bluff. Morais had only been able to identify two words in the message: "VENGEANCE OF". The last word had yet to be identified, and if indeed two or three words were missing then still a number of murders were to come.

The *Herald* reporter's brow knitted. "Marks? Are we talking in terms of letters or symbols here?"

"Uh... letters would be more accurate."

"Roman alphabet?"

"I didn't say that."

The *New York Times* man pressed. "Can you be more specific?"

Argenti held a hand up as he sensed them cornering Jameson. "I'm afraid not. That again would get into the area of too much detail that would leave us open to copycat murders. Suffice that you know, and in turn the Ripper, that we're breathing hot down his neck."

Rousing words. Another grunt of approval from Watkins and a more enthusiastic nod from Latham. The message they'd intended to deliver was going well.

The reporters busily scribbled in their notepads, already shaping the next day's headlines. The *Herald* reporter looked up from his notes.

"And tell us, now that you're apparently so close to catching the Ripper. What sort of man is he?"

Criminal analyst's territory. Jameson answered.

"He's a coward. Nothing more. Nothing less. A coward who preys on women when they're at their most vulnerable. The rest of it – the letters, the body markings – is all just an elaborate cover for his base savagery. He might be able to fool himself that what he's doing is slyly inventive or clever, this game he thinks he's playing with us, but he's not for a minute fooling me, or detective Argenti."

Finley Jameson rubbed the bridge of his nose. He was tired and had trouble focusing at times. He hadn't yet recovered from his spell in the Tombs, the sleepless nights and the mounting anxiety as he'd been cast as prime suspect, and the intensity and pace of the investigation since had been gruelling. There had hardly been a minute to breathe, and now after a 7.00 am meeting with Jacob Bryce to re-examine Anna Walcott's body, for the past two hours they'd been at his house on Greenwich Street reviewing their position.

Lawrence had gone out first thing to pick up that day's newspapers while Alice prepared a breakfast of scrambled eggs, kippers and toast for Detective Argenti's arrival.

Within an hour breakfast was cleared away and the room strewn with newspapers and countless files and books as they desperately searched for anything they might have so far missed on the case.

"That *Herald* report has certainly served us well," Argenti commented. He flicked through the newspaper. "There's a linked story too on page seven. Have you read that as well?"

"Yes. Yes, I have." Jameson had in fact read the headline story twice: "LETTERS FROM A MURDERER – INVESTIGATORS CLOSE IN ON THE RIPPER." The article started by comparing the letters sent to the newspapers, then switched to the other letters now revealed – those marked on the victims' bodies, cleverly fusing the two in the minds' of readers. *"We are now left to wonder just which set of letters will finally be the Ripper's undoing: Those sent to taunt investigators or those he leaves marked in blood on his victims?"*

But the smaller linked article on page seven he hadn't felt so comfortable about, and he'd only quickly scanned it. Headed "A Coward not a Mastermind" it elaborated on his closing comments at the press conference the day before. Their aim was to use the newspapers to draw the Ripper out, a reversal of the Ripper using the press to manipulate them. After all, they knew now from his last letter that his obsession with accuracy and his own image had led him to forego even the opportunity of long-term freedom. That level of vanity could be played upon. But now viewing the article, Jameson worried he might have gone too far. He looked over at Lawrence surrounded by books, many of them half open.

"Any further progress with that missing word?"

"No, sorry. Nothing yet."

Jameson nodded. He should have known that even with Lawrence's encyclopaedic memory it would be a challenge for him to find the word Morais had been unable to, when Lawrence's knowledge of Hebrew was scant in comparison.

"Certainly I think we can discount that last *'Daleth'* mark left on Anna Walcott. I agree with Bryce. The stab wounds are erratic, inconsistent with past victims. It's not a Ripper murder."

Argenti sipped at the last of his coffee. "So, full circle back to the Tierney conspiracy we discussed?"

"Yes. It would appear so." Jameson took a fresh breath. "Shame Colby wasn't able to find any mark on Mary Kelly's body. That might have proved crucial and tipped the scales."

"But as one of the London victims, shouldn't that have featured earlier? This now surely is the last word, or *one* of the last, we're seeking."

"Mary Kelly was in fact the last suspected murder in London."

Lawrence looked up from leafing through a book. "Also, in Hebrew, as with Latin, the principal subject of the sentence often comes first."

"Could Colby have possibly missed the mark?" Argenti ventured. "It's there somewhere on the skeleton or an internal organ, but he's simply overlooked it?"

"If it was anyone else, I might consider that as a possibility, but not Colby. He's too thorough." He shrugged. "Besides, Kelly was the victim where it appeared the Ripper had the least time. So the skeleton or a deep internal organ would have been the last place he'd put a mark. He'd have only had time to put it somewhere superficial, such as her breast or shoulder."

"I see."

They were silent for a moment, only the sound of Lawrence flicking through pages of a large, leather-bound tome, seemingly oblivious to their conversation. Jameson held a hand out.

"Perhaps he intended to put a mark on a deeper internal organ, but got disturbed halfway through so had to abandon the idea. Certainly discounting Kelly as a Ripper victim simply because–" Jameson was suddenly struck with a thought.

Time constraints. If the Ripper hadn't had time to superficially mark the body, then perhaps somewhere close by? He recalled the inscription left on the wall near Catherine Eddowes's body.

"Do you have Mary Kelly's file there?"

It took a second for Lawrence to detach from the book he was reading.

"Uh, yes... I believe so." He searched through a stack of files to one side. He passed it across. "There you are."

Jameson flipped rapidly past the inch-thick wad of notes on top, went straight to the photos, four in total from different angles, each showing Mary Kelly with her guts torn out, lower part of her smock dress drenched with blood and mouth agape in a death rictus. Two of the photos had graced the front of London newspapers four years ago.

Jameson reached for his loop to one side and leant in closer. But he wasn't interested in the body itself, he was looking at the surrounding walls. Finally he thought he'd picked out something. He pulled back and then in again, trying to get the focus tighter, clearer. But it was still indistinct. It could be a mark put there purposefully, or it could be an accidental scuff mark or a patch of damp or dirt. It was hard to tell. He looked up.

"Is there a photographer's near here?"

Argenti was still applying thought as Lawrence answered.

"Two that I know of. One on Broome Street, just off Broadway, the other by Union Square."

They'd been waiting almost two hours, their second vigil of the day, before they finally saw Jeremy Lane emerge from one of the alleyways near the club.

It was Martin who saw him first. Brogan was sitting in a hansom twenty yards from the alley north of the club and Martin was posing as a news vendor by the south alley.

"Read the latest on the Ripper.... Read the latest! Read all 'bout it..."

Brogan had at first smiled at the irony of Martin's repetitive hawking. Then after an hour it had begun to grate. Suddenly it changed.

"Man on the run in Harlem... Man on the run..."

Their agreed warning signal. Brogan turned to see Lane, already seven yards past Martin, heading south down the street with a dark green hacking jacket over his distinctive waistcoat and a matching derby.

Brogan waited for a hansom and a milk truck to pass, then swung his own hansom round in the road and started following.

Lane glanced back briefly, but didn't seem to notice anything amiss. He didn't know Martin, traffic was heavy, and Brogan in the hansom had kept his derby pulled down sharply.

Lane went another thirty yards down the road, then, with another quick look round, went into a bank, Union National.

Brogan pulled into the side. He checked his pocket watch after ten minutes and made a signal to Martin across the road.

Martin was leant nonchalantly against a wall appearing to read one of the newspapers he'd been hawking. Martin couldn't read, but he knew what the signal meant. They'd arranged in advance that if Lane returned the same way, Martin should go ahead of him into the alleyway.

Though they had to wait almost another ten minutes before Lane did so. Martin folded his newspaper and headed back the way he'd come, ten yards ahead of Jeremy Lane.

Lane had checked both the alley and the street as he'd emerged from the back entrance of the club and everything had seemed fine. The alleyway was empty each way, and no signs of Tierney or Brogan waiting outside the club.

As he headed back into the alley, he wasn't particularly concerned by the young man taking the same alley ten yards ahead of him. He was headed away from him and didn't seem to be paying him any attention.

That suddenly changed two-thirds of the way down the alley. The young man turned and smiled at him, holding both arms out as if to block his way. Lane faltered in his step, not sure what to make of it at first. Then as he heard fresh footsteps enter the alley behind him and turned to see Brogan, he knew what it meant.

He looked back and forth frantically for a moment. His best chance was probably with the young man in the hope of rushing him and barging past.

He ran forward, tucking his shoulder and head down as he built up speed. But the young man was stronger than he'd thought. Lane managed to wind him heavily as they collided, but couldn't break past. He felt an arm grappling round him, then gripping tight and swinging him round. He lost balance and sprawled to the ground. The kid straddled him and held a knife by his face.

A second later Brogan was there too. The kid stepped aside and Brogan grabbed him by the jacket collars and lifted him like he was a toy until he was sitting with his back against the alley wall, breathless.

"Why so shy of meetin' us, Jem? Yer know Mr Tierney's been keen to see yer. An' yer also know what happens to those who don't keep their appointments with Mr Tierney."

Brogan slid his own blade out, seven inches long and razor-sharp, and held it by Lane's throat.

"I've been busy," Lane spluttered. "Twice the work to do since Vera left."

"Is that right. So why the hide an' seek act?" Brogan's dry smile quickly dropped. "Look. Tell us where she's gone, and we're outta yer hair. Thas all we're interested in."

Lane looked from one to the other. "I... I don't know. I promise. She didn't leave me any address. She wanted a complete break."

"You expect us t' believe that. Walks out on her club and her girls and doesn't wanna know what's happenin' while she's away. Even if the place burns down?" Brogan shook his head and tutted. He pressed the blade hard against Lane's neck. "One las' time, where is she?"

Lane's Adam's apple pulsed against the blade. "Please... I don't know. I promise."

Brogan squinted at Lane. What was this, blind loyalty to the last? Lane risking his life rather than tell them where Vera was? Or was he calling their bluff, knowing that if they killed him their last chance of finding Vera went with it?

But as he clutched Lane's collar tighter, banging him back against the wall in the hope of knocking some sense into him, he noticed Lane's hand go defensively to his breast pocket, as if eager to shield something there. As Lane's jacket ruffled, Brogan caught a glimpse of paper. Brogan pushed the hand away.

"An' what have we here?"

He fished out the piece of paper and unfolded it, a slow smile rising as he read. It was a bank wire transfer from the Union National Bank to its sister branch in Dover Plains to the account of one Vera Therese Maynard. At the bottom was also her mailing address to be notified by telegram of its arrival: 126 Maple Avenue, Dover Plains.

"My, my. An' here's you sayin' all the time that yer don' know where she's gone."

"What are you going to do?"

Lane's eyes were frantic, though Brogan sensed – loyal to the last – that Lane was thinking more about Vera's plight.

"Now let me think 'bout that a moment." The words had hardly left his mouth before he ran his knife deep into Lane. If left alive, he could warn Vera.

"Hey, *you!*"

A sudden shout and some movement made him look round. A man and woman were by the alley end looking their way, now joined by another man who was moving towards them.

Martin was already backing away, but Brogan had to finish Lane before he left. He went to run his blade across Lane's jugular. Sensing his aim, Lane tucked his chin in at the last second, denying him a clean cut. He went to cut again, but the man was advancing fast down the alley towards them. No time.

He ran off following Martin, already six yards ahead.

"What's this model, if I may ask?"

Jameson perused some of the stock in the shop front while its owner, George Lambert, was busy in the darkroom at the back enlarging Mary Kelly's photos.

Lambert's assistant, a man in his mid-thirties, smiled primly. "This is the latest version of the Eastman Kodet. A folding version of their earlier box camera."

"I see." Jameson watched in fascination as the assistant adjusted focal length by moving the lens back and forth on a small set of leather bellows. "Very impressive."

Argenti glanced aimlessly round the shop, not fixing on anything in particular, but Lawrence's attention had been drawn by what looked like a book on the outside, but opened into a folding camera.

"I haven't seen one of these before," he remarked. "Quite unique."

"Yes. That's newly released too – from a French company. You can carry it just like a book until you decide your photographic subject." The assistant pointed to another camera by the window. "Not too different to the other camera recently released by the Eastman company – the folding Kodak. Which, as you can see, also pulls out bellows fashion from what looks like a small briefcase." He smiled thinly. "Sometimes makes me wonder if manufacturers are somehow ashamed of how a camera looks, so feel the need to–" He looked up as Lambert emerged with a flourish from the back room.

"Ah, has my assistant meanwhile given you the complete history of photography?" Lambert laid four large twelve-by-eight inch prints on the counter-top. "All done to your satisfaction, I pray."

After a moment of inspecting them Jameson commented, "Yes, very good. Considerably clearer."

Argenti nodded his accord, and as Jameson reached to pick one up Lambert advised that they were still slightly damp.

"Try to handle them as much as possible at the back to prevent smudging."

They thanked Lambert and paid, then Argenti and Jameson made their way on foot the four blocks to Morais's Theological Seminary on Broadway while Lawrence brought the hansom round.

They had to wait almost half an hour for Morais to finish a lesson, and he seemed surprised at their presence as he removed his *tallit* shawl from his robe. He'd only seen them the day before.

"Some news?"

"Not exactly," Argenti said. "But I believe we might have found another Hebrew letter in the sequence."

"Please." Morais held a hand towards his study door.

They went through. Seated either side of Morais's desk, Jameson spread out two photos from Mary Kelly's murder scene, pointing.

"Here... and just here I believe are where the letter appears clearest." He passed across his loop. "But you'll probably need this."

366   LETTERS FROM A MURDERER

Morais studied the photos for a moment before looking up. "Appears to be *'Lamed'* – an L."

Jameson glanced at Argenti and Lawrence. "That was our first supposition from the alphabet list you left us. But we wanted to make sure."

"That would certainly be my conclusion." He studied the photos again, as if to ensure he hadn't missed anything. "Even with this mark or shadow intruding on one side, it couldn't possibly be mistaken for any other letter, at least in Hebrew." He sat back. "The *Daleth* you mentioned at our last meeting, you've completely discounted that now?"

"Yes, we have," Argenti answered. "But we wondered now, with the last letter *Daleth* removed and *Lamed* inserted as the seventh letter in the sequence, if it might bring to mind a word in Hebrew?"

Morais nodded. "So remind me. What letters are we now left with?"

Jameson took their notes from the day before out of his pocket. On the top sheet he'd already separated the Hebrew letters they were left with after VENGEANCE OF. Now he crossed out *Daleth* and put *Lamed*. He passed Morais the piece of paper.

Morais took a fresh sheet of paper from his desk and, dipping his quill pen in an inkwell, started writing a series of variations on those letters in different positions.

A Comtoise clock by the far wall ticked loudly, a metronome beat for the scratching of his pen. Morais fingered his beard thoughtfully.

"Do you know how many letters we are missing?"

"Unfortunately not," Jameson said. "It could be one or two letters. It could be five or ten."

Morais poised his pen for a moment before writing again. He wrote down three more possible variations in quick succession, then after a further pause another two. He squinted at them and shook his head after a moment, sighing.

"I'm sorry. I can't seem to find anything immediately. This could take some time."

"I believe it's... it's Asmodeus," Lawrence said.

He hadn't so far seemed too involved, but he'd been looking intently at the letter sequences as Morais wrote them, cross-referencing them in his mind with books that had included Hebrew in Jameson's library.

Jameson looked at him. "Are you sure?" Though from Lawrence's quizzical expression he was reminded of the pure folly of ever questioning his memory.

"Of course. The reference is in fact from one of your very own books, *Pseudomonarchia Daemonum* – The Implied Hierarchy of Demons."

Jameson turned to Morais. "From your standpoint, is that a finding you could concur with?"

Morais wrote down another sequence of Hebrew letters, nodding slowly after a second.

"Yes, it is. Asmodeus was one of the original fallen angels, known as Ashmedai in the Talmud some five hundred years before he appeared in the Old Testament. So his name appearing in Hebrew makes sense. Also, given the nature of these crimes now it's particularly apt."

Jameson's eyes were fixed on the letter sequences Morais had written down.

"How many Hebrew letters remaining to form Asmodeus?" Though he could equally have asked, "How many murders?"

"Just one."

Argenti picked up on the earlier statement. "You said particularly apt. Why is that?"

"Asmodeus is known primarily as the 'Demon of Lust'."

40

The first thing Vicky became aware of was shouting and commotion from nearby. But it wasn't until she heard the sound of a policeman's whistle that she realized something serious was wrong.

She went out the front of the club, and as she looked along the street could see a small huddle of people by the alley entrance thirty yards to her right.

She ran up the street and pushed past them. There were more people still in the alleyway, most of them twenty yards down. As she got closer, she got her first view through a gap in the crowd of Jeremy Lane slumped against the alley wall. Amongst the crowd were two policemen, one of them crouching by the body.

"He's still alive, but only just," he said to his colleague. "Get an ambulance here as quick as possible."

The second policeman ran off. Vicky's hand went to her mouth as she gasped. She'd never seen so much blood. She pushed through.

"I know him," she said. "It's Jeremy Lane. Our club manager."

The policeman by him seemed reluctant at first to let her too close, but at that moment Lane's eyes flickered and focused on her. Lane beckoned with one hand.

"It's okay... it's okay."

She moved close and crouched by his side. Tears welled in her eyes as she looked at him. He held a handkerchief pressed tight against the side of his neck, but still blood seemed to be seeping out and running down his shirtfront.

"Oh, God, Jem. What have they done to you?"

"Brogan," Lane muttered. "Brogan and another man I haven't seen before."

"Bastards!" She shook her head. "I shoulda known once they didn't come round the club any more lookin' fer–"

Lane gripped her hand, cut her short. "Thing is, they know where Ellie is. It's important you get a message to her to warn her."

"Where?"

"Dover Plains. Write down the address."

"I can't." Vicky held her hands out helplessly. "Tell me. I'll remember it."

"One twenty-six, Maple Avenue."

Vicky nodded, repeating, "One twenty-six, Maple."

Lane squeezed her hand tight. "Make sure to get a message to her before Brogan gets there. Warn her!"

"I will. I will."

She got up and started running. But how, she thought. Dover Plains was a fair distance. Then she remembered the man with Argenti who'd handed her his card.

She fished the card out her pocket as she ran into the street to hail a hansom cab.

Jameson was on fire with his thoughts. They were back at his house on Greenwich Street, and he'd done nothing but pace agitatedly back and forth since they'd returned from seeing Rabbi Morais at the Seminary.

"And what was the exact reference on Asmodeus, as you read it from *Pseudomonarchia Daemonum*?"

Jameson meant for Lawrence to actually find the reference and recite it verbatim. But Lawrence merely paused for thought before answering.

"Asmodeus, or Asmodée, is one of seventy-two demons of Abrahamic and Christian religions depicted in the Talmud and Key of Solomon. His adversary is St John, though he was finally thwarted by the angel Raphael. He is usually depicted with three heads – one of a man spitting fire and one of a sheep and a bull – riding a lion with dragon's wings. All of these animals are associated with either lascivity, lust or revenge."

Argenti was pensive. "I think Morais is correct. Given the nature of the murders, it fits perfectly."

"Yes, I daresay it does at first glance." Jameson stopped pacing for a second. "He harbours anger for these women for some reason, so invokes the demon of lust in his attacks on them. Almost as if he's an instrument of that and so not entirely at fault himself, classic syndrome of blame detachment. But it only gives us a clue as to *why* he's doing it, which we'd already mostly fathomed. I recall one of Colby's first lectures along the same line, that the Ripper was driven by some base psychotic anger towards prostitutes in general. This message now tells us little beyond that; it doesn't tell us anything specifically about him."

"Why would it need to?" Argenti shrugged. "Perhaps that's all the message he wishes to convey."

Jameson's eyes shifted momentarily. "I suppose so. It's just that after hunting him for so long, I daresay I expected more. Perhaps just my expectations getting carried away." He called out towards the open door. "Alice! Would you be so kind as to prepare some fresh tea and coffee?"

Alice appeared at the door after a second, smiled primly. "Coming up in just a minute."

"Thank you." Though hardly had Alice left the room before he started pacing again. "What if there's another hidden message behind it as well?"

"Why should there be? Just because you feel this message is too basic or obvious. It certainly took us long enough to find it."

"Yes, it did. But he might have expected us to find it more easily. And remember this is a man with a tremendous ego and vanity, so he might also have expected us to be so smug with our discovery that we wouldn't trouble to look any further. A double bluff, if you will."

"You could also be just fishing. As you said yourself, looking for additional explanations which simply aren't there because you *expected* more."

"Possibly. But why in particular *Vengeance* of Asmodeus? Why not revenge, punishment or wrath?" Jameson suddenly paused as his thoughts coalesced. "An anagram," he said breathlessly. "What if it's an anagram?" He turned to Lawrence. "See what you can come up with – concentrating on personal and place names."

Lawrence picked up a notepad and wrote "VENGEANCE OF ASMODEUS" at the top of its first page. Then he started crossing out letters and reforming them in varying sequences in a chain down the page.

Jameson looked at Argenti. "If nothing's discovered, then I'll accept that my theory is unfounded."

Alice brought in their tea and coffee. Lawrence filled almost four pages with word sequences and they had almost finished them before he finally looked up. He skewed his mouth, didn't seem totally satisfied with the results.

"Nothing for place names. But there are some personal name possibilities: Eugene Samson Cafdove, or Sam Eugene with a double barrelled surname, Dove-Cafson or Cafson-Dove."

The front door knocker sounded. Jameson looked up only briefly towards the hallway before bringing his attention back. Alice had gone to answer it.

"Not exactly conventional names. However, we'll know soon enough if we've struck gold if through immigration records we find–" Jameson broke off as he heard Vicky's excitable voice. He went into the hallway, Argenti close behind him.

"It's okay, Alice. Let her in." Then to Vicky, "What is it?"

She stepped into the hallway. "It's Mr Lane and... and Ellie."

Jameson could tell she was distraught. Her rouge had run where she'd been crying, and she had to catch her breath at one point as she ran ahead of herself frantically explaining what had happened. "He begged me to get a message urgently to Ellie, before Brogan might get to her."

"Lane gave you an address?"

"Yes... yes." She repeated the address she'd been saying over and over in the hansom on the way.

Jameson turned to Argenti and Lawrence. "Do Western Union have an office in Dover Plains?"

Lawrence answered. "No, they don't. The nearest is Hartford."

"Dover Plains police?"

"They don't have a telephone as yet," Argenti said. "Only the main city stations have them, not the smaller towns or provincial stations."

Jameson's eyes darted frantically. "What time's the next train to Dover Plains?"

"I believe four twenty-five," Lawrence answered. "Then every hour after that."

Jameson checked his pocket watch. Only seventeen minutes to spare. He went to grab his hat and cane.

"Okay. Lawrence, you head on to Ellis Island immigration to check those names after dropping myself and Detective Argenti off at Grand Central Station. We've got a train to catch."

Martin looked out as the train prepared to leave. Then at the large clock on the back wall at Grand Central. Three minutes to go.

He was anxious because a police wagon had followed them part of the way along 23rd Street, but they'd hopefully lost them at the junction with Broadway.

They'd seen another police wagon close by the station, and they were worried that some connection might have been made, but no policemen in sight so far. Brogan was too large and distinctive a figure, so Martin had kept a lookout.

"Oh, no – all we need!" Martin pulled his head in sharply as he saw Argenti and Jameson emerge, running along the platform towards their train. "It's the toff and Argenti."

"Are you sure?"

"No mistake!"

Brogan's eyes shifted uneasily. He should have made sure to finish Lane. Obviously Lane had somehow got a message to them.

"Come on." Brogan led the way down the corridor. "They can only be guessin' we're on the train. Let's find a place to tuck away outta sight."

As they leapt onto the train, Argenti clutched at the gun in his inside jacket pocket, worried that it might fall out as they ran.

Heading along Madison Avenue towards Grand Central, he'd remarked to Jameson that he should have stopped by Mulberry Street to get a pistol out of his department's gun drawer. "But we haven't got the time now."

Jameson had offered him his pistol, a Remington 38. He held up his swordstick. "I've still got this. Far more effective at close quarters."

The guard sounded the whistle and the train started moving. They looked along the train corridor each way, already on the lookout for Brogan.

"Let's head this way first," Jameson prompted. "Then we'll double-back and cover the rest."

They went through each train carriage looking keenly side to side. At one point Argenti thought he saw what looked like Brogan a few seats ahead in an open carriage, but as the man turned to a fuller profile it wasn't him.

At the end of the front carriage, they turned back, giving a cursory glance to passengers as they went. As they reached the point where they'd started and moved towards the last two carriages, Jameson seemed unsettled with something. He looked back the way they'd come.

"There are a number of closed private compartments we haven't been able to check. Possibly sleepers for the onward leg to Boston." He'd seen from the board the train's final destination. "We should get a guard to help us check them."

Argenti nodded. "I saw one a couple of carriages back."

They went back, Argenti flashed his badge, and solicited the guard's help to check the train's back carriages. Then they returned with him to check the remaining private compartments towards the front of the train.

The guard rapped sharply each compartment door as they went. A moment's pause and invariably the door would open. If not, he'd call out.

"Excuse me, sirs. It's the train guard. There's something I wish to check."

If the door still didn't open or there was no answer, he'd open it with his universal key. Only on one occasion did he disturb a couple asleep on their beds. The other four compartments he'd opened so far had been empty.

Argenti's hand reached towards his inside gun pocket each time, and after a while the repetitive rapping became unsettling, merging in his mind with the possible exchange of gunfire if Brogan was behind one of those doors.

As they approached the last two carriages and there were only four or five private compartments to check, Argenti commented, "Maybe he didn't take the train after all. Perhaps he's gone by horse and cart. Tierney's brewery has some fast delivery carts."

"The train's still faster. I doubt he'd gain any time."

"Yes, but don't forget he had a half-hour lead on us."

Jameson nodded. "A possibility, I suppose." He was still balancing that in his mind, train plus a half hour versus horse and cart. Lawrence no doubt would have had the answer instantly, as the guard rapped on the remaining private compartment doors.

On the last a man barely five foot high smiled primly at them and was as apologetic as the guard for the disturbance.

"I trust this isn't the man you're looking for either?"

"No. No, it's not." Jameson couldn't resist a dry smile.

"Then I'll be taking my leave of you gentlemen." The guard tipped his cap. "If you require any further assistance, please let me know."

They thanked the guard and ambled back toward the rear carriages where they'd first got on the train.

Jameson pondered whether Brogan could have had sufficient lead time on them to catch the previous train? Unlikely. And if he'd taken a horse and cart directly, the most he'd gain on them would be five minutes. But then that might be all the time needed to dispatch Ellie, he reminded himself. After all, guising as the Ripper he'd killed Anna Walcott within only two minutes.

Jameson suddenly stopped, looking curiously at a washroom door to one side. All but one so far they'd passed had displayed "vacant" on the latch.

"What is it?" Argenti asked.

"This washroom was occupied last time we passed. It might be nothing, but still." Jameson knocked on the door. "Excuse me. When will this washroom be free?" No answer. Jameson waited a few seconds and enquired. "Is there anyone in there?"

Still no answer.

"It could be broken, out of service," Argenti said.

"Yes, could be." But he could see that Argenti wasn't wholly convinced. His hand had reached towards his gun pocket. "You stay here and keep guard. I'll go and get the guard to open it."

The other side of the door, Brogan listened intently. Half the words were muffled and indistinct, but still he caught enough to work out what was going on. In a minute or two a guard would return to open the door and he and Martin would be facing three of them. Whereas if he timed it right, they'd be facing only one.

His hand tensed against the short-handled axe in his jacket. He listened out and timed for when Jameson would hopefully be in the next carriage, out of sight.

Then he swung the door open and swung the axe in the same motion.

The action was so quick that it caught Argenti by surprise. He only had the gun halfway out of his jacket as he saw the glint of the axe blade above his head.

He clutched at Brogan's axe arm, grappling. But Brogan was a surprisingly fast man for his size and had gripped his gun arm a split second before, swinging it back as he threw Argenti against the carriage side. His gun fired, the shot going wild. A startled shout and scream rose from a nearby compartment.

Brogan was stronger too. Argenti knew it was a grappling contest he'd lose. His breath fell short, constricted with Brogan pressing against him. Then Brogan tugged and thrust him hard again against the side like a ragdoll and he felt as if the last air was forced from him.

Brogan's axe arm pulled free, and he knew he didn't have the strength left to parry this time, all he could do was dodge to one side at the last second.

The axe smashed through the window behind him, shards of glass blowing past as they were hit by the buffeting air.

Some people had now come out from nearby compartments, their shouts and screams competing with the frantic noise of the train. Brogan's accomplice looked lost for what to do, so took up position between the closest passengers in case they tried to intervene.

Argenti fought desperately to swing his gun round, but Brogan had his arm gripped like a vice, and now banged it once, twice, against the remaining glass in the window. The glass flew free as his gun fell from his grip out the train.

Brogan raised his axe again, but now not so troubled about his gun arm Argenti was able to wrench it free. He parried with both hands gripping Brogan's arm as it swung down, but even with both he could feel the tremendous jolt and shock, the axe blade halted only inches from his face.

Brogan was grimacing as he pressed down with all his strength, and seemed to be levering and lifting him too so that Argenti was hanging half out of the broken window.

Argenti was trying to work out Brogan's intent, and as that grimace became a leer and he saw Brogan glance to one side, Argenti looked that direction too. The oncoming train was about five hundred yards away, hurtling towards them. If he didn't pull in, it would take off his head and shoulders.

He fought to pull in or wriggle to one side, but Brogan was too strong. He was held firm.

"Let me through... *let me through*!"

Brogan wasn't aware of Jameson's approach at first, but Martin was. He looked anxiously towards Jameson pushing his way through the crowd that had filled the corridor, the guard following.

"Come on! Let's go!" Martin shouted. "It's the toff and a guard!"

Jameson brandished his cane as he thrust past a woman halfway along the corridor, her poodle yapping incessantly with the raised voices and excitement.

Brogan's eyes shifted frantically between Jameson and the approaching train, fifty yards, *forty*. Touch and go whether Jameson reached them first. Yet if they were to make good an escape through the train, he'd need something to give them a head start on Jameson and the guard.

Brogan yanked Argenti back in from the window – Argenti felt the air-rush of the passing train only inches from his head – and threw him towards Jameson as he approached.

Argenti tumbled at Jameson's feet, winded. Jameson almost lost his balance, quickly righting himself and reaching a hand out.

"Are you okay?"

It took a second for Argenti to pull himself together. "Yes, I'm... I'm okay. I'm fine." Then he focused on

Brogan and Martin at the end of the carriage. "They're getting away!"

Jameson led the chase, Argenti and the guard a couple of steps behind as they wended their way past startled passengers in pursuit of Brogan and Martin half a carriage length ahead of them.

At the end of the second carriage along Brogan didn't go straight through, he paused by the door, and Jameson wondered for a moment what he was doing.

Brogan held the door side on and struck the handle on its far side off with his axe; then, shutting the door, he pulled the handle through his side.

The door was jammed. There was no handle Jameson's side to open it.

Brogan turned his attention to the chain links between the carriages. He crouched down and turned the lever to release the screw pressure on them.

The other side of the adjoining carriage door, Jameson frantically banged and rattled at it as he looked through its small glass window.

"What's he doing?"

"Looks like he's trying to separate the carriages," the guard said.

Jameson studied the broken door handle. "Is there any way of opening this?"

"Only if I take the handle from the next carriage door along."

"Okay. Hurry!"

Brogan appeared to pause then, as if he was timing something, and looking ahead Jameson could see a small hillside and a tunnel running through it.

As they got to within twenty yards of the tunnel, Brogan hooked his axe blade under the links; then, as the train hit a bump which brought the carriage buffers together, he yanked the last chain-link loose from the carriage hook.

The front of the train kept going at the same speed, but the back six carriages gradually lost their momentum, finally coming to a halt midway through the tunnel.

The gas line had also been severed as the two halves separated. The back carriages were plunged into darkness, the only light at the tunnel end a hundred yards ahead, an arch through which Jameson observed Brogan waving at them from the receding train.

Jameson looked desperately towards the guard halfway along the carriage. "Which is the quickest way off the train?"

"I think back this way. The exit between the next two carriages."

Jameson and Argenti rushed towards it, but were held up by the dozen or so people bunched by the exit. And as the guard saw the push to make their way out get more frantic and feared a crush, he held up a calming hand.

"Please. Exit in an orderly fashion and make your way alongside the train to the front of the tunnel."

The haste and pushing eased a fraction. But that swiftly changed again as they heard the heavy chug-chug of another steam engine fast approaching.

The goods train carrying iron ore had been a clear three miles behind them.

The next junction signalling had picked up the front six carriages of the train, so registered the track in between as clear. And with the back carriages trapped in the tunnel with their lights out, visibility was nil. Until the last moment.

The driver didn't see the back of the train ahead until it was only thirty yards away. He applied the brakes and there was the screaming of metal against metal as the wheels locked, but the weight of the engine and eighty tons of iron ore behind carried it relentlessly forward.

As it got to within ten yards of the passenger train, he jumped clear, his boiler-stoker following suit a second later.

The scream of grinding metal filled the tunnel, overlaying the screaming of passengers as they frantically ran to get clear.

Jameson and Argenti were forty yards ahead of the front carriage as the goods train hit its rear, a chain of passengers ahead of them and behind.

The carriages were shunted inexorably towards them, seeming to gain five yards for every one they ran. A fireball burst out as the engine's boiler exploded, spewing burning coals towards them like fiery bullets.

They saw five people in the escaping throng hit by coals, two of them struck down. And as that fireball and screaming, grinding conflagration of torn metal pressed down upon them and they could feel its heat against the back of their necks, they feared they weren't going to make it.

They raced hard the last few yards towards the tunnel exit, their only saving grace the cataclysm behind finally losing some of its momentum.

They dived down an embankment to one side, breathless as they watched the tangled and twisted carriages slide past on the tracks just above them.

Three carriages and part of a fourth were shunted clear of the tunnel before the conflagration finally came to a halt.

The third carriage had pushed against the second so that they formed an awkward zigzag partially off the tracks.

A suspended moment as the carriages rocked precariously, then Jameson and Argenti watched in horror as the third carriage finally sheered loose and started tumbling towards them.

Already six yards down the forty-five degree embankment, they started running frantically down the remaining twelve yards towards the adjoining dirt road. But the tumbling carriage was almost upon them and there appeared no possible escape.

41

His favourite city tavern was the St Dennis on the Bowery. In the evening, girls would work the tables and offer private dances naked in side-curtained booths for a dollar, but in the daytime it was more sedate and served strong coffee in earthenware mugs and beef and hog roasts at reasonable prices.

What attracted him most was its mixture of clientele – clerks, sailors, city gents slumming it or those from nearby flophouses out for a treat – and the fact that it was nearly always busy. He could blend in and lose himself amongst the crowd. Nobody would notice him.

It had become almost a habit now. Whenever he thought there would be something interesting in the newspapers, he'd pick up the *New York Times*, *Herald* and *Post* from the news vendor on the corner of Bleecker Street, then make his way to the St Dennis. Over two steaming mugs of coffee he'd read them and by then it would be lunchtime, so he'd order his favourite of roast hog, potatoes and cabbage.

As he came to the article on page seven of the *Herald*, he paused mid-sip of his coffee.

Coward. His eyes seemed to stick on the word. His hand started shaking on his cup and he had to put it down to read the rest of the article.

Is this how he repays me? Risking my neck to save him from the gallows – and he calls me a coward!

He felt his face flushing as his anger rose. He looked round the room, concerned that his rage might have made him more conspicuous.

Life went on as normal. Everyone seemed oblivious to the most ingenious killer that had probably ever been in their midst, the *coward*! He sneered at the irony.

Suddenly he didn't feel so hungry. He paid for his coffee and, as had become his habit, left the newspapers on the table for its next occupants to read.

"Here! Jump in here!" Jameson shouted.

Halfway down the embankment was a sharp-cut foot-high ridge before it continued at the same forty-five degree angle.

Argenti didn't spot it at first, merely followed suit as Jameson dived down and tucked in tight behind the ridge.

If the tumbling carriage hit the edge of the ridge flat-on, it would still crush them, but Jameson had noticed that with each roll it leapt a foot clear of the ground. If they were lucky, it might miss them.

Jameson held his breath as the carriage edge hit the ground only inches from them. He kept his head ducked down and felt its metal surface brush against the back of his jacket as it swept past.

Argenti appeared to have been caught heavier, his jacket torn. He was a second slower in stirring, nursing one shoulder as they both watched in alarm the tumbling carriage hit the road below. Part of it came away, fragments of metal and glass scattering twenty yards past the road.

A horse pulling an open Surrey reared up sharply just six yards short. A hansom twenty yards behind had a better view and had already slowed. Argenti looked towards them.

"We need to catch a lift to Dover Plains, if we can."

But Jameson seemed hesitant, looked back up towards the tangled wreckage and the forty or so people now visible beyond the tunnel end.

"There are people injured who might need my assistance."

Amongst the crowd, Argenti caught sight of a guard in uniform and also a man with a stethoscope kneeling as he tended to a prone body.

"A guard's there and at least one doctor, by the looks of it. There's not much more you can do for them." Argenti gripped Jameson's arm. "But if we don't get to Ellie Cullen on time, it's a certain death sentence for her."

Jameson looked uncertainly towards the stricken train and its passengers a moment longer before nodding in grim acceptance. They started running down towards the road.

Lawrence solicited the help of a young clerk called Harold Mayberry to help him search through immigration files.

The newly constructed Ellis Island terminal was an impressive edifice three storeys high and with the spread of a football pitch, with imposing turrets at each corner and its midpoints.

Castle Gardens had the year before given up the ghost on handling the increasing volume of immigrants, though in its time had processed some eight million of them. The ground floor at Ellis Island was for processing new immigrants, its upper two floors for administration and filing, much of it taken up with those eight million records transferred from Castle Gardens.

There were another eleven clerks at their desks alongside Harold Mayberry in the long filing room. Two were handling other enquiries, but the remainder acted like functionaries in a library reading room, a stark contrast to the noisy bustle of the throng awaiting processing on the ground floor, quietly penning notes and fresh entries. Behind them was a row of wood cabinets seven foot high.

Mayberry closed a large leather bound book on his desk and put it back in its place in a cabinet drawer one from bottom.

"Nothing for Cafdove, I'm afraid." He glanced back at Lawrence as he made his way further along the cabinet row. "The other alternatives were Cafson and Dove, you say?"

"Yes, a double barrelled surname, Cafson-Dove or Dove-Cafson."

"And, again, first names of Eugene and Samson?"

"No. Just Sam Eugene or Eugene Sam."

Mayberry nodded, took out two leather bound books from another drawer and placed them on his desk. Then he went back and took three further volumes from a high drawer further down. He started running one finger down the pages of the first volume.

"Not so many Cafsons. Lot of Caffreys, though." He looked up hopefully.

"No, sorry. Caffrey's not a possibility."

Mayberry ran his finger down two further pages before looking up again. "Only nine Cafsons, but none with the Christian names you gave."

"Do you mind if I look?"

Lawrence held out a hand. Mayberry nodded and swivelled the bound register his way. Thomas, Peter, Elizabeth, Magda... within twenty seconds Lawrence knew there were no possible anagram matches.

Mayberry sighed as he opened the next register. "Dove is going to be another matter. Countless pages of them."

While thorough, Jameson noted the time it took Mayberry to check each page.

"Could I perhaps help you with that, since it is after all my request?"

Mayberry shrugged, as if the help outweighed the irregularity of the request. "Yes, I suppose." He passed Lawrence the remaining volume.

Lawrence ran one finger rapidly down the columns, and had checked over thirty pages while Mayberry was still on his sixth page. Mayberry raised an eyebrow.

"We could do with your help permanently here."

Lawrence simply nodded and returned to checking. Jameson had told him that when people said such things they were invariably joking, but he couldn't be sure.

Three pages later Mayberry commented, "I've found a match on a couple of those Christian names you gave me, Eugene and Samson. But only on the surname Dove. No C-A-F or double barrelled second name."

"What entry date?"

"Twenty-first of October, 1889."

"And what originating address?"

"A place called Hoxton, London Borough of Hackney."

Lawrence nodded. Hoxton was only a mile from Whitechapel. So both the date and the originating address fitted, but that left the CAF unaccounted for. Lawrence kept looking through the remaining DOVE name combinations in his volume, then helped Mayberry check his remaining pages. Nothing.

Lawrence flicked back through the pages to the Eugene Samson Dove entry Mayberry had found. Dove's USA residence was a Brooklyn address, so *everything* else fitted bar those three missing letters. But then that made nonsense of the overall anagram theory, he reminded himself. Transpose or remove any other three letters at random and the name could be anything.

His jaw set tight as he studied the entry. He didn't like being wrong.

••••

When Brogan got to 126 Maple Avenue, he was sure at first he had the wrong address. It was a general provisions store, and when he looked at its three upper floor windows he couldn't discern any movement or activity there.

He looked anxiously at his pocket watch. Dover Plains was a small, peaceful town. They couldn't wait on the street any length of time without looking conspicuous, and they'd already lost six minutes on the train.

The train driver hadn't realized he'd lost the back carriages until twelve miles up the track. Nobody from the front carriages had seen Brogan disconnecting the links, so the driver had obviously assumed it had happened accidentally. He'd stopped the train then, and Brogan feared he might head back. But finally the driver decided to continue on the nineteen miles to Dover Plains station to get help.

Brogan noticed some steps leading up the side of the store. He led Martin towards them and they made their way up to a veranda leading to a door with a side-window. There were also three windows at the back where the veranda wrapped around the building.

Brogan checked each of the windows. Nobody visible, no movement. Again the thought struck that he had the wrong address, but then at the furthest window he spotted one of Vera Maynard's satin burgundy dresses with sequin neck trim laying on a bed. He doubted that anyone else in Dover Plains would have such an ostentatious dress.

"What are we going to do?" Martin enquired.

"We're going to let ourselves in and wait."

Brogan wedged his axe under the sash window to lever it up.

42

Ellie gently rocked baby Sean on her shoulder as she reached with her free hand to lightly ruffle Sarah's hair.

"Now, whaddya say?"

"Thank you, Vera." Sarah smiled tamely up at Vera as she took her first lick at the candy stick.

"My pleasure." Vera gave a broader smile in return. She'd seen the jar of candy sticks at the end of the pharmacy counter after picking up some tonic and hair colouring, and couldn't resist treating the girl.

Ellie signalled her own thanks to Vera with a tight smile as they left the shop. They were mostly silent on the walk back to Vera's place. They didn't talk much in front of Sarah in any case, because invariably it would swing round to Tierney or Brogan or why they were hiding away or what their next move might be. Vera's brother owned the provisions store and the plan was for them to lay low there for a couple of weeks while Vera re-established some old club contacts in Boston, then they'd travel up.

The other subject they stoically avoided was talking about Sarah herself. Not only because they shouldn't talk about it in front of the girl, but because they'd already laboured the subject before finally giving up on getting her to recall what she saw that terrible night.

It was strange. When Ellie crouched down to Sarah's level, it was almost as if the images of what she'd seen were flickering like dark shadows behind her eyes, but she was unable to knit them together as a whole or relate them. And then when Jameson had been released from the Tombs, it hadn't seemed so important any more.

But, small mercies, Ellie thought; a week ago they wouldn't have even raised that tame smile out of her.

"Looks like could be rain later," Vera remarked, glancing up at the sky.

"Hope not." Ellie pulled Sean tighter in to her shoulder, as if to protect him from the grey clouds and the fresh breeze that had risen. "I've still got some washin' out."

They went up the side steps. Vera fished in her purse for the key and opened the door.

Vera Maynard never stood a chance. Brogan ran her through with a long-bladed knife the second she walked through the door.

As Vera sank to her knees, clutching at her stomach, Ellie grabbed Sarah by the shoulder and ran with her and her baby towards the bedroom door opposite.

She slammed the door and turned the lock, stepping back with a jolt as a second later Brogan's shoulder hit the door, a corner of its wood frame splitting.

She laid baby Sean on the bed and leapt for the side drawer where she'd hidden the pistol.

Another bang and the splintering of wood, followed instantly by an axe blade slicing through by the lock. He'd be through any second!

She frantically grabbed the gun and pointed it, hands shaking, towards the door as it burst open.

Brogan stood there, axe in his right hand, knife in the other. It took him a second to focus on what she was pointing at him, and his dawning expression was difficult for her to interpret – disbelief or mock amusement?

She waggled the gun as she glared at him, so that he got the message she was serious. "Now drop the axe and knife!"

She advanced a step. She wanted to move any possible fight as far from Sean as possible.

Brogan didn't drop his weapons, but he did back away a step.

"I said, drop 'em!" she screamed.

Brogan backed away another two steps, still holding the axe and knife. She advanced the same two steps.

"Drop 'em!"

"Whatever you say." He backed away another step and slowly crouched down as he put his knife on the floor. Then his axe. "Jus' take it easy now."

As she came fully out of the bedroom, Brogan glanced to one side, but she was a second slow catching the motion, seeing the billy club only as a faint blur as it swung against her arm, knocking her gun loose.

She realized now why Brogan had so readily backed away. He'd wanted to draw her out of the bedroom. Her gun skittered across the floor. She dived desperately after it, but a second billy club strike caught her shoulder then, knocking her to the ground.

Her breath falling ragged like a landed fish, she saw Brogan's accomplice fully for the first time. She reached a hand towards her gun only feet away, but Brogan's boot came into her line of vision and kicked it further away.

Brogan bent down and picked up his knife and axe. He was in no rush now, could butcher her at leisure.

The first surrey carriage was only going locally, the hansom behind already had two passengers, but a farmer approaching on a surrey a minute later said he could take them.

They offered him a five-dollar incentive to get them to Dover Plains as fast as he could.

He boasted two sprightly fillies, so claimed he'd be able to get them there "As close as dammit," to the train arrival time.

It was a bone-rattling journey at that speed on the rough dirt road. Jameson still felt raw after his spell in the Tombs, and the journey put his nerves on edge all the more, especially with what he knew they might be confronting.

Argenti's teeth were gritted for much of the ride, hanging on to the carriage edge like grim death.

Jameson checked his pocket watch halfway through the journey. Despite their efforts, it looked like they'd arrive at least fifteen minutes after the train. His stomach sank. They weren't going to make it in time. Brogan would dispatch Ellie within the first two minutes, he reminded himself.

Dust rose off their carriage wheels as they arrived in Dover Plains, a few of the local townspeople showing alarm at their speed.

They leapt out as they pulled up in front of 126 Maple Avenue.

Jameson tipped his derby. "Thank you, my good man."

At first, looking at the provision store's front, they thought they had the wrong address too. But then they heard the thud and gasp of someone hitting the floor from an upstairs room. They bolted up the side steps, taking them two and three at a time.

The front door wouldn't open fully with Vera Maynard's body wedged behind, and they had to squeeze through a fourteen-inch gap. Seeing her bloodied, crumpled body, again Jameson feared he was too late, but then through a gap in the lounge door he saw Ellie prone on the floor. Brogan was straddling her, raising his axe.

Jameson burst through, drawing his swordstick blade in the same motion. Brogan had barely registered his presence, head half-turning, as he ran the blade into Brogan's right shoulder.

Brogan groaned like a wounded bear and his arm trembled and spasmed for a moment before the axe fell from his grip, clattering to the floor.

Jameson went to lunge again, but Martin was on him quickly, striking out with his billy club once, twice. The blade fell from his grasp as Argenti rugby-tackled Martin from the side, sending him sprawling.

Brogan turned to Jameson, swinging out with the knife in his left hand. Jameson leapt back from its arc. He still had the stick part of his cane in his left hand and swiftly transferred to his right, parrying the next knife lunge.

Argenti took one billy club blow to the shoulder, but then blocked the next blow, punching Martin hard in the stomach.

Then Brogan did a strange thing. He transferred his knife from his left to right hand. Jameson thought his right hand was out of action. He was focused so intently on the knife that he didn't read the distraction until too late. The left-handed haymaker punch seemed to come out of nowhere, hitting him solidly on the jaw and knocking him halfway across the room.

Everything spun and went black for a second. As his vision fought to clear, Brogan was moving in on him through a dull haze. But Ellie was on her feet again and jumped on Brogan's back, screaming like a banshee as she dug her fingernails into his face, clawing at his skin.

Brogan roared and swung his elbow back at her, knocking her loose. Then a back-handed, ham-fisted punch sent her flying. She fell so badly that Jameson feared at first she'd broken her neck.

Argenti finished Martin off with another blow to the stomach and a nose-shattering face blow, and turned his attention to Brogan as he loomed over Jameson.

Argenti's first punch caught Brogan solidly on the side of the face, but Brogan turned to him, unmoved, as if an annoying fly had bitten him.

His second run-in with Brogan of the day, but this time he hoped to fare better. Brogan only had one arm in use, his right arm with the knife dangled uselessly.

Argenti's first punch though was blocked, and he caught on quickly to strike at the right side where Brogan couldn't block. Two punches connected, but as with the first they hardly seemed to affect Brogan, and as Argenti went for another he was left open and Brogan's return punch felt like a sledgehammer hitting his shoulder, knocking him back three feet.

The trading of punches was fast and furious. Argenti managed to get in five punches to Brogan's two in return, again to his shoulder and chest.

The only problem, as with the first, was that his punches didn't seem to be doing much to Brogan, whereas Brogan's return punches were knocking half the steam out of him. And when a punch finally swung through that struck him squarely in the face, he hardly saw it coming.

The last thing he remembered was laying flat on his back, squinting at the rapidly darkening room, Ellie unconscious a few feet away and Jameson beyond her, struggling to focus and get back on his feet again.

Brogan appeared to make a decision then. Argenti was out of it, and it didn't look like the toff was going to get to his feet quickly, at least not in time.

Brogan turned back to Ellie, switching his knife to his good hand as he poised above her, ready to plunge it home.

The room swayed and tilted as Jameson tried to get to his feet. Knowing he was too late to save Ellie now, he reached an imploring hand towards her, mouthing "I'm sorry", as if it was a last goodbye.

When he heard the two shots and saw Brogan start to topple, he thought he'd already blacked out again and it was all part of a wishful dream.

It wasn't until Brogan slumped against Ellie's body and he saw young Sarah behind holding the small pistol he'd given Ellie that he realized what had happened.

Sarah's hand trembled violently and she pulled the trigger again, just in case. But it struck an empty chamber this time.

In that moment, seeing Brogan poised above Ellie with the knife had mirrored what she'd seen happen with Anna Walcott, the last shadows lifting from her mind. She'd suddenly remembered what had occured that fateful night.

43

The newspapers were full of little else the following day:

Train crash six miles south of North Salem, on the Grand Central to Duchess County line, five killed, fourteen injured. Murder of a forty-two year-old woman, Vera Therese Maynard, in Dover Plains.

Suspect in both cases appears to be one Thomas Errol Brogan, 34, a manager at McLoughlin's Brewery in lower Manhattan. According to Detective Argenti, leading the Ripper case, Brogan is also a suspect in the earlier murder of Anna Walcott, previously attributed to the Ripper. "Some of the trademarks in that case were distinctly different to previous Ripper murders. We will now be looking more closely at Mr Brogan's involvement in that murder also."

Suspect Thomas Brogan is currently in Hartford General Hospital being treated for gunshot wounds sustained in the course of his arrest.

The man sitting alone at a table in the St Dennis read the same headlines as half of New York that morning; except that he read the accounts in all three newspapers – the *Post*, *Times* and *Herald* – and scoured every page for any related articles.

He wasn't used to being referenced as an adjunct to someone else's headlines, but it was preferable to being called a coward, he supposed. At least Argenti and Jameson appeared finally to have got it right with the Walcott murder, though he wondered if they'd have discovered their error without his prompting.

He tapped one finger thoughtfully on the newspapers. If they were close to finding him, as their last reports made out, then they'd probably already worked out his message and how many murders remained. Four years to deliver a single message etched in blood across two continents, but now that it was coming to a close his thoughts were divided. At some stage taunting investigators, playing with their minds, had become as much a part of the game as the puzzle itself, and he wasn't sure he wanted that to end. And how to prompt them about this latest error in their investigation?

He folded the newspapers over on his table and lifted his hand to get the waiter's attention.

Jameson raised a hand in thanks as Alice brought through the tray with a pot of tea and coffee.

"Ah, excellent, Alice. Just what the doctor ordered."

Half the morning spent at Bellevue checking his and Argenti's injuries had been more than enough. Some facial and body bruising and grazed knuckles, but no major injuries; the most serious had been a pulled muscle in Argenti's shoulder and a fracture on the bridge of his nose.

Argenti took a sip of his coffee and glanced at the newspaper on the side table.

"Do you think Brogan will survive?"

"Possible, I suppose. Twenty-two calibre bullets weren't designed to kill men his size, only stop them. Which they did."

"And Ellie?"

"Concussion and a fractured shoulder. They've strapped the shoulder and are keeping her in for observation until tonight." Jameson smiled tightly. "I'll go with Lawrence to see her then, pick her up in the hansom."

Argenti nodded, and reached for a biscuit.

Jameson had earlier contemplated the name Lawrence had found in the Ellis Island records. He picked it up and studied it again.

"So, no Cafson or Cafdove?"

"No," Lawrence said. "Not at least with a requisite Christian name combination."

"And you checked all other possible name combinations?"

"Yes, of course."

"And we already went through all possible place-name possibilities?"

Lawrence was about to answer, then realized it was what Jameson termed a "rhetorical" question. He was mostly talking to himself.

Argenti held a palm out. "What if it is one of the alternatives like 'Revenge', 'Punishment' or 'Wrath'?"

"Not the ideal translation from Hebrew, according to Rabbi Morais."

"But I checked those anyway," Lawrence said. "Nothing on those either."

They were silent for a moment. Jameson studied the name again.

"Certainly both his place of origination, Hoxton, and the time of his immigration fit perfectly. But still we're left with those three stray letters, C-A-F." He took a fresh sip of tea, looking up after a second. "What if it's in code?"

"I tried first a reverse-swap alphabet code," Lawrence said. "Fourth letter from the beginning transposed with fourth letter from end. Didn't leave us with enough vowels. Then substitute letters and progressive alphabet-mapping. No possibilities, I'm afraid."

"If you did the same in Hebrew?" Argenti ventured.

"Then we wouldn't be left with the same Asmodeus link," Jameson said. "Which Morais has already agreed, as the Fallen Angel of Lust, appears to fit the Ripper's modus operandi."

"Yes, good point." Argenti grimaced. He felt a pain twinge where his nose had been strapped and touched it tentatively. "I hope that doctor knew what he was doing."

"I think it was only a junior doctor or intern who strapped it." Jameson smiled. "So don't expect Royal College of Surgeons treatment."

"They don't have that here," Lawrence said. "It's the College of Physicians and Surgeons both together. Attached to Columbia University, I believe."

Then he realized that Jameson had been joking. But Jameson appeared lost in thought, serious. Not his normal indulgent smile when he made such mistakes.

"That's it!" Jameson exclaimed. "It's an academic society initial, like a qualification. CAF… F-C-A – Fellow of the College of Anatomists. Not as well-known as the RCS – Royal College of Surgeons, but a bona-fide association nonetheless."

"Yes, of course," Lawrence said, as if self-admonishing that he should have thought of it himself.

"Don't worry. If it wasn't for the fact that Colby belonged to it, along with half a dozen other obscure medical related associations outside of the RCS, I wouldn't have picked up on it myself."

"They have members involved with *all* anatomical studies, including animals, if I recall," Lawrence commented.

"Yes, that's correct. But it was their pathology member-ship that interested Colby. Much of that stepped outside of what the RCS covered." He picked up the paper with the name again, reading it aloud with more deliberation. "Eugene Samson Dove. FCA. My goodness. Colby might even know him!" Then he quickly sobered that thought as he checked his watch. "But certainly Colby would be the best point to start."

"So you recall him?" Grayling enquired, taking a fresh draw at his cigar.

"Very much so," Colby said. "Though I doubt I would have if he hadn't been expelled from the society. Only days after being struck off the medical register, in fact. I haven't known that to happen before."

Grayling nodded, let out a cloud of smoke. "And they're moving in on him now?"

"Yes. After Jameson received my answer to his telegram about Dove, he confirmed they were arranging a police contingent. An address in Brooklyn, I understand."

Grayling looked out thoughtfully across the restaurant for a moment. They were back at the Café Royal, though this time Colby had called the meeting. Four long years tracking the Ripper, it seemed only fitting that he'd have the final glory of announcing his apprehension rather than Grayling. Also, one meeting which Grayling hadn't called for his own devices; he was no longer in control.

"Certainly that answers the medical expertise you and others suspected the Ripper had," Grayling remarked. "His proficiency with removing internal organs."

"Yes. Indeed it does."

"And what profession did this Dove fellow go into after leaving the medical practice?"

"I heard that he'd in fact become a vet. Obviously wished to keep his hand in with anatomy of some manner. The medical register strike-off doesn't extend to animals."

Grayling nodded with a tight smile and raised his wine glass. "Well, let us hope all goes smoothly in New York with his apprehension."

"Yes, let's hope so." Colby raised his drink and they clinked glasses.

But straight after swallowing, Grayling felt doubt. "And you're absolutely certain they've got the right man?"

Colby smiled patiently. Grayling strove to regain control.

"No remaining doubt. If the evidence compiled wasn't sufficient, then what he was struck off for certainly fits his activities."

Grayling raised his eyebrows in question. "Oh, and what was that?"

"The botched backstreet abortion of a prostitute."

44

They got to the house at dusk.

A compact two-storey wood-frame in Queen Anne style; looking along the road Jameson could see at least eight similar amongst the mixed two- and three-storey houses.

Argenti looked at the brass plaque by its front door. *Equine Physician.*

"In layman's terms, horse doctor," Jameson said.

Argenti rapped on the door hard twice. No answer. No lights visible inside or coming on in its hallway. No discernible movement inside. He rapped again, and after another full minute with no answer or movement inside the house, he beckoned the locksmith they'd brought with them.

Behind them stood Brendan Mann and John Whelan, three uniformed policemen by the front gate and another five in a wagon parked in front. They weren't taking any chances.

They'd emptied the gun drawer at Mulberry Street. Argenti noticed Brendan Mann's hand tense on the pistol inside his jacket as the locksmith finished picking the lock and opened the door.

A long hallway with doors on the right to the lounge, kitchen and a dining room at the back which Dove appeared to use as an office. On the left, stairs led up to the bedrooms and a bathroom while another narrower flight led down to the basement.

They started searching, paying particular attention to Dove's office. As they went through the last few drawers in his desk, Jameson looked up.

"Do you notice anything unusual?"

"What? Apart from the fact that there's hardly anything here to find, unusual or otherwise?"

"Exactly. It's particularly spartan. Minimal displays of silverware and porcelain. No newspapers or clippings and hardly any books. And, most importantly, no photos." Jameson indicated a side table. "The only photos are like these, a couple of racehorses, probably belonging to clients. No photos of himself or family. Nothing to say he's the Ripper, or indeed any hint of who he is at all."

"Perhaps we've got the wrong man. Perhaps Dove's not our man after all."

Jameson shook his head. "No, I disagree. I think the lack of photos and other paraphernalia points more to it being him than *not* being him." As Jameson saw Argenti's forehead knit, he held out a palm. "Think about it. Normally there'd be college diplomas or graduation class photographs on the wall, or something of him with friends or family. We know he's from Hoxton, only a mile from Whitechapel – but how many people in New York or indeed this street or neighbourhood know that? And if they saw a photo of him with Big Ben or the Hackney Empire in the background, they might start asking questions."

"You have a point."

"Look around you. He's buried his background. Become all but invisible."

Argenti dutifully looked, his eyes fixing finally on the horse anatomy chart behind Dove's desk denoting flanks, fetlocks, carpus, patella, short Pastern bone.

"And apart from charts like this," Jameson pointed, "and the rolled cloth of veterinary instruments in his desk's bottom drawer, the indicators of his current profession aren't strongly evident, either. Almost as if he's ashamed of it – reminds him too much of his downfall and what has passed."

As they made their way down to check the last room in the house, the basement, Jameson added an amendment.

"Well, indeed, more evidence of his work here, buried out of sight where nobody can see it."

Thirty or more specimen and bell jars were lined in a row on a bench table that ran one side of the room. Jameson put one hand to his mouth. The smell of formaldehyde was strong, reminding him of the morgue.

Inside the jars were different organs. Spleen, liver, pancreas, stomach, heart. By their size, Jameson guessed they were equine, but as they came alongside a few small specimens, Argenti pointed.

"Do you think these are what I fear they might be?"

"I doubt it. The organs never accounted for were the uterus of Mary Anne Nichols, the left kidney of Catherine Eddowes and Camille Green's liver. But these specimens are the wrong size and form to be human organs. I believe they're either from sheep or horse foals."

On the wall behind the bench were more detailed anatomical charts. Mostly of horses, but Jameson noted also one of a bull, a greyhound and a cat. Then at the end, as if a token acknowledgment of Dove's past medical practice, the bone chart of a human skeleton.

Below the bench row were a series of drawers. Jameson started opening them.

Row upon row of animal bones – tibias, fibulas, ulnas, femurs, tarsals, metatarsals, metacarpals – all numbered and dated and laid out on red baize. The smaller bones were in slim upper drawers, larger ones in deeper bottom drawers. One large centre drawer proudly displayed a horse's skull.

It was impossible for Jameson to tell if any of the bones were human. At first glance, few of them looked the right size and shape and, besides, he couldn't recall bones being missing from any past victims.

He looked towards the end of the room where Argenti had opened the only door leading off. Jameson joined him as he looked in, a cubbyhole three-feet square, nothing there but a few gardening tools and the gas meter.

Argenti closed the door and they stood for a moment in silence, looking around for anything they might have missed. Argenti shook off a shiver. The aura of the room was unsettling with its heavy stench of formaldehyde and hundreds of bones, whether human or not. From above came the creaking of floorboards and muffled voices as Mann and Whelan double-checked the upstairs. Argenti indicated the jars.

"Do you want to take some of these for analysis?"

"Perhaps only one. Any more than that and he'll know we've been here."

Argenti smiled tautly. "Yes. Though perhaps if he appears later while we're still waiting for him, that won't particularly matter."

The shadows in the street seemed to get darker as they waited.

Not just the dying dusk and heavier cloud cover shrouding a half-moon, but the fact that lighting in the street was so poor. The nearest gas lamp was over thirty yards away from the house, and the more they strained their eyes into that darkness, the more imaginary shapes seemed to form out of it.

Jameson rubbed at his eyes and checked his pocket watch.

Two hours they'd been sitting outside the house now with no sign of activity or movement, and only three men approaching who might have been Dove to make them tense and hold their breath – until those men walked to other houses.

One man had got out a hansom almost directly in front, then had walked to a house two away, the others had approached by foot along the road.

Jameson and Argenti sat with Mann and Whelan in an unmarked black wagon with no driver and its interior curtains all but closed.

Tailors, milliners and morticians used such wagons, so it shouldn't draw undue attention. Another similar wagon with four uniformed policeman was parked out of sight around the corner, with the arranged signal that they'd sound the klaxon at the first sign of activity.

They tensed in anticipation as a man in a top hat appeared, but again he walked by. So when only two minutes later another man approached, this time in a dark navy suit and derby, they were half lulled into complacency, and amongst the shadows didn't discern that he'd suddenly turned towards the house until he was halfway down its pathway.

Argenti shook Jameson's arm. "He's here! It's him!"

They leapt out the wagon and Mann sounded the klaxon as he followed with Whelan.

They moved swiftly, drawing their guns as they went. Dove was already at the door, opening it. They'd reached the front gate as he shut the door behind him. He didn't look back.

They saw the light go on in the hallway as they ran the last few yards up the path. Argenti rapped on the door with the butt of his gun.

"Eugene Dove! Police!"

Through a frosted glass pane in the door, it was difficult to tell whether Dove looked their way or not. But they saw him clearly open the door at the side and go down to the basement.

"I said, *police*! Open up!"

Dove wasn't going to reappear. Argenti waited only ten more seconds before shooting out the lock. They burst through the front door and ran towards the basement.

But only four steps down, all the lights went out. Jameson and Argenti froze. It was pitch black. They couldn't see a thing.

"Get the oil lamp," Jameson hissed.

He heard Argenti stumbling back up for it, but couldn't see him. Argenti grabbed the lamp from Mann in the hallway, but they had to move back towards the front door for some weak moonlight to even be able to light it.

Waiting those seconds, Jameson felt the hairs rise on the back of his neck. He could hear movement close by. He drew his sword cane and swished the blade in the darkness. But he knew he didn't stand a chance. He'd only been in the basement once, whereas the Ripper knew it blindfold. He'd be able to run him through in a second and be gone.

His breath felt trapped in his throat, his heart pounding wildly as he heard the rustling draw closer. Then, as Argenti finally swung down with the arc of light from the oil lamp, they saw a rat scurrying away.

Argenti lifted the lamp higher as they made their way down. The arc of light was weak and seemed to dim more as they descended with the cool, damp air. The end of the basement was shrouded in darkness.

They edged forward cautiously, and as the end of the room finally came into view, they looked at each other, perplexed. No Dove in sight, yet they were certain they'd seen him go down to the basement.

Then they remembered the small cubbyhole at the end of the room. He must be there. They edged even more cautiously towards it, breath held. Argenti pointed his gun straight at the door as Jameson swung it open and stepped back.

It was empty.

Jameson glanced at the gas meter to one side. At least they'd worked out what he'd done. "Looks like he turned the gas off. That's why the lights went."

"Yeah." Argenti nodded, eyes scouring the cubbyhole. "Then where the hell did he go?"

Jameson stepped forward, started patting the walls. Solid stone. But then at the back he suddenly hit a patch of wooden board, part of which had a hollow sound.

He knocked and pressed, knocked and pressed. Finally he felt a part of it give. He pushed and it swivelled open to reveal another small cubbyhole no more than two-foot deep. Some coal was piled to one side and at its back iron steps led up to a manhole cover.

Jameson became aware of the light hissing sound in the same instant that Argenti gripped his arm.

"Finley! Dove didn't turn off the gas. He severed the pipe!"

The gas hadn't built up sufficiently yet to ignite, but any second it would. They bolted back towards the stairs, desperate to put as much distance between the kerosene lamp and the escaping gas as possible.

But three steps from the top, Argenti stumbled and cracked the oil lamp against the steps. He still had hold of it, but its side had split open and they watched in horror as the flaming liquid seeped down the stairs.

They ran on, and the burning kerosene met the escaping gas as they were halfway back down the hallway, spewing a fireball up from the basement. They felt the lick of its flames and the intense heat singe their backs as they burst back through the open front door.

After the initial explosion, the flames quickly took hold of the house's wood frame, pushing them even further back. Argenti and Jameson stood helplessly by the front gate as they watched it burn. Mann, Whelan and the four uniformed policemen just behind them, the flicker of its flames playing across their faces.

Whatever clues might have been in there were now lost, which was obviously what Dove had intended.

45

It took him over three hours to find her.

She wore a white linen dress, surprisingly clean given the drab surroundings and her profession. One quick tryst against any of the nearby alley walls and already it would be soiled. Or perhaps she had a place to take clients nearby and she'd undress and carefully fold the dress beforehand.

But it was the red of the carnation pinned at her breast that had first picked her out for him. It matched her lipstick and had no doubt been put there to leave no question about her line of work, even though that should have been obvious from her position at the corner of Peck Slip, only a block from the dockside.

Still he watched her for a while from further down the street to make sure. Dark hair hanging loose almost to her waist, yet a pale porcelain skin, as if she took care of herself or was careful not to toil in the sun. She was perfect. And that splash of red seemed to stand out all the more against her white dress, make her appear the only thing of vibrancy and beauty on the drab, grey street.

He suddenly tensed. Some voices from further down the street broke the night-time silence. He looked round to see a group of men thirty yards down the road spill out of a tavern on the opposite side. Looked like stevedores or dockside porters out for an after-work or between shifts drink.

One of the men also noticed the girl, looked up towards her for a moment.

Dove considered whether to move on, find another girl. The spell between them had been broken, and despite him keeping amongst the heavier shadows his side of the road away from any gas lamps, one of the men might have noticed him. Though he wondered whimsically if that mattered any more, half of New York now knew his name, even if they hadn't yet been able to attach a face to it.

The stevedore pulled his gaze from the girl, brought his attention back to his friends' conversation. A moment later they said their goodbyes. The man lifted his hand in parting and headed away down the street.

Only one of the men walked up the street in the direction of the girl, but he appeared to hardly pay her any attention and kept his side of the road as he turned into Front Street.

Dove waited a moment more for the man to be gone from sight before he approached the girl.

"Have you been waiting here long?"

"Suppose you could say." She attempted a smile. "But probably worth it for the right man."

No doubt a trite line she'd spun to many a man, he thought, but that now was of passing consequence. Up close, she was even more beautiful, sea-green flecks in her hazel eyes and a small beauty spot above her top lip that he was trying to discern was natural or if she'd put it there with mascara or coal dust.

"How much?" he asked. He wanted to get straight down to business, didn't want to spend too long dallying on the street where someone else might come out of a tavern and see them.

"Three dollars, including the lodging house nearby." Then when the shade of doubt crossed his face, she added hastily, "But it's okay, it's safe. A known and listed lodging house."

"I'm sure it is. It's just that I have my own place not far away, which I'd prefer." His turn to dispel her fleeting doubts. "But I'll pay the full three dollars anyway."

She paused for only a second before nodding; perhaps her last chance of a client that night.

He paid her the three dollars and they walked along Front Street, then took the first turn right at Frankfort Street. But as they got closer to the dockside, he sensed a subtle change in her mood, the first twinge of apprehension.

"Your place? Is it a hotel or something?"

Best to keep close to the truth, he thought. Otherwise she might balk at the last moment and he wouldn't be able to get her inside.

"No. It's my office in one of the warehouses. I have a small bedroom there too, because sometimes it's too late for me to make the journey back to my home in Northport."

She meekly smiled her acceptance of his lie, and he returned that smile as finally they reached the dockside warehouse and he opened its door to let her in first.

It took a moment for her eyes to adjust to the darkness inside, and he savoured them widening in alarm at what she saw as he took the cloth from his pocket.

Soaked in chloroform, he clasped the cloth hard over her mouth and rode with her to the ground, watching the shadows in her eyes gradually sink into oblivion.

Curiosity killed the cat. How many other superstitions are there relating to cats? Probably too numerous to mention here.

You should have known not to go snooping on me. Known that I wouldn't leave any trace of me to find beyond what I intended, although it appears to be your forte these days to misread me. A coward? What sort of repayment is that, attempting to label me such after I saved your life?

Do you appreciate the risks I went to for that? As with the other girls, choosing a moment unseen was only part of it. Some of them I butchered only yards from people passing. Ah, but then you'd know that from the girl on the Showboat and the one at the opera, wouldn't you? Killed right under the noses of the two men leading the hunt for me. Do you really believe a coward would have the nerve to do that?

Though now at least we know one thing. if you've finally worked out the puzzle, you'll also know that there's only one girl left. A prize beauty that indeed I already have in my possession. However, in the spirit of the cowardice you mention, I shall give this one a fighting chance.

At nightfall, I shall send you another message telling you where you can meet us. Just yourself and Detective Argenti, no other police presence. If I see other policemen arrive, I shall immediately kill the girl and her fighting chance will have gone. The two of you will have the blood of yet another girl on your conscience.

But arrive alone and you will have a chance of saving her. We shall soon discover just who amongst us are the cowards.

"I don't think we should go," Argenti said. "I think it's a trap."

"That may well be the case. But the threat's very clear. Do we really want the blood of another girl on our hands?" Jameson gestured. "In particular if we sit by and do nothing. His point will have been proven, *we* will be the ones shown as cowards."

The note had arrived mid-afternoon at Jameson's house on Greenwich Street. He'd immediately dispatched Lawrence in the hansom to notify Argenti at Mulberry Street and Argenti had returned with Lawrence just over an hour later. Jameson had checked his pocket watch as they drew up outside. There were, at most, two hours of daylight left. Argenti sipped at a fresh coffee Alice had brewed for him.

"The letter arrived directly through your letterbox, you say?"

"Yes. And of course it's obvious now why, given its contents. I doubt another will arrive at the newspapers. The only way of keeping this meeting secret, simply between us and him."

"Did you see who delivered it?"

Lawrence answered. "Alice first noticed the envelope through the letterbox and gave it to me. I looked out, but there was nobody visible nearby."

"Probably just a street urchin he used," Jameson said. "I doubt he'd have delivered it himself."

Argenti studied the letter again. "As far as I can see, the threat raised is implicit in his trap. He knows otherwise we might not turn up or would call in extra police. He's playing with our minds and emotions, as he has been from day one."

"Yes. You're perfectly correct. But there's another way of looking at this. We partly instigated this situation by calling him a coward. All he's done is alter the scenario now so that it's on his terms rather than ours."

"We instigated the search on his house too, and look how he manipulated that situation to suit his ends. We were lucky to get out with our lives, Finley. He failed to kill us then, so now he wants a second chance at it."

"I don't think so."

"Or, as he makes clear in his letter, he's upset at being called a coward. So this is retribution for that."

"This isn't about us. It's about the girls."

Argenti shrugged. "So he kills this one right in front of us. A showcase murder right before our eyes, then escapes. What better way to prove his invincibility and our incompetence?"

Jameson closed his eyes and gently nodded, a shudder running through him. He knew Argenti was right, but how could he possibly leave it like that? Four years of tracking the Ripper and the succession of mutilated bodies he and Colby had to examine, only to step aside and leave this last girl to die.

Dove would no doubt send another letter to the newspapers making it clear what had happened. They'd be branded cowards and he'd disappear, never to be seen again. His aim would be accomplished. His reputation as the murderer the police could never catch would be enshrined in history.

"I... I don't see what choice we have. We can't just leave this last girl to die." He lifted his voice; a more hopeful tone. "Also, our first chance of seeing the Ripper at close quarters. Seeing what he looks like."

"That's the other strong emotion he's playing on. The desire to see his face after all these years." Argenti sat forward. "Just so long as you keep in mind, Finley, this also might be part of his plan, that his face is the last thing we both see."

The second message arrived just after 10 pm.

Lawrence opened the door seconds after it came through the letterbox and looked out. Nobody visible either way along the street.

"Probably the same street kid as earlier," Jameson commented as Lawrence handed him the envelope. "Their stock-in-trade is to swiftly become scarce. Disappear back into the shadows."

Argenti was two steps behind them in the hallway, looking on expectantly. Jameson opened the note and read it aloud.

"Go to the end of Frankfort Street. Walk to the water's edge at the dockside, then turn and take ten paces to your left. Wait there to receive your next instructions from me." Jameson looked up. "Doesn't leave much time."

Argenti grimaced. "Presumably so that, even if we did feel inclined, we wouldn't have much time to arrange a support force."

"Yes. No doubt he'd be watching out for that in any case. Lawrence, bring the hansom round."

As they sped down Broadway, Argenti commented, "That's by the Brooklyn Bridge and quite an open area, if I recall. Fair stretch of open visibility between the last warehouse buildings and the water's edge."

Jameson nodded thoughtfully. "Presumably too so that he can easier observe whether we've heeded his instructions about appearing alone, without any police contingent."

Turning into Front Street, Jameson pointed. "Park at the end out of sight, Lawrence, and stay with the hansom. We'll walk the remainder. He's specified only police, but I don't want to take the risk with *anyone* additional present."

As they came out onto the dockside, they began to appreciate just how open and desolate it was. A chill breeze off the harbour lightly lifted their jacket tails.

They went to the water's edge, turned to their left and walked the designated ten paces. They could now appreciate the method in Dove's plan, those ten paces took them out of view of anyone watching directly down Frankfort Street. It also put them under the first shadows of Brooklyn Bridge almost directly above.

It was impenetrably dark. The nearest buildings were thirty yards away to their side. Mostly dilapidated warehouses, those that were still occupied weren't active this time of night; deadly silent, only the cool whip of the wind and lap of water at the dock's edge, and not a soul in sight.

"Where is he?" Jameson shuffled his feet, unsure whether the chill suddenly running up his spine was from unease or the cool, damp air.

They looked around, but couldn't see anyone, though had the feeling they were being watched. The dark windows of the nearby warehouses, many of them smashed out, stared back silently.

They waited almost another three minutes, Dove possibly checking meanwhile for any nearby police presence, before a voice finally boomed out.

"Good evening, gentlemen. Glad you decided to come."

They looked towards the warehouses shrouded in darkness. The voice had a slight echo to it as it drifted across the dockside; it was difficult to place its source exactly.

"Now drop your guns where you are and take another twenty paces forward by the water's edge."

They looked at each other uncertainly. Argenti had probably been right, Dove's face would be the last thing they'd see. He'd emerge and simply shoot them where they stood, with the harbour right there to dump their bodies. The voice boomed again, a slight edge to it now.

"If you don't do as I say, then I'll kill the girl here and now and be gone. You won't see me again. *Ever*."

Jameson looked towards the warehouses a second longer, then took the gun out of his inside pocket, crouched and laid it on the ground. He didn't see much choice. Argenti followed suit. Pistol shots at a distance could be awkward. They'd just have to hope that Dove wasn't that good a shot.

"Your sword-cane too, Mr Jameson."

Jameson put its end to the ground and simply let it fall. It clattered in the night-time stillness.

A second later, a boy no more than eleven scampered out from the door of one of the dilapidated warehouses, probably the same boy who'd delivered the earlier notes. He patted Argenti and Jameson down for any other weapons, then nodded as he ran back to the warehouse. A moment later, having collected his last silver dollar from Dove, he scampered off. Dove's voice issued forth again.

"Very good. Now those twenty paces if you please, gentlemen."

With each pace, they felt more exposed and vulnerable. Not only the distance from their weapons, but bringing them closer to that ominous voice. Jameson looked up fleetingly. They were now fully under the shadow of the bridge. Even the few faint lamplights of carriages heading across it visible a moment ago had gone from view.

"That's very good, gentlemen. We may commence."

Finally they saw Dove emerge from the same warehouse door, though it was the girl in a white dress with him who was visible first. She was blindfolded and Dove held her just in front of him. By her left breast was a single red carnation. In contrast, he was dressed in a dark suit and black cape. A derby tilted sharply down on his forehead added to the shadows. His face was barely discernible in the dull light.

They tensed as he approached. They could now see the pistol in his right hand. The closer he came, simply shooting them became more of a proposition.

But Dove appeared to hold the pistol loosely, not aimed at them, and he moved straight ahead towards the dockside rather than their direction. As he finally came to a halt with the girl, he was still a good thirty yards from them, directly on the water's edge.

"One thing you should know about me, Mr Jameson," he called out, "is that I'm a man of my word."

"I don't doubt it for a moment."

"You called me a coward and I said I'd disprove it," he continued unabated, as if Jameson hadn't spoken. "I said I'd give this girl a fighting chance, and I will."

They watched Dove lay his pistol carefully at the girl's feet, as if part of a measured ritual. He then removed her blindfold.

"You may turn around only when I say," he said to her.

The words were barely audible to Argenti and Jameson thirty yards away, but they could see her body trembling even from where they stood. The breeze from the bay lifted at some stray ends of her hair. Dove's claim was right, Jameson considered, a rare beauty. She blinked as she focused on them, eyes imploring; wondering if they might be there to save her, yet still uncertain of her fate. As they were.

Dove started pacing away from her. As he got to fifteen paces away, he turned and called to her. "Okay. You may turn around now." Then, as she turned his way, "At your feet you will see a pistol."

She looked at it and blinked slowly, as if again she was having trouble focusing or couldn't divine its purpose.

Dove pulled open one side of his cape, and Jameson and Argenti saw the glint of the long blade in his grip. Dove raised his voice to reach them.

"What do you think, gentlemen. What are the chances of me reaching her with the blade before she can shoot me?"

"I... I don't know," Jameson answered tremulously, his stomach sinking as the nature of Dove's challenge dawned on him.

"Pretty good, I would say. I'm fast, but in that distance she could probably get in two clear shots, maybe even three. Even odds, maybe even better."

"If you say so."

"Does that seem like a coward to you? A man who'd risk his life to give a girl a better than even chance?"

Jameson didn't answer.

"I asked you a question, Mr Jameson."

"No. No, it doesn't," Jameson answered finally. He could sense that Dove wanted the admission from him, anything less and he might make it tougher on the girl.

Argenti stayed quiet, sensing this game was mainly between Dove and Jameson. Another voice wouldn't help, would only aggravate the situation.

Dove softened the edge on his voice as he addressed the girl again. "Now as I raise the blade towards you, not before, pick up the gun and point it my way. Then fire it at me – as many times as you're able before I reach you."

Jameson looked desperately towards the girl. She was trembling violently, and in her state she'd be lucky to get within a foot of Dove with a shot. And Dove had worked out the distances perfectly. They couldn't get back to their pistols before he reached her, and if they ran her way they'd still be five yards short before he got to her. Unable to help her, but close enough for Dove to run his blade through them once he'd finished her.

He should have listened to Argenti, they were destined to simply be spectators as Dove killed the girl, then they'd probably be next.

Dove raised his blade. The girl lifted and levelled the pistol, her hands shaking wildly. Dove started his madcap run, his cape billowing in the wind.

She fired the pistol when he'd gone only three paces. Missed. And again a second later, by which time he was already halfway through his run.

It was hard for them to tell in the dull light whether she'd clipped Dove on the shoulder or not. His blade arm appeared to drop, though perhaps he'd done that to gain more impetus to his up-thrust as he approached her.

Dove was still at full pelt, his cape flowing wildly behind him. A piece of paper flew from his pocket then, but Jameson paid little attention to it. He could hardly watch, yet felt riveted by the morbid spectacle of it. He felt the desperate need to do something to help her, yet felt rooted to the spot with confusion and fear. Already he could picture the blade stabbing her; and then later he'd be inspecting her on the morgue slab like all the others.

But the splash of red to match those horror images wasn't on her, it was on Dove's face! Her third shot had connected, and Dove's hand clutched at one cheek as it exploded with a spray of blood.

He staggered, but only a yard from her now, he bundled heavily against her. With the darkness and heavy shadows, it was difficult for them to see whether Dove had stabbed her in that last second.

All they saw clearly was the knife fall and clatter to the ground, just before the tangle of Dove and the girl, driven by his off-balance charge, tumbled into the harbour water a yard to their side.

Jameson and Argenti bolted towards them.

They could see nothing in the dark water at first. Then they caught a glimpse of the girl drift to the surface. Her eyes were closed and she looked strangely serene in that brief moment before she started sinking again.

Jameson dived in after her. He lost her for a spell, and wouldn't have spotted her again in the ink-black water if it wasn't for the white of her dress. He caught her eight foot down and frantically started swimming back up with her.

With his sodden clothes and her dress clinging round her deadweight, progress was difficult; and as he felt the bay currents tugging at them, for a moment he feared they wouldn't make it. Her eyes were still closed and it was impossible to tell if she was unconscious or dead. As Jameson finally broke the surface, gasping, Argenti was reaching a hand out to him.

"Pass her here, Finley. Here!"

Argenti clutched under one of her shoulders and together they hauled her out.

Argenti started giving her mouth-to-mouth and Jameson clambered out and assisted, pumping her stomach to push air up through her lungs. They continued for two full minutes and had almost given up before the first water spluttered out of her mouth.

As they sat her up and she coughed and spluttered some more with her first full breaths, Jameson looked thoughtfully back towards the dark water.

No sign of Dove. He was sure he'd seen Dove shot, but it would have been gratifying to have a body to prove that, remove any possible doubt. A fitting end rather than the myth of the Ripper being lost to the dark harbour waters. One final body on the morgue slab to end the saga.

Then, his eyes drifting across the water surface, he thought he saw something, a splash of red against white.

At first he thought it was the girl's carnation against a patch of her torn dress. The carnation hadn't been there when he'd lifted her out the water. But as he focused harder he saw it was a man's face, the red patch where half of it along with his skull had been blown away. Finally, he could make out the dark suit and black cape.

There was no remaining doubt that it was Eugene Dove.

46

"I'd like to offer my resignation. Be relieved of my duty," McCluskey said.

They were his first words as he sat down in Commissioner Latham's office, his eyes still adjusting to the subdued light. It took him a second to realize that Latham was staring at him rather than perusing the folder on his desk, his position when Marsha Talbot had first shown him in. Latham fingered the pen in his hand.

"I hope this isn't because of how this Ripper investigation has turned out, because you feel you've been sidelined. The next case could very well be your turn for glory."

McCluskey smiled tightly. Yes, but how many would carry the same kudos as the Ripper case? Few, if any.

"No, it's not that. My wife has been hankering to go out West for a while, and an opportunity came up in St Louis that–"

"Is that where you're planning to go?"

"Yes. I saw an opening for police captain in the city. I went for the interview while on leave, and they've offered me the position." McCluskey shrugged. "But it would obviously please me if you were also able to offer a written recommendation."

Latham paused only briefly. "Of course. As much as I hate losing good men, it would be my pleasure to do so."

No doubt Latham was thinking that with him gone, there'd be less focus on internal corruption, part of which might reflect on the Commissioner's Office. McCluskey was thinking the same, but for different reasons, less focus on himself also meant less on any possible association with Michael Tierney.

Tierney's threat in the bar that night was still fresh in his mind, then a few nights back leaving his house with his wife and son he'd seen one of Tierney's henchmen, Liam Monahan, watching them from a hansom along the road. A stocky, unsettling figure staring at them through thick-lensed glasses, Monahan ran security at some of Tierney's casinos and clubs and had taken over from Brogan as his right-hand man.

"Thank you kindly, sir. It has been a pleasure working with you."

Latham smiled ingratiatingly, but he didn't return the compliment.

McCluskey got up and left.

Liam Monahan in the end gave up on wearing his glasses and slipped them into his top pocket. He'd gone to see Tierney to bring him up to date on events while Tierney was doing his inspection round at the brewery. Vapours from the mash tuns and vats filled the air and already he'd polished steam from his glasses twice.

Tierney looked up from his ladle test of one of the vats. "Packin' boxes, you say?"

"Yes, that's right. Just this morning; being loaded onto a wagon right outside his house."

"Do yer know where he's going?"

"St Louis, from what I saw marked on one of the boxes."

"Okay. Find out where in St Louis, if you can. With McCluskey off the scene, might not be so important, but yer never know." Tierney put back the ladle and moved further along the row of vats. He became pensive, looked troubled for the first time. "My main concern though is Martin. He's young and the police will put pressure on him. He might talk out o' turn."

"He's in the Tombs. I know two men in there we can use. He'll be dead in his bunk within the week."

"Reassuring t' hear."

He'd felt lost the last few days without Brogan, as if part of himself was missing, but Monahan was proving a worthy replacement. A good seven inches shorter than Brogan, but almost as stocky and wide as he was tall, his thick glasses gave some the impression of him being a mild-mannered accountant. But many a tale abounded of Monahan slipping those glasses into his top pocket before taking apart limb by limb opponents fooled by that initial image.

"What about Tom?" Monahan enquired.

"Tom's solid gold. He'd never say anything."

Even if Brogan was that way inclined, there was nothing the police could offer to entice him. Multiple murder charge, either way they'd hang him or send him to the electric chair. But he should nevertheless make his offer generous to the family Brogan would leave behind. Take care of your own and they'd take care of you had always been his motto. He only hoped his closeness with Brogan wasn't colouring his judgement. After inhaling from another ladle further along the row, he held it out towards Monahan.

"Get the aroma of that. Doesn't it just remind you of the ol' country?"

They made their way up the last spiral stone steps towards the platform in the torch.

Jameson let Ellie go ahead of him. Her breath caught as she took in the city panorama spread before them.

"My, my, Finley. It's beautiful from up here. Thank you for bringin' me."

"My pleasure. When I heard that after all these years in the city you'd never been here, I thought I've *got* to bring you."

He'd only been himself once before, but then he was a recent arrival to New York whereas Ellie had been here since the age of seven.

Though perhaps he'd chosen now to bring her because "liberty" seemed to mirror their situations, his liberty from The Tombs, hers from the threat of Tierney and Brogan, the city from the shadow of the Ripper.

"Looks practically the tallest building in the city," she said excitedly.

"Along with the World Building and Latting Observatory over there, it practically is." Jameson pointed, picking the two buildings out.

"I recall goin' down to Battery Park years ago and seeing 'em building this from there."

"That was just the supporting pedestal," Jameson said. "The main statue came from France."

"From France?"

"Yes. It was a gift from the French to commemorate the freedom they saw enshrined in the American Constitution, which they felt reflected their own Republic. So it was designed over there and part of the statue was in fact displayed at the Paris World Fair in 1878 then later shipped in–" Jameson broke off as he saw her attention drift with his potted history, or perhaps she'd been distracted by a nearby group of schoolchildren with their teacher.

"A gift, you say?"

"Yes. Well, the statue part above the pedestal."

She looked down the dizzying drop to its base. "My. Must have taken a fair bit o' wrapping."

They laughed, and Jameson was reminded why he liked her. Despite her poverty and her dire circumstances, despite the nature of her work to put food on the table for her child, she'd retained her spirit. Her spirit was her liberty.

They stood there silently for a moment, the wind whipping at their hair as they took in the view. Then she said flatly, matter-of-factly:

"I hear that Brogan's survived. Will he be out o' the hospital shortly?"

"Yes. But he'll go straight to the Tombs and won't make it out of there or Blackwell's Island until he hangs."

She nodded slowly. "What if Tierney gets someone else to do his dirty work?"

"Little point. Whatever you or little Sarah might have seen with Brogan will now be of little consequence. He'll hang for the train killings and that of Vera Maynard in any case." He reached out and gently clasped her hand. "Don't worry, you're safe."

They both looked at their hands joined and what it might signify for a moment, and he could swear he felt her hand softly trembling. He let go, quickly changed the mood.

"Come on. Let's go to Bloomingdale's to get you that new dress." He'd arranged to replace the ball gown he'd bought her; albeit a fresh colour and style, the same would have been too much of a reminder of what had happened to Anna Walcott. He checked his pocket watch, two hours before the conference Argenti had convened. "Then I'll have to bid my leave to go to this meeting on Broadway, I'm afraid."

Ellie stayed with Jameson in the end. The conference was being held at Abbey's Theatre on Broadway again because of the number of "interested parties" expected to attend, among which Jameson decided Ellie could definitely consider herself.

The final apprehension of the Ripper was big news. Powder flash bars exploded as they approached the theatre. Inside, the hall was packed and Ellie had to tuck up the back with Lawrence.

It appeared as if half of New York was there, every city official worth his salt, everyone who the path of past Ripper cases had touched, a full contingent of press, and any spare space filled with the "concerned" or simply curious.

On the stage were Argenti, Jameson, Commissioner Latham and Mayor Watkins.

One of the reporters looked up from his notepad halfway through writing down the name he'd just been given.

"Maureen Joanna Blythe? Have I got that right? She was this last intended victim?"

"Yes," Argenti said. "Twenty-four years-old. A resident of Gramercy Park, but working that evening in the Fourth Ward close to the East River Docks."

"And the same profession as the others? A prostitute?"

"Yes."

An agitated murmur ran through the audience, a few faint gasps of shock.

Argenti wondered at the term's capacity to still surprise. Not only given the nature of the investigation but the raw reality of many a city neighbourhood. Did none of them venture onto their own streets? He was reminded why he'd kept Marella's profession from his mother for so long.

"Is this the first girl to have been saved from the Ripper's clutches?"

"It's the first that we know of." Argenti glanced at Jameson. "There might have been past intended victims where he was disturbed at the last moment, but we can't be certain of those. This is the first fully proven such incident."

Jameson nodded, addressing the same reporter. "There were a number of reported close calls in London, plus a handful here. But on those we only had general descriptions, couldn't be sure they were the Ripper, particularly in the absence of any final attack details. To date we've relied mainly on forensic details to identify him."

"So with the absence of that this time, what indeed led you to finally identify the Ripper as this–" He checked his notepad "–Eugene Samson Dove?"

"He wrote a letter to us to arrange this final meeting. His handwriting style was identical to past letters written."

A couple of the reporters looked at each other. A *New York Times* reporter lifted his pen.

"But this was a letter written directly to you, rather than the newspapers first – which he'd done on past occasions?"

Argenti answered. "Yes. And if you look at the nature of that letter–" He'd had copies pressed at Mulberry Street and John Whelan had circulated them along the first two rows at the start of the meeting "–you'll understand why. The Ripper wished this meeting to be private. If he'd alerted the press, it would have been difficult to guarantee others not appearing at the scene, which would then have endangered the girl's life."

They studied the letter again and notes were made. A *Herald* man was first to look up.

"You mentioned also earlier that you had reason to believe this was the last intended victim of the Ripper. Just how did you know that, if I may ask?"

Argenti looked at Jameson. Jameson answered.

"You will recall in a previous meeting I mentioned us following a trail of symbols and letters marked on the organs of past victims. Some of which details were passed from London." He spent a moment explaining the investigative path they'd followed with Colby and Morais. "And then of course as the Ripper ascertained that we'd worked out his puzzle, he confirmed as much in his final letter."

"So the Ripper all but led to his own demise with his letters?"

"Yes. You could say."

A murmur ran through the audience.

"He was also shot right in front of you, I understand?"

"Yes, he was."

Argenti nodded his confirmation. "That was witnessed by both myself and Mr Jameson at close quarters before his body was removed from the harbour waters and transported to Bellevue for autopsy."

"So there's no remaining doubt in your minds that this Eugene Samson Dove is none other than the Ripper? The man known as Jack the Ripper is finally dead?"

"No, there's not," Argenti said.

Watkins and Latham nodded smug approval and a heavier murmur ran through the audience.

But the reporter noticed that Jameson had paused in contemplation. "And is that a finding you concur with, Mr Jameson?"

In that instant Jameson's mind had drifted back to the piece of paper that had flown from Dove's pocket as he'd run towards the girl.

As the morgue wagon arrived for Dove's body, he'd crouched down to pick it up. It was a theatrical programme with the singer Lillian Russell heading the bill and a magician, the Great Bellini, supporting: "SEE THE DEAD COME ALIVE!"

Jameson focused back on the reporter.

"Yes, it is," he said.

Murder. Vice. Pollution. Delays on the Tube. Some things never change...